BLACK SHEEP

Arlene Hunt is originally from Wicklow and, having spent five years in Barcelona, now lives in Dublin with her husband, daughter and mêlée of useless, overweight animals. *Black Sheep* is her third novel.

**Also by Arlene Hunt**
*Vicious Circle*
*False Intentions*

# BLACK
# SHEEP

## Arlene Hunt

HODDER
HEADLINE
IRELAND

First published in 2006 by Hodder Headline Ireland
First published in paperback in 2007 by Hodder Headline Ireland

2

A CIP catalogue record for this title is available from the British Library.

ISBN 978 0 340 92116 6

Typeset in Sabon MT by Hodder Headline Ireland
Printed and bound in Great Britain by Clays Ltd, St Ives plc

Hodder Headline Ireland's policy is to use papers that are natural, renewable
and recyclable products and made from wood grown in sustainable forests.
The logging and manufacturing processes are expected to conform to the
environmental regulations of the country of origin.

Hodder Headline Ireland
8 Castlecourt Centre
Castleknock
Dublin 15
Ireland
A division of Hachette Livre UK Ltd
338 Euston Road,
London NW1 3BH

www.hhireland.ie

*To Andrew and Jordan*

# 1

Gavin Lott whistled until his cheeks ached. He was crying with frustration, and the sudden east wind dried each salty drop on his cheeks. He tramped across the rocky ground, shouting until his voice cracked.

He had been doing this for over an hour, and yet there was still no sign of Flash, his father's prize dog. He had searched high and low all over the Wicklow mountainside. He had climbed craggy outcrops, searched through thick clumps of bracken, hopped across loose shale and lichen-covered walls: nothing.

Gavin dashed at his eyes with his hand, furious with himself. He stopped walking to catch his breath and scanned the heather for miles, desperately hoping to catch a glimpse of the basset hound's white-tipped tail.

Nothing.

He should never have let the stubborn beast off the lead in the first place. He should have known Flash would never follow him. Sometimes he wondered if the bloody dog even liked him.

'Flash! Here, boy!' Gavin cupped his hand to his mouth. 'Here, Flash.'

Although the day had been warm, at this altitude the temperature was dropping, and the shadows down in the valley were growing deeper. He wondered if he had to call off the search. Could the old dog make it through a cold night up here? It wasn't like Flash was used to hardship; he was more accustomed to sleeping flat out in front of the fire or sprawled on one of Gavin's father's many hair-covered, hound-pungent sofas.

'Flash! Here, Flash!'

Damn Sadie, anyway. It had been his wife's idea to take the dog up here. Give him a good run, she had said; exercise those old bones. Hah! Flash would have been just as happy taking a quick trip around the block. And now look: Gavin had lost him. How would he tell his father when the old man got home from hospital? 'Hi, Dad, you're looking well; by the way, I lost your beloved dog, friend and companion of ten years...' Christ, his father would have another stroke. And it would be his fault.

An icy chill spread through Gavin's stomach. What if Flash had fallen and was lying somewhere, whining, with a broken leg or something? Gavin moaned aloud. The thought of Flash suffering sickened him. He spun and half ran, half stumbled towards yet another gorse-filled ditch. He would not give in. He had to find that dog.

'Flash!' He took another deep breath and bawled at the top of his lungs, 'Flash! God damn it, where are you?'

This time he was rewarded with a deep, mournful cry. Gavin tilted his head and was about to call when Flash yowled again. There was no mistaking the sound of a basset in full cry. It was coming from a copse roughly a quarter of a kilometre back down the hill.

'Oh, thank you, God – thank you!' Gavin praised the Lord some more and took off in an ungainly run. He leaped over a wall and pelted as fast as he could down the slope, terrified that the dog would move on.

He cleared the first line of wind-whipped scrub grass and plunged into the gloom of the copse. His footfalls were cushioned by the pine needles scattered across the rocky ground, and the sudden, eerie silence troubled him. No birds called here; not even the wind penetrated through the dense hedges and brambles.

Gavin stopped, waiting for his eyes to adjust to the darkness. The air here was different, too – cooler, with a moist hint of something fetid and tangy. Gavin shivered. Then he saw the white-tipped tail waving furiously from a thick bank of undergrowth, twenty feet away.

'There you are! You total... fucker!' Gavin allowed himself to break his self-imposed ban on swearing. Breathlessly he marched towards the tail. 'You total and absolute fucker of a dog.'

Gavin closed in on the dog, grabbed him by the rump and pulled.

'Come on out of that. What are you looking for, eh? Come out of there, you fucker.'

Flash growled deep in his massive chest and dead-weighted him, throwing all his considerable bulk forwards onto his crooked front legs. Thorns scratched the back of Gavin's hands, and thin points of blood appeared.

'Come out of it!'

Flash ignored him. Gavin shook his head, exasperated.

'Right!' He reached into his coat pocket and took out the lead. God, but his father had this dog spoiled rotten.

He felt along the dog's back and up towards his neck, searching for the ring on the collar. Flash deliberately hampered him by pushing further into the ditch. He began to dig faster, whimpering and growling at the same time.

Gavin flattened down the thorns and nettles with his hiking boots and searched for the ring. His stomach flipped as the cloying stench of decomposition rose from the undergrowth. Gavin pulled a face: probably a dead fox or a sheep or something. No wonder the bloody dog was so interested... Even as the thought went through his mind,

Gavin noticed for the first time that much of the vegetation was dead; many of the branches and plants had merely been thrown into place. Flash unearthed more loose rock and yellow soil.

'Flash, here, leave it – leave it!'

Gavin reached for Flash again but, as he did, Flash lifted his head to growl, and Gavin saw what the dog was so intent on unearthing. He jerked back quickly and stared, his face wrinkling in shock and disbelief.

The hand was small and clenched tightly.

'Oh, Jesus!'

The basset hound was whining harder; his paws flung soil and pebbles backwards, sprinkling Gavin's walking boots like rain. Flash changed position and renewed his frantic digging. In seconds he had uncovered a hank of hair, dark and almost indistinguishable from the surrounding clay. Flash's black nose moved this way and that, snorting and blowing. He moved again and pawed some more. The hair was long, matted and, as Gavin was beginning to see, firmly attached to a head.

Flash threw back another mound of soil, and Gavin saw the top half of a face. It was clearly a woman, but the eyes were closed and sunken, and the skin was mottled and torn in places. Dull pieces of bone showed through a massive gash over the left eye.

More soil slid away and Gavin could tell, despite her state, that the woman had been young. Her mouth was open; a blackened tongue protruded from bloodless lips. The skin around her mouth was stretched and taut, poised in a silent scream; her neck was thrown back as though she had struggled to the surface of this shallow grave and had failed inches from the top.

Before Gavin could react, Flash clamped his teeth around the top of the head and pulled. The head lifted clear from the soil for a second, but pieces of the skin ripped and a small cavalcade of earwigs and other insects charged out from the nose cavity and scurried across the cheek, racing towards the deeper soil.

Gavin's stomach flipped again, but he did not panic. He very calmly leaned in, clipped the lead onto Flash's collar and, with all his might, yanked the hound out of the ditch. He turned on his heel and marched out of the copse, dragging the reluctant and slightly surprised Flash behind him.

When he reached the clearing, Gavin pulled a brand-new mobile phone from his leather-look bum-bag. Sadie had bought it for his birthday and insisted he brought it with him whenever he hiked, in case he fell or had an accident. He dialled the emergency services and asked to be connected to the gardaí. He reported exactly who he was, where he was and what he had found. After assuring the garda on the line that he would wait for them to get there, he hung up and sat down on a flat piece of moss-covered slate.

He scratched gently under the dog's chin. 'Well, Flash, this is another fine mess you've got us into,' he said in his best Oliver Hardy voice, the one Sadie laughed at. Flash whined and began to pant. There were several strands of hair snagged in his teeth.

Gavin calmly and quietly leaned to the side and vomited until his stomach was empty. It was several minutes before his dry heaves subsided.

*

Later that night, as the State Pathologist pulled off her gloves and signalled for the gurney to be brought over, Detective Inspector Willy Lynch, who had been assigned to the case, raised an eyebrow.

'Well?' he said, careful not to sound too optimistic.

The pathologist slipped her mask up onto her head as she approached him. 'I don't know yet. The tears to the skin appear post-mortem – probably a fox; some may have been caused by the dog that found her.'

'Jesus. Well, I shouldn't say it, but thank God for that. I hope it was a quick, merciful death.'

'Oh, I don't know about that, Inspector.' She began to unzip her white overalls. 'The tears might be post-mortem, but the big laceration over her eye is not – and, judging from her hands, I'd say that poor girl fought for her life. Her left index finger and thumb are broken, and so is her right wrist. No; I'd say, whatever happened to that poor creature, it wasn't quick and it sure as hell wasn't merciful.'

# 2

*June Bank Holiday Weekend*

The reception on the small portable television was getting steadily worse. Pat Kenny's face morphed and flickered. Static filled the screen, punctuated by thick green and yellow bands of interference.

JJ leaned out of his seat and banged the side of the television with the heel of his hand. Gradually the picture returned to its feeble, snowy best. Only now the sound was gone.

Triona snorted loudly. She crumpled her empty can of Carlsberg Export and flung it down on the stained carpet.

'Oh, way to go, fuckface. It's totally banjaxed now!'

JJ heard the hostility in her voice. She had been bitching at him all evening, as if it was his fault they had no money to go out. He figured he was two cans away from another row. He curled his left foot up underneath him, while his right tapped against the floor in quick bursts. Unbeknownst to him, he did this every time he was nervous. He'd been doing it a lot lately.

'Lookit!' Triona jabbed his ribs with her bare foot. 'It's bleedin' worse now.'

'Yeah, I see it.' JJ edged further along the sofa. Her toenails needed to be cut and the soles of her feet were filthy.

'I told you not to get this heap of shite!' She jabbed him again, harder. 'Why didn't you get the Panasonic like I told you?'

JJ took a drag of his spliff. He pulled the sweet smoke deep into his lungs and held it there. Maybe if he ignored her, she'd cool down. Certainly, answering back never seemed to be the right thing to do.

'Hey, fuckface! I'm talking to you, you spa!'

Triona kicked him in the arm hard enough to knock the joint out of his hand. It flipped from his fingers in a perfect arc, dropped down between his legs, rolled under the cushions and disappeared from view in a roll of sparks.

'Shit!' JJ leaped up and searched frantically for it. He flicked his dirty blond dreads over his shoulder, pulled the cushions off the sofa and tossed them into the middle of the floor. 'What you have to go and do that for?'

'Piece of shit, this telly. I told you it was when you got it.'

The spliff lay undamaged between an empty plastic sandwich carton and various chocolate and crisp wrappers. It had burned a small dark ring into the once-lemon fabric of the sofa. It wasn't the first such burn to the couch. There was hardly a table or shelf left in the apartment that didn't have the shape of a joint burned into it where JJ had put one down and forgotten about it. JJ didn't care. It wasn't like any of the furniture was his anyway.

He picked the joint up, blew the crap off it and moistened the paper with the tip of his tongue, making sure the fall hadn't loosened it. It hadn't; the joint had gone out, but remained intact. JJ smiled proudly: he knew how to roll a tight spliff. It was his trademark. People always said no one could roll one tighter.

Triona watched him with mean eyes. JJ could feel them burning into the side of his face, but he refused to make eye contact. Here he was, twenty-two and saddled with a bitch like Triona. Man, talk about your fucked-up karma. How had he ever thought she was good-looking? She was dressed, as always, in a grimy fleece top and the mint-green pyjama bottoms that she wore as trousers. She was – he noticed with a jolt of surprise – sort of fat, and getting more so every day. Her bleached-blonde hair was stuck to her head with grease, and it needed a cut desperately. Her face was puffy and she had clusters of spots on her chin and forehead. She hadn't shaved her legs or under her arms in fuck knows how long. She disgusted him. Christ, she was eighteen. What the hell would she be like in another few years?

'What you breathin' like that for?' Triona demanded. 'You gettin' mad or somethin'? Why are you gettin' mad? Don't get mad at me; I'm the one should be mad. I told you not to get this telly, didn't I? But oh, no, you wouldn't listen to me, Mister fuckin' Know-it-all.'

JJ forced himself to relax. The first and only time he'd hit her, she had nearly put him in the hospital. She had at least twenty-five pounds on him and she fought dirty – really, really dirty. She would think nothing of gouging his eyes out or kicking him in the gonads again. Christ, he had vomited half the night, and even now, when he thought about it, he was sure he could detect pain deep in his balls.

'I'm going to head to the shop.' JJ stood up and felt his vision wobble a little. He was stoned off his face. He tucked the spliff behind his ear. 'Do you want anything?'

'Get us some beers and a package of crisps. Salt an' vinegar, and make sure they're King, not Tayto.'

JJ glanced at the collection of empty cans scattered around the sofa and clucked his tongue. 'Shit, Tri, you'd better stall it with that stuff. It's only eleven and—'

Triona heaved her body off the sofa so fast that JJ almost tripped trying to move backwards. She jammed her hands on her hips and stepped close to him.

'Here, you asked me what I bleedin' wanted, didn't you?' She jutted her spotty chin out. 'And I told you, didn't I? What else is there to do in this fuckin' dump? I can hardly even hear the fuckin' telly. Don't you start tellin' me to watch nothin'.'

Triona's head weaved from side to side as she yelled, imitating the trailer trash from shows like *Jerry Springer* and *Ricki Lake* or whoever the hell she watched. JJ hated the way she did that. Recently, she had begun peppering her speech with words like 'dissing' and 'fly', like she was some rap queen or something.

JJ grabbed his hoodie from the back of a chair, ducked around Triona and headed for the door. And the music: 24/7, he had to listen to Li'l Kim and Missy Elliot screaming out their shit on his stereo. When he'd complained, Triona had called him an arsehole and yelled that dance music was 'over', only she'd pronounced it 'ovah'. JJ hated her most for that. Dance wasn't over. It was… evolving.

Behind him, Triona muttered under her breath and threw herself back onto the sofa. 'Can't even see the telly… Useless fucker, tellin' me what to be doin'…'

JJ slipped out into the peaceful night.

He trotted down the main stairs of the apartment building and out into the community car park. The five-building complex was almost twenty years old and starting to look its age. At one point, it had housed a wide variety of professional people and families; but over the years, as the Celtic Tiger roared, spluttered and meowed, the original people had made money and moved to houses with gardens in the suburbs. And with them had gone the sense of pride. Now the paint-work was peeling; the gardens went months without anyone bothering to mow the lawns. The collection of year-tenants, welfare recipients and immigrants living in Kilmainham Heights didn't give a shit if the place fell down about their ears.

JJ flipped his hood up on his head and tried to regain his composure. The moon was brand-new and the sky carried few clouds. JJ fancied he could detect the subtle shift in temperature that brought with it the promise of better weather. And with the better weather came more chances to make some decent money, maybe blow Dublin for a while. Last year, he'd set up on Grafton Street and plaited the hair of southside teenagers and spoiled Europeans until his fingers were numb. This year, he planned to expand the business and provide henna tattoos. If the cops stayed off his back long enough, he might make enough money to check out Amsterdam. He'd heard many cool things about Amsterdam and felt it was high time to pay a visit to what was clearly his spiritual home.

JJ moved off towards the pedestrian gate. God, it felt good to be outside. Maybe he'd sit under the new bridge for a while, relax and have a smoke in peace for a change.

The one-bedroom apartment was a dump. If only he could make Triona get up off her arse and clean it now and then. The week before, he had looked under the sink for something to throw down the toilet and discovered there wasn't a single cleaning product in the flat. He wasn't sure, but he suspected she hadn't changed the sheets on their bed in over two months. They felt grimy and they definitely smelled funny. And the fridge had something growing along the bottom of the door. God knew what she spent her dole on. Christ, why had he ever shacked up with her? He should have known she was no good. That was why her own folks had tossed her out on her ear. They were probably laughing their asses off at him for taking their piece-of-shit daughter off their hands.

Working up a good head of steam, JJ made his way down onto the overgrown towpath that ran beside the canal, slipping further from the streetlight into the shadows.

Who was she to talk to him the way she did – insulting him, giving him grief, making him avoid his own home? The stupid bitch was always on his case about getting a different job, too. As if he had time for a nine-to-five. And when he'd tried to explain to her the need to be around, to be on the scene, she'd laughed in his face and called him a 'dozy prick'.

JJ kicked an empty Scrumpy Jack can into the canal with a ferocity he wished he could use on Triona. He crossed over the tramline and down the bank on the opposite side, away from anyone's prying eyes.

He wished he could get Triona to leave him – then he could go back to being a single man – but as much as she liked to call him names, she never said anything about dumping him. If he had any balls he'd throw her out on her ear, but the truth was he was half… no, he was fully afraid of the crazy bitch.

If only the record companies had given his demo a chance. If only he could get that one break. He could be the next Tall Paul or Seb Fontaine, maybe even a Fat Boy Slim – not that he wanted to be so mainstream. He'd move. Let Triona keep the place; see how long she kept it together without him. He'd rent a loft, a big empty space with bare walls and no neighbours. He'd buy proper decks. He'd hold dance parties – maybe charge a small admission fee, strictly to cover costs. And the girls… well, he wouldn't make the same mistakes again.

JJ sat down under the bridge and rested his back against a cold cement pylon. He relit his spliff, closed his eyes and smoked in peace and quiet.

A car screeched to a halt on the road above. He heard a door open, then another, although the engine stayed running.

Fuck – cops, maybe. JJ pinched out his spliff and flicked it into the dark water. He got up slowly and moved deeper into the shadows, his feet scraping the filthy cement that ran under the bridge, where the junkies shot up and the pissheads fought over cheap hooch. It stank of urine and faeces, both human and animal. He cocked his head and held his breath, preparing to duck if he saw a beam of light.

There was nothing. He was about to exhale when he heard an angry, slurred voice say, 'Stay away from me.'

'Get back in the fucking car.'

'Fuck you!'

He heard a door slam. Then a voice said, 'Hey! Get your hands off—'

JJ Hutton was not the sharpest knife in the drawer, but years of street life had imbued him with an uncanny ability to recognise danger when it presented itself. At those few words, he pressed his body tight against the wall and remained motionless. He heard a curse, and then what sounded like a fight.

Curiosity won out over fear. JJ crept to the edge of the pillar and peered around it.

He could just make out two shapes on the other side of the bank. He squinted: two men, grunting and grappling with each other. The taller man threw a wild fist, and then the smaller one was scrabbling desperately to get his feet under him. As JJ watched, they both fell over the grass verge and rolled down the bank towards the lip of the canal.

'Get off me!'

JJ winced at the sound of flesh on flesh. They were knocking seven shades of shit out of each other. Suddenly the smaller one fell, and even from where JJ stood he could hear the sound his skull made as it cracked against the concrete.

'Get up,' the taller man said. 'Stop fucking around.'

But the man on the ground was stunned. He raised his hand to his head and groaned.

The other man stood up and grabbed him. He was panting as he half dragged, half carried him down the bank, forcing him to the lip of the canal.

JJ stayed perfectly still. He watched as the moaning man tried to resist. What was wrong with him? Was he off his face? Pissed? The moaning man stumbled and fell to his knees. The taller man shoved him; he struggled, but he was too weak or too confused to fight back. After a brief struggle, he slipped over the edge and down into the icy water of the canal.

As soon as he hit the freezing water, the man really began to fight.

He cried out and lurched for the bank, almost making it before he was shoved back down.

'Help…' He disappeared under the water. The taller man grabbed a handful of hair and forced his head under the water. He was panting with exertion, hanging on grimly.

The small man fought violently. Despite the grip on him, he surfaced twice more, thrashing furiously, rising inches over the fetid water, gasping and gurgling for air. But each time the other man pushed him under again. Gradually, he stopped struggling, and within minutes he was still. JJ swallowed hard and closed his eyes, feeling his legs tremble and his bladder ache.

The man on the bank fell backwards. JJ thought he heard him say, 'Jesus Christ,' but before his slightly stoned brain could be sure, the man got to his feet, staggered over to the bridge support and vomited copiously into the water. After a few moments, he wiped his mouth with the back of his hand and reeled away, away from the lip of the canal. He climbed the bank – and, as he did, a car swept past on the road. JJ got one good look at his face before he turned and disappeared from view.

JJ heard his footsteps as he walked over the bridge, not quite running but walking fast, getting as far away from the floating man as he possibly could. A door slammed and the car drove off.

JJ stepped away from the wall and stared into the dark water. In the dim light, he could just make out the man. He had drifted across to JJ's side of the canal, into the tall reeds, and appeared to be snagged there. He bobbed gently, face down.

JJ dithered, hopping from one foot to the other. What should he do? Was that guy really dead? He should get help; maybe he wasn't dead at all. Maybe he should pull him out. On telly, if you did mouth-to-mouth the person sometimes coughed up water and then they were okay.

On the other hand, the water was freezing and it was almost pitch-black down there. And what if the guy was dead and his eyes were open? What if he put his mouth to a dead guy's mouth?

JJ looked at the man doubtfully and pulled a face. He definitely didn't want to do any gross shit. And if he called the cops, there would be all sorts of questions. Nah, man, no way. That was not for him. He was definitely not going anywhere near that gig.

He turned and began to climb the bank towards the road.

Suddenly an idea formed in the wasteland of JJ Hutton's brain. Stunned by this unusual event, JJ clung to one of the stone pillars and held his breath, lest the idea desert him and float away. It didn't.

He trotted back to the lip of the canal and sized up the distance. If he lay on his stomach, he could probably reach the guy's ankles. He dropped down and wiggled out on the bank as far as he could, but no matter how hard he stretched or what angle he attempted, he was a foot or two short. He'd have to get down into the water.

JJ had second thoughts. But he braced himself, pulled off his hoodie, pants and runners and gritted his teeth. He sat down and lowered his legs into the freezing, dark water, making sure to grip the cement ledge firmly in his shaking fingers.

Almost immediately, his teeth began to chatter. The cold was far worse than he'd thought it could be – almost unbearable. JJ hesitated. The water stank, and it had a terrible slimy feel that terrified him.

Something splashed, off to his left, and JJ faltered again. There were sure to be rats in here. He forced himself to stay calm and sank up to his shoulders.

It's only a couple of feet, he chastised himself. You're already wet, so stop fucking about.

He took a deep breath, reluctantly let go of the cement and pushed off, holding his head as high as he could. He could not allow his head to go under that murky surface, not even for a second. Not even if two imaginary naked girls were cheering him on from the banks of the canal. He doggy-paddled to the floating man, grabbed an ankle and towed him backwards towards his clothes.

Teeth chattering uncontrollably, JJ boosted himself out of the water and redressed rapidly. He hunkered down on the lip of the canal and rolled the man face up. His eyes and mouth were open. JJ ignored that and patted him down, his shaking fingers swiftly picking the pockets clean. He snagged a wallet from inside the jacket; in the front pocket of the man's chinos he found a set of car keys and, weirdly, pieces of a mobile phone.

Satisfied he had retrieved everything of value, JJ released the man and watched as he slid silently back into the water and bobbed away, back towards the reeds. He rolled once, his sightless eyes turning in JJ's direction as though in admonishment, before slipping under the surface again.

Unnerved by the dead man's glance, JJ bolted from the canal. He'd gone three streets before he stopped under a street lamp and opened the wallet.

'Holy fuck!'

Jackpot. There were a couple of credit cards and some serious money. JJ skimmed through it quickly: there had to be the guts of a grand in there. Okay, the cash was wet, but it would dry out. He found a car park ticket tucked behind the cash, and his grin got a whole lot wider when he recognised the name of the car park. He opened his palm and looked at the set of keys; there was an Audi logo on the keyring and, beside that, a small silver chain with a silver ball on it. He could dry this ticket out easily and get it.

An Audi. Sweet.

JJ thought about the man's open, staring eyes, his body drifting in the cold water of the canal. Then he shrugged and shoved the wallet into the pocket of his hoodie. No point beating himself up about that. It wasn't like the guy was going to need money or a car now, anyway. No point in letting it go to waste.

Whistling softly under his breath, JJ bounced away, his humour much improved by his unexpected windfall.

# 3

The shopping centre car park was huge. For the second time that hot and humid bank holiday weekend, John Quigley, co-owner of QuicK Investigations, lost sight of his quarry. A black and much-dented Nissan Micra with blinking hazard lights blocked his path. In his attempt to hang back, John had inadvertently allowed the worst driver in the world to scupper his tail.

'C'mon, for Christ's sake. It's not a bus! You've plenty of room there! Lock hard! Lock hard!' John shouted, and tapped the horn.

The red-faced woman craned her neck around to glare at him. This was no mean feat: she must have weighed in at twenty stone, and she was crammed fast in the driver's seat. Her hair was damp and stuck to the back of her neck in ringlets. She gave John the evil eye.

John spread his hands, exasperated. She was trying to park the little car as if it were a Boeing 747.

He tapped the horn again. The Micra jerked and stalled. John slapped his forehead and clenched his jaw.

Finally, the Micra pulled in far enough for John to pass around it. He drove up and down the lanes, narrowly avoiding groups of people pushing trolley after trolley loaded with red and pink geraniums and terracotta-look plastic pots. With a sinking feeling, John pulled his Manta into a handicapped space and climbed out, ignoring the dirty look some old man in a pink-and-green plaid shirt was throwing at him.

'That space's reserved for people with difficulties.'

'I am having difficulties.'

'You're taking advantage of folks with disabilities.'

John ignored him.

The old man clucked loudly. John ignored him some more, scanned the car park and scowled. Where the hell had they gone? The old man shook his head and stalked away, disgusted.

John wiped the sweat off his forehead and cursed under his breath. He blamed the good weather for this sad state of affairs. If every single wannabe gardener weren't out trying to buy bedding plants and bags of topsoil, John might have some chance of tailing Martin Conway and his probable mistress. He shook his head. What sort of a bloke took his mistress to a garden centre, anyway? Men took their wives to garden centres, not their mistresses. What kind of a sicko was this guy?

John grabbed his digital camera off the passenger seat, locked his door and trotted up the outside line of parked cars. Conway drove a distinctive silver and blue Toyota Carina, 03 reg, and John prayed he hadn't left it yet. If he had, John would never find him in the massive shopping-happy crowds. The centre held four different DIY and garden superstores. Conway could be heading for any one of them. There were two furniture shops, too, but so far Conway had always picked the garden places.

Three lanes in, John found the Toyota. It was empty.

'Shit.'

John glanced around hopefully, but there was no sign of either of the lovebirds. Growing steadily crosser, he snapped a few photos of the car, then pulled out his mobile and rang his partner.

Sarah Kenny answered on the second ring. 'QuicK Investigations, how may I help?'

'Have you got a crystal ball?'

'Hi, John, what's up?'

'I've lost him.'

'How?'

'Because some stupid woman got in my way.'

'Where are you?'

John heard the impatience in Sarah's voice and it irked him. 'The big DIY-centre place on the Naas Road.'

'He took her there? My, how romantic.'

'Yeah, not exactly the Love Shack,' John agreed. 'So what'll I do?'

'Look for them.'

'Look for them where? They could be anywhere.'

'Start with one place and work your way through them.'

John spied a McDonald's sign gleaming high in the air over the roof of the nearest superstore. His stomach grumbled loudly. In his mind's eye he saw himself eating a Big Mac and fries and drinking a very large Coca-Cola packed with ice. 'Yeah, well, there's about a million stupid people here. I've got a better idea. Why don't I wait and pick them up on the road outside the centre?'

'John, don't be so bloody lazy. Just have a scout round.'

'I got the photos of them leaving the house.'

'How long was he inside with her?'

'About five minutes.'

'So he was just picking her up, and we need more than that.'

The golden arches had never looked so inviting. John could actually feel his mouth watering. 'I'm trying to use common sense here. This place is stuffed. I could be farting round one shop and they could be in another – or, worse, I could be in one shop and they could be back in the car and heading out again.'

'You're being paid to watch them. So watch them. We need those photos. Mrs Conway wants proof that he's fooling around. Proof, John! That includes when they entered—'

John blew hard into the phone and slapped it against the palm of his hand. 'Sarah? Sarah…can't…what? Brea…up.'

'John, I know you can hear me fine,' Sarah said. 'I said—'

'What? I'm try—' John switched off his mobile and slid it into the back pocket of his jeans.

She could get stuffed. She had dragged him in on a bank holiday Monday, and now she was barking orders at him. It was easy for her to order him around while she was sitting on her arse back in the relative cool of the office. She had probably eaten already. She had claimed she needed to put their files on computer, thus nicely avoiding doing any of the donkey-work. John glanced around the packed car park and shook his head. Screw that. He was going to hit the drive-through, grab a bite, sit in the car opposite the main gate and wait.

He stomped back across the shimmering tarmac and arrived just in time to see the back end of his beloved Manta being inched skywards by a small white tow truck.

'Hey!'

John pelted towards the truck. A skinny man in his forties, wearing sunglasses and a yellow jumpsuit with the name of the shopping centre printed across the back, glanced in his direction. John saw that he was operating a hand-held winch. The driver of the truck, also in his forties, but heavy and swarthy, watched John in the passenger-side wing-mirror. Both men looked hot and bored.

'Hey, stop! That's my car!' John skidded to a halt in front of the man with the winch. He was two inches taller than John. His gaunt face was sunburned and peeling badly around his nose. The sunglasses had brown lenses and were probably prescription.

He nodded his head to the white letters over the parking space. 'Are you handicapped, sir?'

John grinned. 'Depends on what you class as a handicap. I'm not a very good swimmer, and I'm told I can't sing worth a damn – although, personally, I think that last one is a matter of opinion.'

The skinny man didn't even crack a smile. 'So you have no disability that would entitle you to use the restricted space here.' He jerked his head once again to the large lettering over the space.

John dropped his shoulders and attempted his most contrite expression. 'Hey, come on, man. I was here less than three minutes. I'm looking for someone, okay? It's not like I planned to stay. I wasn't shopping.'

Skinny hit the button on the winch again. 'This car park is strictly for patrons.'

The Manta was now fully tilted onto her front wheels. As she rolled gently up onto the ramp, John glanced at her forlornly and tried again.

'C'mon – wait, please. Give me a break, will you? You can let her down. I'm here, aren't I? And nobody needed the space, did they? Look, tell you what: whatever the ticket is, I'll pay now – save you and me a lot of unnecessary bother.' John fumbled for his wallet.

'I'm sorry, sir. Your car will have to be processed.' Skinny turned off the winch and swung it onto the back of the truck. He walked around to the driver's side in slow, lazy strides. The driver handed him a clipboard, and Skinny carefully took down the Manta's registration and filled out the rest of the form.

'We are now impounding your car,' he said imperiously.

'You can't be fucking serious. I was here for three minutes.'

'Yes, you said.'

John looked around frantically, searching for someone who might be of assistance. His eyes found the old man in the plaid shirt, watching the action from the door of Alba Fine Furnishings with a smug grin on his crinkled face. John pointed towards him. 'There, see him? He knows; he saw me come in, he saw me…'

John stopped talking and glanced at the old man again, then back to Skinny. The driver of the tow truck snickered softly.

'Ah, that old bollocks.' John swore some more and glared at the old man. The old man suddenly remembered he had somewhere to be and walked off, head up, shoulders back. One-nil to the oldies. Ignore them at your peril.

'Sir, you may pick your car up at this address.' Skinny passed John a small white card.

'Hey, this place isn't anywhere near here.' John stared at the card in disbelief. 'How the hell am I supposed to follow you and pick it up?'

Skinny paused with his hand on the passenger door. If anything, he looked even more bored than he had when John first saw him. 'I don't know. You can't pick it up today, one way or the other.'

'What? Why the hell not?'

'Sir, it's a bank holiday. Our collection office is closed on bank holidays.' Skinny smiled for the first time. It didn't make him look any friendlier. 'You may pick your vehicle up tomorrow. The opening hours are printed on the card I have given you.'

John stared at him. The hot midday sun burned the back of his neck, and his shirt was stuck to his back. Somewhere deep inside his body, perhaps in his spleen, something popped and fizzled. His shoulders tightened with a sudden surge of adrenaline. His fingers balled the card into mush.

'You're taking my car because I parked it for three minutes in an empty fucking space, and now you're telling me I can't get it back until tomorrow?' The words sounded distorted and muffled, probably as a result of speaking through clenched teeth. People had begun to notice the exchange. Little interested groups were beginning to form.

Skinny's smile stretched a micro-millimetre further. 'Yes, sir.'

John took a step towards him. 'You sadistic prick. You're really enjoying this, aren't you?'

Skinny removed his hand from the door and drew himself up to his full height. 'If you have any complaints about this seizure, you may, of course, take it up with our complaints department. That number is also printed on the back of the card I have given you.'

Whole sections of John's scalp prickled. He recognised this sensation as a warning that his blood pressure was rising rapidly. Using every ounce of restraint he possessed, John forced himself to breathe deeply and step back. He knew that, if he didn't, there was an excellent chance he would be arrested for attempted murder. And there were way too many witnesses for that.

Skinny watched him for a second longer with cool eyes, then turned and climbed into the passenger seat. The driver started the engine and drove off. John saw him laughing, and another piece of his scalp twitched. He stood with his hands in tight fists and watched as his beloved, pristine silver 1985 Opel Manta Berlinetta – a car he had restored from practically nothing – disappeared around the corner with no one but two obvious devil-worshippers to take care of her. Disappointed by the lack of action, the crowd went back to enjoying the beautiful day.

John stalked out onto the main road to the nearest bus stop and waited, in the blistering heat, for a bus he knew would not be on time.

Half an hour later, as John Quigley, detective and potential homicidal maniac, waited, sweating up a storm, Martin Conway and his blonde lady-friend passed him on their way to God alone knows where.

They were laughing.

# 4

Big Jack Lawson hung up the phone and cracked his knuckles. 'That son of a bitch. He's a fucking wee weasel fuck, that's what he is: a weasely wee shite of the highest order.' Big Jack was originally from Fermanagh and, though he'd spent the best part of his life in Dublin, his voice still contained many of its Northern inflections.

He looked as scary as hell at the best of times, but right now, with the beginnings of a bad mood rumbling, he looked terrifying.

At fifty-three, he had lost a lot of his muscle, but he was still only a shade under six foot five and as broad across the shoulders as a young bull. The backs of his massive hands were coated in black hair, and his fingers were as thick as sausages. The hair on his head was dyed an inky black and worn in a slicked-up pompadour, with matching sideburns that could rival Elvis's. He favoured light-coloured suits, which never seemed to fit him properly, and black wing-tipped boots.

But no one laughed at Big Jack's sense of style, at least not to his face. If someone were to make that error, it could easily be his last. Jack's temper was legendary, and his potential for explosive violence was never far from the surface. On top of all that, his brother, Tom Lawson, was known to have links with a certain paramilitary organisation. Big Jack was not a man to be crossed.

And, right at that moment, he was sorely vexed.

'Problems?' Billy Lawson, his nephew, asked in his Northern drawl.

'There's always fucking something. I got to get over to the nightclub now and interview a fucking girl for Serena's spot. Lost another two fucking girls to Stringfellow's last week.'

Big Jack reached into the drawer by his hip, pulled out a bottle of Jameson's and poured a double shot into a filthy tumbler on the desk. He leaned back in his chair and slugged his drink back in one go. The wooden chair creaked alarmingly under his weight. He sighed. Problems... he hated problems. He tried to run a smooth ship. He had eight different legitimate businesses dotted around the city, including a strip joint on Leeson Street, a showroom and garage and two laundrettes – a private joke between him and his brother – and sometimes he felt he was being stretched ragged.

'You need me to do anything?'

Big Jack shook his head. 'Nah. Get going with them cars. Load 'em up at the warehouse – and make sure you don't go breaking no speed limits, you hear?'

'I hear you.'

'Paperwork is good for a quick look, so don't drag any fucking attention to yourself. Sammy's waiting on you down at the port, and he'll have a container ready; make sure there's no fucking about with weight. Get her on and turn about for home. Right?'

'We've been through all this before.'

Big Jack's head swivelled towards his nephew. 'I don't give a shite if we have or not.'

Billy sighed. 'Okay.'

'G'wan, now, away with you. Make sure you get there in plenty of time; no rushing.'

Billy put on a peaked cap and unhooked a set of keys from a chalkboard on the wall.

'Send up the young lad, would you?'

Billy nodded. Seconds later, Mick Quinn knocked on the door.

'Come on in,' Big Jack bawled.

Mick stepped into the prefab office, rubbing his grease-stained hands on his overalls nervously.

Big Jack looked him over appreciatively. Mick was seventeen, a wiry, black-haired young lad who had been working for Big Jack for nearly three years now. He was the son of one of Big Jack's old friends from back in the day, and, as much as it was possible for Big Jack to like anyone, he liked the young lad.

'I got a job for you. Need it taken care of today, pronto.'

Mick nodded but didn't ask any questions. Jack liked that about the lad, too.

Big Jack dug a pen and paper out of his drawer, scrawled something on it in his spidery handwriting and passed the page to Mick.

'That's what you're looking for and where. I don't need to tell you to keep this to yourself, do I?'

'No.' Mick shook his head. He scanned the page, folded it and slipped it into the pocket of his overalls. 'You want me to do it now?'

'Aye.'

'Okay.'

'Good lad. There'll be no one anywhere near the place, but don't take any chances. He's got an office upstairs; you'll likely find it there. I don't want no fuck-ups, hear me? In and out. Don't go fucking with any of his stuff or any of that shit. Just in and out. We clear?'

'Crystal.'

Big Jack grinned. He stood up, came around the desk and grabbed Mick by the back of the neck, his huge hand almost encircling it.

'You're a good wee lad. On you go, now.'

Mick smiled shyly. He let himself out and clattered down the metal stairs. Big Jack watched him go, then he made his way back to his desk and poured another finger of Jameson's.

'We'll see who's giving who the fucking orders,' he said aloud. He lowered himself gently back into the chair and knocked back his drink, his mind already moving and adapting to take control of the state of play. He didn't have a college education or many fancy words, but Big Jack was a clever son of a bitch, and the one thing he was not short of was balls.

*

By the time John Quigley made it back to the office on Wexford Street, he was deeply pissed off. He entered the dilapidated Georgian building and promptly tripped over the empty boxes stacked haphazardly in the hall, left there as usual by the crazy lady who ran the grocery shop on the ground floor. He kicked the boxes furiously and began to climb the three flights of creaking stairs to his office.

On the first floor he passed the door of Freak FM, a pirate radio station owned by local hustler Mike Brannigan. John shook his head at the cacophony of voices coming from inside. Probably half of the local secondary school was in there, playing shoutouts and talking big. Certainly, Mike was never daft enough to show his face around here: too many fingers in too many pies to risk getting snagged by the local cops on something as easy as a pirate raid.

John paused on the next floor to wipe the sweat from his brow. The building was old and in desperate need of ventilation; even after climbing one floor, John could feel the increase in heat. He knew his office on the top floor would be like a sauna.

John tried the door of the second-floor office, giving the handle a good rattle. It was locked, as he had figured it would be. Rodney Mitchell, solicitor, friend and alcoholic, was still MIA. His office hadn't been open for ten days now. John shook his head. Rod had not only fallen off the wagon, he'd been crushed under the wheels.

By the time he made it to the top floor, opened the door and found Sarah holding hands across her desk with a large grey-haired man in a sombre dark suit, John was positively steaming.

Sarah and the man jumped when he slammed the door. The man looked flustered; he pulled his hand back as though burned and cleared his throat twice in quick succession. A dark flush spread rapidly across his already ruddy cheeks.

John nodded to Sarah, pulled a bottle of not-very-cold water from a press and gulped long and hard. Sated, he wiped his mouth.

'Hot as hell out there, isn't it?'

Sarah raised one cool eyebrow and shot him The Look. John put the bottle back, wiped the sweat from his forehead and ignored her.

'John' – Sarah extended a perfectly tanned arm – 'this is James Reid. Mr Reid, my partner, John Quigley. You must excuse his appearance and brusque manner. He's been out on a particularly difficult case all morning.'

John heard the tint of temper in her voice, and it did nothing to make him want to behave any better. He gave Sarah a sarcastic smile. She wore a pale-pink shirt, washed-out Levi's and sandals. She didn't look hot and bothered. She didn't look like she'd spent the morning traipsing around town on a worthless jaunt. Her car hadn't been towed away by Satan's minions.

'Yep,' he said, 'excuse me.'

'Hello.' James Reid nodded to John, looking uncomfortably aware of the crackle of animosity that had just passed between the two detectives.

'Howya.' John pulled off his T-shirt and wiped under his arms with it. He threw it onto his desk, grabbed the bottom of the sash window and hauled at it with all his might. Of course, it didn't budge an inch; it had been painted over so many times that it might as well have been nailed shut. After a few more seconds of grunting and straining, John abandoned the humiliating struggle. He turned and leaned against the window, adopting a casual air that fooled no one.

'So, what we talking about?'

James Reid stared at John and cleared his throat again. He was about fifty, with a kindly, slightly weather-beaten face. He had broad features, to go with his broad frame, and closely cropped grey hair. There was a shaving rash on his neck. He wore a black double-breasted suit, a pristine white shirt and a black tie. The suit looked new, and he wore it like he was under sufferance. John guessed that it wasn't his normal attire.

'Mr Reid has just returned from a funeral,' Sarah said. Her lips were tight with disapproval and her dark-brown eyes flashed dangerously. 'His brother's funeral.'

John stalked across the room and threw himself into his chair.

'I'm sorry to hear that.' If she was trying to make him feel like a heel, she could get lost. How was he supposed to have known? He wasn't a mind reader. He opened the press behind his desk, took out a fresh white T-shirt and pulled it over his head. Still, maybe he had spoken out of turn. If he didn't lay off soon, Sarah would slap his face for him, client or no client.

'My condolences.'

James Reid nodded. 'Aye, well. Thank you. It was a bit of a day.'

John lit a cigarette, gaining level two of The Look from Sarah. Ever since the ban on smoking in the workplace had become law, John had cheerfully ignored it. He cocked his head to one side. 'You from New Ross?'

James Reid glanced at him, surprised. 'Close enough, all right. Near Duncannon.'

'Thought the accent sounded familiar.'

'Do you have people down that way yourself?'

'Nope.' John blew out a stream of smoke. 'I bought some parts for my car from a guy from New Ross. Never forgot the accent. He talked like he could charm birds out of trees; then the fucker stiffed me. If I ever see him again, I'll wring his scrawny neck.'

'Aye, well. There's a lot of that kind of carry-on around the country.' James Reid somehow managed to look even more uncomfortable. 'Fierce, the way some folk carry on, so it is.'

'Before you… returned, John,' Sarah said, 'Mr Reid was—'

'You can call me James.'

'Ah, okay.' Sarah smiled. 'James was telling me that he'd like his brother's death investigated.' She spoke in a perfectly neutral voice, but John knew her too well to be fooled. He could tell she was close to boiling point. Time to quit acting the idiot.

He pulled out a notebook and pen and waited, his hand hovering over the paper. 'Okay. We can do that. So what are we looking at?'

'His brother died last week in a drowning accident.'

'It was no accident,' James said. 'That I can assure you. My brother did not drown in an accident.'

Sarah glanced at him, then back to John. 'The gardaí are involved, but James believes they're satisfied that it was death by misadventure.'

'What's the name of the officer handling the case?'

'Detective Inspector Jim Stafford. He's in Kevin Street.'

'Never heard of him.' John looked at James Reid. 'If the police are looking into it, why do you need us?'

'Like I said, I don't think they're really looking for anyone.'

'Why not?'

James Reid took a couple of seconds to reply. Then, as if deciding something, he sighed heavily. 'At first they thought David might have been robbed, and he either fell or was pushed into the canal.'

'What made them think that?'

'His wallet was gone, he had a head injury and they reckon they found traces of his blood on the path near where he was found.'

'So why aren't they looking for the mugger?'

'Exactly!' James Reid nodded vigorously. 'That's exactly what I said!'

'Now, though,' Sarah said firmly, 'the gardaí say he might have been robbed earlier in the evening.'

'Why?'

Sarah shrugged.

'Oh, aye,' James said angrily. 'Oh, aye; then he was walking home, fell, slipped into the canal and drowned.'

'What makes them so keen to mark it as an accident?' John asked.

'You might as well know that they're saying he was drunk. I said that was b— well, sure, what if he was? David liked a drink, but he could handle it. I don't think I ever saw him falling around drunk in my life. They did a test, got a blood alcohol reading, and it was high, right enough; but there was no way it was high enough for him to just fall into a canal and drown.'

'What was the reading, do you know?'

'Point two; that's what the coroner reckons.'

John and Sarah exchanged glances. That was more than high. David Reid must have been trashed.

'And another thing,' James said. 'Why is his car missing?'

John raised an eyebrow. 'Is it?'

'No trace of it. Does that sound fishy to you?'

'It would certainly have me asking questions.'

'Like I already said, the gardaí haven't ruled out the possibility that he was mugged earlier; his car keys could have been taken then,' Sarah said firmly.

'What kind of car is it?' John asked.

'Brand new Audi Quattro, silver. He'd only bought it a few months ago.'

'Definitely missing?'

'No sign of it anywhere.'

'That's interesting.'

'That's what I think.'

John scribbled 'Missing Audi and wallet, possible mugging' at the top of a clean page. 'What do you think happened that night, Mr Reid?'

'I think my brother was murdered.'

John wrote 'Murdered?' and underlined it. He glanced at Sarah. She inclined her head ever so softly to the right. Her long dark hair fell off her shoulder. John understood her expression immediately: she had already heard the story, and she didn't buy it. John felt a twinge of sympathy for this big, awkward man.

'Was there any sign of a struggle?'

'He had a bad head injury, didn't he?'

'No, I mean any other sign – bruising, torn clothing, anything that might suggest he was assaulted rather than just fell?'

James exhaled sharply and rubbed his hands along his thighs. 'No, nothing like that. But his mobile was all smashed up. The cops found bits of it in his pockets.'

John frowned. That was strange. If he had been attacked, why would someone smash up his phone? Why wouldn't they rob it, along with the wallet and car? 'Were there any witnesses? Nobody heard anything?'

James raised his head and glanced imploringly at John. 'No, no one heard anything or saw anything.'

'I'd like to see a copy of the incident report. Was there a post-mortem?'

'I'll get you a copy of the report.'

'Thank you.'

'Would your brother normally drink if he was driving?' Sarah asked.

'No, never. That's why their theory' – he spat the word out – 'is that he got drunk, left the car in town, started walking home and had an accident. But that doesn't make sense. Why would he have walked across the bridge if he was coming from town? He lives on the town side of the canal.'

'Who says he was in town?' John asked.

'One of his friends met up with him earlier that day.'

'What's his name?'

'Max Ashcroft.'

John wrote that down too. 'Do you have a number for this man?'

'I'll have to have a look for it. Or you could ask Larry Cole – he's David's closest friend. He's a solicitor. Himself and David know each other a good couple of years now. They play golf together.'

'Okay. Get that number and we'll talk to him.'

'Well… that was it. They said he most likely walked home from town and fell over the bridge; because he was so drunk, he couldn't find his way to the bank and drowned.'

John wrote 'bridge'.

'Did you ever hear the like? They tell me he drowned in less than five feet of water. Sure, even that doesn't even make sense. David wasn't the tallest, to be sure, but…' James balled his huge hands into fists and opened them again. 'I don't understand how he drowned. It doesn't make sense.'

'Unless he was unconscious,' Sarah said softly.

Something about this story triggered John's overheated brain into action. He glanced up. 'Where did this happen?'

'Not two miles from here, over in Kilmainham.' James ran his hand over the raised, angry skin on his neck. 'Them fuckers are going to try and return a verdict of death by misadventure, I know they will.' He glanced at Sarah. 'Sorry for swearing.'

'That's okay.' Sarah smiled. 'I'm sorry to have to ask, but was there any suggestion or possibility of suicide?'

'No.'

John put out his cigarette. Now he remembered. He had heard something about this on the news. He remembered thinking that the guy must have been pretty smashed to die like that. A twinge of guilt joined up with the one of sympathy. Pretty soon he'd have a whole set.

James yanked at his tie and opened the top button of his shirt.

'Look, I told the cops this and I'm telling you the same: something was up. The last few weeks, David… well, he seemed to be a little under the weather. He wasn't suicidal, not by a long shot, but there was something going on with him. I spoke to him on the morning he died, and he was in good enough form – told me he'd be coming down the following weekend, and that he'd been thinking of taking a bit of a break towards the end of September.' He glanced at John. 'It sounded to me like he was feeling better in himself.'

'What do you mean, he was under the weather?'

'Just not himself. Something wasn't right, I know it.'

'What about his friends?' Sarah said. 'Did they notice anything unusual in his behaviour lately?'

'I don't know, they never said… I suppose you'd be better off talking to them yourself. There's a gang of them go golfing regularly.'

'Is there? If you could get me the names and numbers, that would be great.'

'I only have Larry's number. I don't know the rest of that shower at all.'

'Shower?' John said. 'You're not so fond of them?'

'Ah, I met them a few times… they're all full of themselves, you know.' James shrugged, suddenly looking very tired and defeated. 'Wouldn't be my sort, now, I tell you. You might find their numbers at David's house.'

'I have the keys to David's house,' Sarah said to John, by way of an explanation.

'I haven't been back to the house myself since the first day I found out,' James said softly. 'I – I just haven't.'

John nodded sympathetically. 'Not to worry, we'll have a look and have a word with his friends.'

Sarah leaned forward in her chair. 'The night of his accident, did your—'

She flinched as James rose to his feet so fast that his chair toppled over. Two spots of colour flared high in his cheeks. 'It was no accident. I keep telling you that, I keep telling the gardaí. Someone must have attacked David, they robbed him and they threw him in the fucking canal!'

He straightened his shoulders, righted his chair and sat back down. 'Look, I want you two to find out what happened. I don't give a shite what the gardaí say. My brother was no suicide. He wasn't a drunk, either. I want you to find out what the hell happened that night. I want to know why my brother is dead. I want some answers!'

Sarah said nothing. John felt a trickle of sweat run down his back and into his soggy underpants.

'Can you do that for me?'

Sarah sat back in her chair, her face stony. 'Mr Reid, there's no need for you to get so upset. We're investigators; it's our job to keep an open mind and to consider all possibilities. Including the possibility that what happened to your brother was an accident.'

'I know. I'm sorry. I shouldn't have shouted like that.' James ran his hands through his hair, his expression one of bewilderment and embarrassment. 'I'm sorry, but no one wants to listen to me. I know something happened to him. I can't explain it; I just know. I can feel it in my gut.'

Sarah glanced over at John. He waited. It was her call. It was a good minute before she sighed and said, 'All right, we'll take your case.'

'Thank you.' James tried to smile, but it was a desperate parody.

'I know you've explained to me already,' Sarah said, 'but tell John everything you know again, from the beginning. Everything you noticed about your brother's recent behaviour.'

James tugged at his shirt collar and glanced at the window. 'It's hot in here. Can I give that window a try?'

'Knock yourself out,' John said. 'It hasn't been open since we took over this office. I doubt the devil himself could—'

James stood up, seized the window frame and flexed his massive back. There was a sharp cracking sound, and the layers of gloss paint splintered and gave way. The window slid open.

John stared at it. Sarah swallowed.

James leaned on the sill and took a deep lungful of fresh air. 'Ah, that's better.'

Then, with a dignified grace that belied his anguish, he settled back into the chair and began to fill them in on the remarkably little he knew about his younger brother.

'I suppose, in a way, David was always different. My father, God rest him, used to call him the black sheep of the family…'

# 5

As soon as James Reid left, Sarah read over her notes. 'God, where do we even start with this? I mean, what can we do that the gardaí aren't already doing? I really don't see what we can do with it.'

'Then you can tell him. Jesus, that guy's as strong as an ox.'

'Poor man. He's obviously distraught.'

'He's probably right, though.'

Sarah glanced up. 'You think someone killed his brother? On purpose?'

'I don't think he decided to go for a dip himself.'

'John, for heaven's sake—'

'What?' John looked blankly at her.

'Do you have to be so glib? The man is dead.'

'Right, so he won't care what I say.'

'John.'

'What? I'm just saying. I'm still allowed to talk in this office, aren't I?'

Sarah flung her pen at him and missed by a mile.

'Nice shot.'

'Shut up and give me my pen back.'

'Look, I don't buy the idea that he was murdered any more than you do, but he would have been an easy target for a mugging.' John threw the pen back to her. 'Think about it: the man was blotto, he had a point-two blood reading and he's staggering home from God knows

43

where. He gets jumped and winds up in the canal. It's not beyond the realm of possibility. And we're all about the possibilities, aren't we?' he added, mimicking her slightly.

'He could have lost his wallet earlier that evening; the broken phone suggests he might have slipped more than once. He walks home, falls into the canal and is so plastered he can't get out. It happens.'

'Does it?'

'You know, not everything in life has to be complicated.' Sarah wore a thoughtful expression as she perused her scrawled notes. 'Sometimes accidents happen. It's sad, but it's a part of life.'

John watched her chew her bottom lip and thought how cute she looked when she was concentrating. 'What?'

'I'm not sure. The car being gone is a puzzle.'

'Well, there you go, then.'

Sarah Kenny was one year younger than him. She was tall, five foot ten in her socks, and slim without being too skinny. She had thick, almost-black hair that she wore long and straight. She had deep-brown, intelligent eyes and perfect Cupid's-bow lips. She was sharp-tongued and clever in a way that most people found irritating – but if she cared what other people thought of her, it didn't show. She was ferociously loyal and fair and would always fight for the underdog, but she didn't suffer fools. She walked with a slight limp where she had been shot the year before by a drug dealer named Patrick York, although it was improving dramatically since she had taken up Pilates. She was an intense person, private and reserved. Although he had known her for most of his life, sometimes John felt he hardly knew her at all. She was his best friend, and he loved her desperately.

They had dated when they were first free from school, and had been happy until John had blown it in a spectacular fashion. Because of him and his betrayal, Sarah had left Ireland and spent years in England doing God knew what with God knew whom. Her two older sisters, Jackie and Helen, hated John with an unbridled passion and couldn't understand why she worked with him. For her part, Sarah never spoke about his betrayal or her time away; and, although John was sometimes curious, he never pushed for information she didn't offer to share. He was just happy she was in his life, and he saw no need to rock the boat. He figured she would open up when she was ready.

John popped another cigarette into his mouth and lit it.

'You know it's against the law to smoke in here,' Sarah said. 'This is a place of work.'

'So arrest me.' John scanned down his own page.

David Reid had been forty-four when he'd drowned. He was a bachelor and had lived at 428 South Circular Road, Dublin 8. He had worked as a furniture designer; he and his business partner, Lillian Daly, ran a small workshop in Dundrum that had made pricey handmade furniture for over ten years. James Reid thought it was a successful company, not in the big league, but easily carrying its own weight. David Reid had no ex-wives, no children, no pets and no girlfriends, and no close friends that his brother knew about, except Laurence Cole and the group of golf buddies. David's only interests appeared to be cars, clothes, work and golf weekends.

'Not much to go on, is it?' John said.

'Not really. What if he did have his car; what if he he was driving—'

'Drunk as that?'

'—and he was attacked? Someone might have flagged him down. Maybe he was attacked for the new car.'

'A carjacking, in Dublin?'

'It happens, doesn't it?'

'Not very often.' John glanced at his watch. Across town, some of his mates were having a barbeque. He could still make it. There were plenty of hours left in the day; it wasn't too late to soak up some rays and down a few cold ones. 'So…what do you want to do?'

'Let's go take a look at where he drowned.'

'Today?

'Yes, today!'

Visions of ice-cold beer shimmered, then vanished. John sighed. 'I don't have my car.'

'We can take the Fiesta.' Sarah looked up. 'Wait – what happened to your car? Were you carjacked too?'

'A car park Nazi happened.'

'Ah! No wonder you were so touchy earlier. Let me guess: did you park in a handicapped space?'

'Sarah, why don't you—'

'Did you at least get a picture of Conway with her in the car?'

John shook his head. 'Just coming out of the house.'

'Dammit!'

'It's not that easy to follow him.'

'Now we'll have to wait until next time he arranges a trip.'

'I'll get the money shot.'

'Mrs Conway wants proof, John.'

'I know. I said I'll do it.'

'You missed him last Saturday, too. We can't keep charging Mrs Conway for a job that should have only taken an hour or so.'

'I told you already, I didn't know the mistress had a car too. I thought they were walking somewhere. By the time I'd run back and got my car, they were gone.'

'Still.'

'Still what?'

'We need a photo of them actually... you know.'

'Getting it on?' John said, grinning.

'At least catch them kissing. She said she'll take kissing.'

'I said I'd get it.'

Sarah relented. 'Why do you think they always go to shopping centres? That's just weird.'

'I dunno.' John stubbed out his cigarette. 'Maybe they're not having an affair at all. Maybe they are just friends.'

'Then why does he lie about seeing her?'

'Doesn't want the missus to get jealous.'

Sarah shook her head. 'No, there's definitely something kinky going on.'

'I've never seen them as much as hold hands.'

'It's a strange one, all right.'

'Do you really want to go look at that bridge now?'

Sarah switched off her computer. 'Yes, I do.'

'It'll still be there tomorrow.'

'John.'

'All right, let's go. But I'm driving.'

Sarah snatched the keys off her desk and dropped them into her shirt pocket. 'Uh-uh, hotshot. My "piece of shit", I drive.'

'It's the company car.'

'Nice try. You'll still have to ride shotgun.'

'Forget it, I'll walk.'

'Suit yourself.'

'I will.'

'Fine.'

Sarah grinned, and John scowled at her. He knew she knew he would fold. He always folded. That was why he was sitting in the office, on a hot June bank holiday weekend, instead of lying on his back over at Dollymount Strand with the lads, drinking Becks from a cooler, playing football and getting sunstroke. Sarah had guilted him into working because he had missed Conway on Saturday – and now, because some Nazi had impounded his car, he had missed Conway again and he had no ammunition to ward off Sarah's zeal. He knew she would make him wear a seatbelt; he knew she would slow down for every orange light; he knew she would park carefully. He knew she would be silently laughing at his cross face. John wondered what horrible things he had done in a past life to deserve days like this.

'Well?'

John heaved himself out of his chair. 'You drive. I don't feel like it anyway.'

'Right.'

'Ah, shaddup.'

*

At the bridge, Sarah leaned over the side and frowned. 'Where do they think he fell in from?'

'I don't know.' John stared at the huge pillars holding up the new Luas line. He squinted at a plaque overhead; it read 'Ann Devlin Bridge'. 'Who's Ann Devlin?'

'She was Robert Emmet's girlfriend.'

John looked surprised. 'How do you know that?'

'I read.' Sarah tilted her head. 'It looks pretty shallow to me. Do you think the water level's dropped because of the good weather?'

'Probably.' John, below her on the cement towpath, squatted down on his hunkers and skipped a small stone across the still surface. The water was unusually clear, and he could see all the crap and disused trolleys sticking out of the silt at the bottom. A lone swan paddled about a few feet from him, keeping a wary eye on the action.

'I'd be surprised if it was even five feet,' Sarah said. 'If it had been the other side of the lock, I'd understand; water's pretty deep there.'

'It was probably deeper here last week, though. There was a good bit of rain on the Thursday, the day before he drowned.'

'Wow, how can you remember that?'

'Because I washed the car and then it bloody rained on it.'

Sarah laughed. 'Okay then, I believe you.' She looked at the water again. 'We need something to measure it.'

'Why?'

'To see how deep it is.'

'What difference does it make? We know he drowned here; that's not in dispute.'

'I just want to know. I'm going to the car. Wait there.' Her head disappeared from view.

John sighed and sat down on the grass. The sun beat down mercilessly and he was feeling more and more irritable by the second. Maybe, after they measured the damn water, he might still make it to the Strand in time for a hot dog...

'Okay, I've got a tape – here.' Sarah tossed a bright-yellow tape measure over the side of the bridge. It landed with a solid thump, inches from John's feet. 'Stick it in and see how deep it is. Make sure you give the bottom a good poke.'

'Excuse me?' John started to laugh. 'And you a convent girl.'

'Oh, ha ha.'

'What are you doing with a tape measure in the car, anyway?'

'I have all sorts of tools in the car. You never know what you might need on a job.'

'Did you learn that from this week's copy of How to Be a Detective?'

'Just see how deep the water is!'

'And what are you going to do? Direct?'

'I'm going to have a look around on the opposite bank.' She disappeared again.

John went to the lip of the canal. Underneath the bridge, in the cool shadows, a dark shape scuttled along the wall and slipped into the water, casting a minor ripple. John crunched over broken glass and watched, disgusted, as a sleek black body exited the water on the opposite side and disappeared into the thick reeds.

The lads were probably starting the barbeque about now. There would be beefburgers, hot dogs, fried tomatoes, fried onions, lashings of sauce – John's stomach gurgled just thinking about it – and here he was, sharing his day with rats and whatever other filth he could rustle up from the bottom of the canal with a yellow tape measure. Sweet. This could have waited until the following day.

He unrolled the tape and dipped it into the water. It slid down, deep into the silt. John pushed until the tape buckled.

'Four feet, eight inches,' he yelled.

'What?' Sarah came into view on the opposite back.

John repeated the measurement.

'So not even five feet.' Sarah stared into the water and frowned. 'How the hell did he drown?'

'Sarah, it doesn't have to be deep. He had a head injury. And, like I said, if he was blotto drunk, he could easily have drowned. What we need to do is get a good look at the accident report.'

John rolled up the tape and flung it across the canal to Sarah. He stepped back out into the sunlight and sat down on the grass.

Sarah picked up the tape and scanned around the dried grass, pushing a few wilting nettles back with her foot. She bent down and peered at every scrap of paper and cigarette butt. John watched her, feeling the sun burn the back of his neck and scalp. He was getting a headache.

'The cops already looked around.'

'I'm just looking.'

'What are you looking for, Sarah?'

'I don't know. Just give me a minute.'

Sarah worked her way slowly along the line of the bridge, down to the water's edge, and then retraced her steps slowly. 'If he didn't fall, then what the hell was he doing here? It doesn't make any sense.'

'What do you mean?'

'James Reid is right: David's house is on this side of the canal. If he had been coming from town, he wouldn't have passed this way. So where was he coming from?'

'I don't know.' John watched her and knew she was trying to visualise that night. He saw her look up the bank and frown.

'Even if he did fall, how did he end up in the water?'

'If? Now you think he was attacked?'

'It's all about the possibilities,' she threw back at him.

Overhead, the Luas rumbled by. John glanced at his watch again. He could grab it as far as Connolly and then take a bus to Dollymount, be there by two…

'It looks like there are drag marks here.' Sarah pointed to a faint line in the dry grass with her big toe.

'So? Could have been kids playing about, could have been someone hauling a bag of rubbish to the canal, could have been anything.'

'Could be drag marks. John, just take a look around. If someone was here, maybe—'

'Maybe they were good enough to leave an address?'

'Will you just look?'

'I thought the cops said he fell off the bridge.'

'They said that was the most likely scenario. "Most likely" doesn't mean anything to me.'

John sighed. He knew from her voice that he might as well forget about escape. The day was a complete bust. He climbed to his feet. 'All right, I'll take a look.'

'Thanks.' Sarah resumed her study of the bank.

John stepped back into the shadows. He waited for his eyes to adjust to the gloom and looked around. There was plenty of evidence that the bridge was used as shelter: cigarette butts, crushed cans and bent spoons littered the pockmarked cement, along with some aged dog crap – at least, John hoped it had come from a dog. The place stank to high heaven.

John walked through the tunnel out into the sunlight on the other side. Why would a furniture designer have walked under this bridge at night? Was he on his way home from somewhere – walking back from a party, a friend's house, maybe? It wasn't exactly the safest of places. Even in the broad light of day, it made John a little uneasy. But late at night…

'John!'

John turned and made his way back under the tunnel. 'What?'

'I've found something.'

Sarah was kneeling, reaching for something in the dock leaves and dandelions growing at the foot of the stone plinth supporting the bridge. She cleaned it on the hem of her shirt and stared at it.

'What is it?'

'It's a globe.'

'A globe?'

'Yes, a globe.' Sarah turned it over in her hand. It was a small silver globe, a little bigger than a marble. The words 'Meridian Club' were printed in relief across it. A small chain was attached to a link where the North Pole would have been; the other end of the chain was broken. Sarah bounced it in her hand. 'Heavy, too.'

'Is it off a necklace?'

'I don't know. This looks like it's solid silver.' Sarah held it up for him to see.

'It's more like a key chain.'

'I doubt it's been here too long; it's still shiny.'

'Nice catch.'

'Thanks.' Sarah bounced the globe in her hand again. 'Come on, let's go.'

'Where?'

'To his house, of course.'

'Now?' John glanced at his watch. 'Sarah, it's a bank holiday. Can't this wait until tomorrow?'

Sarah slipped the globe into her pocket and brushed her hands on the legs of her trousers. She regarded John across the water. 'You were the one who said you thought this man might have been attacked. Don't you think we should go take a look at his house? Learn a bit about him?'

'Yes, but why can't it wait until tomorrow?'

'Got something on?'

'Only a serious case of thirst. Andy Cosgrove is throwing one of his legendary barbecues.'

'Andy Cosgrove? You're kidding. I thought he almost poisoned half your crowd the last time he cooked?'

'Yep, lamb à la arse of fire.'

'And you're letting him cook again?'

John nodded. 'Yep.'

'God, you all deserve each other.'

John rubbed his hands together and glanced wistfully towards the road. 'So? Can we do this tomorrow?'

'Sure, go ahead.'

'Cheers. Promise I'll make it up to you.'

'Just make sure you're in tomorrow.'

'Scout's honour.'

'You were never a scout,' Sarah said. 'You need a lift?'

'Nah, I'm good.'

'You sure?'

'Yep.'

'Okay, see you tomorrow, then.'

'Thanks.' John galloped up the bank.

Sarah heard him jogging down the road and out of earshot as she dusted the last of the clay off her hands. She should have known John would have something on. It was a bank holiday and he had a life. Bank holidays, work days – they were all the same to her. She didn't have anywhere to go, except home. Maybe she'd call one of her sisters… She dismissed that thought as soon as it entered her head. Frankly, the idea of spending a glorious afternoon like this one with Jackie or Helen was not her idea of fun. Listening to them lecture her about her life, and how she should settle down, find a man, get a real job… ugh. Better to be alone than endure that. Maybe she'd grab a bite to eat in town, or go to the cinema, or something. Maybe she'd call over to her mother's house, see how she was. She had fallen the week before and sprained her wrist. It wasn't terribly serious, but it was sore, and she had been a bit off lately – nothing Sarah could put her finger on, just off. Sarah felt increasingly guilty about not spending more time with her.

'You want to come?'

Sarah looked up. John was standing on the footpath, his hands on his hips.

'What?'

'Do you want to come to the barbecue? I can't guarantee there won't be drunkenness and social degradation, maybe even some flesh shown, but they're a good bunch of lads.'

Sarah hesitated for a second, but then she smiled. 'Thanks, but I've got a ton of stuff to do.'

'Like what? Think fast, now.'

'I'm meeting Helen.'

John pulled a face. 'Bleagh. Rather you than me.'

'Stop that; she's still my sister,' Sarah said, but she couldn't help smiling.

'Okay, here comes the tram. Catch you tomorrow.' He waved and was gone.

Sarah scrambled slowly up the bank. Her ankle was hurting slightly, and she didn't want to put too much weight on it. By the time she'd made it to the top, John was boarding the Luas. He waved at her as he went past, his boyish, good-looking face beaming.

Sarah waved back, then dropped her head until the tram vanished around the corner. She pulled her mobile from her pocket and dialled her mother's house.

It was picked up almost immediately.

'Mum?'

'Sarah?'

'Jackie?'

'Hello, angel.'

'What are you doing there?'

'Well, it's a beautiful day. We thought we might take Mum out for a bite to eat. Barry thought it might do her good to get out of the house for a while.'

'Oh, is Barry there too?' Barry was Jackie's fiancé; Sarah couldn't stand him.

'Sure. What are you doing today? Would you like to come? We're just thinking somewhere local. We'd love to see you.'

We, we, we, all the way home, Sarah thought, somewhat uncharitably. 'No, I can't. I've got a job on. How is Mum?'

'She's fine, darling. Her wrist is looking a bit better. Want a word?'

'No, I'm… Tell her I called, and I'll give her a buzz later on.'

'Okay. Are you sure you won't join us? It seems ages since we've seen you.'

'No, honestly – I'd love to, but… another time. Well, tell Barry I said hi, won't you?'

'Of course.'

'Bye.' Sarah hung up and slipped the phone back into her jeans.

There had to be something she could do to keep herself occupied. Those kitchen cupboards – she'd been promising herself for weeks she'd give them a good clean-out…

She rested her arms on the bridge and stared into the water, thinking of her little one-bedroom apartment on Patrick Street. It was small, neat and incredibly quiet. When she'd first returned from England it had been her haven, but lately she'd begun to resent the quiet, had started putting the radio on as soon as she got home. And why, suddenly, did the thought of spending the afternoon watching a group of sweaty, semi-naked men eat undercooked meat and drink beer seem so appealing?

What the hell was wrong with her?

She pulled the globe from her pocket again and twirled it, letting it catch the light. Meridian Club. A travel agency, maybe? She didn't know why, but for some reason she felt sure it was connected to David Reid.

She dropped it back into her shirt pocket. She knew what she would do: she would go and check out David Reid's house herself, seeing as she was in the neighbourhood. After all, when the chips were down, she had nothing else to do except work, and she knew it. She could lie to John until she was blue in the face, but she couldn't lie to herself.

# 6

Sarah parked the car across the street from the two-storey, red-brick Victorian house and climbed out. It was cooler here, under the leafy canopies of the tall beech trees that lined the street, and Sarah leaned against her car and took a moment to enjoy it. Bank holidays were so quiet. There was hardly any traffic, none of the usual ruckus. The air was scented by flowers in the nearby gardens and the steady hum of distant lawnmowers filled the air. A bumblebee droned past, and Sarah watched his impossible, erratic flight with a smile.

She locked the Fiesta, tucked her handbag under her arm and crossed the street. She unlocked the front door with the spare set of keys James Reid had given her and stepped into a silent, cool hall.

The hall was spacious and airy. The floor was polished wood, a sisal-covered stairway ran along the left wall and at the bottom of this was an ornate phone table with a sleek silver cordless phone. Two reception rooms led off the hall; the kitchen, she could see from there, was to the rear of the house.

Sarah opened the first door and stepped into a nice-sized living room. A huge rubber plant in a teak and bronze stand dominated the bay window. Sarah touched the dark-green leaves, mildly jealous of its magnificent vitality. She had killed every single house plant she had ever bought, either by over-watering or by not watering enough. The only plant to survive her onslaught was a small supermarket cactus with plastic flowers that sat, dusty and neglected, on the window ledge outside her bedroom.

The furniture was inviting and tasteful: an antique davenport, brown leather armchairs and a matching sofa, and a hand-woven rug in front of an antique fireplace. A wide-screen TV and a stereo system that Sarah was fairly certain cost more than she earned in a year took up most of one corner. A recessed bookshelf groaned under the weight of bestsellers – hardbacks, all of them, and all without a single crease in their spines. She pulled out *The Da Vinci Code* – illustrated edition – and sniffed the virgin print: the pages had never been touched, much less admired. Clearly David Reid was more of a collector than a reader.

She replaced the book and flipped through the CD collection, smiling as she recognised some of her own favourites: Callas, Carreras, Tosca, Puccini, Montserrat Caballé. There was also a collection of 80s classics and six CDs of Elaine Page and Andrew Lloyd Webber, which Sarah didn't smile at. The teak magazine rack was full of newspapers and men's magazines – so at least he read something, Sarah thought snottily. A tall, slender sideboard with glass doors held elegant glasses and at least forty bottles of wine. Sarah ran her hand over it. It was a beautiful piece of workmanship, highly original and yet classical in its simplicity. Sarah wondered if David Reid had designed it himself.

She opened the connecting double doors and stepped into the next room. It was a dining room, but it looked like it was hardly ever used. Again, the furniture was beautiful and looked handmade. A large gardenia sat in a stainless-steel pot in the centre of the table. Sarah brushed her fingers against it. The delicate white flowers and silky green leaves glowed with good health, and the scent was intoxicating. How the hell did people do it?

She opened the door leading back to the hall and stepped into the kitchen. It was a nice kitchen – nothing fancy, but clean and homey, with pale marble worktops and Shaker-style units. Narrow sliding doors led out to a small, sunny patio. There were hanging baskets and terracotta urns filled with flowers, all bursting with colour; the high wall was covered in jasmine and Virginia creepers. There were two recliners facing south, and Sarah imagined that on sunny afternoons there would be nothing nicer than sitting out there with a book and a glass of cold, crisp wine, listening to the birds sing and letting the world pass on by. It occurred to her that most of these plants would surely die if James Reid didn't take care of them. That saddened her.

'God, stop being so maudlin,' she muttered under her breath, surprised at herself. What was wrong with her today? Now she was upset over the plants of some man she'd never met. Jesus, maybe John was right; maybe she did need to get out more.

She climbed the stairs and did a brief layout check. There was a master bedroom to the front of the house and two smaller guest bedrooms to the back. Another single bedroom in the centre had been converted to an office, and it was here that Sarah turned her attention first.

David Reid's office was a masterclass in simplicity and efficiency. It was clean and uncluttered, painted a pale primrose-yellow. Framed sketches of antique furniture covered the walls and a mechanical drawing board was pushed against the far wall. Under the one long window was a vast mahogany desk with a green leather inlay. The desk was neat: it held an Apple laptop, a flip-top calendar, a Rolodex and a silver-framed photo. Sarah sat in the swivel chair and ran her hands over the wood. It was smooth and highly buffed. She coveted it, then felt guilty as she recalled its owner's demise.

Sarah picked up the photo and studied it. It had clearly been taken on one of the golf trips James Reid had mentioned. Four suntanned men grinned back at her from an immaculate fairway. Sarah picked out David immediately. It was easy; he looked quite like his brother, although where James was big and slightly ungainly, David looked dapper and handsome in his golfing whites and sun visor. He was the shortest of the four men in the photo and wore a neat little black moustache. For some reason, Sarah thought with a grin, he put her in mind of a modern-day Hercule Poirot.

Sarah turned the photo over and unclipped the back. Just as she had expected, the names were neatly written in black ink across the back of the photo. 'Larry, Max, Clive and me, La Manga, '98.'

Sarah returned the photo to the frame and stared at the faces again. These men looked like friends. They might have known if David was depressed about anything – or, then again, they might not; it was Sarah's experience that men seldom opened up like women would.

She put the picture down and flicked through a couple of bills she found in the top drawer. Gas, electricity and phone – everything was paid up and paper-clipped together. A company chequebook was half empty, every stub filled in with the same tidy handwriting. She found an old ledger in the bottom drawer, lifted out the top sheet of paper and read it. It showed a recent order to supply forty ornate sideboards to a hotel in Wales.

Sarah drummed her fingers on the desk and glanced around the neat room. She was beginning to get a feeling for this man.

She hesitated for a second, then, feeling slightly intrusive, she turned on the laptop. The battery sign showed that the power was low, but Sarah soon realised she wasn't going to do much snooping anyway: David Reid's computer was protected by a password. Sarah typed in 'furniture', but it was rejected. Sighing, she turned the laptop off again. She had never been any good at that type of thing.

She checked out the master bedroom. It was bright and spacious, with honey-coloured floorboards. On one wall, two pieces of modern art took pride of place. The furniture was handmade from a deep, rich cherrywood. The sleigh bed was covered in a dark-red, hand-embroidered Chinese bedspread; the curtains were heavy suede, red silk and sand-coloured muslin, draped across the bay window in a looped, elaborate ensemble. It was a bit over the top, but Sarah was impressed at David Reid's sense of style. His whole house intrigued her.

She thought of John's bachelor pad in Ranelagh and huffed a laugh as she compared the two. She doubted John even noticed things like furnishings, and as for pieces of art, forget about it. If it hadn't been for his sister Carrie, he wouldn't even have curtains on the windows. And even at that, Sumo, John's beast of a dog, had managed to pull down the ones in the bedroom twice.

Sarah opened one of the wardrobe doors. David had had expensive taste in clothing, too. She ran her hands over the Armani suits and silk shirts that hung inside. Expensive house, top-of-the-line clothes, golfing trips and a new car; clearly David Reid had been doing something right.

On top of his bureau there was a large silver hand mirror, a set of gentleman's brushes that Sarah guessed were antique and a silver carriage clock. Next to that sat a basket of cufflinks and watches and another silver-framed photo. Sarah picked it up and recognised David again. He was younger in this picture, in his late twenties. He and a man with floppy blond hair sat on a wall, grinning broadly at the camera. David's arm was casually thrown over the other man's shoulder, but, casual or not, Sarah recognised the intimacy between the two men, and something clicked in her brain. The house, the style, the exquisite finishing... God, it was such a cliché, but David Reid had most likely been gay. James had never mentioned it. Maybe he didn't think it mattered, maybe he felt uncomfortable discussing his brother's sexuality. Either way, Sarah would bring it up next time they spoke. She didn't like being kept in the dark about anything pertaining to a case.

She looked around the room for another few minutes, but nothing jumped out at her, certainly nothing that would indicate why James Reid thought David might have been murdered. He seemed to have lived a quite normal life, had a moderately successful business and a small band of friends, enjoyed music and his garden. What was there to suggest anything had happened to him, other than a horrible, tragic accident?

Sarah ran her hand over the vibrant bedspread. She wondered who would be the recipient of all these wonderful things. James, probably. She didn't know him, of course, but somehow she couldn't imagine him savouring all these things with the same pride that his brother had obviously felt.

But then, trappings weren't everything. Had David Reid been lonely? Had he sometimes wished to have someone to share his things with? Had he had someone? Had he wanted more, or had he been happy with his place in the world? What had happened to him that night?

She was still musing over David Reid's belongings when someone kicked in the kitchen door.

# 7

'Fuck it, I cut me arm,' Sharpie Quinn said. He lifted his arm in disgust and licked the droplets of blood.

'I told you that glass would go everywhere. Should've broke the lock like I told you.' Mick Quinn – older by a mere two minutes – looked at his brother with world-weary resignation. He was beginning to regret ever telling Sharpie about his mission. 'Big Jack's gonna fucking go mental. He said not to make it look obvious.' Mick looked around him. 'This is bleedin' obvious.'

'Yo, fuck him. Why you always worrying what that dickhead thinks?'

'These fancy doors, they're easy. Would've only took a minute to unlock it. No need for the noise. I told you, he said no damage. You never listen.'

'Mick, you're giving me a pain in me hoop.' Sharpie pulled a two-inch shard of glass out of his skin. He held it up to the light and wrinkled his nose at it. 'Yo, look at that.'

'We're lucky there was no alarm.'

'Shit, bro, I told you there wasn't no alarm.' Sharpie tossed the shard behind him. 'Come on, man; let's do this thing.'

He kicked away the rest of the glass and climbed in through the door, taking care not to damage his brand-new runners. Mick followed. Once inside, they dusted each other off rapidly, checking for nicks and cuts.

'Here.' Mick handed Sharpie a pair of latex gloves and slipped on a pair of his own.

'Yo, this is real CSI shit.'

'Come on. We've got to move fast.'

They were almost identical in appearance, but as they approached adulthood, significant differences made them easy to tell apart. They were seventeen years old, black-haired, with brilliant blue eyes framed by long, luxurious lashes. They should have been handsome, but somehow they were not.

Mick wore his black hair short and usually dressed in jeans and Kicker boots. He didn't wear any earrings or jewellery, and his fingers were stained with oil and grease that wouldn't come off, no matter how many times he washed them with Swarfega. His hours of hard work as an apprentice mechanic had given him a wiry, muscular build. Ever since he was a little boy, Mick Quinn's passion had been cars.

Sharpie had a seven-inch scar running from below his ear to under his jaw. He wore his hair in cornrows, which he had redone every three months at a small African hairdresser's off Camden Street. He was also beginning to bulk up. He did weights regularly and guzzled protein powders and shakes in his quest to gain a body like that of his hero, Fifty Cent. The body wasn't the only thing he strove to mimic. Sharpie Quinn had found his place of worship on MTV Base, tickled green by the obscene wealth displayed by rappers like Snoop, Dre and The Game, but it was Fifty whom Sharpie adored above all others. So Sharpie wore huge jeans that hung halfway down his arse, snow-white runners, basketball tops, bandannas under baseball caps and a huge diamond earring – fake, of course, from H&M. He was, in his opinion, hard to the core, pure gangsta.

They had been raised single-handedly by their mother, a big brute of a woman with arms like two sides of beef, after their father had flown the coop back when the boys were three. Rose Quinn worked as a cleaner five nights and two mornings a week. She had never accepted a handout from anyone, and she liked to let everyone know it. She was sparing with her affections, quick to slap or sneer. It was an idyllic life for Sharpie, who cheerfully ignored her most of the time, and an uncomfortable one for Mick, whose very presence seemed to stoke her ire.

The two brothers hung around almost exclusively together. From an early age, they had shunned any attempts at friendship from other kids – not that many attempts were made in the first place. Folk might have tried to get to know Mick, but there was something about Sharpie – an unsavoury cast to his eyes, a sneer on his lips – that made people avoid him. It wasn't something anyone could put a finger on, but whatever it was that inspired unease about Sharpie, it spilled over onto Mick. They went everywhere together, with the exception of work.

Neither of the boys had finished secondary school, but while Mick was gaining a skill in mechanics, Sharpie was learning a craft of his own. He was a runner for an established gang, and was paid for his services in cannabis, which he resold from the back of a bike in his area. He robbed just about anything he could lay his hands on. He was banned from half the shops in the city centre, and his home was the first port of call whenever a break-in occurred in the neighbourhood. He had a juvenile record as long as his arm, including joyriding, theft, two arrests for assault causing actual bodily harm and three for carrying a concealed weapon. His stints in Pat's and his ability to keep his mouth shut had gained him cred amongst his peers, and other older hoods in the neighbourhood were starting to take note. They might have taken him on, but for his hair-trigger spasms of violence. Word was out that Sharpie was more trouble than he was worth. The only people who were happy dealing with him were a small gang made up of Nigerian immigrants and inner-city kids – and even they insisted he deal far away from their main areas.

Sharpie liked to pretend he had received his scar in a fight – he often held his head cocked to the side, so people could see it and be intimidated by it – but the truth was that he'd been sliced open by a junkie looking for fix money as he crossed a patch of waste ground in Ballymun. It had happened on a bright, cold morning, as he and Mick made one of their rare trips to school. They had been thirteen years old. The scar had faded to faint silver over the years, but Sharpie knew that had it not been for his brother – who was less than one minute behind him, having stopped to cadge some smokes from a group of lads he knew – he would have bled to death. When Mick had found him, he had been lying on his back, gasping for air, the front of his coat saturated with dark blood. Mick had stripped off his coat and jumper, ripped his vest off and wrapped it tight around his brother's neck, and carried him – actually carried him over his shoulder – to the nearest house. They made it to the hospital two minutes after Sharpie's heart had stopped. The doctor who revived him told Rose Quinn that if Mick hadn't acted so intelligently, Sharpie would almost have certainly have died. Mick even had his picture in the paper.

But Rose Quinn hadn't seen it quite the same way. When the photographer left, she had slapped Mick upside the head hard enough to make him stumble and fall. She told the ashen-faced boy, in a low, dangerous voice, that she held him responsible for the attack, that if he had been there in the first place, the attack might not have happened. She said brothers looked out for each other. She said that by letting his brother get attacked, Mick had as good as stabbed Sharpie himself.

Mick had never spent a day since then free from guilt. Especially since it had become clear that the post-attack Sharpie was not the same kid who had walked onto the waste ground that day. Something had changed in him – maybe from shock, maybe from the lack of oxygen, but from that day forward Sharpie was prone to strange moods and terrible temper tantrums that left him shaking with rage. Sometimes he blacked out; other times he acted like he didn't recognise those closest to him. The first time he attacked someone, the doctors said it was delayed shock, an oversensitive fight-or-flight response. They said it would get better over time.

It hadn't. And now, at seventeen, Sharpie Quinn was as dangerous as the loaded Glock he kept hidden in his bedroom.

Sharpie had ambitions. He was making good money for a kid his age, but he was just biding his time until he could move up into the big leagues and get a crew of his own together. That was where the real money was. Unbeknownst to Mick, Sharpie had recently purchased the Glock handgun and a round from a Nigerian crack-dealer called Ngolgo, who lived in a basement flat in Parnell Square. He had told Ngolgo he needed it for protection, because his business was the street. Ngolgo had given him a sly grin, shrugged one shoulder and pocketed the eight hundred euros. He didn't care what the kid wanted it for. Stupid kid had paid twice what the gun was worth, and that was fine by him.

Sharpie had developed a swagger of epic proportions after that purchase, even if most of the time he kept the gun under the floorboards in his bedroom. People noticed the new bravado and attitude. And when Sharpie fronted up to an older, bigger hash dealer and bitch-slapped him around the road for straying onto his turf, people knew: Sharpie was starting to believe his own hype.

'Where we goin'?' Sharpie asked.

'He said it was probably upstairs, in the office. Nice-looking gaff.'

'Kinda pouffy-looking.' Anything faintly effeminate angered Sharpie. To be considered a pouf was the worst thing he could think of. He had once stomped a guy half to death for 'making eyes' at him in a park.

'I like it.'

'You bleedin' would.' Sharpie's nostrils flared. 'I swear to God, Mick, sometimes I wonder about you. You're turnin' pussy on me.'

'I'm what?'

'You heard.'

'Yeah? I'm not the one wearing jewellery.'

'Fuck off.'

They made their way to the front hall and began to climb the stairs. Mick paused and stuck his head through the sitting room door. He spotted the music centre and gave a low whistle.

'What?' Sharpie stopped halfway up the stairs and looked at him.

'Nothing. He's got a nice stereo, that's all.'

Sharpie came back down and brushed past Mick. 'Nice! Worth a few quid.'

Mick's face fell. Why had he bothered to mention it?

'You want it?'

'Nah, come on. He said not to take anything, only what we came for.'

'Fuck him. You ain't his bitch.'

'Sharpie, I don't want it.'

'Suit yourself, man. But you want it, I'll take it for you here and now, straight up.'

'I said no.'

'Your loss.' Sharpie led the way upstairs, licking at the blood on his arm again. The cut wasn't so bad. The real pain came from the blistered skin on his forehead. He touched it with his fingertips and winced. 'I'm burnt to shite, so I am.'

'Told you not to fall asleep outside. Why do you want to be so tanned, anyway?'

'Better than that fuckin' milky look you got going on. When you take off that T-shirt you're gonna look like a ghost.'

'So I won't take it off.'

'Gotta take it off sometime.'

'Least my skin will stay on my body. You'll be peeling before the weekend.'

'I won't. I'll go brown.'

'You won't.'

'I always go brown. I got sallow skin.'

'You've the same fucking skin I got, and I ain't sallow.'

'Huh!' Sharpie pulled a face. He didn't like to be reminded of his milky-white complexion.

'Ma should've called you in.'

'Her and that bitch from next door were out gabbin' over the wall. I hate that bitch – always stickin' her nose into other people's business, goin' on about that bitch daughter of hers.'

'Which one?'

'The nurse. Always tryin' to rub Ma's face in how good that bitch turned out, as if being a nurse was somethin' special. Any cunt can be a nurse. Look at all the immigrants. They're nurses and doctors, aren't they? Shit, can't be that hard.' In spite of the fact that his greatest wish was to wake up one day as black as Fifty Cent, Sharpie's dislike of immigrants was almost as great as his dislike of gays.

'Still an' all, she should've been keeping an eye out.'

'Yo, be cool.' Sharpie clicked his fingers. 'Which one's the office?'

They found the office and searched it quickly, riffling through the drawers of David Reid's desk and then the filing cabinet.

'It's not here,' Mick said after a few minutes.

Sharpie slipped the laptop into his duffel bag and grinned. 'Easy money, baby.'

'Sharpie, he said—'

'Yeah, yeah, he said, "Suck my dick," and you said, "For how long?" Look, we can get readies for this. You gettin' so much you gonna turn down easy money?'

Mick shook his head.

'Hold up. We might as well have a look round this crib, now that we're here.'

'Sharpie—'

'That frame look silver to you?'

'Huh?'

'The frame on the desk. Give it here.'

Mick picked up the frame and looked at it. Big Jack would be furious if he found out stuff was missing from the house. 'I don't think this is such a good idea.'

'Ain't no one gonna miss shit like that. Give it here, I'll do it.'

'No.'

Sharpie glowered at him angrily. 'Look, the door's busted anyhow, what difference this gonna make?'

Mick opened the frame and removed the photo of David Reid and his friends. He slipped the frame into the bag with the laptop. 'I'm going to take a look around, see if he has it somewhere else. Try not to break anything else.'

Sharpie grinned. 'You the boss.'

Mick worked his way through all the rooms methodically, finishing with the master bedroom. Shaprie followed him in. His eyes gleamed when he spotted the jewellery on the bureau. He bounded across the floor in two steps. 'Yo, Mick! Look at all this shit.'

Mick was rifling though the locker by the bed. 'What?'

'All the fucking shit stashed here.' Sharpie picked up a watch, held it aloft and whistled. 'Is this a fucking Rolex?'

Mick lifted the mattress and peered underneath. Nothing. He glanced around the room appreciatively. He really liked this house, despite what Sharpie said. It was clean and quiet, not like his ma's house – big prints, fake flowers and scuffed lino, everything smelling of the deep fat fryer. He'd like a place like this someday; this place was the business.

'What do you think?'

'Could be fake.'

'Nah, man, this is the real deal.' Sharpie grinned. He clipped the watch onto his wrist and nodded at how it looked against his sunburned skin. It was a player's watch, straight up, exactly like the ones the guys wore in the videos. 'Yeah, this is bleedin' class,' he said, forgetting to be gangsta for a second in his delight.

'We'd better get out of here.'

'Hold up. It's not like that guy Reid's gonna be needin' any of this shit no more, right?'

'Sharpie, come on. I was told not to touch nothing, just get it and get out.'

'How's anyone gonna know if we took shit or not? You think anyone's gonna report a fuckin' busted door to the cops? You think they gonna care 'bout it?'

'Jack will find out. He always finds out. Then it's my fucking arse on the line.'

'So what if he does?' Sharpie's face darkened and his eyes took on that look, that look that said the red mist was coming down. 'Fuck, you're doin' him a favour even bein' here. Man ought to be kissin' your ass for what you're doin' for him, know what I'm sayin'?'

Mick scratched at the back of his neck. 'I don't know, Sharpie—'

'I don't give a bollocks what you don't know, Mick. I know shit. I know we got us a golden opportunity to make some money. I know the guy is dead and won't be needin' this shit. I know we're here right now. I know I'm takin' it. You don't want any, that's your lookout.'

'I didn't say that.'

'I knew it. Here, then, open the bag.'

Mick did as he was told. Sharpie put the clock and the silver set in first, then emptied the teak basket and threw everything in on top. 'We got a right, Mick, a fuckin' right. We're the ones doin' the work, ain't we?'

'S'pose.'

'There you go, then. Stop harpin' on about shit all the time. Jaysus, you gotta learn to relax, bro.'

Mick grinned sheepishly, and Sharpie cuffed him gently behind the ear. Although he was the younger brother, Sharpie was the natural leader. He decided where they went and what they did when they got there. Mick knew Sharpie was right: he was too cautious. He acted like a beaten dog sometimes, cringing, waiting for the next blow.

'Look at that picture. Didn't I tell you he was a bleedin' queer?' Sharpie lifted the photo and stared at it, his upper lip curling in disgust. 'Man, that shit is fucked up.' He bounced the picture in his hand. 'Frame's probably worth a bit, though. We bring this silver shit to Clanbrassil and we can get something for it. We'll try Bo.'

'Yeah, he might go for it an' all.'

'He'll go for it. Bitch's always lookin' to make money.'

Sharpie bashed the picture against the corner of the bureau. The glass shattered, scoring the wood and sending shards everywhere. He ripped the picture from it and tossed the frame into the bag.

'Probably got more money for it with the glass.'

'Too late now.'

'Why didn't you just open the back of it?' Mick asked. 'Take the picture out?'

'Dunno. Just like smashin' things.'

'We'd better go.'

Sharpie looked at the bed thoughtfully. 'Yo, man, that cover is dope. Think Ma would like something like that?'

Mick glanced at the bedspread. It was beautiful, and he knew his mother would love it. He also knew it would end up full of fag-holes, toast crumbs and stains. 'Too bulky to carry.'

'But she would, though, wouldn't she?'

'Sharpie—'

'Fuck it, I'm takin' it. Wait here.' Sharpie went downstairs. Mick heard the sound of drawers slamming, and then Sharpie was back carrying a plastic binliner. He grabbed the Chinese bedspread, yanked it off the bed and folded it as small as it would go, then stuffed it into the plastic bag.

'It's not going to fit.' Mick watched him force a third of it in and shook his head. 'You never listen.'

'C'mon.'

'You'll never get over the wall with it.'

'The wall? Fuck that shit! If it ain't locked, I'm goin' out the front door.'

'What?'

'You spacin', Mick? You really are a stupid motherfucker. It looks less dodgy if we walk out the front door. Better than climbin' over a bleedin' wall, so it is.'

'What if somebody sees us?'

'So what if they do?' Sharpie looked over his shoulder and grinned at Mick. 'People won't even notice. People never notice when you do shit that's ordinary. Walkin' out a door, that's ordinary. It's when you act all shifty that people remember shit. Someone sees us climbin' the back wall, they're gonna remember that.'

'Still an' all, we gotta be careful. If he gets wind—'

'You know your problem, Mick? You worry too much about this and that. You're gonna give yourself a stroke worryin' about shit all the time, for real.'

'Yeah, yeah.' Mick hefted the bag onto his shoulders and trailed downstairs after his brother.

\*

As soon as she heard the front door slam, Sarah scrambled out from under the bed. She had spent the last few minutes uncomfortably squashed up against the far wall, barely breathing and praying that they wouldn't look under the bed. When the one called Sharpie had started to yank the bedcover off, she had almost cried out in fright, but she had clamped a hand over her mouth and held perfectly still.

She smoothed her shirt and straightened her hair out. I'm okay, I'm okay, she told herself over and over again. But her heart was hammering hard in her chest and the back of her shirt was soaked through. Ever since she had been shot, Sarah had had an extremely acute understanding of how dangerous people could be. What if they'd discovered her? What if she'd been standing in the kitchen when they broke in? Who were they?

Descriptions!

She ran to the window and peered out through the muslin, taking care not to move it or cast any shadows. The two men were walking away from the house. Sarah watched as they crossed the road and walked – not too fast, not too slowly – along the footpath. They were dark-haired and about the same height. One was dressed like Ali G. She could see they were young – little more than kids, really. From the conversation she had overheard, they appeared to be brothers.

So what had they been looking for? And who had sent them? It hadn't been a random break-in; that much was clear. She'd heard them mention Reid's name. And one of them was worried about someone called Jack.

Sarah watched until they disappeared from view. Then she glanced around the bedroom, dismayed at how bare it looked without the bedspread. She hurried out to the landing and did a quick check of the other rooms.

Sarah stood in the door of the office and swore softly under her breath. The laptop was missing – the space on the desk mocked her. She went to the desk and sat down heavily in the swivel chair. She opened the drawers. The business files were scattered all over the floor. Those two guys had been looking for valuables, no doubt. She picked up the photo and studied the handsome face of David Reid.

'What in the name of God was that about?' she asked him.

What had been on that laptop that was so important someone would send two yobs to steal it on the same day David Reid was buried? Who the hell was Jack, and how was he connected to David Reid?

Sarah dug into her handbag and pulled out her notebook. She'd better write everything down before she forgot a single word.

# 8

'And, of course, the sergeant handling the case was delighted to hear James Reid had hired us.'

'What's his name again?'

'Stafford.'

'Yeah? Cops are always like that.' John yawned and scratched at his stubble. It was ten past ten and another scorcher of a day. John was so hung over he could hardly blink. He leaned forward and rested his head in his hands. He was trying very hard to convince himself that he was fine and not going to puke any second. The barbecue had broken up at four that morning – well, not so much broken up as passed out. A Corporation refuse truck collecting the bins on the pier had woken them up at seven. Andy Cosgrove had dropped John home, where he had immediately vomited, drunk a litre of water, vomited again and passed out on his bed in his clothes. It was only the persistent ringing of his phone two hours later that had forced him back to consciousness. It had come as no surprise to find his sister Carrie on the other end of the line, reminding John that he was meeting her new boyfriend later on that evening. No matter how much John had pleaded with her, she had remained unmoved, hanging up on him with the spine-chilling words, 'You'd better be there or I'll come round to your house and drag you out by your balls.' He believed her. Only an older sister, John decided, would be that malicious.

He slumped down into his seat, pulled two Nurofen out of his top pocket and swallowed them with a mouthful of water. His hands shook and his head felt like someone was dancing the mambo up there in spike heels. He was not just hung over – he was beyond hung over. He was convinced he was knocking at death's door, only Death, being a selfish bastard, was ignoring him, content to let him suffer.

'What did this Stafford guy make of the break-in?'

'He was interested enough,' Sarah shrugged, 'but he said there's been a spate of break-ins in that area recently, and if crooks know there's a funeral and no one will be at the house, that makes it all the more vulnerable. They said they'd look into it, but they doubt there's any real connection with David Reid's death. More opportunistic than planned, seems to be their thinking on it.'

'Even with the missing car?'

'Even with that.'

'Did you tell them what you heard?' John's face darkened momentarily. '"He" this and "he" that? Did you mention the name Jack?'

Sarah nodded.

'And?'

'And nothing. He said they'll look into it, and if they learn anything someone will be in touch.'

'And James definitely never heard David mention that name?'

'He says not.'

'I can't believe they weren't interested. Shower of loafers. Why is it I pay tax again?'

'Because you have to.' Sarah finished the last of her yoghurt and dropped the pot into the bin. John was not a fan of the gardaí. A few of their members had given him a terrible time a few years back, when he had worked on an adultery case, and now he held the unshakable view that 99.9 per cent of them were complete and utter arseholes. 'Poor James. It was a terrible shock for him, considering the day that was in it. But it had him all the more convinced that the drowning was no accident. I have to say I'm starting to think that myself.'

'I told you it was suspect from the word go.'

'All right.' Sarah rolled her eyes. It was more than she could stand to be wrong at the best of times; to have John gloat was too much.

'So now what?'

'Now we need to find out who Jack is and why those kids took the laptop. I'm going to talk to David's business partner, too. Maybe she can throw some light on it.'

John nodded. 'I'll ring Steve, see if he can get anything about our two boys. I mean, Sharpie and Mick. They've got to be in the system.'

'I hope so.'

'Weird that James wouldn't confirm if his brother was gay or not.'

'No, he didn't want to talk about it. Got quite cool with me when I pushed a little, said David was a bachelor, and that was all he knew.'

'He knows, so.'

'Yeah, that's what I figure. I wonder, could Jack be a boyfriend or something? Maybe there was something on the computer he didn't want anyone to see.'

'That's stupid. Why would a boyfriend get a couple of gougers to break in? Why wouldn't he go get it himself?' John yawned. 'We should check with David's friends, see if they noticed David acting unusual lately. When are you going to go talk to his business partner?'

'I have an appointment with her for this morning. I made it before you dragged your sorry arse out of bed,' Sarah said, bristling slightly. She had spent most of the evening sorting through the masses of paper-work she had taken from David Reid's house, going over his credit card bills and phone records, searching for anything that looked out of the ordinary. She had been on the phone half the morning, trying to get reports and talking to James Reid and making appointments. It was a bit rich for John to suggest she do anything, or that any of her suggestions were 'stupid'.

'What are you going to do?' she asked, a bit more sharply than necessary.

'I told you, I'll run the names Sharpie and Mick by Steve.'

'And?'

'And I don't know yet.'

'They're probably about eighteen or so, maybe younger. Now that I think of it, they could even have been twins.'

'Twins? Right, that should narrow it down.'

'Also Bo, on Clanbrassil Street. Run that too.'

'Bo?'

'I told you!' Sarah flipped open her notebook. 'The one called Sharpie said this Bo might offer them money for the silverware they took.'

'Right, no need to shout.'

'Maybe it's a nickname. The carriage clock should be easy to spot. It was small but heavy, probably antique. It had a crest over the twelve, a sort of shield with two swords crossed under it.'

'Shields – got it. Bo could be a pawnbroker or an antique dealer. Clanbrassil Street – there's a pawnshop there.'

'Will you check it out?'

'Sure, soon as I get my car.'

'Okay. Then we talk to the friends.' Sarah clapped her hands together. 'Okay then, let's get rolling.'

John groaned at the sound. It hurt to talk and it hurt to move his head. The water seemed to be sitting on top of his stomach in a fetid, steaming puddle. He was trying not to visualise it. Sarah watched him suffer without an ounce of sympathy.

'Good night, was it?'

'Yeah.'

'Did you get over in time to get some food?'

John nodded weakly.

'Did Andy make burgers and hot dogs, with lashings of cheese and onions? Hate to think of all that juicy meat turning in your stomach. Hope he cooked it all the way through, didn't leave any of it raw and bloody. It would be easy to cover up semi-raw meat with all those greasy toppings.'

John stared at her. He swallowed loudly. What little colour he had drained from his face. 'Sarah, please stop.'

'I'm sure it was fabulous – an oily, greasy feast of sensations.' Sarah smiled maliciously. 'Glad you enjoyed your evening.'

John closed his eyes. It was all he could do not to throw up on the desk.

'Want a lift over to the car pound?'

John kept his eyes closed while he shook his head.

'Okay then, see you later. Ring me if you need me for anything.' Sarah grabbed her car keys and sailed out the door.

John winced, half expecting her to slam it, but she didn't. He heard her whistling as she went down the stairs, and his shoulders slumped. He leaned forward and rested his thumping head against his desk, willing the pain to subside.

Semi-raw meat?

John jumped out of his chair and ran down to the next floor, where he barely made it to the communal toilet before he vomited for the third time that day.

*

Sarah found the small workshop eventually, after taking five or six wrong turns. She parked her Fiesta in the small staff car park and climbed out. She heard the sound of saws and sniffed as the dry, clean smell of sawdust and shavings drifted along on the warm air.

In the outer office, a secretary with short red hair and 60s-style glasses stopped typing and glanced quizzically at her as she entered.

'Can I help you?'

Sarah approached the desk. 'Hi, my name is Sarah Kenny. I called earlier. I have an appointment with Lillian Daly.'

'Oh, yes. She's down on the floor. She's expecting you.' She pointed to a door. 'Go through there, follow the hall and you'll come to another door that leads out to the main factory floor.'

'I've never met her before. What does she look like?'

'You can't miss her.' The secretary grinned. 'She's the only one wearing a skirt.'

Sarah opened the door at the end of the hall and stepped into a room about the size of a large school gym. The smell of chemicals and wood was almost overpowering, as was the noise. Men operated huge saws, sawing vast logs of wood in half and sending the pieces down a production line to other huge machines. Three men were bent over tables, sanding small pieces of wood and passing them down along the line. Another man wearing blue overalls was carefully buffing a mahogany cabinet with a soft rag.

Sarah saw Lillian Daly immediately. She was about forty and wore a sharp, tight, black pencil skirt and a pristine fitted blouse. Her pale-gold hair hung straight almost to her waist. She was deep in conversation with a huge man in dungarees with yellow goggles pushed up on his head.

Sarah approached them. 'Miss Daly?'

Lillian Daly glanced around. Her expression was one of impatience and mild irritation. She was barely five two in her incredibly high wedge heels. Her eyebrows were perfectly sculpted and the same pale gold as her hair. Her eyes were of the palest blue. 'Yes?'

'Sarah Kenny.'

'Oh, right. Give me a moment. We'll talk in the office.' She turned back to the massive man. 'Now make sure that delivery leaves on time. The interior designer will be there from five to six, and I don't want that little weasel throwing a hissy fit because his pieces are late.'

'Yes, Lilly.'

'Good man.'

She smiled and patted him on his massive chest, and he beamed at her as though she had informed him he'd won the lottery. She turned back to Sarah, and the smile vanished. 'Okay, I'm under pressure time-wise, so let's do this quickly, hmm?'

'Whenever you're ready.'

They climbed a set of aluminium steps and went into a tiny, paper-filled office that overlooked the main floor. Lillian proffered the only chair to Sarah and sat on her desk, her legs swinging easily. Sarah recognised the move: she wanted to be above Sarah when they spoke. Talk about your overcompensation.

'You're here about David?'

'Yes, his brother has asked our firm to investigate his death.'

'Why? What is there to look into? I thought David drowned.'

Sarah frowned slightly at the abrupt tone. For a woman who had recently lost her business partner of ten years, she wasn't exactly wringing out the hanky.

'His brother believes the drowning may not have been accidental.'

Lillian snorted a laugh. 'God, typical James.'

'Excuse me?'

'And you thought you'd take the the case, huh? Even though the gardaí have as good as said David drowned because he was blind drunk.' Lillian hopped off the desk and strode to the window to look out. 'Wouldn't make much sense to tell David's brother it was an accident and do yourself out of a job.'

Sarah felt her hackles rise. 'It had nothing to do with keeping the job.'

Lillian turned around. 'Oh?'

Sarah let the snide tone slide. Power games were not her thing, and this little rip was clearly trying to push her buttons. She pulled her notebook out of her bag. 'I have a couple of questions.'

'I'll tell you whatever I can.'

'Do you know anybody by the name of Jack?'

Lillian shook her head. 'No, I don't think so.'

'What about Mick and Sharpie?'

'I know about fifty Micks. There are two working downstairs right now.'

'This guy would be young, about eighteen or so. Black hair. He has a brother called Sharpie.'

'No, I can't say that I do.' But now Lillian was obviously curious. 'Who's—'

'And how was David lately? Did you notice anything unusual about his behaviour? Did he seem down or depressed?'

'Not really.' Lillian frowned slightly. 'I mean, he might have been a little quieter, now that you mention it, but hardly anything dramatic. Why do you ask?'

'His brother thought he might have been a bit troubled of late. I thought you, working so closely with him, might have noticed.'

Lillian shrugged. 'Well, if he was, I didn't notice anything outlandish.'

'Does David have an office here?'

'Sure, next door to mine.'

'Do you mind if I see it when we're done talking? I'd like to take a look around, see if I can get a feel for him.'

'You don't really think his death was anything other than an accident, do you?'

'I don't know yet. That's why we're investigating.'

'James was upset yesterday at the funeral, but...' Lillian paused and gave Sarah a coolly appraising glance. 'I'd hate to think of anyone taking advantage of him right now. He is grieving, after all.'

'I'm aware of that,' Sarah said sharply. 'Someone broke into David's house yesterday and stole some items, including his laptop.'

That got Lillian's attention. She unfolded her arms and took a step away from the window. 'Are you serious?'

'Very. Add that to the fact that his car went missing and his mobile phone was smashed to pieces on the night he died, and I'd say a little investigation is in order.'

'His Audi is missing?' She had completely dropped her attitude. 'That stupid car was David's pride and joy. He'd only had it a few weeks, never stopped going on about it. Of course you can look at his office. But David hardly spent any time there. He wasn't exactly the sort of guy who coped with being office-bound. In fact, he mostly worked from home.'

'If you don't mind my asking, what did he do, exactly? His brother mentioned he did most of the design work…'

Lillian ran a hand through her hair. 'Oh, yes, David was an incredibly gifted designer and an excellent networker. He knew everybody – and what a gift of the gab he had. Somebody would commission a table from us, and by the time David was finished with them, they'd be ordering chairs, beds, wardrobes, God knows what else. He was a tremendous salesman.' She laughed, with a bitter twist to her mouth. 'But, like a lot of creative people, he was incredibly dismissive about the actual business end. David hated to be here in the factory, hated the noise and the sawdust. Fortunately, that suits me fine. I'm not exactly what you might call a people person. But I know how to run a business efficiently.'

'You were a good team.'

'I suppose you could say that.'

'What will you do now?'

Lillian shrugged one shoulder. 'We have enough commissions to keep going for a while. Then… I'll find another designer, I suppose, and a salesman. It's unlikely I'll ever find anyone who can do both.'

'Yes.' Sarah raised an eyebrow. 'It must be a real inconvenience for you.'

'Oh, I see. You think, because I'm not weeping and wailing, I'm not upset about David's death? You don't know me from Adam. Who are you to pass judgment on me?'

'I'm sorry.'

'So you should be.'

Sarah knew she had crossed the line. 'I didn't mean to upset you.'

Lillian swung away and looked out the window again. Sarah sensed her struggling to compose herself. She watched the rise and fall of her shoulders, wishing she had kept her big mouth closed. Lillian Daly was right: who was she to judge?

'I wouldn't say we were friends, exactly,' Lillian said after a moment had passed. 'But we knew where we stood with each other. Sometimes that's better.'

'Can you think of anyone who'd want to hurt David?'

'No, I honestly can't. He was a very affable man, charming, easy company.'

'What about his personal life? Did David have a girlfriend?'

'Girlfriend?' Lillian barked a laugh and looked over her shoulder at Sarah with genuine amusement. 'David wasn't interested in girls. He was as gay as Christmas. Surely James told you that?'

'I see. No, he didn't mention it.' Sarah was glad to have confirmation at last. 'A boyfriend, then?'

'Nobody current – well, not as far as I know. Not that he'd tell me. He could be very coy about his private life.'

'His brother mentioned he was a keen golfer.'

'Totally. He was mad about that stupid game, he and that bunch of twats he hung around with.'

'That would be Laurence Cole and…?'

'Yes, Larry – everyone calls him Larry. And Clive Hollingsworth and Max.'

Sarah jotted the names down in her notebook. 'Max?'

'Ashcroft. Mr Alpha himself.'

'Huh?'

'That's how Max sees himself. The alpha male of the pack, the big cheese.'

'You think they're like a pack?'

Lillian sniffed and raised one of her perfect eyebrows. 'Oh, I know that sounds harsh, but you'll see when you meet them. They all think they're God's gift. Insufferable bores. Smug, self-satisfied bunch of cretins. David was the best of the lot, but that's not saying much.'

'You didn't like them, then.'

'Not particularly. But, like I said, I'm not exactly a people person.'

'Did you ever hear David mention something called the Meridian Club?'

'No. What's that?'

'Probably nothing.' Sarah shrugged. 'What does Laurence – Larry Cole do?'

'Do? Hah! Not much, I gather. He's a solicitor. Took over his father's firm a few years ago.'

'He's not very good?'

'He's not, but the firm his daddy built up is, so Larry made the only wise move I'd say he ever made in his life: left the family name on the business, handles Mickey Mouse property stuff from time to time and plays a lot of golf.'

'And the others?'

'Oh, I don't know. Max is involved in stocks and takeovers and all that stuff. Clive runs a German corporate bank or something. Money-men – the most boring people on the face of the Earth.'

'Where did David fit in with them? I mean, where did he know them from?'

'He and Larry know each other for years. He probably met the others through golf, or at some country house or other. David travels… travelled in some very high societies. You needn't look quite so sceptical. We make bespoke furniture, you know. The only people who can afford it are the rich.'

Sarah hadn't realised she was looking sceptical. She hastily rearranged her features, although Lillian Daly was really starting to give her a pain in the arse.

Lillian leaned back against the window ledge and studied Sarah intently for a moment. 'He really was a nice man. I can't imagine anyone hurting him. Do you really think his death wasn't a accident?'

'I don't know yet.'

'But what do you think?'

'I don't think anything just yet.'

'But if you had to hazard a guess.'

'I wouldn't.'

'Jesus, you don't give much away, do you?'

'I don't have anything to give away at this point.'

Lillian rolled her eyes and stood up. She went around her desk and took a key from a hook on the wall. She tossed the key to Sarah without warning, but Sarah reacted fast and snatched it out of the air. Lillian's mouth twitched.

'David's office is next door, if you want to take a look. Just leave the key on my desk when you're finished.'

\*

John was positively steaming by the time he had retrieved the Manta and paid the fine. He drove back across town, his mind a cauldron of bubbling rage and resentment. A hundred and fifty euros they'd charged him to reclaim his car. It was robbery, daylight highway robbery. Clampers were the scum of the earth, he raged silently.

His headache had subsided, but his exhaustion was increasing by the second. He wanted to go home and climb into bed so badly that he visualised doing just that at every red light.

But no. The old John might have skedaddled; the john who had promised Sarah he would pull his weight had work to do. He parked on Clanbrassil Street, climbed out of the Manta and jaywalked across the road, heading for Whelan's Fine Jewellery & Antiques. The shop was inconspicuous, its black paintwork caked in dust and the one grimy window covered in chicken wire. Most people probably walked past it daily without ever noticing it, but when he'd worked in the bar trade John had often heard it mentioned.

He placed his finger on the tarnished brass buzzer. Through the bubbled glass he watched as an old man poked his head through a pair of brown velvet curtains towards the back of the room and squinted at him for a few seconds. John waited. Finally the old man shuffled out from behind the drapes, reached under the counter and buzzed him in.

The shop was an old-fashioned affair. The wooden counter ran in an L-shape and the dusty glass shelves underneath were crammed with a selection of gaudy rings, bracelets and old-fashioned necklaces. Behind the counter were more shelves, crammed with items all the way to the ceiling, all locked behind chicken-wire doors. The room was dark and stank of mould and dust and mouse droppings. A radio played softly in the background.

The old man was as round as he was tall. He wore his brown cord trousers high on his waist, held up on his Buddha belly by frayed green braces that criss-crossed his vast back. Wisps of white hair had loosened from his comb-over and stood up inches from his scalp, like fronds of seaweed. He rested two gnarled hands on the counter and peered over his bifocals at John.

'What can I do you for?'

'Are you the owner?'

'Brendan Whelan, aye.'

John stepped close to the counter. The old man's nostrils twitched slightly, and John knew his pathetic attempts that morning – brushing his teeth twice, liberal splashes of aftershave – had done nothing to soften the fumes of alcohol that emanated from him in waves. He cleared his throat. 'My name is John Quigley. I'm a private detective with QuicK Investigations.'

The old man didn't look particularly impressed by this announcement so he pressed on.

'I'm investigating some stolen items.'

'So naturally you came here?'

'I was wondering if you know anyone, or have anyone working for you, called Bo.'

At this, the old man looked even less impressed. He straightened up. 'Are you trying to be funny, son?'

'No.'

'Why don't you go back out the way you came in?'

'Do you know anyone by that name?'

'Look, get out of here. You little bastards – always the same nonsense! I told you lot before: don't come back in here no more.'

John wrinkled his forehead in confusion. 'What?'

'You think you're being clever?' For some reason, the old man was beginning to get pretty annoyed. 'Go on. Get the hell out of it. Go on, you little shit, you!'

'You need to calm down.'

'Get out.'

'Sir, I can assure you I have no idea why you're so angry. I'm only—'

'Oh, aye, you're only here to sell your shit to that little feckless ingrate. I warned your lot before. I said I wouldn't put up with it any longer! Coming in here reeking to the high heavens. Go on! Go on before I call the gardaí!' He began to wheeze. 'Get out, I tell you!'

'Look, relax, will you? I'm not trying to sell anything. I'm just looking for someone called Bo. Do you know anyone called Bo or not?'

The old man's face had gone the colour of beetroot. He whipped off his glasses and wiped at his eyes, but his breath became more laboured. He glared at John and batted his chest with his hand.

'Are you all right?' John was beginning to regret ever opening his eyes that day.

The old man bent forwards and put his hands on his knees, still trying to catch his breath, but at John's voice he shook one fist in agitation.

Although John had no idea what he'd said or done to cause such upset, he realised his continued presence was only exacerbating the old man's distress. He took a step back from the counter. 'Hey, calm down. I'm going, okay?' He reached into his pocket and extracted his wallet from his jeans.

'Get out!'

John took out a card and tossed it onto the counter. 'My number is on that card. You want to ring the cops to check up on me first, go ahead. Then, when you stop having a heart attack, call me.'

The old man coughed and spluttered, but John had a fair idea he was repeating his demand that John leave. And, on that note, he figured he might as well do as he was bid.

He stepped outside into the bright, warm day and stood there with his hands on his hips. He glanced back in, but the old man was already disappearing back through his curtains, his massive back juddering with coughs and heaves.

John lit a cigarette with trembling hands, took a long drag and let it out slowly. His headache was returning. It moved behind his eyes, its spidery fingers agitating his senses.

What the hell had that been about?

He pulled out his mobile and called Sarah.

'Yep?'

'Okay, you're going to have to talk to the pawnbroker.'

'Why?'

'I don't think he and I hit it off.'

'Imagine that. Does he know who Bo is?'

'Probably, if Bo is a feckless ingrate.'

'What are you talking about?'

'Bo. I'm talking about Bo.'

'John, you're not making any sense. Did he say he knew him or not?'

'He knows him. I left my card with him, but I doubt he's going to call, and there's no way I'm going back in to talk with him. I'd end up calling him an ambulance.'

'Well, I'm about to leave here. I'll meet you back in the office.'

'Learn anything?'

'David Reid was very nice and definitely gay, but I'd kind of figured that part out already.'

'Anything else?'

'Nope.'

'Useful.' John took another drag of his cigarette. 'That was a pretty shitty thing you did to me earlier.'

'What was?'

'Talking about food. You made me sick.'

'Oh, John.' Sarah started to laugh. 'Stop it, you're breaking my heart.'

John hung up. On another day he might have been able for her, but today she had him licked and she knew it.

He tossed his cigarette away and wearily made his way back to the car. All he wanted to do was lie in the back garden with the dog for a few hours, dozing in the sun.

God, life was cruel.

# 9

Larry Cole hung up the phone and sat staring out the window of his Georgian house, staring across his landscaped garden to where his wife Dee and her sister Nancy sat sipping green tea in deckchairs, under the vast umbrella Dee had ordered from somewhere. Larry didn't need to be out there to know what they were talking about. He knew from Nancy's hand movements that they were having one of their endless, boring conversations about weight loss. What fad was it this week: Atkins, South Beach, colonic irrigation? He watched Nancy's mouth moving and Dee's dark head nodding vigorously, and he clenched his back teeth. The fact that both women were skin and bone seemed to escape them completely. Dee had always been slim, but lately she looked like a good strong breeze might knock her over. She had lost her breasts, and when he slipped his arm around her at night he was sure he could feel her bones move beneath her skin. Not that she allowed much contact these days, anyway. She always claimed she was too tired.

Larry ran a hand through his thinning, light-brown hair and closed his eyes. He wished Nancy would bugger off, give him some peace in his own damn home. No wonder her husband had left her. She treated his house as though it were her own, always opening doors and snooping around, and lately she'd taken to spending the night, claiming it was too late to drive home or she had had too much to drink. It infuriated him to come downstairs in the morning and find her slumped across the nook in the kitchen, clutching a mug of coffee like it was the last refuge of the damned. And she smoked constantly. The whole house reeked of her menthol cigarettes. Disgusting. But when he'd complained to Dee, she had turned on him.

'She's my sister! Her husband has left her and run off with that awful tart. What do you want me to do? Turn her away? She needs me now. How can you be so callous?'

So Larry tried to be patient. He supposed it was hard for Dee. They were at a bit of a loss since their youngest had left to go to college the previous September. Despite phone calls and pleading from her mother, she was spending longer and longer away. Their son lived in Canada with some awful Nebraskan girl and rarely came home, despite the fact that he frequently hit them up for money. Dee was still adapting to the emptiness of the house, the new routine, or rather lack of one. He understood that. But filling that void with Poison Nancy, with her snide remarks and sly glances? She made Larry feel nervous, impotent. And really, there was only so much one man could tolerate of that glass-shattering faux laugh.

She was a cuckoo in the nest – his nest – and she was starving him of his own wife.

It wasn't like they were so old, either. He was only forty-four, and Dee wouldn't be forty until October. They had married young and worked hard all their adult lives; now they should be thinking about enjoying the peace and quiet, taking some holidays, going travelling – not drifting along, barely talking and wasting all their precious energy emotionally supporting her wretched sister. After all, he was practically retired from the firm these days, although he wasn't fool enough to pretend that it had been by choice. He wanted to… What did he want? What was it? Why did he feel so listless, so anxious, so…so under siege?

Larry glanced out the window again. He ran a hand over the lower half of his stomach and pressed gently. The phone call had upset him; he didn't like to be threatened. He didn't feel well, hadn't felt well in weeks. He had himself half convinced he was getting an ulcer. Maybe he should go get it checked out, but the truth was, he didn't really want to know. Maybe it was an ulcer, maybe it wasn't. Maybe it was something worse.

Well, it was no less than he deserved. Especially after…

He shut his eyes, squeezed them tightly closed. He didn't want to think of that. Max had warned him about that, had told him to put it out of his head. And Max didn't seem to be fazed. Clive claimed to be okay too, although Larry had detected a sliver of hysteria in his voice earlier that day. But that could be just wedding nerves. Less than a week till the joyous occasion. God, how would he cope with it? All those people – the smiles, the jokes and jovial air. How could he go through with it? It had been easier when he'd had David to talk to. But David was gone…

Stop.

He opened his eyes and glanced out again. The women had stopped talking. Dee looked like she was dozing. Her head was pressed back against the deckchair, her knees raised and slanted over to one side. Her skirt had ridden high on her slender hip and Larry let his eyes linger on her soft, pale skin. He had made the mistake, one drunken night, of talking about their lack of sex. Clive and David had politely listened, knowing he was drunk and morose and in need of letting off a bit of steam. But Max – Max had reacted with mocking scorn.

'I wouldn't put up with that shit in my house. You put a ring on her finger, didn't you? Least she can do is stick to her end of the bargain. It's not "love, honour and hold off on the sex". We put a roof over their heads, food on the table. I blame feminists, bunch of man-hating lesbians. They've destroyed the Western world. It's time we fought back.'

'You talk foreplay like that to Laura?' David had laughed, spilling some of his wine. 'What do you do for the encore? Threaten to chain her barefoot to the kitchen sink? You old charmer, Max. My, no wonder she always looks so cheerful.'

Larry remembered how he and Clive had tried, unsuccessfully, to smother their laughter. It was a running joke amongst the men that Max's wife Laura was unnaturally dour-faced for a pretty woman in her twenties.

But Max had been incensed. He had lunged at David, threatening to break his neck. Only for the fact that he was so drunk he could barely stand, he might have pulled it off. David had apologised, of course, but Max had been furious and remained brooding for the rest of the evening, refusing any apology, resisting any attempt to draw him into the conversation. They had broken up early that time.

Larry watched Dee sleep and knew deep in his heart that despite her gradual withdrawal from him, he would never speak to Dee that way. He loved her, would always love her. He would do anything in this world to protect her from harm, to protect her from hurt.

His stomach burbled uncomfortably. Larry groaned. He tried to contain it, but his bottom lip betrayed him. It wobbled, and when he tried to stop it, it wobbled all the more. Finally Larry Cole dropped his forehead onto his fist and wept silently.

*

Max Ashcroft was in his office. And, unlike Larry, he was having a grand old time. He and Atlee Cross, his boss, were drinking aged brandy and closing a particularly fine bit of business together.

'You're one tough old son of a bitch. A regular pit bull!' Atlee chortled, slipping lower into the plush leather seat. 'Sure glad to have you on my side.'

Max scrawled his signature across the bottom of the document and slid it towards Atlee. Atlee read through it swiftly, chortled again and slipped the document into the inside pocket of his jacket. Then he raised his glass.

'A toast to sons of bitches, and to the biggest son of a bitch I've ever laid eyes on.'

'Cheers. Long may this son of a bitch make money.'

'Damn straight.'

Max raised his glass and took a sip. Modesty didn't suit him, so he didn't bother with it. At forty, he was the very embodiment of success. He was a tall man, fit from golf and the twice-a-week racquetball games he played with ferocious concentration. It was still early in the day, but already his jaw was shadowed heavily. He had dark-green eyes and thick hair that he wore slightly longer than men his age could normally get away with. It was still dark, but greying at the temples, a look that his wife assured him only made him look more distinguished. He wore a sharply fitted pinstriped suit, a scarlet Bill Blass tie and fine black handmade shoes.

Atlee raised his glass again. 'I never saw such balls. Had those good old boys from the board running for their chequebooks like giving you money gave them a hard-on. By God, I swear I never saw the like.'

'They know I'll get them a good return on their investments.'

Atlee laughed and slapped his thigh. 'Sure would be something to see that old bastard's face when he finds out you're buying his company out from under him.'

Max tilted his head and smiled, his eyes sparkling with malice. 'Yes, he should have taken our first offer when it was still on the table. Stubborn fool. I'd like to be a fly on the wall for that particular moment.'

'Lordy, it sure would be a sight.' Atlee grinned. 'Bet you anything you'll be up for CEO after this.'

'Really?' Max also thought so, but it seemed prudent to keep Atlee on his roll.

'Sure, why wouldn't you? I'll personally recommend you. But, shoot, we mustn't get too carried away just yet. The old bastard is down but not out.'

'Mortally wounded, though.'

'Yeah, he's drawing his last breath. Fuck him; should've gone for the merger. All these old-school assholes can't be taught nothin'. So, know what I say?'

'No.'

'I say fuck 'em. Let 'em learn the hard way. No progress, no second chances. This is a kill-or-be-killed business, Max. There ain't no room for sentimentality in business. Don't I always say that?'

'You do indeed.' Max smiled indulgently. He must have heard Atlee say that a hundred times – that and 'If your ducks can't fly, might as well roast 'em,' whatever that meant.

'Damn straight. Anyway, he ain't exactly going empty-handed, now is he? He can go retire, learn to play bridge or some shit.'

Atlee drained the last of his brandy and hauled his skinny ass out of the chair. He was sixty-one and head of Balta QEC, one of the largest mergers and acquisitions companies in Alabama. Aside from his holdings in the States, Atlee had an office in Dublin, one in Madrid and one in Cairo, but it was Dublin he called his home. Atlee claimed the climate suited him, although Max guessed the tax incentives suited him even better. He wore his usual attire: a pale-blue shirt – which, depending on the weather, would be either brushed cotton or fine cotton – tucked into deep indigo denim jeans, a cowboy belt and stacked cowboy boots. He was a walking stereotype of the Southern gentleman farmer. When Max and he had first been introduced, two years earlier, Max had actually glanced down to see if he wore spurs, and had been mildly disappointed to find he didn't.

Atlee paused by the door. 'You and that pretty wife of yours ought to come on out to the house this weekend. I'm throwing a barbecue, teach you Irish cocksuckers how to flame meat. None of your Irish crap, neither: prime Argentinian beef. Should see the job Wanda's done on the garden. Shoot, you'd hardly recognise the place.'

'Atlee, we'd be honoured.'

'Say about three in the p.m.?'

'You got it.'

Max put down his glass and raised his left eyebrow as high as it would go. His mother swore he was the spitting image of a young Roger Moore, and Max had spent many an hour in the bathroom perfecting the eyebrow-lift. 'Should we bring anything?'

Atlee winked. 'Nope, just you and the little lady. And bring the kiddies, too. My niece is coming with her brood. There ain't nothing better than having family around.'

'Great idea,' Max said, thinking he would rather stir-fry his own balls than listen to a bunch of kids screaming all afternoon. But he kept the smile in place. Atlee was big on family. 'We'll be there… Oh, no, wait. Damn – I can't.'

Atlee cocked his head sideways. 'No?'

'No, I'm going to a wedding. Wow, I had completely forgotten. Clive Hollingsworth – you know, one of the lads I play golf with. His wedding.'

'Well, doesn't matter. Another time, then.'

'Of course, any time.'

When Atlee had gone on his loping, jaunty way, Max Ashcroft reclined in his chair, threw his feet onto his desk and smiled at the ceiling. What a day it was turning out to be. First he had smashed an old rival with an underhand bid on a huge tract of valuable land. And now he had been invited to Atlee's home. He didn't know which of the two gave him greater satisfaction. Of course, it was a shame that Clive's wedding was on the same day, but he was confident there would be other invites.

He raised his glass again and toasted himself silently. He had an eye-catching wife who kept herself in shape, and a beautiful house near Howth that had been featured in *House and Garden* magazine. His kids – two sons, a three- and a two-year-old – were becoming more and more like him every day; the older one could already do the eyebrow trick. He felt blessed. Business was booming. The Celtic Tiger had been good to him; money was pouring in. He was at base camp, ready for the final push to the top. Max basked in a sense of achievement so overwhelming he got an erection. It seemed like a shame to waste it.

He hit the intercom on his desk. 'Hey, Angie, c'mon in here a second, would you? I've got something I want you to look at.'

'Be right there, Mr Ashcroft,' Angie's breathy voice replied.

Max grinned. Man, this new secretary was such a little goer. Twenty-one, blonde, with tits like melons. All he'd had to do was take her out for two meals, and she had dropped her knickers as though they were burning an extra hole.

Angie shut the door behind her and paused there, letting Max give her a good look over. She was wearing a tight blouse, straining at the buttons, and a tight black pencil skirt – exactly the way Max had told her he liked women to dress.

Angie smiled at the look in his eye. She had not set out to seduce her boss, not intentionally, although she had thought he looked really sexy. The fact was, she could hardly believe he was even interested in someone like her. But when, after a drunken going-away party for one of the partners, he had told her that his wife was frigid and that they were together solely for the sake of the boys, she had been thrilled. Julia, the stuck-up cow of an accountant, had pulled her aside the next day and warned her to be careful around Max – but what did she know? She was probably jealous. With any luck, if Angie played her cards right he'd see she totally understood him, and he would leave his wife and start dating her, out in the open, like regular couples. It happened, didn't it? Look at Bridget Jones. That would really give the other women in the office something to talk about. Angie smiled, imagining the envious glances and hushed tones.

Max grinned at her and unzipped his fly. He jiggled his eyebrows.

'Oh, Miss Hart, I've got something that needs your undivided attention.'

Angie locked the door and slid across the room, trying hard to do the provocative wiggle she'd practised.

Max watched her performance and his grin widened. God, she was pretty, all right, but dumb as a stump. He wondered how long it would be before he'd have to fire her.

*

Clive Hollingsworth was seated on a purple couch, watching his fiancée try on shoes. He was hot, he was bored and he was starving. And he was sick to the back teeth of spending every spare minute shopping for and talking about his upcoming wedding. Sometimes it seemed like it had taken over his life.

'These would be perfect for the going-away night, wouldn't they?' Sylvia turned one delicate ankle in his direction. Clive glanced down at the strappy sandal. To him it looked exactly the same as every other sandal she had tried on since they had come into Brown Thomas.

'Yes. It's perfect.'

'Would this one be your favourite?'

'Yeah, probably.'

'You don't sound so sure.'

'Sylvia, it's lovely.'

'But the heel isn't right, not really. I was thinking more of something with a wedge.' Silvia frowned and glanced at the salesgirl. 'Do you have them in this style, but with a wedge heel?'

The sales assistant, a tall, good-looking girl with long chocolate-brown hair and the patience of a saint, smiled politely. 'I can check for you.'

Clive rolled his eyes. 'What's wrong with those ones, Syl? They're exactly the colour you were looking for.'

'But the heel is all wrong.'

'Who cares about the heel?'

'I do.'

Clive threw his hands up in the air, exasperated. 'It's just a heel.'

'It is not just a heel!'

'I have to get back to work.'

'You don't have to be back in the office until three.'

Clive glanced at his watch and swore under his breath. It was ten to two; he'd been in Brown Thomas's shoe department for almost forty minutes. 'Syl, I need to get something to eat. I can't sit here all afternoon while you look at shoes. What the hell do you need more shoes for, anyway? You must have hundreds of pairs of shoes.'

Wrong, wrong, wrong. As soon as the words left his lips, he knew he had made a mistake. Sylvia yanked the sandal off and flung it into the box. 'Jesus Christ, Clive! We are getting married in less than a week! All I ask is that you give me a bloody opinion on some shoes! How can you be thinking of food, anyway? You know, I've been working flat out organising this wedding, making sure everything's perfect, making sure everything's under control, talking to caterers, florists, even the damn priest! So, if you don't mind, all I want from you today, Clive, is an opinion on some goddamned shoes!'

Sylvia swept a lock of gold hair off her forehead and turned back to the salesgirl. 'I'll try the wedge if you have it.'

The salesgirl picked up the box and expertly ghosted away. Clive watched her go, sighed and slumped down further on the sofa. Ever since he had slipped the ring on Sylvia's delicate finger, one year before, he had felt more and more under the cosh. He loved her, but she could really push his buttons.

Sylvia was tiny, five foot tall and slender with it, with big pale-blue eyes and expensively highlighted honey-blonde hair. She worked in advertising and could charm the birds straight out of the trees when she felt like it. But lately – or was it just lately? – Clive had detected just a hint of her mother in her voice, and it made him want to run, run anywhere. Of course, as soon as he thought that, he felt guilty. It was understandable; she was, after all, under pressure. They both were. And it didn't help that, because Sylvia's father, Judge Ambrose Cockburn, was paying, the wedding was fast becoming the biggest social occasion of the year. Every which way they turned, the judge had his spoke in. Clive was beginning to understand why people eloped.

Clive's mobile vibrated in his pocket, and he resisted the urge to take it out to see who was calling. It was probably the office. Lately it seemed he was snowed under with work. Not that he had any objection: he was being made partner in a month's time, the youngest partner in the firm's history. At thirty-four, he would soon head up the Irish office of the biggest international branch of the KeiserBundes banking organisation. It was an honour and a credit to his dedication and hard work. Between the partnership and a society wedding, Clive Hollingsworth should have been deliriously happy.

So why wasn't he? Why couldn't he enjoy his success? Why did he wake up every morning and feel the black cloud roll into place? What was the point of…

The mobile vibrated again. Clive groaned and pulled it out. A text message from Larry. It read, 'Call me. Urgent.'

He put the phone back into his pocket and closed his eyes.

'Clive?' Sylvia sat down beside him and picked up his hand in hers. 'Clive, sweetheart, what is it? Are you okay? You're as pale as a sheet.'

She looked at him, her huge blue eyes concerned and trusting. Clive smiled wanly at her.

'I'm fine, Syl, but I need to get something to eat. I've been on the go since early this morning, with nothing more substantial in me than a cup of green tea.'

'Why don't you go ahead and see if there's a table available at the Troc? I'll follow you down.'

'You don't mind?'

'I think I can manage.'

Sylvia smiled then, and in the radiance of that smile Clive felt the cloud break, if only for a little while. He leaned in and gave her a kiss on the forehead. 'I'm sure whatever you pick will be just perfect, just like you.'

'Oh, get out of here, you charmer!' Sylvia laughed and kissed him back. 'My God, the things a man will say to get out of shoe shopping.'

Clive laughed and stood. 'See you in a few?'

'Sure. Order me the crab salad, would you?'

'You bet.'

Sylvia watched him go, and the smile slipped from her face. Whatever was up with him lately, it terrified her. He wasn't himself at all. She knew he was under immense pressure at work and with the wedding and everything else, but she couldn't help feeling there was something else eating at him. He wasn't sleeping; he wasn't eating; he looked troubled. Even her mother had commented on how pale and irritable he seemed. Clive had brushed it off as too many nights out with the boys, but Sylvia knew that wasn't it. Ever since the stag night, it seemed Clive had been seeing less of the boys – not that she was completely unhappy about that. As far as Sylvia was concerned, the less time her fiancé spent with Max Ashcroft, the better. Of course, David's terrible accident had completely devastated Clive but even before that, something had been wrong, she was sure of it.

She wished he would confide in her. She wished he would tell her what was on his mind. She hoped he wasn't having second thoughts about the wedding; she would die if that turned out to be the case. She loved him, more than she wanted to admit even to herself.

'You're in luck: we have one pair of wedge heels left in your size.' The dark-haired girl returned and proffered the shoes.

'Oh, they're perfect!' Sylvia exclaimed. And all thoughts of what might be bothering her fiancé vanished.

*

Clive dialled Larry's number as he walked to the restaurant. 'What?'

'I've just had that bastard on the phone,' Larry said, his voice high and frightened.

'And?'

'He's insisting we pay the same price.'

'But… how? How? We can't cover David's share.'

Larry sighed heavily. 'We have to, Clive. What choice do we have?'

'Jesus Chist, Lar, when will it end? That man will have a hold on us for the rest of our days.'

'He won't. He'll sign, and that will be it. I'll talk to you later. I need to get hold of Max.'

Clive hung up and walked miserably on. He no longer had an appetite.

# 10

Back at QuicK, Sarah and John were grabbing a bite to eat.

'That's weird. Why do you think he got so upset over the name if it was nothing to do with him?' Sarah was eating a chicken and tomato sandwich while she listened to John describe his morning. 'And why did he say, "I told your lot before"? What lot? Who did he think you were?'

'Don't know, but whoever it was, I don't think he likes them much.'

'Did you get hold of Steve?'

'Yep, he says he needs a bit more to go on than a nickname and a guy called Mick.'

Sarah finished her sandwich and dabbed at her mouth with a napkin. 'I'll talk to the old man, try a different approach.'

'I don't think it'll help much.'

'People don't get that freaked out unless they're scared of something. Trust me, I'll get him to help.'

'What are you going to do, put him over your knee and spank the information out of him?'

'Do you think that might do it?'

'It would for me.' John grinned. He was still feeling rough, but the Big Mac and fries he was stuffing into himself were gradually putting some much-needed sustenance back into his body. He licked cheese off his fingers and gulped down some of his Coke.

Sarah tried to ignore his gobbling. 'The numbers for the friends are on your desk. I got them from David's office. Make appointments to see them. Also, I've contacted the credit card companies to see if there's been any movement since the night of David's death. If his wallet was stolen, maybe we'll get lucky and someone will use the cards. I'm also going to keep hassling the gardaí about the missing car, make sure they know that if anything turns up, we're to be contacted immediately.'

'My, you have been the busy little bee.'

'Max Ashcroft's the one who saw David the day he died. We should probably see if we can find out where they were drinking, if David was planning to meet up with anyone else, what time they left at – that sort of thing.'

John balled up the take-away bag and tossed it into his bin. 'Right, boss.'

Sarah made her way towards the door. 'I want to talk to them face to face, not over the phone. Don't mention anything about the break-in to them, either – not yet.'

'If you hold up a hoop, I'll jump through it for you too.'

Sarah snorted and left.

John lit a cigarette and picked up the phone. Man, she could be a real ball-breaker when she wanted.

* * *

Sarah walked to Clanbrassil Street, enjoying the exercise and the unbelievable weather. The sun, she decided, made everything look different. People smiled at one another, windows were open everywhere and gardens were in full bloom. Everything looked cleaner, brighter and more vibrant. If only, Sarah mused, the summer in Ireland lasted longer than a couple of days.

She skirted around a skip, stepped off a kerb and stumbled, jarring her bad leg. Wincing, she bent down and rubbed at her ankle. As she did, she thought she glimpsed someone turn fast and duck around the corner house at the top of the street. Sarah stood up slowly and stared at the building.

It was probably nothing… yet she waited a little bit longer, until she was sure, glad John wasn't around to notice how spooked she was. Patrick York – the man whom she had shot and who had shot her – had a lot of friends and business partners back in Holland, and the gardaí had warned her and John to keep their wits about them for a while.

She counted to twenty, and when no one appeared she set off again, feeling stupid and paranoid.

'You are officially starting to lose it,' she admonished herself under her breath. But, stupid or not, after a few steps she took another quick look over her shoulder. Nothing. She scoffed at herself as she crossed a car park and stepped out onto Clanbrassil Street.

She was buzzed into the pawnshop immediately. She stepped into the gloom and stood there blinking, waiting for her eyes to grow accustomed to the dark. The shop appeared to be empty.

'Hello?'

'Hello to you.'

Sarah jumped. She turned and saw two huge, watery eyes, swimming behind a pair of bifocals, staring at her from behind the counter. She approached and peered over. Seated on a hard-backed wooden chair, polishing a candlestick with Brasso, was the man John had described.

'Hello, I'm looking for Brendan Whelan.'

'That would be me, so.'

'Are you the owner, Mr Whelan?'

He squinted up at her and smiled. 'That's right. What can I do for you?'

'Sir, my name is Sarah Kenny. My partner came to see you this morning.' She put her card down on the counter.

The smile vanished. Whelan put down the candlestick and hauled himself slowly to his feet. 'Well, then I might as well tell you the same thing I told him: get out of my shop.'

'I take it you called the gardaí and checked that we are who we say we are.'

'I didn't ring no one. Now, I said get out. I told that other fella, and now I'm telling—'

'Please. Hear me out.' Sarah raised her hand. It was interesting that he hadn't checked on them. 'I'm investigating stolen items and a possible murder. The name Bo has come up in relation to our inquiries—'

'A murder?'

'I know there is someone called Bo connected with this shop,' Sarah said, mentally crossing her fingers. 'If you don't talk to me, I'm going to talk to the gardaí. I am not going to be happy. I'll have to explain to them why I'm asking, and I don't like dragging the gardaí into my business. Do you?'

'Will you just tell me what murder you're talking about?'

'My client's brother was killed just over a week ago. His house was burgled yesterday, the day of his funeral, by two men. Young, late teens or very early twenties. One was really thin, and they both had dark, almost black hair. About five seven or thereabouts. They could have been brothers. One of them was dressed like a rapper. Sound familiar?'

Whelan shrugged.

'We have it on good authority that the items stolen were fenced to somebody called Bo. When we checked, Bo came up as being connected with this shop. You want to tell me about that, Mr Whelan?'

'I don't know anything about any stolen goods.'

Sarah sighed. 'Fine, have it your way. I'll ask the gardaí.'

'You like threatening an old man?'

Sarah crossed her arms. 'No, I don't. But I don't like people stalling, either.'

Whelan glared at her, his face puffy, his watery eyes filled with open hostility. But after a few seconds his shoulders sagged, and the fight drained out of him like old bathwater.

'Tell me what is this about. How did your client…die?'

'Client's brother.'

'Right. How did he die?'

'He was drowned.'

'But this Bo didn't have anything to do with that, did he?'

Sarah gave a noncommittal shrug and tried her hand at a bare-faced lie. 'Who knows?'

The old man closed his eyes for a moment or two. He was breathing heavily, and Sarah noticed his colour was very high. 'What kind of stuff are we talking about, anyway?'

Sarah pulled out her notebook and flicked it open. 'There was a man's Rolex and jewellery – bracelets, rings; one very ornate man's ring, heavy, with Chinese writing on the front. There was also a carriage clock, a couple of silver picture frames that I think were probably antique, a silver brush set and a laptop.' She ripped the page out and put it onto the counter. 'Here, you can have this.'

'Look around you – there's nothing like that here!'

'Not yet.'

The old man leaned on his hands and scowled. He ignored the list. 'You don't really have anything on this Bo, then, do you?'

'I want to talk to him. If the goods are passed on to him, I want to know.'

'And if you can't talk to him?'

Sarah looked him straight in the eye. 'I will talk to him; you can be sure of that. See, I know you know who I'm talking about. I'm here as a courtesy. The moment I leave here, I'm going straight to the gardaí – see if they're a bit more forthcoming.'

'Here!' A voice to the side rang out. Sarah turned just in time to see a tall, wiry, heavily tattooed man come flying out from behind the curtain and vault the counter.

'No – stop!' Whelan shouted.

Before Sarah had a chance to react, the man grabbed her by the shirt and swung her into the wall. Sarah gasped in pain.

'You want to talk to me, bitch? Here I am. Who the fuck sent you here? Who the fuck are you to be talkin' to me old lad, tellin' him shit, talkin' about the fuckin' gardaí? Go fuck yourself! You won't find nothin' here. I didn't do no fuckin' robbery, and I sure as fuckin' shit didn't do no murder.'

He emphasised each 'fuckin'' by slamming Sarah into the wall.

Sarah tried to catch her breath. 'Get your hands off me!'

'Let go of her.' Whelan was coming out from behind the counter, wheezing and panicked. 'Stop it!'

'Please,' Sarah said. 'I'm just—'

'You're just fuckin' leavin', that what you're doin'.' Bo grabbed her by the arm, so hard she knew she would have a bruise for weeks, and dragged her towards the door. He opened it with one hand and flung her out so hard she fell onto her knees.

'You stay the fuck away from here.'

He slammed the door closed.

Shocked and sore, Sarah pulled herelf slowly to her feet. The left knee of her trousers was ripped and her knee was bleeding. She dusted herself down and limped away from the door, afraid that he might come after her again. When she got around the corner, she sat down on a step and pulled her mobile from her bag. She dialled the office.

'John?' she sniffed.

'What is it – what's wrong?'

'Can you pick me up?'

'Sure. Are you all right? You sound upset.'

Sarah brushed some hair from her face. 'Will you just pick me up, please? I'm around the corner from the pawnshop, outside the laundrette.'

'I'll be there in two minutes.'

Sarah turned off her phone and tried to pick some of the grit from her hands. Suddenly the day didn't seem so sunny.

# 11

Brendan Whelan locked the door of the shop. He made his way into the back and slowly climbed the stairs to the second floor after his son. He peered into the gloom of a back bedroom. He could make out his son's bare back and one heavily tattooed arm as he pulled on a pair of boots.

Whelan swallowed and tried to stop the shake in his hands. He was a hard-working, honest man. He had raised his son single-handed, ever since the day his tramp of a wife had run off with some piece of shit from the docks, back in the late 70s. He had tried his best to instil a sense of decency in the lad, a work ethic, a sense of pride in a hard day's work. He had failed miserably in every respect. That failure sapped almost every ounce of strength from his body.

'You shouldn't have done that.'

His son ignored him.

Whelan made his way carefully across the cluttered floor and pulled back the curtains. 'I'm talking to you.'

'What time is it?'

'Time you answered a few questions.'

Bo fumbled for his watch, which lay on top of the bedside locker, half hidden amidst wads of tissue paper, empty cigarette boxes and four glasses of water of varying heights and dust levels. He grabbed it and brought it to his face. 'Fuck.'

Whelan pushed some clothes off a chair and lowered his body carefully onto it.

'Listen to me, now. Have you been dealing with those Quinn boys?'

'What? What are you on about now?' Bo pulled on the second boot and began to lace it. He was a scrawny, unkempt-looking man of thirty-two. His hair was a nondescript mousy brown, thin and ragged in places, and his skin was acne-scarred and pasty. Both arms were fully tattooed, and he had a ring through his left nostril. 'Have you been drinking or something?'

'They're the only ones call you Bo. How would the detectives know that?'

'I don't know nothing about no murder.'

'She also wants to know about a break-in that happened yesterday. A break-in that involved two little bastards fitting the description of the Quinns. She found a connection to someone called Bo. You following me?'

'What connection? What are you talkin' about?'

'I'm telling you what she said. It's them Quinns, isn't it?'

'Da, listen, I swear, I haven't seen either of them Quinns.'

'You promised me. You swore you wouldn't deal with any more stolen gear. I could have been shut down last time.'

'And I haven't. Look, just 'cause someone was talking about me don't mean I'm involved. I don't know what the fuck some bitch, whoever she was, thinks she knows, but Da, I'm telling you, I swear to you, I don't know nothin' about any of this shit.'

'If I find out you're lying, I'll go to the gardaí myself. I just want you to know that. If a single dodgy piece turns up downstairs or with any other of the dealers I know – say some silver picture frames, or a carriage clock, or a Chinese ring, or any stuff like that – I promise you, Brendan…' Whelan lifted a trembling finger and jabbed it in the air. 'If that happens, or if I hear from anyone that you've been selling, I'll report you myself. Do you hear me, lad? You need to sort this mess out. D'you hear me?'

'Yeah, I hear. Relax, there's no worry. Look, what the fuck makes you think I've done something, anyway?' Bo lit a cigarette with a match and watched his father warily through the smoke. 'Why would I? I'm straight now.'

His father closed his eyes for a long moment, breathing heavily. Bo stared at him, his own heart beating loudly in his chest. He knew the old boy wasn't fooling around.

'Da, I swear, I don't know what that bitch was on about.'

Whelan stood up and shuffled out the door. He had heard that voice before, the night his wife had told him not to worry, that she would be back, that there was nothing going on. Suddenly, he felt terribly old, an old man, defeated by the bad genes that had given him a weasel and a liar for a son. He stopped at the door and looked back. 'Just make sure you heed me. One word, and you and me are through.'

Bo waited until he heard the heavy tread on the stairs before he moved. He yanked open the trunk at the foot of his bed and removed the blanket on top. Underneath was the rucksack given to him by Sharpie Quinn not twelve hours before. He opened it, stared at the goods inside and swore. This shit must be hotter than the gates of hell if detectives were involved. Fuck – he'd never be able to move it now, and he needed the money it was supposed to bring in. He had paid Sharpie five hundred for the lot, almost every last penny he had, knowing it would fetch four times that amount once it was all broken down, banking on being able to move it in twenty-four hours. Now he was fucking stuck, out of pocket and seriously inconvenienced.

He wasn't going to put up with this shit, no way. Sharpie had sworn to him that no one would miss this lot. He would hold on to the laptop – he might be able to line up a safe buyer for that in an hour – but the silver and shit, that had to go back. He couldn't afford to be out of pocket.

Bo found his jacket hanging on the back of the chair, pulled out his mobile and began to dial. 'Sharpie, listen up. We got a problem.'

\*

'That motherfucker!'

Before the call, Sharpie had been lying on his back listening to Tupac, his mind and body chilling from the joint he was smoking. Now his afternoon was blown. He sat up, picking absentmindedly at a piece of peeling skin on his forehead, and dialled Mick's number. Nothing; the phone was ringing out. Cursing furiously, he got up off the bed, grabbed his baseball cap and ran down the stairs.

His mother glanced up from her afternoon soap opera as he searched the hall table for his house keys. 'Where you off to?'

'I'm goin' out.'

'What time you back at?'

'Later.'

'I'm goin' to work. You want dinner?'

'Leave it in the microwave!' Sharpie bawled back. He raced out the door and made his way, as fast as cool would allow, to the Luas.

# 12

'Where is he?' John leaned across the counter, his knuckles whitening as his hands bunched into fists. He spoke in a tight, barely constrained way that made Brendan Whelan nervous. He looked like he was about to run upstairs and tear the place asunder. He looked like a man barely in control.

Whelan was right: John was so angry that he could hardly breathe. He had brought Sarah home and paced her little apartment, ranting and raving, while she changed her trousers and used Dettol to clean her wounds. It had taken her the whole time, including the journey back to the office, to convince him not to go to the gardaí and not to find Bo and kill him.

'He's not here,' Brendan Whelan said.

'Where did he go?'

The old man sagged a bit further behind the counter. He wiped at his eyes with the sleeve of his shirt. 'What are you going to do?'

Muscles bunched and unbunched in John's jaw. 'She's not going to press charges, if that's what you're worried about. She should, but she's a fucking nice person.'

'Oh.'

'But you tell that little prick, if I ever come across him, I will break his neck.'

'Look, please – he didn't mean to hurt her.'

'Bullshit.' John leaned in closer. 'Now you listen to me. Sarah was very clear about this. She thinks you know the two boys who broke into David Reid's house. She wants their names. I want their names. We clear? You give us their names, and she doesn't press charges and I don't break your fucking son into fifty pieces.'

They stood looking at each other over the counter for a minute. John read uncertainty in the old man; he was wondering if Whelan was ever going to open his mouth again when he took a huge deep breath, took off his glasses and wiped them on the hem of his sleeve.

'If I give you their names, will you leave my son out of this business? He's not a bad man... he's just weak. He likes a flutter, you see, and, well...' Whelan raised his hands helplessly. 'I try to keep him straight, but I'm nearly seventy. I can't be watching him night and day.'

'I'll do my best, but if your son has those items, I want them returned – especially the laptop. There could be evidence on it.'

Whelan hesitated, still polishing his glasses slowly. John knew he was stalling, and knew now was not the time to push.

'If I do find this stuff for you, say if it turns up somewhere – not saying my boy has it, or anything like that but, if it does, are we agreed you'll keep his name out of it?'

'I said I'd do my best.'

He fidgeted for another moment or two. 'Mick and Shane Quinn. Reprobates, the two of them. They're twins. They used to be in and out of here all the time, until I barred them.'

John nodded. That sounded about right: Mick and Shane, Shane being Sharpie. 'They're friends of your son?'

'Friends?' Brendan Whelan snorted in disgust. 'Users like that don't have friends, just poor saps they can get something out of.'

'And what did they get from your son?'

'What do you think?'

'They were pawning stuff that didn't necessarily belong to them.' John glanced around. 'Passing stuff through here, no doubt.'

'Found out when some old one spotted her late husband's pinky ring in the window and came in here screaming blue murder.' Whelan sat down wearily. 'Brendan swears blind he didn't know, but, well, those two little shits would rob the sight out of your eye if you weren't careful.'

'Oh, yeah, and your son's a choirboy.' John pulled out his notebook and wrote the names down. 'Any idea where they live?'

'Up in Inchicore somewhere.'

'Can you get their address for me?'

'I'll ask.' Whelan suddenly looked older and tired. 'Tell your friend I'm sorry about what happened. I've tried to keep Brendan straight. But I can't be on top of him all the time: he's a grown man. What can I do? What can I do?'

John put his notebook away. 'Nothing, I suppose. A piece of shit is a piece of shit, no matter what you do with it.'

Whelan shrugged. John knew he was uncomfortable talking about his son, and again felt a little sorry for him. But then he thought of Sarah and his sympathy vanished. At the end of the day, it was the likes of this man's son, profiting from other people's misery, who kept thieves in business. John wondered how many other homes Mick and Sharpie Quinn had fleeced. How many people had returned home after a hard day at work and found their homes violated, their belongings stolen, their peace of mind shattered? It made him mad even to think about it.

'Call me either at the office or on my mobile the moment anything turns up.'

The old man nodded, but he didn't look in John's direction. He looked defeated and old, sitting there in his dusty shop with the smell of decay all around him.

\*

'What are you doing here?' Mick, who had been daydreaming about driving a Subaru Impreza across Europe, came reeling back to Earth with a wallop when he saw Sharpie huffing and puffing across the yard, carrying a can of Red Bull in one hand, his chains swinging in all directions. Mick experienced that familiar sense of dread he got in the pit of his stomach whenever he knew someone had pushed his brother's buttons too hard.

'We gotta talk.'

'What's wrong?'

'Man, what the fuck is up with your phone?'

Mick frowned. 'It's in my bag. What's wrong?'

'That fuckin' Bo called me. He's tryin' to pull out on our deal.'

'Sharpie, you've got to get out of here. If Big Jack sees you, he'll go fucking spare.'

'Didn't you hear me? Bo wants his money back.'

Mick glanced out the door of the shed. There was no sign of Robbie, the other mechanic. That was good, because Robbie hated Sharpie and would squeal him out as soon as Jack got back. 'Why is Bo freaking out?'

'He's a fuckin' chickenshit motherfucker, says the gear is too hot. Says someone's askin' questions about it.'

'Asking questions?' Mick said, alarmed. 'Who? How would anyone know to ask—'

'How the fuck should I know? I'm tellin' you, he's just freakin'.'

'Didn't he tell you?'

'Says we'll talk later.'

'I don't like this.' Mick chewed on his lip thoughtfully. 'He can't make us take it back, can he? A deal's a deal. I don't want to be stuck with it either. If Big Jack finds out we took it, he'll kill me.'

'I ain't givin' nothing to no one.'

'What did he say, exactly?'

'Goin' on with some shit about connections.'

'Connections? What connections?'

'I don't know, do I? Usual fuckin' bull 'bout money.' Sharpie rolled his eyes. 'Then he says his old man more or less told him the stuff is hot, and he never even saw it nor nothin'.'

'Then how's he know about it, if he never saw it?' Mick said, growing more confused by the second. He threw down the ratchet he had been holding and wiped his hands down the front of his overalls. 'How does his old man even know he's got anything?'

'That's the question, fo' real. He's tryin' to sting us somehow.'

'Shit, you don't think the cops are giving out pictures and shit of the gear?'

'Mick, you saw that stuff; it wasn't that fuckin' special. It's that fuckin' gimp Bo, wanting his money back 'cause he's got scared or some shit.'

'Shit.'

Mick shook his head. He'd already put his share of the money in the bank that morning. He'd been saving more or less every cent he had for the best part of a year now. As soon as he turned eighteen, he was buying an Impreza. There was a guy on Viking Quay who owned one, blue with gold trim. Mick worshipped that car. He had stopped to look at it that morning on his way into work, admiring its clean lines, almost drooling at the double exhaust. That sleek piece of machinery was the reason he got up every day and dragged his tired arse into work. Big Jack had even said he'd help him out with the insurance.

'Ringin' me up at my crib, givin' me lip, makin' threats,' Sharpie was saying, his face closed in and mean. 'He think I gotta take that kind of shit? Me? I don't take shit from no one.'

'I knew this would happen. I knew we shouldn't have taken that other stuff.'

'Fuck that. Fuck it for real.' Sharpie thought of the Rolex hidden in the bottom of his wardrobe. He could have picked up serious money for it, but it was the most beautiful thing he'd ever seen and he couldn't bear to part with it. 'We need to make sure Bo stays quiet and keeps our names out of anything.'

Mick blanched. 'You think he would give anyone our names?'

'Who the fuck knows? Stupid bastard probably shafted someone, and now he's lookin' to drop us into whatever hole he's dug for himself.'

'I don't want no one snooping around after me. Big Jack warned me: in-and-out job. He—'

'Fuck Big Jack!' Sharpie exploded, grabbing Mick by the top of his skinny arm. 'I don't give a shit what that Elvis-lookin' motherfucker thinks.'

Mick shook him off. 'Easy for you to say, 'cause you don't work for him.'

'Shut up a minute and let me think.'

Mick rubbed his hands through his hair and sighed. He should have known there would be trouble; there was always trouble when Sharpie did things his way, always. Or maybe it was his own fault. After all, he had told Sharpie about the job Big Jack had asked him to do. What had he expected?

Sharpie gulped back the rest of his can of Red Bull, belched and jiggled his mobile at Mick. He looked agitated and mean; his blue eyes danced. He was thinking of the way Bo had spoken to him on the phone, the dismissive way he had demanded Sharpie undo the deal; he was thinking of the gun back in his bedroom. 'Ringin' me, demandin' shit from me, who does he think he is? Nah, we gotta make sure no one connects us with Bo. We gotta make sure Bo don't involve us in anything.'

'Look, we can sort this. There's no need to get, you know, freaked out.'

'I'm not freaked out, bro,' Sharpie said, in a flat and oddly calm voice that made Mick break out in a sweat. 'But I'm tellin' you this: I ain't gonna have no fuck threatenin' me. I'm gonna take care of that bitch, for real.'

'What are you talking about?'

'Nothing. I'm gonna call him, get him to meet us here this evening.'

'Here?' Mick took a step backwards. 'Why here?'

'What's wrong with here? You got a key, don't you?'

'Sure, but—'

'But nothing. We're blood, Mick. We ain't gonna let no bitch threaten us.'

'Sharpie—'

'I'm gone. We'll talk later.'

Mick watched as his twin turned and bobbed his way back across the yard. He felt that knot of anxiety grow larger, until it sat in his chest like a bowling ball.

# 13

'What's the matter with you? Keep your goddamned voice down.'

Max Ashcroft lowered his glass and glanced over his shoulder. He, Larry and Clive were seated in the Octagon Bar at the Clarence Hotel. It was too early for the place to be busy, and Max noticed the barman looking in their direction. He held up three fingers to signal another round.

'He rang the house before my mobile,' Larry said. 'I saw the number when I got home. Dee might have answered.'

'So fucking what if she had?' Max snapped.

'And now detectives too… It's a nightmare.' Larry was growing paler by the second.

Clive shook his head. 'I don't want Sylvia hearing about this, either. She's pretty wound up right now.'

'Oh, for fuck's sake!'

'Don't "fuck's sake" me – you of all people,' Clive said angrily.

'What's that supposed to mean?'

'You know what I mean. If it wasn't for you, we wouldn't be in this—'

'Oh, so it's my fault, is it?'

'Yes, actually, Max, it fucking is!'

'Stop it!' Larry clasped his hands together between his knees.

The moment John had hung up, Larry had called the other two and suggested they meet. Now he wished he hadn't bothered. Why had he ever thought Max might have something useful to say?

'It's probably nothing, just James kicking up a bit of a stink.'

'Yes, but it's strange, isn't it? What is there to investigate?'

'Exactly, so why are you sitting there gibbering like a fucking retard?'

'Max, there's a little more to—'

'We said we wouldn't talk about that. It's got fuck all to do with David being pie-eyed and falling arse over tip into the canal.'

'It has everything to do with it,' Larry snapped.

Clive took out a Rennie's tablet and popped it in his mouth. His lunch sat heavily in his stomach and his indigestion was playing havoc. 'We have to talk about it. We need to keep our story straight.'

Max snorted. 'What fucking story? You think I'm going to tell some detective what David and me talked about that day?'

'Of course not, but—'

'I don't want to talk to him,' Clive said suddenly. 'I don't want to talk to anyone.'

Larry drained the last of his drink and sighed heavily. 'Me neither, but it'll look worse if we don't. He said he wants to ask a few questions about David, that's all. It's perfectly natural.'

'But like what? We were his friends, we played golf together, and that's really it.'

Larry raised an eyebrow. 'And if he wants to know why you didn't go to his funeral?'

'I was sick,' Clive snapped. 'You know I was.'

'What does any of it matter?' Max said. 'We say, yeah, great bloke for a shirt-lifter—'

'Max!' Larry said. 'Watch your mouth.'

'Well, he was, wasn't he?' Max said, trying to make it sound like a joke. 'Anyway, great bloke, played a mean game of golf and could sell sand to a rag-head—'

'Oh, Jesus.' Clive shook his head.

'We don't have to talk to him, I suppose.'

'Yeah, head in the sand,' Max sneered. 'That's a great solution. Nice one, Larry.'

'You don't get to speak to me that way. If it wasn't for me—'

'Yeah, yeah. Relax, you're my hero.'

They brooded for a while in silence. Then Max leaned in and whispered savagely, 'Course, there could be more to it. I mean, who knows what they found at David's house – a diary or some shit...'

'Or the contract?' Clive looked like he was about to faint.

'I have the contract,' Larry said. 'I'm a solicitor, remember? David thought it would be better with me.'

'But a diary—'

'He didn't keep a diary. Max, stop making things worse.'

'Ah, Christ, I don't bloody know, do I? He was acting strange. Who knows what he did?'

Clive sat up straighter. 'But how did this guy sound, Larry? Did he sound, I don't know, did he sound like he thought there was something odd about David's death?'

'I don't know,' Larry said miserably. 'I was so shocked that James was actually having it investigated, my mind almost went blank.'

Clive and Max exchanged worried glances, but before either of them could say anything, the waiter brought their drinks. They waited until he left. It was Clive who spoke first.

'Look, all right, we can see this guy, get a feel for what they're thinking. At the end of the day, what difference does it make? I mean, we spoke to the gardaí and they seemed content to go with mugging. Even if there was something odd about David's death, we didn't have anything to do with it. What harm can a quick talk with this crowd do?'

Larry plucked at his beer mat and began to shred it. 'What if...what if something, well, happened to David because of the girl?'

Clive visibly blanched. 'Oh, Jesus, are you fucking serious? You think he was deliberately—'

'Shut up, Larry,' Max hissed. 'I warned you before about that. Forget the fucking girl.'

'I was just—'

'I said shut up. I don't want to talk about that fucking girl ever again. This is what we're going to do. We will meet this guy individually, and we will say we knew David, he was a pal, he was great at golf, and that is it. We don't know anyone who had anything against him. But he was inclined to get shit-faced, and if he was mugged or he drowned it was a tragic accident, and we all miss him terribly. We won't mention any fucking girl and we won't mention a thing about our friend's other problem. Shit, even dead he's a fucking pain in the arse.'

He leaned in even closer, his darkly handsome face vivid with menace. 'I have worked my arse off to get where I am today. I have a great fucking job and a wife and kids. I am not going to throw it away for anyone, and that includes our pal David. If either of you shitheads opens your mouth about that girl… well, you can kiss your wedding goodbye, Clive; and you, Lar, old boy, can say adios to your house and that wife of yours. We'll be finished. We'll go to jail. And I have no intention of letting that happen. We're in this together. Do we understand each other?'

Larry sat back, trembling, his face moist with sweat. Clive chewed another Rennie's.

'Do we understand each other?'

'Yes,' Clive said eventually. 'We do. But, Jesus, Max, I don't like any of this.'

Max shrugged. 'Me neither, but if we keep out wits about us we can walk away from it. Right, Larry?'

'Right, right.'

'Okay, then. Give that guy a call back and give him our numbers. Let's put this bitch to bed once and for all.'

'I knew that fuck would be late.'

Mick shrugged and cleaned under his nails with a piece of plastic. His nerves were humming, and he wished he didn't feel so jumpy and ill at ease. He wished he had said no to meeting at the garage. Robbie had only been gone an hour; he could easily be close by. He glanced up. There was something wrong with his brother, too. Sharpie was too restless for Mick's liking. He was jumpy, wired. He smoked incessantly, picked at his skin and repeatedly kicked an empty Coke can around. The noise was driving Mick up the wall, but he held his tongue. He knew from his brother's face that he was in a dangerous place right now.

He hoped Bo didn't show up.

'We should have met him someplace else. If Big Jack finds out, he'll kill us.'

'Man, how can you stand working for that fat piece?'

'He's all right. You pull your weight, he leaves you alone.'

'It's bullshit. Look at you, sitting there all filthy and shit. You should come in with me. Man, together we could work up a serious patch. Know what I mean? I can't be everywhere at once.'

'I've only another few months to go before I'm fully qualified.'

'And then what? You still gonna be graftin' for shit rest of your days, another fuckin' nine-to-five loser.' Sharpie crushed the can under his foot and came to stand in front of Mick. He pulled out a packet of John Players and lit another cigarette from the butt he was holding.

Mick glanced at his watch, eager to change the subject. 'You like that new Snoop song?'

Sharpie snorted in disdain and held his hand up, palm flat. 'Man, quit right there. That motherfuckin' sellout. *Deep Cover* was the dope; now he's all mainstream and shit. I mean, duets with Justin fuckin' Timberlake? What's next? Him and J-Ho, like that other shit Fat Joe? Nah, Mick – damn, he sold it on. He ain't street no more.'

Mick nodded. He wanted to add something, to keep the atmosphere cool – Sharpie was always cool when they spoke about rap – but unfortunately he had used up his knowledge reserve, and seconds later his brother's eyes were dancing again.

'Sayin' he's gonna pull our deal,' Sharpie said, pacing. 'Has to be a load of bullshit. Even if someone did see us, why would the first place they go be the pawnshop?'

'So why doesn't he want the gear all of a sudden?'

'Maybe he couldn't offload it or some shit.'

'He knows guys into that kind of stuff. He's never had any trouble before.'

'Yeah, but maybe the old man's pulled a clampdown. I've never known Bo to pull a stunt like this, looking for his cash back. You thinkin' that could be it?'

Mick shrugged again. 'Dunno, but we're about to find out. Here he comes now.'

Bo slipped in through the gate and made his way over to the twins, with his queer gait. Mick watched him coming, thinking that Bo always moved like his shoes were too small or he was uncomfortable using the balls of his feet. He wore tight black jeans and a tank top that could have done with a wash. He carried a small blue backpack over his shoulder, and his tattooed arms seemed to glow in the darkening evening.

Sharpie grabbed his arm and jerked him into a complicated, hand-slapping, shoulder-walloping greeting. 'All right, my man, what's the story?'

'All right.' Bo stepped back from Sharpie faster than was necessary.

'Bo.' Mick nodded to him.

'All right, Mick, how's it going?'

'Good. What's all this about, Bo?' Mick sat on an upturned oil drum. 'Someone's looking for us?'

'Not looking for you personally. Looking for me.'

'Okay, what's that got to do with us, then?' Sharpie said. He was grinning, but Mick could hear no trace of humour in his voice. Sharpie was buzzing, and that was not a good thing.

'I can't move this shit.'

'So?'

'So it ain't worth shit to me now.'

'So what?'

Bo balled his hands. 'Look, you need to take this shit back. They were looking for Bo. Not many people call me that. Fact is, you two's the only ones that does.'

Sharpie shrugged, but Mick felt a tremor of unease. 'Who were they?'

'Detectives.'

'Jakes?' Sharpie said, scowling.

'What?'

'Cops,' Mick translated.

'Nah, man, private. Look, the deal's fucked. It's too boogie that they were in looking for Bo the day after you sold me all that shit. They mentioned all the shit – picture frames, clock and the laptop. You've been fucking rumbled.'

'Coincidence,' Mick said.

'Bollocks. I should've known that shit was too hot. They're looking for me because somehow they know we do deals. My old lad is having a meltdown. He's threatening to turf me out on my ear and everything.'

'No one knows nothing,' Sharpie said, growing angrier.

'They were in the shop. That wasn't my fucking imagination. They was looking for me; how long do you think before they're looking for you?'

'So sit on it a while, give it a chance to cool down.'

'I can't afford to be out of pocket till that shit's cold. I need my money back. Look, the computer – no hassle, I got a buyer lined up; but the rest of the shit... Passing on silver takes time. I—'

'Are you fo' fuckin' real, man?' Sharpie snorted a laugh. 'What the fuck makes you think we still have the money to give?'

Bo ignored him and kept his eyes focused on Mick. 'You and me go back a good way; you know the score. I gotta be able to move the gear on, you know that. And I can't move it if it's hot.'

'Business is business,' Mick said, beginning to clean his nails again. 'We don't have your money, Bo. It's gone. Best thing you can do is pass that shit on to another buyer.'

Bo shifted from one foot to the other. 'Look, Mick—'

'No, you look,' Sharpie said, seething now. Who was Bo to talk like he wasn't even there? 'We find shit sometimes, and we sell it to you. Now, that's our end of the business finished. I don't care if you gotta flush that shit like waste. Got it? Anyone comes in your bleedin' shop askin' for us, you don't fuckin' mention us, all right? Fuck, man, you know this.'

'I need my money,' Bo said, in a strangely firm voice.

'You fuck, you.'

'Bo, there's no point crying to us. It's a… what does Big Jack call it?' Mick said, trying to lighten the tension.

Sharpie was watching Bo through narrowed eyes. 'I don't know, Mick. What do he call it?'

Mick smiled nervously and tossed the piece of plastic over his shoulder. 'A buyer-beware situation.'

'I need that money, Mick.'

'I can't help you.'

Bo bounced on his heels. 'What are you saying?'

'We're saying no, homie. You wasted or something?' Sharpie said in a cold, flat voice. 'You deaf?'

'I'm sorry to hear that.' Bo nodded. 'Very sorry.'

Sharpie's nostrils flared. He stepped close to the older man and grabbed him by the front of his T-shirt. 'Here, I don't like the fuckin' gob on you. You're sorry? What are you sorry about? Didn't you hear my brother? We're done, this deal is done. What are you sayin' sorry for?'

Mick slid off the oil drum. 'Sharpie—'

'No, what's this fucker tryin' to say? He says he's bleedin' sorry, I want to know about what.'

'He's not trying to say anything – are you, Bo?'

Bo tried to wrench his arm free, but Sharpie suddenly let go and shoved him away. 'You gonna tell me what the fuck you're so sorry about?'

'I need that money.'

'"I need that money,"' Sharpie mimicked. He curled his free hand into a fist and swung it. It caught Bo behind the ear and he staggered backwards. Sharpie advanced on him. 'You fuckin' bollocks, you don't fuckin' threaten me! What, you think I'm your bitch now?'

'Sharpie, leave him. He's not going to open his gob.'

Sharpie swung his fist again, but Bo leaped out of the way and threw a punch of his own. It was a wild swing, but it caught Sharpie flush on the side of the head, knocking his baseball cap into the dirt. Mick jumped on his brother and hauled him back. Sharpie's teeth were bared and he slapped at his twin.

'Yo, Mick, let go of me! I'm gonna fix that motherfucker.'

'Sharpie, stop—'

Sharpie backhanded Mick hard across the mouth, splitting his lip. Mick grunted and fell, landing hard on one knee.

But Bo Whelan was in the grip of something neither brother understood. It had been over a week since he'd placed a bet, and he was deep in hock to a man who wasn't interested in excuses. Not only that, but earlier that day he'd received a tip on a sure thing running in the three-thirty the next day. His old man wouldn't lend him any more money, he hadn't a red cent to his name and he knew that, short of knocking off some old biddy for her pension, he was not going to see any more cash for at least another week, maybe longer. He was afraid, panicked and in the throes of an addiction so fierce and all-encompassing it dwarfed his fear of confronting the brothers.

Desperation can make men do stupid and dangerous things. Bo Whelan was about to do something spectacularly stupid.

'You fucking little bastards! You think you scare me, Sharpie? If you don't give me my money back, I'm going to fucking do you. Give me my money back.' He dropped his backpack, and it hit the ground with a distinctive clang. Mick winced. If the clock was in that bag, it was probably broken now.

Sharpie glanced at Mick. 'Yo, bro, you hearing this?'

'I want my fucking money!' Bo lunged at Sharpie and shoved him hard in the chest. Sharpie, caught off guard, went sprawling.

Mick got to his feet and wiped at the blood on his lips. 'Bo, stop!'

'I've got all your—'

Incensed and winded, Sharpie scrabbled to his feet and charged Bo, catching him around the waist and trying to head butt him. Bo brought his elbow down on the back of Sharpie's exposed neck and Sharpie went down again, grunting. Bo kicked at him and caught him in the ribs, lifting him off the cobbles. Sharpie rolled away, filthy and coughing.

Mick spat blood and jumped in. He pinned Bo's arms and wrestled him away, forcing him back one step at a time, his hard, wiry muscles more than a match for him, more than Sharpie's show muscles any day.

'Bo, stop it – stop! You're fucking out of line here. Stop!'

'I need that money!' Bo yelled, spraying spittle all over Mick.

'All right, you'll get your money. Calm the fuck down, man! Cool it.'

Behind them, Sharpie climbed slowly to his feet. He looked down at his threads; he was covered in oil stains and bits of crap. His ribs ached and he was taking shallow breaths. He looked over at Bo and cracked his neck, and as he did so, a steady white noise began to build behind his murderous gaze.

'You shouldn't have done that, homie,' Sharpie said. The noise rose and reached its peak; then it stopped. And now he was calm.

Bo held up his hands, and Mick released him. 'Look, Sharpie, I don't want no aggro with you, you know? But you're not giving me much of a choice here, you know? I can't sell the gear on. What am I supposed to do? I need that fucking money.'

Mick watched his brother. Something had happened. Something was going on behind those flat, dead eyes. Mick felt his guts twist up inside him.

'I just want my money.'

But whatever chance Bo had had of doing any kind of deal with the Quinn brothers had gone the moment he struck Sharpie. Mick began to sweat. His brother was staring at Bo as though Bo were some kind of species he had never seen before. Mick wanted to tell Bo to get the hell out of there, but it was too late. Sharpie stepped in closer, a serene smile on his face.

'All right, Bo. Ain't no need for us to be hatin'. I'll give you what you want.'

Bo glanced between the brothers, his weasel face puckered with uncertainty. 'Yeah? Straight up?'

'Straight up.'

'Really?'

'Yeah, you're gonna get it right away.'

'We don't carry cash around,' Mick said nervously. 'Maybe later we—'

'Situations change, bro, don't they?'

Mick turned back to Bo, a sick feeling in his stomach. 'Bo, this is fucking gash. Just sit on the gear and keep your mouth shut. You'll be shot of it in a couple of weeks. You know you will.'

Bo shrugged. 'I can't, man. I'm bleeding sorry. If there was anything else I could do, you know it, I would. But, shit, I really need—'

'You need the money. Yeah, you said.'

Mick looked at Sharpie and felt his stomach flip. What he saw was the other Sharpie, the one who made decisions – decisions that he would not be talked out of. Decisions that would no doubt come back and bite them both in the arse. 'Sharpie—'

Sharpie put his hand behind him, up and under his shirt, and when he brought it back around, it held the Glock.

Mick groaned. Bo blinked stupidly at it, as if he didn't know what it was.

Sharpie pointed the gun at Bo, making sure he turned it sideways, the way all true gangstas held their guns. 'Yo, man, you see this Gat?'

'Jesus, Sharpie, where did you get that?' Mick asked. 'Put it away.'

'You think you can threaten me, bitch? Step to me, beat me down?'

The blood drained from Bo's face and he took a stumbling step backwards, holding up his hands in front of him. 'Sharpie, man, I swear, I – I was just letting off steam, you know? Relax, man, take it easy. I'm sorry – I'm sorry.'

'You take it easy. I'm cool, I'm chillin'.'

'Look, I don't… we don't have to, you know. I'll shine it on. It's cool. I'll sort it.'

'What? You think you can get all up in my grill and 'spect me not to step to you? Think you can slap me? Think you can step to this and walk away?'

Bo looked at Mick, tears forming in his terrified eyes. 'Mick, please, tell him, please. I didn't mean anything by what I said. I didn't mean to—'

'It's all right, Bo, relax.' Mick waved a frantic arm at him and turned to his twin. 'Listen to him, he—'

Sharpie squinted and pulled the trigger.

The explosion made both of the twins jump. The bullet nicked Bo's right index finger, punched a hole the size of a fifty-cent piece in his cheek, then ricocheted off his cheekbone and travelled upwards into his frontal lobe, where it cut a swathe through his brain and exited through the top of his skull.

Bo's eyes rolled upwards. He said, 'Uh.' His legs buckled and he collapsed into a twitching heap.

'Sharpie...' Mick stared at Bo in horror, his mouth hanging open. Eventually he managed to croak out, 'What the fuck? What have you done?'

Bo shuddered; his heels jerked and rattled on the cobbles. A pool of blood began to spread out from behind his head. Mick groaned.

Sharpie, who had almost dropped the gun from the recoil, tried hard to play it cool. But he was so excited he could hardly speak. Right up until the moment he squeezed the trigger, he had believed he was just going to scare Bo, and then... and then it was like somebody else had taken over, someone who said, Fuck this motherfucker, waste his ass. 'I warned him, man, I told him not to fuck with me. I iced his ass.' He started to giggle uncontrollably. 'Ooh, he iced. Fo' real.'

Mick stared at his brother. 'You fucking lunatic. Oh, man, oh, man, you've fucked us – oh, man, you've completely fucked us. Oh, man, oh... we've got to call an ambulance.'

Sharpie stopped giggling. 'Are you for real? Call and say what? We found this shot dude where you work? Shit, Mick, that is some stupid shit.'

'Oh, Jesus – oh, Jesus. Someone will have heard it, the cops are probably on their way...' Mick started pacing in circles, pulling at his hair. Every so often he stopped and stared at the rapidly growing pool of blood spreading from under Bo's ruined head. And he said, 'Oh, Jesus,' again.

Sharpie put the gun back in the waistband of his jeans and pulled his top down over it. 'Mick, chill. We need to get rid of him.'

Mick kept walking. 'Where the fuck did you get that gun?'

'I bought it.'

'You bought it? Oh, Jesus.'

'Stop with that Jesus shit.'

'We can say it was, I don't know, some kind of accident or something, or a joke. It went off by accident. We could—'

'We need to get rid of him.'

Mick stopped pacing. 'How, you fucking eejit? You think of that? How? Where? This isn't the fucking films. What the fuck are we gonna do? Oh, Jesus – oh, man.'

Sharpie looked around. 'Shit, Mick, you got cars here, don't you? We wrap him in plastic, put him in one of the cars and dump him somewhere.'

Mick stopped walking and sat down on the ground with his head in his hands. He was afraid he was going to faint.

'Did you know you were going to kill him? Before you came here, did you know?'

Sharpie ignored that. 'We can clean this shit up, hose it down and shit, then we're cool. No one knows we met him—'

'I asked you a fucking question.'

Sharpie stopped talking. He took a deep breath and looked at Mick full on. 'All right. I thought it wouldn't come to that – but, shit, then he hit me! What was I supposed to do? What if he'd squealed us out? Huh? I ain't going back to Pat's, no way, not over some fucking silver and shit. Then he hit me, man. I can't have no disrespect.'

'Pat's?' Mick felt sick. His head was reeling. 'Disrespect? But you killed him. We'll get life for this.'

'Not if no one knows about it,' Sharpie snapped. 'That's why we gotta get movin'. We need to cleanse this motherfuckin' place, for real. C'mon, I saw this shit on *CSI*. We can—'

'Are you fucking crazy?' Mick shook his head. 'I'm not doing shit. I'm not cleaning nothing! You dragged us into this fucking mess, and you—'

'Yo, you dragged me into this deal, takin' me with you when you was robbin' that guy's crib.'

'I didn't take you, you fucking came.'

Sharpie shrugged. 'Not how your boss is gonna see it, now is it? You know it, Mick. What's Big Jack gonna say when he come in tomorrow and see this dude lyin' here?'

Mick groaned long and loud. As bad as his day had become, he knew it would be a whole lot worse if Big Jack got wind of this. He had no choice: he had to get rid of Bo.

'All right. You stay right here. I'll get some plastic seat covers and see if I can get the Fiat to work.'

# 14

'I mean, bad enough that you can't smoke in a bar, but does anybody in this godforsaken hole drink any more?' John asked, turning the wheel and reversing into a parking space. 'You should have seen the state of him. Sparkling water, sparkling water. Who goes to a pub and orders sparkling water? It's the stupidest thing I ever saw. What kind of a man sits there and drinks fucking sparkling water? It was embarrassing.'

Sarah nodded. She had a splitting headache, and she wished John would stop ranting on about Carrie's new boyfriend. He'd been going on about him all morning, and she was heartily sick of listening.

She glanced at her watch, wondering how much longer it would take Steve Magher to come up with an address for the Quinn brothers. She was itching to call him again, but she didn't want to hassle him. As Steve had already pointed out to her that morning, he was a sergeant in Tallaght, not QuicK's personal assistant. Detective Sergeant Steve Magher was a no-nonsense Corkman, and he was never thrilled to be roped into one of their jobs, but John had once pulled off a crucial surveillance job for him, and, for all his grumbling, Steve had never let them down.

Sarah sighed. She didn't mind talking to David's friends, but she really wanted to get hold of the Quinn boys and ask a few questions. With John. She wasn't feeling up to any more rough stuff.

'"Sparkling water",' John mimicked, falsetto. 'Jesus, this country's going to the dogs.'

'John, it was a Tuesday night. Maybe he just didn't want to have a head on him today.'

'Bollocks. Sitting there with that puss on him – you should have seen him. And Carrie acting all twittery and clinging onto his arm every time he opened his mouth. I've never seen the like.'

'Oh, Christ. Give it a rest, will you?'

'She giggled. Carrie doesn't giggle!'

Sarah sighed.

'I'm telling you, Sarah, there is something wrong with a man who won't have a drink with you. It's not like he's teetotal or anything. I asked Carrie.'

'Maybe he was trying to make a good impression.'

John snorted.

'I hope you didn't say anything nasty to Carrie about him.'

'Ah, give me a bit of credit, will you? She'd have knocked my block off. I'll have to wait a while before I can do a number on him.'

They were parked around the corner from the Morrison Hotel, just off Ormond Quay. The traffic was heavy and stalled. John jaywalked across the road, narrowly avoiding being struck by a motorbike whizzing through the gaps. The courier swore at John; John swore back.

Sarah watched their outburst with little interest. She was tired, having spent much of the night twisting and turning, and she was sore. She was thinking about her mother, who had called her twice the night before to chat, and who, despite Sarah's attempts to get off the phone, had rambled on for over an hour each time about a litany of seemingly unconnected things. And when, finally, Sarah had said she had to go to bed, her mother had snapped at her and hung up. Sarah had called her back, but the phone had been off the hook.

What was that about? Nothing, probably, yet Sarah was worried.

Her mother had always been flighty, prone to fits of depression alternating with almost hysterical joy. But she had never been vicious or abusive. Maybe she was in pain – the fall had certainly shaken her. Perhaps, Sarah thought guiltily, she was just lonely.

She turned the collar of her jacket up and waited for a proper break in the traffic. How could it be so cold and miserable, after the heat wave of the few days before? She looked up at the sky: it was going to lash any minute. The clouds were the colour of day-old bruises, and so low it seemed as though you could raise your hand and brush them with the tips of your fingers.

'Hey, come on, will you?' John called.

Sarah followed him across the street and into the Morrison Hotel. Larry Cole had given John a good description. They found him seated in a brown leather chair in the bar, reading a newspaper, with a cup of steaming coffee in front of him. Though he was expecting them, he looked startled when John walked over and tapped him on the arm.

'Yes?'

'Hi.' John held out his hand. 'John Quigley. This is my business partner, Sarah Kenny.'

'Hello.' Sarah offered her hand.

'Oh, I didn't realise there would be two of you.' Larry shook hands with both of them and then clasped his hands together.

Sarah tried not to pull a face; his hands were disgustingly clammy. She wondered why he looked so nervous. Maybe this was simply his natural state. What had Lillian Daly said about a pack? This man was more of a poodle than a wolf.

John and Sarah sat down opposite him. Larry asked if they wanted coffee or tea; both of them declined.

'So, well now, what can I help you with? I don't have very long, I'm afraid. I must say, I thought it a bit strange when I heard James had hired detectives, most strange.'

'Really?' Sarah said. 'I don't see why. The circumstances of his brother's death are a little odd.'

'Well, yes, there is that.'

'David Reid was a close friend of yours, wasn't he?' John said.

'I've known David almost twenty years now. We met at college.'

'And you've stayed friends that whole time?'

'Well, initially we met sporadically, but then we started bumping into each other more often. Really, we've been close for about the last ten years. Golf – we both play…em, played a lot of golf.'

'I heard he was a keen golfer.' John pulled out a notebook and flipped it open. 'It's just a bit of background we're looking for. Anything you can tell us about how David was in the weeks leading up to his death would be great.'

Larry smiled stiffly. 'How he was? I'm not sure what you mean.'

'Like, did it seem like there was anything troubling him? You know, how did he seem – was he depressed or anxious in any way?'

'No – gosh, no. He seemed fine. His usual self.'

'His brother thought he seemed troubled,' Sarah said.

'Troubled?' Larry blinked and took a sip of his coffee. 'Really, I never noticed.'

'He never mentioned anything to you about…' John shrugged. 'Oh, I don't know, owing money or being in a jam, or anything out of the ordinary?'

Larry shook his head slowly. 'No, no, nothing like that. This all sounds rather ominous. What's the deal here?'

'James Reid doesn't think his brother's death was an accident,' Sarah said simply.

'Really?' Larry Cole looked queasy. He flapped his hands at them, took a gulp of his coffee, half scalded himself and finally squawked, 'What on earth would make him think it was anything else?'

Sarah and John exchanged glances. John leaned forward slightly. 'Are you all right?'

Larry Cole nodded. 'Yes, of course. The coffee's too hot.'

'Right,' John said.

'But… so, does James think David was… what? Murdered?'

Sarah and John exchanged glances again. 'I don't think he thinks he was murdered,' John said, 'but he thinks some foul play was involved, yes. He might have been mugged or carjacked.'

'Really? How… extraordinary.' Larry cleared his throat and took another gulp of his coffee.

'It's not that odd,' Sarah said, narrowing her eyes. 'His car is missing. And his house was broken into on the day of his funeral.'

He didn't flap about this time; he looked genuinely shaken. 'Excuse me?'

'His new Audi has been missing since the night of his death. And two men – kids, really – broke in and ransacked his house on Monday.'

'The gardaí never mentioned it. I had no idea. And I have absolutely no idea where the car could be. How odd. Poor David.'

'And the wallet and keys weren't found on the body.'

'No?' Larry winced at the word 'body', and Sarah felt a pang of guilt. Perhaps she was being too cool with him. 'Oh, God. David was a carefree sort – great with people, really. He was exactly the type of person who would strike up a conversation with a stranger.'

Sarah nodded slowly. 'You knew he was gay, of course.'

'Well, yes. He was very open about it.'

'Did he have any boyfriend trouble – jealous lovers, anything like that?'

This question actually seemed to relax Larry Cole, and for the first time he stopped twittering and looked Sarah straight in the eye. 'Oh, no, nothing like that. As far as I know, David never really got that seriously involved with anyone. He had a relationship with a fellow a few years ago – a hairdresser, Marcus something or other – but after they split, I don't think he wanted anything permanent. I think David preferred to be unfettered.'

'Where did this Marcus guy work?' John asked.

Larry gave them the name of a city-centre hairdresser's. John wrote it down.

'Did David drink a lot?'

'Not particularly. I mean, we can all knock back a few when the mood catches us.' He tittered for a second, but stopped abruptly when neither of the detectives joined in. 'But I wouldn't have said he drank excessively.'

'And what about your other friends?' John asked. 'From what I can make out, you and Max Ashcroft and Clive Hollingsworth were all very close, but James told us Clive didn't attend David's funeral. Why was that? Had they fallen out?'

'No! No, nothing like that – God, no. As a matter of fact, David was to have been Clive's best man at his wedding in a few days' time.'

'Yeah? Strange, then, that he was a no-show at the funeral,' Sarah said.

'He would have attended if he could have. He was terribly sick – stomach bug. He rang me that morning. He was dressed and everything, but he was so ill he almost fainted. Sylvia – that's Clive's fiancée – told me she had to practically force him into bed.'

'I see.' Sarah nodded. 'How long have David and Clive known each other?'

'David and I met Clive at a charity golf game about eight years ago, and Max sort of joined our little crew a few years later. Golf again; we're all keen golfers.'

'Tell me something,' John said. 'Did David normally drink and drive?'

'No. He'd have one, of course, but that would be his limit. He needed to travel for business, he would never have risked losing his licence.' Larry ran his hand through his thin hair. 'This is very strange. I don't understand where the car would be.'

'Did he have a garage somewhere?' Sarah asked.

'Not that I'm aware of. Why would he need one?'

'I don't know,' Sarah said. 'It's got to be somewhere, hasn't it?'

John glanced at her. She was cranky today, and he could tell she was getting a little exasperated with the lack of progress.

'Was everything going well with his work, as far as you know?'

'I believe so. Lillian can be a trial sometimes, but they got on quite well, in a business sense.'

'She'll be sole owner of the business now, won't she?' John said.

'Yes.'

'That business must be worth a pretty penny.'

'Actually, without David's input it won't make nearly as much. Look, you have to understand: Lillian is the master organiser, but David was incredibly gifted with people and with design. Between the two of them, they built that business from scratch. Now she'll have to hire a designer and a separate sales rep and try to keep hold of all David's old contacts. It won't be easy. Certainly Lillian, shrew though she is, wouldn't have wanted David gone.'

Sarah believed him. Miss Congeniality was going to find it very tough to woo the clients without him.

'Does the name Jack mean anything to you?' Sarah asked.

'Jack? No, I can't… Jack?'

'Jack, yes. You don't remember David ever mentioning the name?'

'No, never.'

'What about Sharpie, or Mick?'

'Mick?' Larry shook his head, looking more and more confused. 'Sharpie? Er… no. Why do you ask?'

'They're the names of the two boys who broke into his house.'

Larry Cole looked like he had been slapped. 'You know who broke into his house?'

'We know their names,' Sarah said, frowning. 'That's all.'

'Well, that's…that's something, at least.' Larry Cole glanced at his watch. 'You know, I've really got to get going. Was there anything else?'

'Not this minute,' John said, standing. 'But if we need you, we'll call.'

'Will you be seeing Max and Clive today?'

'Yep, Max in about half an hour and Clive after that.'

'Poor James.' Larry collected his coat and scarf from the chair beside him. 'I suppose he needs closure. It must very difficult for him right now.'

John nodded and slipped his notebook into his pocket. 'It's hard losing a family member, especially a younger one.'

'Have you ever heard of a place called the Meridian Club?' Sarah asked suddenly.

Larry grinned at her, showing a lot of gum. 'Of course.'

'Can you tell me what it is?'

'It's a golf club in Colorado.'

Sarah took the globe from her pocket and passed it to Larry Cole. 'You ever seen one of these?'

Larry took it. He put his glasses back on and stared at it for so long that John and Sarah exchanged glances.

'Mr Cole? Are you all right?' Sarah asked.

'I'd forgotten about these stupid things.' He lifted his face, and Sarah could see he was genuinely upset. 'We got them made up, you see – a sort of commemoration of our first golfing trip away together. David's idea, I think. He called us the golfing globetrotters.' He closed his hand around the globe. 'Where did you get it?'

'I found it at the accident site.'

Sarah gave John her 'I told you so' look. John rolled his eyes.

'Poor David. He always carried it on his car keys.' Larry passed it back to Sarah and took a deep breath. 'Well, if you can excuse me…'

Sarah stood up and offered her hand. 'Thanks for taking the time to see us. I'm sorry about the circumstances.'

He shook her hand. Sarah had to force herself to keep the smile in place. His hands were slimy with sweat.

'Yeah, thanks.' John shook next. He surreptitiously wiped his hand on the back pocket of his jeans when he got it back.

'If you need me for anything else, please don't hesitate to call,' Larry said, sadly.

\*

Larry Cole wasn't sure if he could dial the number, his hands were shaking so much. He sat behind the steering wheel of his car, taking great gulps of air and forcing his mind to think.

Finally he mastered the phone and dialled Max's mobile. The phone rang and rang; eventually it was picked up by a disgruntled and breathless Max.

'What?'

'Max, it's me. Oh, God, it was awful.'

'Larry, I'm in the middle of something here—'

'David's car is missing, it's been stolen. And the house was broken into on the day of his funeral.'

Max didn't say anything for a second, then, 'Hold on.'

Larry heard him talking in the background with someone else. He came back on the line almost a minute later. 'The house was broken into?'

'The day of the funeral.'

'Fuck. You know who did it, of course.'

'It had to be Lawson.'

'Bastard. Okay, tell me what the fuck they think they know.'

'They asked me if I'd ever heard the name Jack! The girl, she said they knew the names of the two boys—'

'What boys?'

'The ones who broke in. Jack wouldn't do it himself.'

'She knows their names? How the fuck can she know their names?'

'I don't know. I – I never even asked, it was such a shock when she asked about Jack.'

'No second name?'

'No, just Jack. And then she asked me about the Meridian Club.'

'Why were they asking about the club? What has that got to do with anything?'

'The girl – she found David's keyring where he drowned. I almost died when she mentioned it. I don't want them checking into it. Don't you remember? We were joking at the hotel – Christ, Max, don't you remember? We booked the dinner table in that name, for a joke. We toasted it, for Christ's sake. I wish to God we hadn't used that name. It was so stupid.'

'They found his keyring? But what difference does it make?'

'I don't know. I wasn't thinking straight. I don't want any connection to the hotel, that's all. What if they're checking out David's movements and they think of checking under "Meridian Club"?'

'Calm down, Larry, and listen to me. The club doesn't matter. It was five years ago, for fuck's sake. Why the hell would they go around looking for bookings under that name? And even if they did connect him to the hotel, so bloody what? We were there – it was Clive's stag!'

'I know, but if—'

'If nothing. Larry, I mean it: you need to calm down.'

'I know, I know, I'm sorry. I was just... I wasn't expecting to be questioned, really. I thought I was, but I wasn't. And seeing David's keyring like that... it upset me, that's all.'

'Yeah, I know,' Max said, sounding genuinely upset for a second. 'Look, it's going to be hard, but that's the way it is. Eventually, this shit will all blow over and we can get back to normal again.'

Larry nodded. 'Right, you're right.'

'All right, take it easy. Look, I gotta go here. I'll call you after I talk to them.'

'Okay.' Larry hung up and closed his eyes, wishing that for once he could have Max's unwavering faith in tomorrow being another day.

# 15

Mick looked down at his hands, his breath coming from deep within him in short, sharp bursts. He was crying and there was blood all over him. He tried to pat himself down. He was convinced that he had to be bleeding from somewhere, but where? His hands were... The blood wasn't his.

He turned his head. Bo was standing there, his arms splayed out in front of him. He was talking, but Mick couldn't make out the words. Was it even English? Bo: that was where the blood came from. His eyes were full of blood. It dripped down his cheeks and onto his chest.

Mick turned his head. Sharpie was there, with the gun in his hands, but it wasn't Sharpie; this thing was bigger and had a muzzle, like a bear. Mick could smell him. He smelled of wet fur, mixed with the stench of rotting leaves. The creature looked once at Mick, its black eyes flat and cold, then back at Bo. It drew its muzzle back, exposing long, yellow canine teeth that glistened in the dead air.

'Sharpie, no!'

Mick tried to run, but his feet were so heavy he could barely lift them. He watched as the Sharpie creature pulled the trigger.

'No!'

The bullet ripped through Bo's face, shattering bone and ripping skin. Mick could smell smoke and burning flesh. A spray of blood arced out and struck his face. The Sharpie creature licked its lips and turned towards Mick. It leaned in and licked the blood from his face. Its breath was hot and fetid—

Mick screamed.

Then he woke up.

Sharpie was asleep in the next bed, flat on his back, a sunburned arm thrown across his face. Mick willed his heart to slow down. He swallowed hard and lay there panting, listening to the sound of his heart mixing with the sound of rain slamming against the window.

He stared at a patch of light moving slowly across the ceiling of their room. The light was a mystery to him; he'd never noticed it before. He wondered idly what was causing it. A truck outside, perhaps, maybe the reflection of headlights on the rain-soaked road. Think of lights, think of sunburn, think of anything except…

He sat up and felt a sharp pain in between his shoulder blades. He was surprised by it momentarily, but then he remembered why it hurt. He had pulled a muscle or something when he had fallen trying to haul Bo's body over the ditch. Mick lay back down again, all of the air vanishing from his lungs as though an invisible hand had punched him squarely in the chest.

They had murdered Bo and dumped his body in the Dublin Mountains. Worse than that, they had stolen Big Jack's Fiat Punto to move the body, and on the way back it had stalled. They'd had no choice but to push it behind the Superquinn centre in Templeogue. They had taken the plates off, set it on fire, caught a taxi back to Big Jack's yard and tried to make the lock look as though it had been tampered with. It had been almost four before they had reached home.

Big Jack. Mick groaned loudly.

It wasn't like the films or video games. When you killed a man, he didn't just fall over and die. He didn't soundlessly exit the world as though carried away on a cloud. No, it was brutal and violent and it reeked of piss and blood and fear. Bo had bled and bled. His legs had kicked and twitched for what seemed like an age as the almost-black blood spread over the dirty cobbles of the yard.

Mick closed his eyes and tried to inhale, but the leaden sensation only worsened in the dark. He opened his eyes again and forced himself to concentrate on the light.

How would he do it – how would he go to work and act normal? How would he try to pretend everything was the way it had been yesterday? How would he act when he was questioned about the car?

He turned his head and looked his brother over carefully. He could see the blood beneath Sharpie's fingernails, even though they had scrubbed their hands for almost twenty minutes upon their return home.

Mick closed his eyes again, trying to force the image from his mind. The triumphant look on his brother's face. The strange sound the bullet had made as it punched through Bo's skull. The spray of warm blood that had lashed him across the cheek like a whip. It was all so vivid, so horrifically vivid. The look on Bo's face when he saw the gun aimed at his head, the terror in his voice as he had begged for his life, pleading with Mick to help him. The way, when they had lifted him, pieces of skull had stuck to their hands.

Mick threw the duvet back and ran for the bathroom. He made it to the toilet and vomited until his stomach was empty, and then he dry-retched until every last drop of saliva was gone.

'What's the matter with you?'

His mother stood at the bathroom door, watching him suspiciously. Her pink fluffy slippers were shaped like rabbits. An unlit fag hung from the corner of her mouth.

'Nothing.' He reached over and flushed.

'Why aren't you in work?'

'I'm going in now, in a minute.'

'You're very late. It's past eleven now. Must have been some night. What happened to your arm?'

'What?'

'Where'd you get all them scratches on your arm?'

Mick glanced at his arm and, sure enough, there were two ferocious-looking tears from the top of his shoulder to just behind his bicep. He had got them fetching branches and bushes to cover Bo.

'Oh, that. It's nothing. Got hurt in work yesterday.'

'Your face is all bashed up, too. Is that a cut lip?'

'I told you, I hurt it in work.'

'Doin' what?'

'Lifting corrugate or something, I don't know. Stop asking me questions.'

His mother pulled her lips into a thin line. She didn't believe him. Mick spat and wiped his mouth with the back of his hand. He felt faint, light-headed. He wished she would go away.

'Where were you two last night?'

Mick shrugged. 'Just out.'

'What were you doin', anyway? I thought I heard you and your brother wafflin' at all hours. What were youse doin' in the bathroom?' She pushed the door open with her foot and glanced around.

Mick followed her gaze. He had wiped down every surface and sprayed the whole place clean last night. They'd hosed the yard down before they left with Bo, and done their best to remove any trace of his blood. But as soon as they had arrived home they had been amazed to see just how much more blood remained on their clothes and even in Mick's hair. They'd had no choice but to use the bathroom to wash off, despite the risk that their mother might discover them.

She exhaled hard. 'You're late for work.'

'I'm going now.'

Mick closed his eyes as the full weight of the trouble they were in came crashing down on him. He had fucked about with the lock of the Fiat a little, but was it enough to make it look like the car had been nicked? And what about the boot? Would the cops be able to tell there had been blood all over it? It had burned well, but who knew? Didn't they have forensics and shit?

Oh, Jesus – they'd probably be able to read the chassis number. The cops would trace it to Big Jack the moment they checked the registration.

Mick groaned out loud. Big Jack would go fucking spare if he ever figured out they had taken it. He'd rip Mick's head off for sure.

'What're you makin' that sound for? What the hell's wrong with you?' His mother was now giving him her undivided attention, her eyes narrowed with suspicion. Mick's stomach flipped again.

'Are you sick?'

'Ma, just leave me be, will you? I'll be grand in a minute. Probably a dodgy burger or something.'

'Burger, my eye.' His mother pulled a face, and Mick knew she thought he was sick from taking acid, or ecstasy, or whatever drug she thought they took behind her back.

'Ma, I'm grand.'

'Make sure you don't go gettin' puke all over me carpet. If you do, you'll be the one cleanin' it. I'm warnin' you.'

When she had made her way back downstairs, Mick ran the taps and washed his pale face. He stared at his reflection in the mirror. He looked terrible.

He went back to the bedroom and shook Sharpie.

'Come on, wake up.'

Sharpie rolled over onto his stomach. Mick jabbed him in the back, hard. 'Sharpie, what am I gonna say about the fucking car?'

Sharpie opened one eye and stared blearily at his brother. 'What? What is it?'

'The Fiat! There's going to be fucking murder when Big Jack finds out it's missing.'

Sharpie rolled over and sat up slowly. He rotated his shoulders, one at a time, and winced. 'Yo, man, what gives? I'm fuckin' wrecked, yeah?'

'Sharpie—'

'Fuckin' relax! I thought we already talked about this. Look, they'll see the car is gone, see the busted lock and figure out it was stolen. Then, if it turns up all burned out and shit, we just be doin' what we doin'. Nothing to do with us.'

'We should never have fucking taken it.'

'What the hell else were we gonna do – leave him there for Big Jack to discover? Yeah, that would be something.'

'I don't know if there are fingerprints or fuck knows what in it!'

'It's burned to a fuckin' crisp, Mick. They won't find nothing.' Sharpie yawned and scratched his balls. 'You gotta relax.'

'You relax. They have all sorts of shit to check these days. Ah, man, this is a fucking nightmare. What happens if they find the blood? What happens when they find Bo? They'll put it together.'

'Look, it's cool. Even if they find him, ain't no one gonna connect the two things. The jakes are gonna think Bo got stiffed by moneylenders. Shit, you know he owes money all over the gaff.'

'People looking for money don't kill the people they're looking to get the money from.'

Sharpie scowled. He didn't like Mick contradicting him; that wasn't the way it worked. 'Yeah, well, it still don't got a thing to do with us. There's nothin' to connect us to him.'

'Apart from Big Jack's fucking car! You think Big Jack is gonna be okay with the cops knocking on his door asking about it?'

'He'll just claim it off insurance,' Sharpie snapped. 'Keep your fuckin' voice down. You don't want Ma hearin' you.'

Sharpie reached for his cigarettes and lit one. He blew out a stream of smoke and searched Mick's face with his sharp eyes. 'What's the matter with you, anyway? You look like you spacin'. Your eyes are all weird and shit.'

Mick reeled off the bed and started to search for his clothes. 'What do you think?'

'Yo, fuck that shit. You cryin' over that bitch Bo? You need to be flushin' that shit like waste. I had to do it – you know that, you saw how it went down. I had to protect us, our deal. If he went to the fuckin' jakes, we were fucked – and not just from the jakes, neither. You know how it is.'

'Yeah.' Mick pulled on a pair of tracksuit bottoms. 'Course, this way is so much better.'

'Mick—'

'Look, I'm good, okay?' Mick grabbed his boots and hauled them on. 'I gotta get to work. I'm late as it is.'

'Hey, don't bleedin' forget: Bo pushed us to this.' Sharpie sat up and jabbed his finger through the air. 'He fuckin' threatened us, Mick. No way I was gonna let anything happen. We had to get rid of him. You want a stint in Pat's? Me bollocks, bro. They probably wouldn't even put us in Pat's this time, we'd be bumped up to the big house. I ain't doin' that.'

'I'm going downstairs.'

'It needed to be done. I thought we was cool on that.'

'I didn't agree to anything. I didn't even know you had a fucking gun. Where did you get it from?'

'From my peeps, you know. I had to take care of us, yo, for real. You should be thankin' me, not bustin' my grill.'

Mick scowled and continued dressing.

'You need to step up, bro. You need to be watchin' my back.' Sharpie flung the duvet back and swung his legs out. He was angry now. 'I want you to say it. Say it was the right thing to do.'

Mick yanked a relatively clean T-shirt out of the pile of clothes at the end of his bed. 'I'm going downstairs. I need a cup of tea.'

Sharpie watched him leave the room and felt a knot of anxiety in his chest. Mick never willingly went downstairs to get tea or anything else. Going downstairs meant spending time with their mother, and that was usually the last thing he wanted to do. Sharpie ground out his cigarette, got up and dressed quickly. It was the car; had to be. Mick was probably worried about the car. Stupid fuck, always worrying about some shit. After the shit with the car died down, he would chill, and then they were home free.

Mick's mobile rang, vibrating on the locker between their beds. Sharpie looked at the screen, his heart beating a little too fast for his liking. It was the garage – probably Robbie wondering where Mick was. He must have noticed the car was gone by now, too.

Sharpie turned down the volume on the phone and blew out through his teeth. It stopped vibrating, and Sharpie saw there had been five missed calls already.

The ball had started rolling. All Mick had to do was play it cool for a few days, and they'd be home free.

He lit another cigarette and noticed the thin line of brown under his thumbnail. He ran last night's actions through his head. The car breaking down was a bad thing and a pain in the arse. But they had kept their money, and Bo was taken care of. Sharpie took another drag and blew a series of perfect smoke rings. He had taken care of the problem. He was the man.

He glanced over at the movie poster of Fifty's *Get Rich or Die Trying* that hung over his bed. It was a brilliant shot of Fifty's massive, tattooed body, his arms outstretched, a gun in one hand, a microphone in the other – not the dumb one of Fifty holding some kid that the cinemas had eventually gone with. The original poster was the bomb, in Sharpie's opinion, and they should have used it, instead of giving in to fucking whingers protesting about glorifying violence and shit. Didn't them bitches know that violence was real, that it was the street, the way of the soldier? That was what he, Sharpie Quinn, was: he was a street soldier, for real. He had taken his first scalp.

He'd never imagined killing could be so easy. It was like one minute you had a problem and, the next, the problem went away. That was the real deal. You boiled it down, that was how it went. It made him feel different – kind of like he felt when he got away with shoplifting a whole load of shit, but better, more powerful. It was knowing that he could do it, knowing that he could rid himself of any fucker who crossed him. Knowing he had the capacity. At the end of the day, one fucker's skull was just that; they all cracked the same. Sharpie shivered. He felt so alive, so powerful, so... He didn't know what he was feeling, only that, whatever it was, it felt good. It felt right.

Sharpie Quinn had found his calling. He had crossed over the line most people avoided, and he liked it. He saluted Fifty and swore an oath. From that day on, he was gonna be the shizzle; he was gonna be all that. He had stepped up to the big time.

# 16

If Sarah had thought the interview with Larry Cole was a waste of time, she was fast learning that talking with Max Ashcroft was a hundred times worse.

He was exactly the sort of man she despised – rude, boorish, speaking almost exclusively to John – and when he wasn't treating them as mindless pariahs, he was busy ridiculing James Reid, their client and brother of his supposed good buddy, for being 'an anxious culchie'.

'Got to say, I thought this was all bullshit when I heard,' Max was saying to John. He linked his fingers together on his desk; his gold wedding ring glinted. 'Open and shut, isn't it? Coroner said he drowned, right? I know what these country folk are like. James doesn't want people thinking David was a lush or anything. Stuff like that can drag the family name in the mud. That's why he won't accept that his brother was skulled when he drowned. I mean, I knew as soon as I heard what had happened.'

'You weren't surprised that he drowned?' Sarah said, amazed at his flippant tone and unable to keep a trace of anger out of her voice. His smug, self-satisfied face was really beginning to get her goat.

Max glanced at her and raised one dark, tufted eyebrow. 'Sure, I was surprised that he'd drowned, but I'm saying I wasn't surprised that he'd had an accident. You got to ask, what was he doing lurking around a bridge at night?'

'What does that mean, exactly?'

'Look, I knew David. He was a risk-taker. David drove like the clappers, liked a drink, always had an eye out for a bit of action, you know what I mean? What do they call it? Cottaging?' He grinned and winked lasciviously at Sarah. She felt the hair on the back of her neck bristle. 'I know his brother disapproved of his lifestyle, but David was a real party animal.'

'There was no evidence or mention of any partying,' Sarah snapped, appalled.

'Well…' Max shrugged.

'James said David could handle his drink. He claims he never saw David that drunk.'

'Yeah? James never came with us on any of our nights out. Trust me, sweetheart, David could lose it like the rest of us mortals.'

'What time did you meet that day?' John asked.

'Around seven or thereabouts. Look, I told the cops all of this.'

'I know, but we're just trying to get a picture of his day.'

Max rolled his eyes. 'We went to Bar Mizu for a bite to eat. Then I left around eight.'

'Were you both drinking?'

'We had a few. Nothing too heavy.'

'David was driving?'

'I assumed so.'

'And how did he seem to you that evening? Was he acting in an odd manner? Did it seem like there was anything troubling him?'

'Course not. He was in great form.'

'Did he say where he was going? Was he on his way home?'

'No, but I gather he was heading over to the George.'

'His car is missing,' John said. 'Any ideas?'

'Really? No, I have no idea.'

'His house was broken into on the day of his funeral,' Sarah said in a cool voice.

Max shook his head. 'Bastards. Is nothing sacred? You hear about shit like that all the time. A garda friend I play golf with said scumbags look out for obituaries in the paper, then hit the house.'

'You think that's all it was?'

'What else could it be?'

'Did David ever mention any argument or disagreement he might have had with anyone?'

'Nope.'

'Did you ever hear him mention anyone by the name of Jack?'

'Not to me.'

'What about Sharpie or Mick?'

Max shook his head. 'Don't ring any bells.'

'Do you think it's possible that anyone would try to harm David?'

'Of course not.' Max paused for a moment and lowered his eyes. 'He was an absolute gent, and anyone who knew him will tell you the very same thing. No, what happened to David is a tragedy, a real loss to us all, but there's no point trying to make it out to be anything other than a terrible accident. Time to move on.'

'I found this.' Sarah took out the globe and put it on the table.

Max looked at it and shook his head. 'We had them made up for a golfing trip a few years back.' He fingered it softly. 'Poor David.'

Sarah studied him. Despite the hand-wringing and facial dexterity, there wasn't an ounce of sincerity in his voice, as far as she could tell. She folded her arms and sat back in her chair. 'So, in your opinion as his friend, David left you, got drunk, went looking for some sex, fell down, slipped into the canal and drowned. That about size it up?'

Max lifted his head and gave her the benefit of his complete attention for the first time. 'More or less.' He jiggled the eyebrows again. He held up his hands. 'I'm not making a dig. Nothing to do with me how he got his jollies, long as it wasn't round me. I'm just saying.

Anyway, I wouldn't be a hundred per cent surprised if, all jazzed up like he was, he was looking for a bit of company. Who knows what type, huh? You know?'

Sarah had taken about as much as she could take, and she wanted to get the hell out of that office before she said something she regretted. She stood up. 'Well, if you have nothing else to offer, thank you for your time, Mr Ashcroft.'

'Any time, sweetheart.'

She resisted the urge to pop him one on the nose.'John, we'd better go. We're going to be late.'

John knew they had plenty of time. He glanced at her and recognised the murderous glint in her dark eyes. Time to go, all right.

'If we have any more questions, we'll be in touch.'

'No hassle.' Max came around the desk, shook John's hand and slapped him on the back. 'You ever play golf, John?'

'Not any more. Used to play a bit with my dad, when he was alive.'

'Still got a set of clubs?'

'I do. They're dusty, but they work.'

'You should come on out to the K Club if you ever get a chance, have a round.'

'The K Club?' John laughed. 'Ha! More chance of me getting into heaven than into there.'

Max threw back his head and laughed. It was a deep, throaty, manly sound that Sarah suspected he practised. It made her want to punch him in the thorax.

'You ever fancy a round, I'll put you down as a guest.'

'Okay, I might hold you to that one.'

Max showed them to the office door. 'Nice talking to you both. Sorry I couldn't be more help.' He pumped John's hand and tried the same with Sarah, but she wrested her hand free. Max acted like he didn't notice. Or maybe he did, and he just didn't give a damn.

As they made their way down the stairs, away from the doe-eyed secretary who watched them surreptitiously over the top of her computer, Sarah muttered fiercely, 'My God, what an arsehole.'

'Bit of a cold fish, I suppose.' John dug a cigarette out of his box and flicked it into his mouth. 'I didn't think he was so bad.'

'You wouldn't.'

'What's that supposed to mean?'

'I don't like him.'

'Because he didn't ask you to play golf?'

'He barely even spoke to me.'

'Not being funny here, but I don't blame him. You were giving him the evil eye from the moment he opened his mouth.'

'No, I wasn't!'

'Right.'

'I can't believe he called me "sweetheart". Twice! And the disgusting way he spoke about David Reid… He doesn't seem to be the least bit sorry his friend is dead. And since when is being gay the last gasp of iniquity?'

'In what now?'

Sarah buttoned her coat up, her face drawn into a tight knot of disapproval. 'Why did he mention sex to us? What has that got to do with anything? It's almost as if he enjoyed putting David Reid down.'

'Tell you something else: Larry Cole was lying about not recognising the name Jack.'

Sarah snapped around, surprised. 'You noticed that too?'

'Hard not to.' John grinned. 'He looked like someone had shoved a poker up his arse when you mentioned it.'

'What do you think that's about?'

John shrugged. 'Don't know. But we'll find out.'

'Damn right.' Sarah chewed on her lip for a moment.

'You okay?'

'I'm fine. Just sore and pissed off. We seem a bit stymied. I wish Steve would get back to us with the address of those boys.'

John lit a cigarette and blew out a long, thin stream of smoke. 'We'll catch a break. Next stop is Clive Hollingsworth. You want to grab a coffee? We're kind of early.'

'I'm sick of coffee.' Sarah pulled open the door to the street and glanced out at the rain as it hammered down with such force that it bounced off the cement. 'It really bothers me that nobody seems to give a damn about this man – not his friends, not his business partner, not even the cops. He had a whole life here, and now he's gone, and no one apart from his brother really seems to care.' She paused and sighed, her anger dissipating rapidly. 'It's kind of sad, don't you think?'

'What?'

'This case.'

'I suppose so,' John said, but then he frowned. 'Why?'

'Imagine going through life and then that's it – and everyone keeps carrying on as if nothing happened. Like he was never here at all. Makes you wonder what's the point of trying.'

John leaned against the wall. 'I guess some people don't make that much of an impact.'

'I think that's really awful.'

'That's the way it is sometimes.'

'It shouldn't be.' Sarah shook her head. She was no longer thinking of David Reid. She was thinking of herself.

\*

'Where you going with the truck?'

Robbie McHugh swore softly under his breath. He had hoped to make it out of the yard before his boss showed up. He shut off the engine and pulled up the handbrake. What was he doing in at this hour? Robbie swallowed dryly.

'Howya, Boss.'

'What about you?'

Big Jack closed the door of his bottle-green Mercedes and beeped the alarm – an unnecessary action, since the car was perfectly safe parked in the small courtyard to the front of the garage. He rolled his shoulders and cracked his neck.

'You got a job on?' Big Jack walked through the rain with his strange, loping strid, towards the driver's side of the truck.

Robbie nodded. 'Just came in there ten minutes ago.'

'Pick-up?'

'Pick-up.'

'Anyone we know?'

'Yeah, the Reynolds one.'

'Which one is she?'

'The woman with the buck teeth?'

'What happened?'

'From the way she described it, clutch's gone again, I reckon.'

Big Jack nodded and looked around the muddy yard. 'Where's the other fella?'

'Not in yet.'

'Not in?' Big Jack raised a huge paw and squinted at his watch. His head swivelled back towards Robbie. His face was immediately thunderous, his grey eyes flinty. 'Why the fuck not? Did you talk to him? He sick? He call?'

Robbie swallowed. 'I called a few times, but he's not answering the mobile.'

'Fucking dosser.' Big Jack ground his teeth together and glanced at his watch again. 'How long will it take you? I've got to head back over to the salesroom.'

'Not too long, 'bout half an hour or so.'

'Go on and pick up that car.' Big Jack stepped back and slapped the roof of the truck. 'I'll hang on here till you get back.'

Robbie took a deep breath. This was the moment. This was the time to talk to him about the missing Fiat.

'Er—'

He was saved by the high-pitched shrieking of the yard phone, the copper bell rattling hard on its beam. Big Jack waved him off and turned towards the metal steps that led up to his office.

Sighing with relief and feeling his bladder unclench, Robbie high-tailed it out of there. Mick could go be damned. He didn't buy the fucking Fiat being stolen. The lock had been tampered with, all right, but as far as Robbie was concerned it didn't take a genius to work out which light-fingered little shit was behind its disappearance.

Bloody Sharpie Quinn. Robbie despised the little shit. Mick was all right, might even be a decent little mechanic one day, if it wasn't for the influence of the other little bollocks. Robbie grunted as he changed into third. Well, it was going to be interesting watching Mick handle this mess.

Big Jack stepped into his ramshackle office, which always smelled faintly of diesel and oil, no matter what air-freshener he used. He picked up the phone.

'Hello?'

'Jack?'

'Speaking.'

'It's Dennis here.'

'What about you, Dennis!'

'I was looking for you down at the showroom, they said you might be there. Jesus, Jack, you can be a whore of a man to track down. What's wrong with your mobile?'

'Ah, nothing. The old battery is fucked. If it comes loose at all, it knocks itself off.'

Dennis Keogh owned one of the largest firms of haulers in the country, and he was a long-time friend of Big Jack. Dennis, like Jack, was from Fermanagh. He had been involved in trucking for over four decades, and Big Jack had helped him out in a number of ways over the years. Back in the early days, half of Dennis Keogh's rigs had been made up of parts 'acquired' by Big Jack Lawson.

'How the hell are you, Dennis?'

'Oh, sure, fair to middling.'

Big Jack laughed. It was the standard reply from Dennis, no matter what the occasion. 'What's the craic with the king of Dundalk? What can I do for you?'

'You know my youngest lad, Rory?'

'I do indeed. A credit to you, he is. Never laid eyes on a finer young man. He still hurling?'

'He is that. Come here till I tell you. Rory's turning eighteen next week, and myself and a few of the lads were thinking of throwing him a bit of a bash, d'you see what I mean?'

'Eighteen? Jesus, where does the time go?' Big Jack sat down behind his desk and rubbed his face. 'I remember him, and he only a pup, weaving in and out amongst the legs at your father's funeral, may the good Lord rest his soul.'

'Oh, sure, time marches on, all right.'

'So' – the chair creaked under his massive weight – 'a bit of a bash, you say?'

'And I was wondering if, you know, if you could provide a bit of the, er, entertainment.'

'You want to hold his birthday down in the club?'

'No, no, we'll be throwing a bash for him up here in the hotel. But later himself and a few of the lads are talking about heading down to Dublin, so I said I'd talk to you – maybe you could organise something.'

'How many girls we talking about?'

'Well, say a couple of young ones that wouldn't mind a bit of craic.'

'A couple?'

'Say five or six.'

Big Jack pulled out a notebook and flipped it open. 'This would be a private set-up, Dennis. I don't want no hotels and shit. Not for that kind of gig.'

'No, no, there'll be no hotels – all done private, like. I'll let him use the apartment up in Christchurch.'

'I'm sure we can arrange something, so. I'll talk to the girls.'

'Good man. Try and make it a blonde for the young lad. He has a thing for the blondes.'

'Sure, don't we all?' Big Jack wrote 'Blonde – Shirlie' on the notepad. 'When would this be for?'

'Saturday.'

Big Jack whistled. 'You're cutting it fine.'

'I know, but sure, he only mentioned this the other night. I'll send someone down to fix up with you on the Friday.'

'Grand.'

'Same price as before, is it?'

'It is.'

'Don't suppose there'd be much chance of a reduction on a few of them?'

Big Jack laughed. 'Ah now, Dennis, if it's quality you're after, you have to pay. These girls are like supermodels. Sure, they wouldn't get out of bed for any less.'

'All right, so.' Dennis didn't push the matter. 'I'll give you a shout during the week, sort out the times, and so on.'

'Good man, Dennis.'

'Good luck.'

'Good luck.'

Big Jack hung up, settled back into his chair and did a quick calculation. Five or six girls hired privately for the night worked out at a tidy sum. He hitched his hands behind his head and threw his feet up onto the desk. Maybe things were starting to look up again.

And they had looked grim there for a while, when the little Ukrainian one had passed on. Ivanka. What a hot little piece she had been. Nineteen and ripe for the picking. He'd had his eye on her himself, truth be told. Tom, his brother, had thrown a blue fit when he'd heard. She had only been in Belfast a fortnight, and Tom had paid a fortune for her over in London. Big Jack shook his head sadly. Sure, these things happened, but what a waste. Poor creature.

Big Jack's sentimentality was as false as his hair colour. He did not think of the girl's unclaimed body, lying in the freezer of the morgue. He never thought about the family whose faint hopes diminished as week after week passed and they heard nothing of their daughter. And he was wrong about her age. Petra Noviska – for that was Ivanka's real name – had been only seventeen years old when she accepted an offer, through an agency, to work as a nanny in the UK. She had a two-year-old son and she lived with her parents and three younger siblings. She had lied about her age to get a permit. The woman who had taken her details knew she was lying, but she didn't care one iota.

Petra didn't know, on that freezing day in November, that she would never return home. When she left home that morning, she was not to know that it would be the last time she saw her parents, that she would never play with her son again, that she would never make the money to put herself through college and become a beautician. Within twenty-four hours of signing the agency form, Petra Noviska would be beaten, robbed of her passport and shipped to Germany and from there to the UK, where she would be moved from one place to another and forced to work as a stripper and prostitute. Finally, in February, she had been sold to Tom Lawson and brought over to Belfast, and in March she had come south to work for Big Jack, Tom's brother.

Big Jack had promised he'd give her passport back once she made back the money his brother had spent on her. Petra didn't know whether to believe him or not, but he seemed fair. He didn't hit her and didn't mess with the girls too much, and she was allowed to keep almost one-third of what she made. It wasn't ideal, but she figured it was her only chance of going home again. At least he seemed to care.

She was wrong.

Petra now lay grey and abandoned on a slab in Dublin City Morgue, alone, unclaimed and far from home. And Big Jack couldn't have cared less.

# 17

Max stood by the window and watched John and Sarah run across the street and climb into a silver Manta. He ran a hand through his hair. 'Did you get Clive?' he asked into his phone.

'He's not in the office and he's not answering his mobile.'

'You've got to get him, he needs to be warned not to react. What the fuck was Lawson thinking?'

'Did the girl ask about the Meridian Club? You don't think they'll connect it, do you?'

'Frosty bitch. She mentioned it in passing. Look, never mind the club.' Max watched as the car pulled away. 'It's Jack Lawson we need to be concerned with. How did they get his name?'

'I don't know. At least it's only his first name.'

'Maybe David had something in the house. Look, you've got to keep trying Clive.'

'I'm halfway to Carlow to meet a client.'

'I've got two meetings back to back this afternoon, and a fucking phone conference with Atlee any minute!'

'Maybe she won't mention it.'

Max ground his teeth together. Larry sounded exactly like the petulant, weak-kneed bitch Max frequently thought he was. Say what you like about David, he thought furiously, but at least he owned a decent set of balls. 'You okay?' he asked.

'I'm fine.' In truth, Larry was close to tears. The day had turned very sour, and the interview had upset him in many ways. 'Did she look at you as though you were guilty of something? She kept staring at me as though she knew I'd done something wrong.'

'She did that shit with me, too – probably some kind of thing they learn. But I don't think they know a thing. If it wasn't for David's brother, no one would be bothering their arse about any of this.' Max closed his eyes. 'It will all die down, you'll see.'

'I didn't realise the car was missing. The whole thing is very odd.'

'Yeah. I wonder where the hell it is.' Max turned away from the window, sat down and drummed his fingers on the desk. Two lines were flashing on his phone, and he was sure one of the calls was Atlee. 'Look, Lar, you'd better keep trying Clive. Make sure you give him the heads-up. I've got to go here.'

'Okay. I'll call you later.'

'Talk to you.'

Max hung up and massaged his temples. He had a building headache that was sure to cripple him for the rest of the day. He pulled open a drawer and swallowed a couple of Solpadeine with a deep gulp of Ballygowan. Though he felt the meeting with the detectives had gone okay, he hadn't liked the way the girl had looked at him. But she looked like she was that sort anyway – a stiff bitch. Damn David's stupid culchie fuck of a brother, anyway. Why couldn't he let sleeping dogs lie? And how the fuck had they come up with Jack's name?

\*

Clive Hollingsworth strode through the crowds and the rain, hurriedly making his way back to the office. He had spent – no, wasted – another morning, this time with his mother, searching for the perfect tie to go with his wedding suit. He was tired, he was mildly hung over and he was fed up to the gills with people hassling him. He wanted desperately to go home and lie down. The last thing he wanted to do was meet two detectives to talk about David Reid. He shook his head. Talk about your dog days.

He pushed open the revolving glass door to his office building and made his way to the elevator, ignoring the receptionist, who was waving at him. Sylvia had already called him four times that morning, and he had had enough. He had switched his mobile off after the last call, and he was damned if he wanted any of her no doubt countless messages. All he wanted was a few minutes' peace and quiet. All he wanted was a few minutes to think undisturbed. Was that too much to ask?

He stepped into his outer office. Clodagh, his secretary, stopped typing. She looked up with a slightly strained smile.

'Good morning, Mr Hollingsworth. Your appointment is here.' She tilted a fine pale hand in the direction of the chairs where Sarah and John sat waiting, somewhat damp and steaming.

Clive glanced at his watch. 'You're early.'

John stood up and offered his hand. 'John Quigley. How you doing? We finished up with your pal Max Ashcroft a bit earlier than we expected, so we thought we'd come on over. This is my partner, Sarah Kenny.'

The dark-haired girl stood and offered her hand. Clive shook it, a little unnerved by her unsmiling expression and the way her dark eyes scanned his face, as if she could read his every thought.

'Well, since you're here, you might as well come on in. Would you like a coffee, or tea?'

'No, thank you,' Sarah said. She had a deep voice for a woman and a strange accent, slightly clipped.

John shook his head. 'I'm good.'

Clive relaxed. The guy's accent was pure Dub, and at least he was smiling.

Due to the sensitive nature of the documents and information Clive dealt with on a day-to-day basis, he always locked the door of his office when he left it. Now, as he shrugged off his coat and patted his pockets for his keys, he felt more and more uncomfortable under the detectives' gaze.

'Can never find anything when I need it,' he said jovially.

'I'm like that,' John replied. 'Head like a sieve, haven't I, Sarah?'

Sarah said nothing, just watched Clive coolly with her unreadable expression.

'Right, right.' Clive finally located the keys and unlocked the door. He ushered Sarah and John in and showed them to seats, hung up his coat and dropped the keys into a teak bowl on his desk.

'Sir,' Clodagh came to the door. 'May I have a word?'

'What is it?'

Clodagh smiled stiffly. 'Mr Cole is on the line. He's called several times.'

John and Sarah exchanged glances. Clive saw them and tried to keep his smile from slipping. 'Did he say why?'

'No, sir.'

Clive ran his hands through his damp hair. What could it be now? Was there never a moment's peace? He glanced at the detectives. How would it look if he took the call – better or worse? 'I'll call him back in a while. Please tell him I'm in a meeting.'

'He says it's urgent.'

'Larry Cole?' John said. 'We saw him earlier.'

'His firm's handling some work for some of our clients,' Clive said. 'Everything is urgent. You don't mind if I take this, do you?'

'Fire ahead,' John said.

Clive picked up his phone and punched a button. 'Larry? Hi, it's Clive… Really? No, those files were sent over to your office weeks ago… Oh, ha ha. Snail mail indeed… Not at all, I'll get right on it, don't worry. And thanks for calling.'

He hung up and smiled at Sarah and John. 'Now, where were we?'

'Larry does work for your firm?' Sarah said. 'I didn't realise he practised much. Lillian Daly told me he was practically retired.'

Clive blinked. 'Oh, he does a few bits and pieces, here and there, you know.'

Sarah leaned over and scooped out the set of keys Clive had dropped into the bowl. 'You've got one of those globes on your keyring too, I see. From your golf trip, am I right?'

'Oh, yes. That was a terrific trip, Colorado. David said we should mark the occasion, so we got these made up.' He smiled sadly. 'Seems silly now.'

'Why?'

'I – I don't know. It's just... well, silly.'

'I hear you're getting married?' John said.

'This Saturday.'

'Nice,' John said. 'Congratulations.'

'Thank you.' Clive smiled and bobbed his head.

'Yes, congratulations,' Sarah said. 'I believe David Reid was to have been your best man?'

'Yes, he would have been.'

'Were you very close?'

'He and Lar knew each other longest, but he was my best friend in many ways. A good man, very funny.'

'Were he and Max close?'

Clive glanced at her. 'We were all friends.'

'It's just that Max has a few theories about what happened to David that night.'

'Oh?'

Sarah nodded. 'Yeah, he thought David might have been... what did he call it, John?'

'Cottaging.'

Clive frowned. 'I don't—'

'Looking for casual sex,' Sarah said, watching him carefully.

Clive flushed and sat back in his chair. 'That's ridiculous!'

Sarah shrugged. 'That's what he said.'

John leaned forward in his chair. 'James, David's brother, thinks David was upset recently, that something may have been troubling him.'

'Really?'

'Did you notice anything out of the ordinary? Did David express any concerns recently that you can think of?'

'Like what?'

'I don't know. Did he seem more anxious than usual?'

Clive drummed his fingers on the desk. He was clearly rattled. 'Anxious? Really, I can't say I've noticed. Mind you, I've been a bit anxious myself, what with the wedding and everything. It's been all systems go for weeks now. Are either of you married?'

'No,' John said.

'Well, if you do get hitched, do yourselves a favour: elope.'

John and Sarah smiled politely. Sarah leaned forward. 'Did David ever mention the name Jack to you?'

'Jack? No, no Jack. Why do you ask?'

'What about Sharpie and Mick?'

'Who?'

'Why do you think someone would break into his house on the day of his funeral and steal his laptop?'

'What?' Clive shook his head. 'I didn't – I mean, I don't know. I never…' He looked like he had been slapped, and Sarah and John both noticed that Clive Hollingsworth was extremely uncomfortable with this line of questioning.

'Would he have confided in you if anything was troubling him?'

'Of course. I was his closest friend.' Clive looked imploringly at John. 'Look, I can't tell you anything. I don't—'

'Were you?' Sarah turned slightly in her chair and smiled. 'And yet you didn't go to his funeral.'

'I was sick. I could hardly stand, I was so ill. What kind of thing is that to say?'

'Would David have driven his car drunk?'

The jump seemed to confuse him. 'What? No…no, he needed his car for work.'

'Max Ashcroft met David that Saturday, and they were drinking together. David had his car with him. Now the car is missing.'

'His car?' Clive drummed his fingers again. He noticed what he was doing and placed his two hands flat on the desk. 'Are you sure? He must have parked it somewhere. Maybe he grabbed a cab home or something.'

'If he'd grabbed a cab, why would he be walking across that bridge he supposedly fell from?'

'I don't know.' Clive cleared his throat. He had regained a good deal of his composure, and he was all business again. 'Look, what happened to David was a tragedy – but, really, I can't imagine what else anyone can say about it.'

'Of course, you know he had a head injury,' John said. 'He might well have been attacked and drowned.'

Clive blanched. 'Jesus.'

'Do you have any idea if he was upset or acting weird lately?'

'No. Look, the only thing on my mind was my wedding, then David had his accident. It's been… really very difficult.'

'If it was an accident,' Sarah said. And this time she was sure that Clive Hollingsworth looked like he was going to be sick.

'So, if there was anything, anything at all…'

'I don't… if I think of anything, I'll call.'

'Cool.' John laid one of his cards on the desk. 'Even if it seems trivial, we'd appreciate it.'

John and Sarah stood. After a moment, Clive stood too and flattened his tie. 'Well, goodbye.'

He didn't offer his hand.

After Sarah and John left, Clive flopped back into his chair and held his head in his hands. He felt sick to his stomach. Jesus Christ, that bastard Lawson...

'Mr Hollingsworth?' Clodagh tapped the door gently and looked at him. Her face was etched with concern. 'Are you all right?'

'Yes, I'm fine.'

'Your fiancée is on line three.'

'Tell her I'll call her back.'

'I did say you were in a meeting, but she seemed very insistent. She's called a number of times today.'

'Clodagh, please, tell her I'll call her back.' Clive rummaged around in his drawers looking for the packet of Rennie's. He seemed to have been chewing on them constantly for weeks.

'Of course.'

Clodagh backed out the door and closed it gently. She wished Clive would hurry up and get married already, because the strain was really beginning to tell. And people said the brides were nuts.

# 18

'Hey.'

Sharpie glanced askance at his brother for the second time in as many minutes. Mick sat slumped in his seat, silent, brooding, ignoring all attempts at conversation.

'Hey. Mick.'

Mick continued staring out the window of the tram with a sour puss on him. Sharpie didn't like being ignored. It was making him angry. He punched Mick in the side – not hard, exactly, but hard enough to get his immediate attention.

'Ow! What?'

'You gonna keep this shit up?'

'What shit?'

'This silent shit. I don't like it. You're buggin' me.'

'I'm late for work. Why are you coming in, anyway? Why didn't you just stay at home?'

'I got my reasons.'

Mick scowled and rubbed his ribs. Sharpie's eyes skittered in his head and he was clearly expecting to talk. Mick tried to edge further away, but he was trapped with no room to move.

'If Robbie asks why you're late, say you was playin' pool over in Rathmines, then you went to Ma's crib and watched a video. You didn't go nowhere all night. You sat up watchin' videos, and that's why you slept in.'

'Yeah.'

'Yo, we clear on this?'

'I said yeah.'

They got off the tram at Heuston and crossed over the bridge. The wind was rising, whipping the rain so hard that it drove at them almost horizontally. Sharpie stomped along, his hands tucked deep into his pockets as though he was impervious to it. Mick followed behind, feeling sick to his stomach. Robbie wasn't the idiot Sharpie thought he was. He was never going to buy that story. If only he'd got up early, if only he'd got in to work at a normal time, maybe it wouldn't have looked so suspect when they discovered the car was gone. Now it looked dodgy from the word go.

They walked up Bridgefoot Street to the gates of the yard. Mick was dismayed to see Big Jack's Mercedes parked under the all-weather tarpaulin.

'Bollocks – Big Jack's here.'

'Be cool, bro, be cool.'

'Shit.'

Mick had hoped the boss wouldn't show his face until a good deal later in the day. Now he'd missed his chance to plant some ideas about the missing car in Robbie's head.

Sharpie grabbed him by the arm and yanked him back behind the pillar of the gate. 'All right, remember: just stick to the—'

'There you are! What the fuck time do you call this to be arriving into work at?' Big Jack was leaning on the metal railing overlooking the yard. His massive face looked like it was hewn from granite. His pompadour was starting to sag in the damp air, making him look even more malignant than usual.

'Hey, Jack.'

'Don't you fucking "hey" me. Get up here.'

Sharpie released Mick's arm and stepped into view. He jerked his head towards Big Jack. 'Yo, Jack. How you doin'?'

Big Jack came down the steps with impressive and frightening speed, and towered over the two brothers. 'You, get the fuck out of here. And you, where's my fucking car?'

'What car?' Mick said, wishing his voice didn't sound so screechy and high.

'What car? The fucking Fiat!'

Sharpie lowered his eyebrows and looked first at Mick and then at Mick's boss, his expression a perfect example of puzzled innocence. 'What you talkin' 'bout? What Fiat? Why would we have a Fiat?'

'I'm not talking to you.' Big Jack turned his murderous gaze back to Mick. 'What's this fucking gombeen doing here, anyway? Didn't I tell you about that before?'

Mick was so scared that his mouth could hardly create the moisture needed to speak. 'He was on his way into town, Jack. We…we came in together, that's all.'

'Hey, don't be talkin' 'bout me like I ain't here.'

Big Jack lurched forward. Mick flinched and took a step back. Sharpie held his ground, even though he had to crane his neck to keep eye contact.

'Yo, man, you need to back the fuck up.'

'Shut up.' Big Jack pushed him aside with the greatest of ease and grabbed Mick by the collar of his T-shirt. 'You telling me it wasn't you took the car out of the yard last night?'

'If I'd taken the car, I'd have driven it in. But I wouldn't take it. Not without askin' you.'

'Then where the fuck is it?'

'I don't know. Did you ask Robbie?'

'It was Robbie who told me it was gone!'

Sharpie stepped into view again. 'Yo, man, he's telling you he don't know where it is. Why you all on it?'

Big Jack ignored Sharpie. 'It didn't just fucking disappear, did it? The yard was locked.'

'I don't know,' Mick said. 'I swear.'

'Lock's been fucked with, but…' Big Jack frowned. He shook Mick hard enough to make his teeth rattle. 'Here, what happened to your face?'

Mick touched his hand to his split lip, but before he got a chance to answer, Sharpie spoke again.

'Hey, yo, I'm talkin' to you. Let go of him, you fat-ass motherfucker. He said he don't know nothin', so you don't need to be harassin' my blood. What, you think you can push us around like that? You need to step off.'

Big Jack's head swivelled towards Sharpie. He looked the lad up and down. Had he heard right? Had this kid – standing there in a yellow hoodie, giant pants and huge, unlaced trainers – had this kid just called him a fat motherfucker?

'What's that now?'

'Sharpie, shut up, will you?' Mick pleaded. 'Just go where you're going.'

'Nah, man, he can't talk to you like that. You told him you—'

Big Jack's eyebrows were now so low they seemed to obscure his eyes. 'Kid, you're starting to give me a pain in my prick.'

But Sharpie smiled a sly smile. He heard the noise in his head. He was the soldier. He was pure gangsta. He was so hyped up on his own sense of newfound power that he didn't understand that the wolf is no match for the bear.

'Yeah, you need to be showin' some respect. My bro works for you, that don't make him no bitch. You can't hang your shit on him. Fuck, that alco you got working for you probably sold the motherfuckin' thing. Why you all up in Mick's grill?'

Mick felt faint. He turned to Sharpie, bewildered and terrified. He knew Big Jack, he had witnessed what Big Jack could do. He was almost crying. 'Sharpie—'

'Nah, Mick, he needs to back—'

Big Jack reached down and slapped the side of Sharpie's face. The sound was muted in the damp air. Sharpie staggered a little from the blow, but before he fell, Big Jack grabbed the front of his hoodie, bunched it tight and lifted him clean off the ground. 'You fucking shit-talking cockroach. You ever speak to me like that again, I'll rip that fucking head clean off your shoulders and stuff it up your arse for you.'

'Big Jack.' Mick's voice was strained but firm. Despite his genuine terror, Mick was not about to let the man mangle his brother. 'Listen…'

'What?'

'Look, I don't know shit about the Fiat, but I'm late because I had a nixer this morning.'

'A nixer?' Big Jack repeated, still keeping Sharpie's big runners dangling a good five inches above the ground. Mick could see Jack's handprint on the side of Sharpie's cheek, as clear as day. Sharpie looked dazed and white with rage. Mick knew the situation was about to go nuclear.

'Yeah, a nixer.'

'Nixer?' Big Jack hissed the word out. He turned his head to look at Mick, his massive face red as beetroot. 'I don't fucking pay you to do nixers.'

'Big Jack, look, I'm sorry about being late an' all, but—'

'Shut your trap.' Big Jack lowered Sharpie to the ground and shoved him so hard that he went flying onto his arse, covering the back of his hoodie in muck. 'You clear off. If I even catch a whiff of you around here again, I'll fucking skin you alive.'

He turned to Mick. 'I'm not running a fucking charity here,' he snapped. 'I pay you to be here at nine o'clock. Robbie had to go on a pick-up, and if I hadn't been here, the yard would have been shut. I don't want my yard standing idle during a working day. I've no option: I have to dock you a day's pay.'

'You're gonna wish you hadn't done that,' Sharpie said behind him.

Big Jack stiffened and turned around slowly. 'What did you fucking say?'

'You deaf or somethin'?'

There was something strange going on. Normally, if Big Jack pulled the whammy on a kid Sharpie's age, the kid started snivelling and pissing himself, but this little bastard, with his chain and his pansy hair, was actually staring him in the eye. And Big Jack was no fool: although he recognised some fear there, there was also a defiant loathing – and something else, something he couldn't identify.

'Get moving. I won't be so polite next time.' Big Jack jabbed his thumb at Sharpie's upturned face. He was surprised. The kid was a gabby little mouthpiece at the best of times, but this was different. He glanced at Mick, who looked pale and washed out, as usual, but Sharpie... there was something different about him. His sneer was a little more cocky than usual, and his eyes showed nothing but naked hatred.

'Fuck you, dawg.'

'You dirty wee shite, what the fuck did you say?'

Mick stepped between them, forcing Sharpie back a step. 'Nothing – he didn't say nothing, Big Jack.'

Big Jack never took his eyes off Sharpie. There was an almost unbearable stand-off, Sharpie breathing hard, Big Jack clenching and unclenching his fists. Finally Big Jack snorted.

'Get him to fuck off out of here, Mick, and then get on with your work. You need to get started on the Ford Focus. Robbie will give you a hand with it when he's finished the job he's doing.'

'Okay, Jack, okay.' Mick was sweating heavily. He prayed that Sharpie would just keep his mouth shut for another few moments. 'Be finished with it today.'

'All right, then. Get on.'

Big Jack gave Sharpie another glowering look before he turned and went back inside. He climbed the stairs, but he stopped on the landing and watched the two brothers in deep conversation for another few minutes, reading their body language and observing their shared looks and gestures. He didn't believe that Mick was telling him the truth about the Fiat. Robbie said that the lock to the main gates had been tampered with, but that, in his opinion, it was almost impossible to open without a key.

Big Jack sighed. He had known the boys' father back in the day and had had a fair hand in his eventual disappearance – a fact he kept strictly to himself. A whiff of guilt had led him to hire Mick when he turned fifteen. He had recognised Mick's passion for cars, and it was cheaper to keep the little shit around and teach him as an apprentice than to pay a fully qualified mechanic. Anyway, the lad wasn't dumb, and he had a natural aptitude for mechanical work.

Mick had other talents, too, as Big Jack had suspected he might. He was a champion car thief and as light-fingered as any conjuror. And, since a very large part of Big Jack's empire consisted of recovering vehicles and chopping down cars for parts – legally or illegally, didn't make any difference to him – the boy proved invaluable. Big Jack could give Mick a car reg and an address and know that, no matter what make of alarm was installed in it, within twenty-four hours that vehicle would be sitting in a lot over in Ringsend, waiting to be moved north or disassembled. The number of ringers Jack provided rose steadily, and his export business was an absolute goldmine. Up north first, then over to England, on to France, down through Spain and finally to the African coast. It was a beautiful system.

Big Jack was a shrewd man. He knew you were only ever as strong as your weakest link. That was what had kept him ahead of the game for so long. He needed to know he could trust the people he dealt with, right down to the smallest cog of his empire. And now one of his cogs had come loose.

Mick was trying to calm Sharpie down. 'Look, you antagonised him. Just forget about it.'

'Forget about it? Motherfucker put his hand on me. He messed up my gear. You gonna stand there and defend him?' Sharpie spat, glaring furiously at his twin. 'We're blood. You saw what he did. He disrespected me, he disrespected you.'

'Sharpie, you were giving him lip. You know what he's like.'

Sharpie pulled himself up to his full height and ran his hands over his cornrows. 'Yo, fuck him – and fuck you too, man. End of the day, you and me, we're fuckin' brothers. I would never let some Elvis-looking wannabe put his hands on you. You're a fuckin' disgrace, man, a low-down dog.'

Mick sighed. 'He's my boss.'

Sharpie looked over Mick's shoulder to where Big Jack was watching them. 'Yeah? Well, let me tell you somethin', bro: no one puts his hands on Sharpie Quinn, not 'less he wants them hands cut the fuck off. Yo, he gonna pay for dissin' me, for real.'

He whirled on his heel and walked off, bouncing and rolling down the road, his jewellery swinging and his head full of revenge.

# 19

'Wow, Lillian Daly was right: they are a pack, all right – a pack of bloody freaks.' Sarah jerked her seatbelt around her and snapped it into the lock. 'I wouldn't believe any of that lot if they told me it was Wednesday.'

John glanced at her. 'But do we think they had anything to do with David Reid's death?'

'I don't know. Between the slimy hands, the twitchy body language and that Max guy and his innuendos… He really took the biscuit – so bloody quick to paint his friend as a deviant. I mean, what was that about?'

'So do you think Max Ashcroft had something to do with David Reid's death? Or Larry Cole or even Clive Hollingsworth?'

Sarah hesitated briefly before she shook her head. 'No. I just wonder what the hell they're all lying about.'

'They're definitely hiding something.'

'Oh, for sure. Clive Hollingsworth looked like he was going to faint when I mentioned the name Jack.' Sarah chewed her lip thoughtfully. 'But what the hell are they hiding?'

John shrugged. 'And is it connected to David's death?'

'Jack. It has to be something to do with whoever the hell this Jack is.'

'I'll call Steve again, put a flame under his arse. We find Mick and Sharpie, we find this Jack person who everyone's so keen to peretend they've never heard of.'

'I hope so. John, pull over and let me out.'

'What? It's lashing rain.'

'I can see that.'

'Where are you going?'

'Max Ashcroft said he met David in Bar Mizu, didn't he?'

'Yes.'

'And then he went on to the George.'

'Right.'

'Well, then, you check Mizu and I'll check the George, see if anyone remembers seeing him. And another thing: if David did have his car with him before he got rat-faced, chances are he probably parked it somewhere around there, maybe in a car park.'

John popped a cigarette into his mouth, although he didn't light it. 'You don't want to search every car park in the city centre? Please tell me you're not thinking of doing that.'

'Not every single one of them. The ones around Stephen's Green, George's Street, that sort of area. Look, what else have we to do, anyway? Until either Steve or Brendan Whelan gets us an address, we're stuck.'

John looked out the window at the heavy rain. 'Sarah, there are a lot of car parks around there.'

'I know. That's why, if we split up, we can halve the time.'

'But even if we do find it, what then?'

'Then at least we know that David Reid wasn't attacked for his car. I'll start with Stephen's Green. You do the one on Drury Street.'

John put the indicator on. 'All right, but it's a lot of walking around. How's your leg today – still sore?'

He saw Sarah pause. But then she set her jaw in that way she had, and he knew the deal was sealed. Walking it was.

*

Max Ashcroft closed his mobile phone and tried to look as though he was concentrating on what Michael Durkin was saying to him. Michael, a partner in the firm, was busy discussing some new takeover in the pipeline, with all the fervour of a devout Christian in a village of heathens.

'Not even close to the original offer…'

Max stared at his lips and nodded where he thought it was appropriate, but in his mind he was replaying the interview. He hadn't liked the girl one bit, and he didn't trust Larry – or Clive, for that matter – not to break if he was questioned too often. No, something had to be done to ensure their safety. By breaking into David's house, Jack Lawson, the fat bastard, had somehow managed to stir up trouble that Max had hoped they had left behind.

Something was going to have to be done.

*

Clive Hollingsworth was debating whether to leave a message on Larry's phone or not when he heard a commotion in the outer office. He looked up in time to see his door burst open and Sylvia's furious face bearing down on him.

'What the—'

'God damn you!'

'What the hell's going on?'

Clodagh appeared in the open doorway, behind Sylvia. She looked startled and apologetic.

'You're here!' Sylvia said.

'Of course I'm here, Sylvia.' Clive put his mobile down. 'The big question is, what are you doing here?'

'I'm here because we were supposed to be meeting with the priest this afternoon. Fifteen times I've called this bloody office today! Fifteen times. I had to let him go in the end. I will not be fobbed off like that, Clive.'

Clive blinked and looked at his secretary. 'Was that today?'

'I'm sorry, sir. I did remind you earlier, twice.' Clodagh glanced at Sylvia and back at him, mortified to be hauled into their problems.

Clive felt a flicker of shame. 'It's all right, Clodagh. Thank you.'

He waited until she closed the door before he turned his attention to Sylvia. 'Honey, I'm—'

'Do you have any idea how embarrassing it was for me? Sitting there with him and Mum, waiting for you, calling your stupid mobile and office again and again and again?'

'Sylvia, what can I say? I'm so sorry. It completely slipped my mind.'

Red rag and bull. As soon as the words left his lips, he knew it.

'How can something so important slip your mind? We're getting married in a few days!'

'I'm sorry.'

'Honestly, I could die. The shame of it, the absolute shame of it. What must Father Roche have thought?'

'I'm sorry.'

'And poor Mum – she's known Father Roche all her life. He baptised me, for Christ's sake! Clive, can you imagine how she felt?'

'Oh, shut up, Sylvia.'

'I—' Sylvia gaped at him. 'What did you say?'

'I said shut up!' Clive stood up and slammed his hands onto the desktop. 'I am so fucking sick of talking about the fucking wedding, sick of it. I said I was sorry. We can arrange another meeting with Father bloody Roche. Just stop fucking hassling me.'

Sylvia stared at him, her eyes huge and brimming with tears. 'Don't shout at me.'

Clive sat back down and leaned back in his chair, his anger seeping from his body, leaving him shaken and guilty. 'I'm sorry, Syl, but I'm up to my eyes here. I'm sorry I forgot, okay? I'm sorry for shouting.'

'You're sorry.'

'Yes, I'm bloody sorry.'

'You don't sound bloody sorry!'

Sylvia turned on her heel and stormed out, slamming the door so hard that Clive's picture of water crashing around a lighthouse fell off the wall, shattering the glass and splitting the frame.

Clive thought about chasing after her. But in the end he remained sitting there. After all, what was the point in apologising? She was right: he couldn't force himself to sound sorry. He had meant every word he said.

\*

Sarah walked up George's Street and crossed over to the other side. The barman in the George had recognised David, but he couldn't be sure if he had been there on Saturday night or not, as the bar had been packed solid. He had given her the name of the other barman who had worked that night, and Sarah planned to call him as soon as she got back to the office.

John called just before she reached the Stephen's Green shopping centre.

'How you doing?' he asked.

'Nothing so far. You find anything?'

'Not in the car park, but Bar Mizu was a hit. Showed his picture to the waitresses and asked if anyone remembered seeing him.'

'And did they?'

'Oh, not just him, but – as the very nice Australian waitress put it – the big jerk he was with, too.'

Sarah grinned. 'Ah. She didn't by any chance mean Max "Jiggle Me This" Ashcroft?'

'The very man. She said he kept calling her "darling" and "pet", and he found some way of putting his hand on her whenever she brought drinks.'

'Gross. Go on.'

'And she can't be certain, but as far as she remembers, David Reid wasn't that drunk. But he was drinking heavily. She also remembers that he and Max had a hell of an argument, so bad that she had to ask them to keep it down.'

'Really? Dear old Max never mentioned that. Does she know what they were arguing about?'

'No, only that David said, "I won't do it," several times. After she asked them to keep it down, Max stormed out. She said David just sat there and had another drink, then, after a while, he left too. She said he seemed a little embarrassed. Tipped big as he was leaving, to make up for it.'

'Yowza. I bet my last cent they weren't fighting about any bloody golfing trip.'

'Suspect, isn't it?' She heard John light a cigarette. 'So, what now?'

'Car parks.'

John groaned.

Sarah grinned. 'Unless you have a better idea?'

'Not really.'

'You do Drury Street. I'm just at the back of the shopping centre.'

'Sure thing, boss.'

She ended the call and carried on, but her mind was burning with questions. Why were David's friends lying to them? Were they trying to protect David from something? Were they trying to protect themselves? They were successful, wealthy men, with good careers and families. What the hell could they be hiding? Or was she reading too much into their manner?

She made her way into the shopping centre and rode the elevator to the top floor of the car park. It took her twenty minutes to work her way down to level C, and as she let her eyes run over the next line of cars, she began to realise there were more silver Audis floating around Dublin than she had thought.

She was growing tired when John phoned.

'How you doing?' he asked.

'Well, you were right about the walking. This place is an awful lot bigger than I thought it was. And there's a lot more Audis than I expected, too.'

'Tell me about it. How's your leg holding up?'

'It's okay.'

'You sure?'

'Yes.'

'I'm finished here, so I'm going to go down to the Brown Thomas car park. Follow me down when you finish there. Oh, and I'll give the pound a call, maybe they picked the car up. It's clamper central down here.'

'Good idea. I hadn't even thought of that.'

'I'm not just a pretty face, you know.'

'You're not even a pretty face,' Sarah said, laughing. She hung up.

Seconds later, the mobile rang again.

'You think of a good comeback?'

'Excuse me?' a woman's voice said.

Sarah winced. It was her eldest sister, Helen. 'Oh, hi. I thought you were John.'

'Do you use this number for business?'

'You know I do.' Sarah could sense the waves of disapproval drifting down the line.

'Then you should be more careful about how you answer it. I could have been a client.'

The sarcastic tone made Sarah's hackles rise. 'Helen, I'm in the middle of something here. What is it?'

'Jackie and I were talking—'

'Ah, Jesus.'

'—and we want you to come over to Jackie's house tonight. We need to talk with you about something.'

'About what?'

'I don't want to discuss it over the phone.'

'Helen, you know I hate this sort of cloak-and-dagger crap. If it's about me, just tell me now. I don't want any lectures about work or anything. I'm doing fine – in fact, I'm in the middle of a case right now.'

'This isn't about you, it's about Mum.'

'Mum?' Sarah blinked. 'What about her?'

'Not now, Sarah,' Jackie said, her voice vibrating with irritation. 'We'll talk tonight. What time suits you?'

'I don't know. Eight, nine?'

'Pick one.'

'Eight, then.'

'Okay. I'll see you then. Where are you, by the way? The echo on this line is terrible.'

'I'm in a car park.'

'I thought you said you were working.'

'I'm looking for a car in a car park.'

'That's your job?'

Sarah could feel the colour rising to her cheeks. No matter what she said or did, Helen had a way of making her feel nine inches tall. 'Look, Helen, I've got to go.'

'Yes, I'd better let you get back to it,' Helen said. 'I'll see you later.'

'Goodbye, Helen.'

Sarah pocketed her mobile and raked her fingers through her hair. She didn't like it when Helen and Jackie said they had to talk to her. Usually, that meant she was about to hear something she didn't want to hear.

# 20

Big Jack discovered the whereabouts of his Fiat at four minutes past five that evening, when, as he was getting the float ready for the bar in Juicy Lucy, he got a call from his wife. He listened in disbelief as she recounted everything the gardaí had told her.

Big Jack hung up and rang the garage. Robbie answered.

'Hello?'

'Robbie.'

'Howya, Jack?'

'Where's Mick?'

'He's round the back there. Do you want me to get him?'

'No. They found the Fiat. The fucking cops were on the phone, saying they've got it up on the back of a van.'

'Where'd they find it?'

'Burnt out in a fucking supermarket in Templeogue.'

'Templeogue?'

'Yeah.'

'Jaysus, that's a shame. The little shits.'

'The gate – you sure it was messed about this morning?'

'Someone had been fucking with the lock, all right.'

Big Jack looked at his reflection in the smoked mirrors behind the bar. He looked like the world's scariest gargoyle come to life. 'If I find out Mick had anything to do with it…'

'Mick's a good lad, Jack. If he had've borrowed it, he wouldn't have burned it out. And the keys were here, remember?'

'That other fuck, though, he's not a good lad. And he's the one calling the shots.'

'The brother?'

'Aye. He was there today, acting the big man.' Jack patted his hair. 'Look, I've got to get on. I have to go down to the fucking cops now and sort out the details for the insurance.'

'Okay.'

'You keep an eye about you there. I don't want that other fuck anywhere near the yard, you hear me?'

'I hear you.'

Big Jack hung up and sat down on a bar stool. Katie, his floor manager, gave his shoulders a squeeze as she went past.

'All right, Big Jack?'

'Aye.'

She carried on walking. Normally he liked making a bit of small talk with Katie, but today he was preoccupied. Either some little fuck had broken into his yard, which was worrying enough, or Mick had stolen his car. But why take it to Templeogue? And if someone had broken in, why would they rob a nine-year-old Fiat Punto when there were better cars in the shed?

It didn't make any sense. And now, because of it, he had to deal with the fucking gardaí, and the last thing Big Jack liked doing was dealing with that shower.

*

'Everything all right?'

Robbie wiped his filthy hands on an even filthier cloth and looked at Mick. 'Big Jack called. They found the Fiat.'

'Yeah?' Mick tried to look like he was only curious.

'Yeah,' Robbie said, watching him closely. 'You want to know where?'

'Sure.'

'Templeogue.'

'Oh.' Mick swallowed. 'What did Jack say?'

'He's pissed. Keeps asking me about the gate.'

'Yeah? He's probably worried that they'll come back and take something else.'

'Don't give me that shite.' Robbie flung the rag down and folded his arms. 'There's no way anyone could have got that car out of here last night unless they had a key, and old Jack doesn't exactly hand them out, now does he?'

'Maybe the yard wasn't locked up properly.' Mick tried to keep eye contact and found he couldn't. Robbie's expression was one of real scorn, and it made him feel about three inches tall. 'Maybe it—'

'Don't even bother. I was last out yesterday, you little prick. I locked up, and it was still locked when I came in here this morning.' Robbie took a step towards him. But he didn't look angry any more, just resigned and a little worried. 'Look, Mick, I don't know what kind of eejit you think I am, and I don't care, but don't fuck with Big Jack. You hear me? You got a good thing going here, don't go fucking it up.'

'I'm not. Look, Rob, I didn't take it, if that's what you're thinking.'

'Well, it didn't walk out of here, did it?' Robbie jabbed an oil-stained finger in the direction of the road. 'You and me know it was no more fucking stolen than it vanished into thin air.'

'I got to get back. I got to fix that Ford.'

'Big Jack's going to fix you if he ever finds out you took his car. I don't know what you and that other fucker were up to, but it better not come back here. You'd do well to remember that.'

Mick turned and walked back into the shed, feeling more and more dejected with every step. He genuinely liked Robbie, and the look of disappointment on the older man's face was burning through him.

He went back to work, but he could hardly concentrate. He was scared. Everything was messed up so badly – and something was different about Sharpie. When Jack had knocked him over that morning, he had looked half crazed. Where killing Bo had sickened Mick – every time he allowed himself to think about it, he almost vomited – the same act had transformed Sharpie. It was almost as though it had unleashed some power in him. He was acting like he'd discovered something, something within himself that ate his fear. Not that Sharpie had ever carried much fear to start with.

Mick didn't know a thing about destiny or fate or anything else along those lines, but he recognised trouble when he saw it coming and, despite Sharpie's reassurances, he knew trouble was on the wind. It was like that time they'd let old Dicky Gaffney's pit bull out of the yard, for the laugh, only to watch it terrorise the whole neighbourhood for over two hours before the dog pound came and looped it. A loose pit bull, unleashed and fearless, was not an easy thing to control.

\*

'Well? Please tell me you had better luck than me.' Sarah climbed into John's car and pushed her damp hair back from her forehead. She was pale as a sheet, John noticed, and she looked exhausted.

'Not a sausage. No word from any of the pounds, either.'

'Okay. The barman at the George wasn't sure if David was there on the Saturday night. He gave me the number of the other barman. I'm going to give him a shout when I get back to the office, see if I can meet him and have him take a look at the photo.'

'Give the number to me, I'll call him.'

Sarah looked surprised. 'Why?'

'You know how I love talking to gay barmen.'

While investigating a missing persons case the year before, John had been kicked silly by a little gay man wearing nothing more than very small stripy undies. It still rankled a bit.

Sarah laughed tiredly. 'Okay. Just don't let this one karate-chop your kidneys.' She gave him the number and name.

John glanced at his watch. It was ten to six and he was gasping for a coffee. 'I haven't heard anything back from Steve about the Quinn brothers yet, either.'

'You should call him again.'

'He'll be all right. I'll give him a buzz in a while, butter him up a bit – you know how he gets.' John started the engine.

'Would it be okay if I don't go back to the office?' Sarah asked.

'Sure. Everything all right?

'I'm going to go home and clean up. I've been summoned to Jackie's house this evening.'

'Oh?'

'By Helen. They want to talk to me.'

'I see.' John wrinkled his nose. 'Do you want me to give you a lift home?'

'Nah, it'll only take me a few minutes to walk from here.'

'I'll give you a call if I hear anything in the meantime. Who knows, maybe Steve will favour us with an address for our light-fingered boyos.'

'Maybe.' Sarah opened the door. 'Wish me luck.'

'Good luck. Give the she-wolves a kiss for me.'

Sarah laughed, got out of the car and slammed the door.

\*

John parked the car just off Camden Street and walked back to the office. He made a cup of coffee and sat down to make his calls. He rang the barman first.

'Hi, my name is John Quigley, I'm a private investigator with QuicK Investigations. Sam, your manager, gave me your number. I hope you don't mind my calling? … Oh, he called you already? Well, better safe than sorry. I wonder if I could meet you today, have you look at a photo for me? … Sure, that's no problem. Give me your address… Perfect, meet you there in an hour. Thanks.'

He had just put the phone down when the door opened and a short, swarthy man with greying hair and caterpillar-like eyebrows stepped in uninvited.

'Help you there?' John said.

'I'm Detective Inspector Jim Stafford. Are you the Quigley I've been hearing about?'

'Probably,' John said and popped a defiant cigarette into his mouth.

'I want a word with you. You've been riling up James Reid.'

'"Riling"? Would that be the same as stirring?'

Stafford stepped in and grabbed the back of the nearest chair. 'Oh, great – a smart-arse. Just what I need this evening.'

'Sit down there, Detective, and take a load off,' John said, reaching for his lighter. 'I've got a feeling this might take a while.'

# 21

Sarah pulled up outside the gates of Jackie's Victorian semi in Rathgar. She switched off the radio and turned off the engine. The silence that followed was deafening.

She rested her forehead against the steering wheel. The rain had stopped twenty minutes before and the evening had become bright and warm. Droplets of moisture twinkled on the leaves and railings, and the sky was a dusky pink.

Sarah lifted her head and glanced at the glossy red front door. She groaned as a wave of depression hit her.

She was here now, she told herself, might as well go in. And yet her fingers kept gripping the steering wheel and her eyes stayed glued to the road. She could see Helen's black Land Rover Discovery (subtle) parked behind Jackie and Barry's Volvo (safe), and she fought against the sensation of… what was it?

Entrapment.

'Calm down,' she said aloud to her reflection in the rear-view mirror. 'They are your sisters. And. You. Can. Always. Leave.'

The last part worked a charm. Her fingers relaxed enough for her to prise them free from the wheel and get out of the car.

'Ah, here you are,' Jackie – second in command to Helen, and only two years older than Sarah – said in an over-bright, almost jovial voice. The second Sarah heard it, she flinched and knew that a) Jackie was already slightly sozzled, and b) they had been talking about her when she had rung the doorbell.

'Hey, Jackie.'

She leaned forward and kissed Jackie's cheek. She noticed that Jackie was wearing the Dior perfume she had given her for Christmas, and she wondered if that was some kind of statement, a trick to butter her up for some reason… Oh, God, what was wrong with her – why was she so suspicious? Her sister wore Dior, there was no parlour trick. 'Good to see you.'

'Oh, you too, angel. It's been too long.'

Jackie embraced her so hard and so long that Sarah felt claustrophobic. When she finally extracted herself from the bear hug, Jackie sighed and stood back, her dark eyes roaming over Sarah's face.

'You look tired. How's your ankle?'

'Doing okay.' Sarah said nothing about her 'fall' the day before.

'Really?'

'Really.'

'Come in, come in, we're out the back on the deck. Can I get you a drink?'

'Sure, I'll have a Coke.'

'The weather's been crazy, hasn't it? Hot one minute, cold the next.'

'Yeah, crazy.'

Jackie swayed off into the kitchen, and Sarah followed. She was always surprised by the sheer size of Jackie's kitchen. They had extended it three years before, and now it was nearly as large as her whole apartment.

Jackie picked up a half-empty glass of red wine from the marble counter. Sarah and she stood looking at each other, observing.

Jackie wore a long raw-linen skirt, a black cowl-necked top and a turquoise pendant with matching earrings. Her long hair was looped up in a messy yet graceful coiffure. She taught art at a local secondary school and was, despite her modest protestations, becoming a bit of a name herself for her private and yet deeply touching portraits. Her artist's eye was somehow able to extract the essence of a person and transplant it onto oil and canvas.

'Want anything with the Coke?'

'Will I need it?'

'Now, honey. Don't be like that.' Jackie smiled and changed the subject. 'Wait until you see the new trees I ordered to act as a wind-break. They're Japanese – very unusual, but so pretty.'

'I'm sure they're lovely.' Sarah bent down to tickle Albert, Jackie's old tabby cat, under the chin. He purred softly at her touch, and for a second Sarah remembered another kitten she'd once had. The sudden pain of that memory shot through her so hard she snapped back upright, gasping for breath.

'Are you all right?' Jackie took a step towards her.

'I'm fine,' Sarah said, holding up a hand to ward her off. 'My foot… the damp. Let's just go and get this over with.'

Jackie's garden was large and very old, a lucky inheritance from the previous owners, but Jackie had recently added a new deck and she was, rightly, very proud of it. Jackie, Sarah thought irritably, did not suffer from the black thumb Sarah seemed to have when it came to plant life.

Through the French doors she could see Helen and Barry sitting in garden chairs on the deck, talking softly. Helen's back was to the doors. Her dark hair had been cut into a severe bob, and it glinted under the storm candles Jackie had strung artfully along the wooden veranda. Sarah watched her, feeling the tension rise. What was it about her sisters that did this to her?

'Is Paul coming to this little tête-à-tête too?'

Paul, Helen's husband, was a handsome, overbearing orthopaedic surgeon with dry hands and a roving eye. He was the prize possession of the Kenny family, a shining example of a good catch. Sarah disliked him in the same way she disliked snakes: they were obviously intelligent, and fascinating to watch, but she wouldn't like one within striking distance.

'No, darling,' Jackie said, slopping more red wine into her glass, 'he had to work.'

'The devil must have taken the night off.'

'He's very busy these days. Helen says she hardly ever sees him.' Jackie rolled her eyes. She opened her fridge – a silver, double-doored Smeg with ice-maker, the kind that probably cost more than Sarah's car – and produced a Coke. She grabbed a glass from the draining board, flung some ice cubes into it and handed it to Sarah.

'Voilà.'

'You know, maybe I will take something with this,' Sarah said. She was stalling and she knew it. 'Have you got any brandy?'

'Of course.'

'That, then.'

'I'll get you a fresh glass.'

'This one is fine.'

'Are you sure you want to put brandy over ice?'

'Does it matter? I won't like it anyway.'

While Jackie fetched the brandy from the sitting room, Sarah watched her eldest sister through the doors. She loved Helen, of course – that was never in dispute – but she was hard to like. Helen was prickly, bossy and always right – at least as far as she was concerned. She seemed to disapprove of everything Sarah did, but she saved most of her venom for John Quigley and Sarah's continuing relationship with him.

Sarah sometimes felt that Helen wanted to run her life for her. She wanted Sarah to take after her, find a man, settle down, get a cosy job, be secure. To Helen, security was almost as important as oxygen. And Sarah's decision to work with John Quigley – or, as Helen put it, 'the likes of John Quigley' – clearly rankled.

'Here you go, darling.' Jackie returned and handed Sarah a bottle of Torres. Sarah mixed herself a hefty one and took a deep breath.

'Ready?' Jackie said, over-brightly. Her voice was strained, despite the wine.

Sarah looked at her and felt the sharp taste of panic in her mouth. 'Jackie, please, what's going on? Is she gunning for me again?'

'Sarah, you shouldn't always think the worst of her.' Jackie lowered her voice and placed her thin, pale hand on Sarah's arm, her expression soft and deeply troubled. Sarah looked at her, noting – as always – that, of the three girls, Jackie looked the most like their mother. She wasn't as tall as Helen and Sarah; she was curvier, softer, and her features were less defined. They all had brown eyes, but where Sarah's and Helen's were almost black and slightly owlish, Jackie's eyes were a soft hazel.

'Come on, we'd better go out.'

Sarah followed her sister out into the garden. She paused by the door and closed her eyes. The rain had left a faintly earthy tang in the air, and the jasmine trailing tendrils over Jackie's garden shed was beginning to let down its heavy evening scent.

'Hey, Sarah.'

'Hello, Barry.'

Barry stood up and embraced her clumsily. Sarah stiffened in his arms.

He was a short, boring, harmless man who worked in IT and was forever pulling at his earlobes. He had, Sarah noticed in a moment of spite that left her giddy with guilt, grown alarmingly fat in a repugnantly feminine way. Beneath his white shirt, his man-boobs were flourishing, and his hips were taking on that soft, wide-load-bearing look that expectant mothers get in the seventh month.

'Hello, Helen.'

Helen stood up and brushed her lips through the air two inches from Sarah's cheek. She was wearing an olive-green suit and a deep-red silk cami. Her shoes were the exact colour of her skirt, and her long, slim legs were uniformly tanned. Sun bed, thought Sarah. She couldn't imagine Helen lying outside long enough to get a colour that even.

'Hello. I was beginning to wonder what was keeping you.'

'No doubt.'

Helen passed a critical eye over her younger sister. 'You look a little thin. Have you lost weight?'

'Not a pound.'

'Well, you look thin. And exhausted.'

Sarah sat in the chair next to Helen and took a sip of her drink. 'You look great.'

Helen made a pleased sound; she was always a sucker for a compliment. 'How's work? Did you find the car?'

'Work's fine, and no, I didn't.'

'Is that what you're doing now, searching for lost cars?'

Sarah bristled and smiled nastily. 'It's part of an ongoing investigation into a suspicious death.'

'Oh, Sarah, do be careful,' Jackie said as she sat down. 'I hope you're not taking any silly risks.'

'I know what I'm doing, Jackie.'

'Do you?' Helen said.

'Yes. So,' Sarah said quickly, 'are we waiting for anyone else? Or can we get this show on the road?'

'Why? Are you in a hurry to get somewhere?' Helen said sharply.

'No. But you obviously have something to say, so let's hear it.'

Helen and Jackie exchanged glances, and Sarah felt a prickle of unease. Clearly they had planned to ease her into whatever they wanted to talk about, and she had put them on the back foot.

Helen lifted her wine glass and took a sip. 'This is excellent wine, Jackie. Wherever did you get it?'

'Oh, it's South African, very nice vineyard. I think I bought it in O'Brien's. I can check for you, if you like.'

'Do. You should try a glass, Sarah.'

'I don't want any. I just want to know what's going on. You asked me to come meet you, and I'm here. You said this was about Mum, and Mum isn't here, so what is it about?'

Jackie leaned out of her seat a little. 'Darling, now don't get all defensive—'

'About what?'

'Well, about nothing. We want you to hear us out, that's all.'

'So shoot.'

'We don't think Mum can manage on her own any longer,' Helen said.

'What are you talking about?'

'She had that fall last weekend and hurt herself quite badly—'

'She sprained her wrist,' Sarah said. 'I called in to her Sunday evening and she was a little sore, but that's it.'

'And, after discussing it, Jackie and I—'

'After discussing what?'

'If you let me finish, I'll tell you,' Helen said, her voice rising hard.

'Sarah, please,' Jackie begged. 'Just hear us out, my darling.'

'And Jackie and I feel that, with her mobility problems, it might be better if Mum went to a care facility.'

Sarah stared at Helen as if she'd been slapped. It took her a couple of seconds to get control of her vocal cords again.

'A home? You want to stick Mum in a home? Jesus fucking Christ, Helen, she sprained her goddamn wrist. Are you serious?'

'Yes,' Helen said, and put her glass down on the table, harder than necessary. 'Very.'

'You can forget it. I won't agree to it.'

'You don't have to.'

'It's completely ridiculous. She's sixty-five years old, she's too young to be in a home.'

'Sarah, she has ever-decreasing mobility, and, in case you haven't noticed, she also has a very serious problem with depression.'

'She's always had that.'

'It's getting worse.'

'She has a few bad days—'

'She has more than a few. And another thing: I'm sure you've noticed the other changes in her lately.'

'What changes?'

'The way she acts, the way she talks… you can't sit there and tell me you haven't noticed!'

'I haven't.'

But Sarah was lying, and even as she said the words she felt an icy grip tighten around her heart. In truth, there had been a big difference in her mother in the last three months. She was constantly ringing up, sometimes crying, other times accusatory, complaining that she couldn't remember where anything was in her own house, accusing the sisters of moving things. She had locked herself out so many times that both sets of neighbours had keys. And there were other signs, too. The fortnight before, when Sarah had called over to bring her to collect her pension, her mother had refused to let her into the house, claiming she didn't recognise her. It had taken over half an hour for Sarah to convince her to remove the chain from the door – and then she had acted like nothing had happened. Sarah hadn't mentioned that one to anyone. She had hoped it was a once-off. Now she was starting to realise it wasn't.

'You know,' Helen said. 'She's so forgetful, and half the time she can't tell me and you apart. She called me Sarah twice last week – and, before you say she always did that, I don't just mean she called me your name; she seemed to think I was you.'

'It's that damn medication. She gets confused.'

'The medication she doesn't take, you mean? Three different prescription bottles in her bathroom, two half empty and one full. The seal hadn't even been broken.'

'Who told you that? Who found them? Jackie?'

'Excuse me?'

'Well, come on, Helen, how would you know what tablets she had? It's not like you ever spend any real time with her.'

Two spots of colour rose in Helen's cheeks. 'That's not fair. I—'

Sarah raised her hand. 'All right, so she's forgetful.'

Jacie sighed. 'Angel, it's more than that. She's becoming… unbalanced.'

'Everyone in this fucking family is unbalanced!'

Helen sat forward in her chair. 'I'm serious, Sarah: she's getting worse every week. Every day. She can't manage on her own any longer. It's only a matter of time before something terrible happens, an accident or something.'

'I won't let you do this. You can't make me agree with you. Who are you to decide anything?'

'For God's sake!' Helen threw her hands into the air. 'What is wrong with you? This isn't about me, or you, this is about what's best for Mum.'

'Sticking her in a home is not what's best for her!' Sarah shouted, hot tears forming unbidden in her eyes. 'She'd hate it.'

'She wouldn't. She'd have activities, people to wait on her hand and foot. It's not like the old days, Sarah. She would get excellent care.'

'No.'

'They're not really homes. It could be an active community care programme.'

'Jesus, calling a fucking duck a mallard doesn't make it any less of a fucking duck.'

'Sarah—' Jackie said, but Sarah cut her off with a swift flap of her hand.

'I don't want to hear it.'

'She can't stay in that house alone,' Jackie persisted. 'Sarah, what if something happens to her? We can't watch her every minute of the day. I brought her over a casserole last week, and I found it still in the fridge on Friday, she hadn't touched it. I don't know what the hell she's eating half the time. I don't know if—'

'I'll move in with her.'

'You?' Helen threw her head back and laughed. 'What about your flat?'

'I'll sell it.'

'What about your job? Are you going to be available twenty-four hours a day?'

'Of course not, but—'

'Well, that is what our mother needs, Sarah! Someone she can depend on, twenty-four-seven.' Helen turned to Jackie. Her face, so like Sarah's, was a tangle of anger and frustration. 'Jackie, please, back me up here.'

'Darling, we're not trying to railroad you, but it's true: lately Mum's been getting much worse. You don't know the half of it. She's very disorganised. She's forgetful, distracted. The fall is just a very minor part of a much bigger picture.'

'So she's getting a bit scatty. Christ, I'm a bit scatty myself.'

'She's more than a bit scatty, my angel. Last week she went into town to go shopping and she couldn't remember her address. She had to get the taxi driver to drop her off here.'

'Maybe she wanted to come here.'

'She was still in her slippers. She'd been wandering around town in them. She had no purse, I had to pay the driver.'

Sarah groaned and buried her head in her hands. 'Jackie, please stop. You don't understand. You've had her. I'm...I'm only getting her back again. I don't want to lose—'

Helen cracked her knuckles. 'I think we're going to have to face the fact that our mother is showing all the signs of the onset of Alzheimer's.'

Sarah reeled back in her seat as if she had been electrocuted. 'Oh, my God. You don't know that, Helen.'

'I haven't got it confirmed because I can't get her to go see a neurologist. But I've spoken to Dr Heffernan, and he agrees with me that all the signs are there. We need to get her to a specialist.'

'You spoke to Heffernan about this? When?' Sarah felt betrayed somehow. Dr Pat Heffernan had been the family GP for as long as she could remember.

'Week ago, when I realised Mum was getting worse.'

'You never told me.'

'I didn't want to worry you.'

'Ha! Right, you didn't want to worry me, but springing this on me is so much better. Well done, Helen.'

'I knew you'd do this,' Helen said, her face tight with anger. 'I knew you would find a way to turn Mum's health into a personal attack on me. Well, think what you like. Mum is suffering, and we—'

Sarah lowered her head into her hands. 'Jackie, tell her to stop.'

'No, darling. We all love Mum, but we need to talk about this, we need to find some way to agree on a course of action.' Jackie wrung her hands together and glanced forlornly at Helen. She knew Helen had agonised over this decision and was struggling to keep everything together. If only Sarah realised just how much Helen loved her and wanted to protect her… 'The places we've looked at have been really very lovely. Helen brought some brochures, if you'd like to have a look at them.'

'You've already looked at places?' Sarah was reeling.

'Look, if it's about money,' Barry piped up, 'don't worry. We understand you're not in a position to pay. We've already agreed that we'll cover the expense, at least until the house is sold.'

'Barry,' Helen said sharply, glaring at him so fiercely he wilted, 'this is not the time to talk about money.'

Sarah lifted her head slowly and looked around at the three faces, her eyes resting last on her eldest sister. 'You have it all sorted. Wow, I don't see why you bothered to include me in this at all.'

She stood up, pushing her chair back so fast that it toppled over with a clatter.

'Sarah, wait—'

'Seems to me you have it all fucking worked out.'

'Darling—'

'No, Jackie. Brochures, selling the house, I see what this is. Don't fucking mind me. You pack of vultures have already decided.'

'Oh, Sarah, grow up!' Helen stood too. 'We asked you here to discuss our mother's health. We've shielded you for long enough, it's time for you to grow up and face some facts.'

'Shielded me? Oh, that's rich. Thank you so much, Helen. I can rest easy in my fucking bed tonight, knowing how shielded I am.'

'Watch your mouth, Sarah,' Helen said. 'You don't need to speak to me that way.'

'You're right, I don't. In fact, I don't need to speak to you at all.'

'Sarah, please, just wait – you haven't even given us a chance to explain…' Jackie reached frantically for her hand, but Sarah yanked it back as if Jackie's touch scalded her.

'Fuck off, Jackie. I know you're not behind this, but for once in your life I wish you'd put down the fucking bottle and grow a damn spine.'

Jackie's hand flew to her mouth.

'Hey,' Barry said.

'Hay is for horses!' Sarah screamed at him. Barry's mouth closed with a snap. Sarah whirled back to Helen. 'I won't let you do this. You don't get to decide this!'

And with that she tossed back the rest of her drink and ran out of her sister's house.

Without even thinking, she climbed into the Fiesta and drove straight to her mother's house.

\*

The house in Clontarf was a modest affair. It was semi-detached, with three good-sized bedrooms, a front and back garden, a lounge-cum-dining-room, a kitchen and two bathrooms. Nothing special, really, but worth a fortune in the current market, especially as it was near to the coast and in a middle-class area.

Sarah parked the car outside and sat in it for a few minutes, breathing hard, trying to gain control. Those assholes, she thought, ambushing me that way. Who do they think they are? She began to cry, stupid, fat, unstoppable tears. Bastards, heartless, selfish bastards.

But, as she looked at her family home through fresh eyes, she felt her heart lurch. She dashed furiously at her tears.

How had she not noticed before? Compared to the neighbouring houses, her mother's was more than a little shabby. Even though the girls took it in turns to mow the lawns and cut back the box hedges, the garden looked neglected and overgrown. The net curtains could have done with a wash, the gate needed to be scraped back and painted with a rust-guard and the front door needed a coat of varnish. Sarah sniffed loudly as she noticed the gutter was barely hanging on. The decay was setting in. The old house and its owner were losing some fundamental battle and slipping away, back to the elements.

Sarah dried her face and climbed out of the car. She walked up to the front door and let herself in. The door was sticking, and she stepped over a pile of mail.

When had her mother stopped picking up the mail?

'Mum?'

No answer, although Sarah could hear the television in the lounge.

'Mum, it's me.' She picked up the mail and leafed idly through it. Junk, mostly, one or two bills. She put it down on the hall table.

'Mum?'

She opened the door to the lounge. There was no one there. The television was on with the volume turned down low, and two of the lamps burned dimly, but there was no sign of her mother. A sensation of unease crept along Sarah's spine. She walked though the dining room into the kitchen. The sink was filled with dirty dishes. Sarah frowned at the debris-covered worktops and the mountain of dried-out teabags by the sink.

'Mum?'

She checked upstairs, moving faster now, trying to keep calm but becoming more agitated by the second. She glanced at her watch: ten past nine. Where could her mother be at this hour?

She ran back down the stairs and opened the back door. To her immense relief, she saw the light in the shed at the bottom of the garden was on. She ran across the damp grass and yanked open the shed door.

'Mum, there you are. What are you doing?'

Her mother was standing three rungs up on a rickety wooden fruit ladder. At Sarah's voice, she turned around slowly. The ladder creaked alarmingly under her weight. She was in her nightdress and she was barefoot and filthy. Her long grey hair hung straight down her back, covered in cobwebs and splinters of wood. Scattered around the floor were various rusty tools and tins of dried-up paint. It was a tetanus nightmare.

'Oh, hello there.'

'Mum, what in the name of God are you doing? Get down from there. What about your wrist?'

'Yes…' She looked down. 'It was very sore earlier, but I had to look and then I couldn't find them.'

'You couldn't find what?' Sarah went to her and guided her down, taking great care to support her mother's weight with her shoulder. God, she seemed lighter – or did she? The skin around her hand was black and blue, and the whole joint was swollen and shiny. Where in God's name had the bandage gone? Sarah wondered. Had she been wearing it at all? Was she taking the anti-inflammatory tablets?

'There were pigeons. They used to be in here. I saw it on National Geographic this evening, and we had the exact same ones. I just wanted to see if they were the same ones.'

Sarah half lifted her mother off the last step. 'You don't have any pigeons.'

'They were here, Sarah,' her mother said, in an irritated voice that was not like her. 'The racing ones were nearest the top. And the breeders were below them. I wondered if they were the same ones, that's all.'

'Oh.' Sarah's mind reeled. Finally she understood. Her father had kept pigeons for a while, when she was a little girl. But then a ferret or a cat had made its way into the shed and decimated the birds. Her father had come in the next morning, cleaned up the feathers and bloodied bodies, and sold all the survivors to a man from Wexford. He had given up on them. Anthony Kenny had always preferred to do things that way. It was always easier to give up than to start again.

'Come on, Mum, let's go inside. You must be cold.'

'Nonsense, it's very warm for this time of year. Don't you find it very close?'

'No.'

'Your hair.' Her mother smiled, reached up and stroked Sarah's head. 'I thought you cut it short?'

'That was Helen, Mum.'

'Yes, of course it was.'

'Come on.'

Deirdre Kenny allowed Sarah to lead her into her house. Sarah got a basin of warm water from the kitchen, washed her mother's feet and redressed her wrist. She seated her mother in her comfy chair by the gas fire, elevated her wrist on cushions and made her a cup of hot chocolate with full milk, the way she liked it. Then, once she was certain her mother was snug and safe and secure, Sarah tidied up the shed. She cleaned up the kitchen, gave the bathroom a quick going-over, stripped her mother's bed and put on fresh sheets. When she was finished, she sat on the end of the freshly made bed and cried until her face ached.

# 22

Sarah yawned. The office seemed unbearably stuffy. 'Good old Steve. He really is a good sort.'

John shrugged and threw his feet up onto the desk. 'Maybe so, but he says I now owe him, and I'm very worried about how that Cork loon might want to cash in.'

Sarah grinned. 'Don't worry, I'm sure it won't be anything too terrible. So tell me, what did the barman say?'

'He said Saturday night he was swamped. He remembers the bouncers throwing David out, but not whether David was with anyone or not. He thinks he saw him arguing with a guy at one point, but by the time he looked again, the guy was gone.'

'Lot of arguments David had that day. Could the barman describe the guy he was arguing with?'

'Not really. He said he might have been blondish.'

'Blondish… wow. Struck out.' Sarah sighed. 'I can't believe the cops actually called here. Unheard of.'

'Stafford was all right, for a short-arse.' John laughed softly. 'Straight-talking, at least, for a bluebottle. Says we need to keep him in the loop if we find anything.'

'Is he going to return the favour?'

'He's a cop, Sarah. I wouldn't trust him if he told me his balls hung to the left.'

'He really thinks we're barking up the wrong tree?'

'He says there's been a spate of gay-bashings up that end of the canal.'

'Maybe that asshole Max was right,' Sarah said slowly, rubbing her eyes with the heels of her hands.

'Maybe. Maybe he wasn't. That still doesn't explain the break-in.'

John didn't like how tired and defeated she sounded. He didn't comment on Sarah's pale face or the bruised shadows under her eyes. He figured if she wanted to talk, she would – and she didn't like it when people pushed. But he disliked Jackie and Helen another sliver more than he had the day before, and that was saying something.

'You okay?'

'I'm fine.' She didn't say anything for a second. She was almost afraid to look at John. She could hear the concern in his voice, and she was sure if she looked at him she'd start crying. 'John, look, I'll be staying at the house in Clontarf for the next few weeks so, if you need me for anything, that's where I'll be, okay?'

'Sure.'

'Just for a few weeks, until Mum's wrist gets a bit better.'

'Okay. Tell her I was asking for her.'

'Sure.' Sarah lowered her head and began looking through her note-book. She needed to regain her composure. 'How come it took Steve so long to get the address?'

'They're only seventeen, and only one of them's in the system: Shane Quinn. He's acquainted with the inside of St Pat's like I'm acquainted with Guinness. Full-on tealeaf, but he's racking up the beefs for violent conduct too. The other one is clean as a whistle, as far as Steve can tell. No mention of him anywhere.'

'There were two of them in that house. Let's go see these Quinn lads, see if we can find out what the hell they were doing that day.'

'I did a check on our friend Bo,' John said. 'He's got a record too.'

'You ran his name?'

'I did.'

Sarah looked pained. 'I thought you told the father if we got the stuff back, we wouldn't bring Bo to the attention of the gardaí.'

'I didn't mention what it was in connection with. I gave Steve Magher a bell to see if he had the Quinn brothers' address for me, and while I had him on the line, I ran Bo.' John shrugged. 'I had to do it, Sarah.'

'Okay.' Sarah ran her hands through her hair. 'What did Steve have to say about Bo?'

'Arrested eight times for handling stolen goods and three times for shoplifting.'

'Light-fingered.'

'The last time he was pulled was over a year ago.'

'Leopards, spots.' Sarah shrugged. 'That doesn't mean anything except that he learned to be more careful.'

'True.'

Sarah rolled her chair sideways, pulled David Reid's slim file out of the top drawer and slipped the Quinn boys' address into it. She flicked through the file. It was slender, but at least they were getting somewhere. 'You think the Quinns will talk to us?'

'Maybe if we tell 'em we're turning them over to the cops for the break-in.'

'I don't know,' Sarah sighed. 'I know we need to find out who Jack is, but I don't like the idea of confronting those two – especially the one with the record. One roughing-up a week is my limit.'

'You can stay here if you want.'

'No way.'

John rolled his eyes. He should have known better. 'We need leverage. You haven't heard from Whelan or Bo yet, have you?'

'No.'

'It'll be easier to push the Quinns if we have something to push them with.' John tapped his pen on the desk, thinking. 'At the moment, it's just your word that they were in the house. You didn't even get a good look at their faces.'

'I know what I saw, John. I'd recognise them again.'

'Try the old man, see if anything's turned up.'

'Not a hope of Bo using the shop, knowing we're looking at him,' Sarah said, but she dialled the number for the pawnshop anyway. It rang for ages. Finally a gruff, tired voice answered.

'Hi, Mr Whelan? It's Sarah Kenny here, from QuicK Investigations. Good morning. Any word on what… What's that?'

John looked up at the tone in her voice.

'Since when? … I see…I see… Are you sure? … No. No, of course not. No, sir, I'm sure it's nothing like that… Mr Whelan, you need to calm down. Please, stop shouting—'

She replaced her receiver. 'He hung up on me.'

'What's going on?'

'He says Bo is missing. He claims he hasn't been seen or heard from since Tuesday. He's not answering his mobile, and no one's seen him.'

'Great.' John shrugged. 'Bo knows we were looking for him, and he's lying low for a day or two. Or else the old lad's acting to get us off his back.'

'He sounds pretty worried.'

'Maybe he's a really good actor.'

'Let's go find out.'

'Now?'

'It's on the way to the Quinns', isn't it?'

John unfurled his body. 'All right, come on.'

*

But Brendan Whelan was in no mood for questions. He was angry and he was very frightened. He couldn't put his finger on why, exactly, but he was. When he let John and Sarah into the shop, he was already wheezing slightly.

He railed against them for being there and accused them of harassment, then he railed against them for causing his son to be missing in the first place. He directed much of his anger at Sarah, claiming that if she hadn't threatened him with the police, none of this would have happened.

'None of what?' Sarah said, exasperated. 'Your son attacked me, remember? Anyway, you don't know that anything's happened.'

'I do.' Whelan hit his chest with his open hand. 'I can feel it. You, making me think he was involved in all sorts. You got me to put pressure on him, and now look – he's gone.'

'You seemed pretty sure he was involved the other day.'

'I wasn't sure of anything. You made it sound as though he was up to his neck with those two little shits. You made me doubt my own son.'

'Let me get this straight,' John said, leaning on the counter. 'Your son attacks my partner when he hears the word "gardaí", you speak to him about handling stolen items and he does a runner. And somehow this is our fault. Am I missing something here?'

'You don't know what it's like. You do something wrong, and then you're a marked man. Brendan was trying to change. He was done with that sort of stuff.'

'He's done a runner, that's what he's done.'

'Something has to have happened. He wouldn't just up and leave without saying anything.'

'Sure he would,' John said, 'especially if he's worried that he's going to do another stint in jail for handling stolen property. We looked into his background. You can say what you like, Mr Whelan, but your boy's no angel. Got quite a file on him, the cops do.'

'You'd no right snooping around after him!' The old man glared first at John and then at Sarah. 'You said you'd keep his name away from the gardaí!'

Sarah tightened her lips. 'I didn't say a word about him, to the gardaí or anyone else. Look, where might he have gone?'

'Nowhere. And I'm telling you, if he knew he wasn't going to be home for the night, he'd have called. He always did. And it's been two nights now.'

'Well, maybe he's just lying low,' John said, 'hoping we'll go away.'

'He'd call. He wouldn't have me worried like this. I'm telling you, something's happened to him. Sure, where would he go? He doesn't have any money, he doesn't have anywhere else.'

Sarah folded her arms and leaned back against the shelves. Whelan's anxiety was beginning to rub off on her; he was so utterly certain that something had happened. 'Have you called the gardaí?'

'Oh, aye,' Whelan almost spat. 'And tell them what? That the day you crowd come into my shop accusing my son of stealing, he goes missing? Oh yes, that would really make them come running.'

'Well, then, I don't know what you can do. What was the last thing he said to you?'

'Nothing.' The old man ran his hands over his head. 'But he was going to meet up with them two Quinn boys, I'm sure of it.'

Sarah looked at John. 'What makes you say that?'

Whelan closed his eyes, and his shoulders slumped. Every line and wrinkle on his face seemed to exude fatigue.

'What makes you say that?' Sarah said, a little more firmly this time.

'I heard him. I heard him talking to one of them on his phone.'

'Did you hear what they said?'

'No, I only heard him say, "Sharpie". It was right after he, well, made you leave.'

'You sure he said "Sharpie"?' John asked.

'I said so, didn't I?'

Sarah and John exchanged glances. The old man sat down and tried to calm his breathing.

Sarah figured he had given them everything he could. 'If you do hear anything, or if Bo gets in touch, will you give us a call?'

Whelan looked at Sarah, as if to see if she was pulling his leg, but her face was earnest. He leaned forward on the counter and took a great shuddering breath.

'I wouldn't call you if I was dying of thirst and you had the only water in town. Now fuck off out of here and take this reprobate with you.'

*

John and Sarah sat in the car for a few minutes, watching the traffic, neither of them speaking.

After a few minutes, John sighed. 'You all right?'

'I'm grand. It just wasn't nice seeing the old lad upset like that.'

'Bo's probably lying low till this shit blows over. Maybe he sold the gear on and he's flush. Or maybe he was worried you were going to press charges.'

'Why do people have to be such arseholes?'

'You want to go to the Quinns' house, light a bit of a fire under their arses?'

Sarah nodded. 'More than anything.'

'Okay, then.' John started the car. 'Then let's do it.'

# 23

John smiled. 'Hello there. We're looking for—'

'What have they done now?' The florid-faced woman who had answered the door scowled at them.

She was squeezed into a pink velour tracksuit, and her feet spilled out from a pair of pink flip-flops. Her hair was short and dark, and the ash hanging from the cigarette clamped in the corner of her mouth dangled at least an inch long. Her upper arms, Sarah couldn't help noticing, were thicker than the tops of Sarah's legs. She looked like she could snap either of the detectives in half if the mood took her.

John frowned. 'Who do—'

'You're lookin' for Sharpie and Mick, right?'

'Yes, but—'

'You the police?'

'No, I'm—'

'Who are you, then?'

John took a card from his pocket and handed it to her. She read it and snorted. 'Private detectives, huh? What's this about?'

'Look, we'd really like to talk to… er, are they your sons?'

The woman refolded her massive arms. The ash finally gave up and fell onto her chest. 'Yeah. What do you want to talk to them about?'

'We're investigating a burglary that happened Monday. We thought—'

'So who sent you here?' She pulled herself up, her eyes mean, and removed the cigarette. 'It's that old Galvin bitch from round the corner, isn't it? Every bleedin' time something happens, she's out, pointin' the finger this way. Well, I'm sick of it. I'm a hard-workin' woman' – she jabbed herself in the chest with her thumb – 'two jobs I hold down, and no handout from no one. Raised them boys single-handed. You think that's easy?'

'No,' John said, wishing she would stop spitting all over him. He took a step backwards.

'Cops don't want to do nothin' but blame me sons for every fuckin' thing that happens round here. Lazy-arsed bastards. I work hard! I shouldn't have to be puttin' up with this shite! You want to talk to the boys, you go find 'em. They're not here.'

'I see. Do you—'

'Mick's at work. Don't know where the other one is. All right?'

'Where does—'

'Garage on Bridgefoot Street. You can't miss it. You tell him I'm sick of this shit, you tell him I don't want this kind of thing on my doorstep, you tell him I don't need it. Now, you gonna keep me standin' here all day, or what?'

'No. Thank—'

She closed the door in their faces with a bang.

'—you for your help,' John said to the knocker. He turned to Sarah and pulled a face.

'Let's go find this garage,' Sarah said.

'Yeah,' John agreed. He wiped a glistening piece of spittle away with his sleeve.

*

Twenty minutes later, they parked opposite the open gates of a large enclosed yard that John assumed was the garage. Certainly, there was nothing else on Bridgefoot Street, apart from some run-down flats.

'This must be it,' John said.

'Hang on – Lawson Motors? I've seen that name somewhere...' Suddenly Sarah snapped her fingers. 'This is where David Reid bought the Audi! The paperwork is in his file. Well, well, another connection between the Quinns and David Reid.'

Her mobile rang. She looked at the screen and turned it off. John noticed, but he didn't comment.

'Let's go,' she said.

In the yard, a small man in grease-splattered overalls was working under the bonnet of a car. He looked up when they approached. He had a sallow, weatherbeaten face and bloodshot eyes. Sarah knew from the look of him that he was a good friend of the bottle.

'Can I help you?'

'Hi,' John said. 'We're looking—'

'If it's for a car, you've come to the right man, but the wrong place, my friends. You need to head on over to the showroom.'

A bear of a man with dyed black hair and an ill-fitting green-grey suit advanced on them. He was huge and he was beaming.

'What can I do for you folks?' he said, looking them up and down. 'Something reliable, for a good price? Now that I can provide! You leave it to me, I'll take care of you. Hire purchase not a problem, finance sorted within twenty-four hours.'

'We're not looking to buy a car, Mr...?'

'Lawson. Call me Jack, Big Jack; everyone does.' The big man didn't look quite so jovial, now that they weren't buying.

'Jack?' Sarah and John said at exactly the same time.

Jack Lawson frowned. 'Yes.'

John recovered fast. 'My name is John Quigley, and this is my partner, Sarah Kenny. We're private investigators.' John held out his hand and watched as it disappeared into Big Jack's paw.

Big Jack kept the smile in place, but his eyes had turned cool and watchful. 'Private investigators? Like Magnum PI, eh? Well now, not often we get glamour down these parts, is it, Robbie?'

Robbie grunted. 'No.'

'So what can I do for you, folks?'

'We're looking for—'

'We're looking for a car,' Sarah said suddenly. 'An Audi Quattro.'

Big Jack looked confused. So did John.

'An Audi? Well now, I have a few up at the showroom.'

'No, I'm sorry, I'm not explaining this very well,' Sarah said, but her eyes were focused on a young man who had appeared in the door of a nearby shed and was watching them with an anxious expression on his pinched face. 'You see, Mr Lawson, we're looking for a particular car.' She pulled out her notebook. 'Ah, here it is: a silver Audi Quattro.' She showed the registration number to Big Jack. 'I believe it was purchased from you back in February.'

'From me?'

'I believe so. You own Lawson Motors, right?'

'Aye.' Big Jack was watching her very carefully now.

'Well, I'm fairly certain David Reid – that's our client's brother – bought his car from you.' She looked past him again to where the boy stood. Same black hair, same build… it had to be him.

'He must have bought it from one of the sales lads. I only own the place, I'm not really there much of the time,' Big Jack was saying. 'David Reid – I'm trying to place the name…' He followed Sarah's gaze to the door. 'I'd have to look back through the sales sheets. We sell a lot of cars, don't always remember everyone personally. This guy's car stolen, then? He looking to sort out details for insurance?'

'He died almost two weeks ago,' John said.

'Died? Really? That's… Who did you say you were working for again?'

'His brother James. We're helping to tie up David Reid's estate.'

'Right, right.' Big Jack and the mechanic exchanged glances. 'And you reckon the car's missing?'

'It's missing, has been since the day David Reid died, and we thought, well…' Sarah looked at John and grinned sheepishly. 'It was a long shot, but we were hoping that maybe David had brought it in for a service or something.'

'A service?'

'Yes.' Sarah nodded. 'I know, it's stupid, really, but frankly, Mr Lawson, at this stage we're at a loss as to where it could be.'

'Ah, I see. Well now, Robbie here would be the main mechanic, he could tell you if he'd worked on it. You done any work on an Audi Quattro lately, Robbie?'

'No. Why would a new car need a service, anyway?'

'Mick? Come here a minute, will you?' Big Jack yelled without turning around.

The young man in the doorway jumped slightly. Then he walked towards them, moving slowly, warily.

'Yeah?'

'You didn't work on an Audi lately, did you?'

Mick looked shyly at Sarah and John and shook his head.

Big Jack nodded. 'Well, I don't know what else I can tell you.'

John sighed. 'I know. Like Sarah says, it was a long shot.'

'And there's no sign of this car at all?' Big Jack said.

'No, it's vanished.'

'That's a strange one, all right.' Jack shook his head. 'Well, sorry I couldn't be more help to you.'

'That's okay.'

'Do you have a card there handy? Maybe if I hear anything…'

John dug a card from his wallet and handed it over. While Big Jack squinted at it, John tried not to notice that the card looked like a postage stamp in his hand.

'QuicK?'

'That's us,' Sarah said. 'Listen, we won't take up any more of your time. Thanks again.'

Big Jack gave them the once-over again. 'Not at all. You're ever in the market for a good-quality car, you remember Big Jack.'

'Sure will.' Sarah hooked her arm into John's and steered him towards the gate.

Big Jack watched them until they drove off.

'What the fuck was that about?'

'Dunno,' Robbie shrugged.

'David fucking Reid.' Big Jack scowled. He turned on his heel and made his way to the stairs. 'Mick, get your wee arse upstairs. I want a word.'

Mick followed him up. 'Yeah?'

'When you did that job for me the other day, no one saw you, right?'

'No, Jack.'

Big Jack caught him by the back of the neck and dragged him so close that their noses were almost touching. 'You did what I said – you didn't touch anything, did you?'

'No, Jack.' Mick could feel his knees trembling.

'You didn't touch his fucking car?'

'No, Jack! I swear I never even saw it!'

'All these vanishing fucking cars. I don't like coincidences much. I find out you're lying to me, I'll fucking string you up by your guts, you better believe me, lad.'

Mick nodded.

Big Jack released him. 'Get back to your work.'

*

'Well, we wanted a Jack and we got a Jack,' John said as they waited at the top of the road for the lights to change.

'Doesn't know David Reid, my arse. He knew who I was talking about the moment I said his name. You saw his face, right?' Sarah said excitedly. 'And that kid, Mick – it was him. He's definitely one of the guys who broke in.'

'You sure?'

'Positive.'

'Okay, then. We now have a Mick and a Jack. All we need is a Sharpie and a reason for all this, and we're home clear.'

Sarah clapped her hands together. 'Oh, I love when we get a whiff of something.'

'Yeah, great. A whiff of what, though?' The lights changed and John drove on. 'Why would Jack Lawson send his mechanic to rob a computer from a guy who bought a car from him?'

'I don't know yet, but I know he lied about knowing David, and I know Clive Hollingsworth nearly shat himself when we mentioned the name Jack. There's something going on here, John.'

John glanced at her. She looked animated and excited, a far cry from earlier. 'All right, what do we do next?'

'Next, John, next we look into Jack Lawson. I want to know what the connection could be between him and David Reid.'

'We need to talk to that kid,' John said. 'I might swing by later, see if I can get a word out of him.'

'Okay, but be careful. That guy Jack looks like he could tear you to pieces.'

'Big bloke, all right.'

# 24

While John parked the car, Sarah headed up to the office. She found James Reid waiting on the stairs. He was casual today, wearing jeans and a grey T-shirt. Sarah couldn't help noticing his muscular arms bulging from the thin material. He looked like he hadn't been getting much sleep. There were puffy pockets of skin under his eyes that she hadn't noticed on the Monday.

'Hello,' she said. 'Been here long?'

'Half an hour, no more.'

Sarah unlocked the door and glanced at James again. He was clearly agitated.

'What is it?'

He followed her into the office. 'I got a call this morning from the solicitor handling David's estate.'

'Oh?'

'He's drawing up the probate, so naturally he's been looking through David's financial records. There's over forty thousand euros gone from David's savings account. It was drawn out the day before his death.'

'Really?' Sarah sat down. 'Any idea where it went?'

'None. That's almost every penny David had saved. That's a whole shitload of money to be gone, isn't it?'

'It sure is.' Sarah frowned. 'And he never mentioned anything to you about it? Never said he was thinking of, I don't know, maybe buying another property or something?'

'He never mentioned anything. Look, this money was drawn out in cash – I've checked. He made a special order for the withdrawal.'

'Give me the name of the bank and whoever oversaw the transaction.'

'What do you think is going on?'

'I don't know.'

James wrote down the names of the bank and the manager who had handled the withdrawal. Sarah took the page and stared at it, her thoughts racing. Forty thousand quid was too much money to simply vanish into thin air. What the hell had David Reid done with it?

James ran his hands through his hair. 'None of it makes any sense. David made good money. He has a mortgage, but it's not huge. What the hell would make him take out every penny like that?'

'I don't know.'

'I wish I knew what was going on.' He paced to the window and then back again. 'You know any more about them two jokers that broke into his place?'

'I know who they are and where one of them works. I even have a fair idea who sent them.'

'Really?' James sat down, looking hopefully at her. 'What did they say? Who are they?'

'Actually, this is where it gets a little weird…' Sarah proceeded to tell him about the Quinn brothers and Big Jack Lawson, and as she spoke James Reid grew more and more bewildered.

'And this is the garage where David bought his car?'

Sarah took out David's file, found the receipt and showed it to James. 'There it is – Lawson Motors. As soon as I saw the name, I remembered where I'd seen it before. I'd only just flicked through the paperwork before we left.'

'But I don't understand. Why would this fella send that young lad into David's home? What were they looking for?'

'I don't know,' Sarah said truthfully, 'but I intend to find out.'

'What the hell is going on?' James stood up and paced around the room again. 'Jesus, I want to go over there right now and wring that young lad's fucking neck. Make him talk.'

'I know, but if you do, you'll tip Jack Lawson off that we know about his connection to the robbery. We don't know if that robbery has anything to do with David's actual death or not.'

'It must have.'

'But we don't know it.'

'It's so… maddening!' He balled his work-roughened hands into fists.

'I know it is. But it's only been a few days. We will get to the bottom of this, but for the moment we need to play our cards close to our chests.'

Eventually, a very angry but resigned James Reid gave Sarah his word that he was not planning to do anything too hasty, such as driving to the garage and wringing the truth out of Mick Quinn's scrawny neck and taking a hurley to Big Jack Lawson. After he'd gone, Sarah dialled John's mobile.

'Hey, where are you? I thought you were coming straight up after you parked the car.'

'I'm around the corner, talking to Mike Brannigan.'

Sarah rolled her eyes. Mike owned Freak FM, the pirate station on the first floor. He was a local hustler and small-time crook who had probably never done an honest day's work in his life. For some reason, John loved talking to him.

'Well, tell Mike I said hi, but get in here. James Reid just left.'

'I'll be there in two seconds. Mike's telling me about something interesting.'

'John—'

'Sarah, I'll be there in a few minutes.'

He hung up on her. Peeved, Sarah put the phone down and went back to staring at the piece of paper in front of her.

Everything connected with her client's brother seemed to be missing: forty thousand euros gone, car gone, computer gone; David Reid, gone. Where – and why?

Sarah took out the globe she had found by the bridge and spun it from its chain. It glittered in the sunshine that threaded its way though the windows. What if her suspicions about the friends were just that – the paranoid wonderings of a woman who suspected the worst in everybody? Or was there some connection between their jumpiness and the missing money, or Jack Lawson?

She thought of Larry Cole's slimy hands and Clive's frightened eyes. What had they been afraid of? What the hell could the connection be? James Reid was right: it was maddening. God, she felt like such an amateur sometimes.

The phone on her desk rang.

'Hello, QuicK Investigations, how may I help?'

'He's dead.'

'What?' Sarah gripped the receiver tightly. 'Who is this?'

'They shot him – they shot my boy in the face.'

'Mr Whelan?'

'They shot him in his face.' He was sobbing now. 'He's dead.'

'Oh, my God. I'm so sorry, Mr Whelan. What—'

But he had already hung up. Sarah was left with nothing but a dead line.

When John came in a few minutes later, she was on the phone with a contact at the coroner's office.

'Thanks a million. I will; I'll call back.' She hung up and pinched the bridge of her nose with her fingers.

John clapped his hands together to get her attention. 'Hey, guess what?'

Sarah raised her head slowly.

'That guy, Big Jack? Mike Brannigan knows him – and not only is he the owner of Lawson's Motors, he also owns Juicy Lucy's down on Leeson Street. You know, the strip club.'

'What?'

'Juicy Lucy's; he owns it. What if there's a connection between David Reid and Jack through the club?'

'Why would there be? He was gay.'

'So? All I'm saying is, we should keep it in mind. I mean, there has to be some reason Jack Lawson had the Quinns ransack Reid's house, and I don't buy that it was over a car.'

'John, Bo Whelan was found. He was shot.'

'What?' John stopped grinning. 'How do you know?'

'His father called me.'

'Oh, shit. What happened?'

'I don't know everything yet, but there's no doubt it's him. His father identified him.'

'Jesus.' John sat down behind his desk and lit a cigarete. 'His old man said he was going to see Sharpie Quinn, right?'

'He said he spoke to him,' Sarah said, thinking of how frightened Brendan Whelan had seemed earlier. The poor man. She felt terrible. Even though Bo had attacked her and thrown her out of the shop, she would not have wished that fate on him.

John stood up suddenly. 'Sarah, you see what you can find out about Jack Lawson.'

'Where are you going?'

'I'm going to talk to Mick Quinn.'

'John…' Sarah looked nervous. 'I don't know. I don't think you should let that Big Jack character know you're sniffing around, not just yet.'

'Look, this Mick kid is clean, right? I might be able to get him to talk.'

Sarah nodded and took a deep breath. 'Okay, but be careful.'

'You know it.'

# 25

John sat in the parked car for almost an hour before he spotted Mick Quinn leaving the garage and making his way down the street towards him. The young lad was walking in a fast line towards the quays, head down, deep in thought.

John waited until he was only a few feet away and tooted the horn. Mick glanced up and looked at him, blankly at first, then with growing alarm.

John rolled the window down. 'Hey, come here – I want a word with you.'

'I can't. I've got to—'

'Come here.'

Mick hesitated, and then his shoulders slumped. He dragged his feet, but he did as he was told.

'Get in,' John said.

Mick opened the door and slid into the passenger seat. 'I don't know nothing about no stolen car, man, I swear to God.'

'You know anything about breaking into a house last Monday?' John said.

Mick swallowed. All the colour drained from his face, but the back of his neck flushed red.

'House?'

'Yeah, David Reid's house.'

Mick looked away. 'I dunno. I—'

'Sure you do. You and Sharpie, is it?' John lit a cigarette and offered Mick one; he noticed the kid's hand trembled violently when he took it. 'Look, Mick, from what I hear you're not a bad lad, but you've got to help me out here.'

'I can't,' Mick mumbled, so softly that John almost didn't hear him.

'Why, 'cause of your boss? We know Big ol' Jack sent you in there. The question is, why?'

Mick raised his head and stared at John in amazement. 'How…?'

'You were seen.'

Mick nodded softly. He said nothing for a while, but John could almost hear the cogs of his brain whirring. At last he put his hand out and rubbed the dashboard. 'This is a nice car.'

'It is.'

'You do the restore on her?'

'Most of it.'

Mick nodded again, as though he approved of this. 'She fast?'

'Two-litre, what do you think?' John said, but he smiled.

'I bet an Impreza could take her.' Then Mick grabbed the handle of the door and opened it.

'Hey, where you going?' John said. 'I'm talking to you.'

'I can't.'

'Hey, kid, I want to know why you and your brother were there. Either you talk to me or I talk to Jack. What's it gonna be?'

Mick patted the car once more. He smiled at John, then, with such breathtaking sadness that John got a start, he said, 'Nice job. I gotta go and grab my lunch.'

'Hey—'

Mick closed the door and walked away, his steps no longer hurried, his shoulders hunched against the world.

Robbie, who had watched the exchange with interest from the gate of the yard, slipped back inside, a bad feeling growing in the pit of his stomach.

*

Mick leaned against the wall and lit a cigarette. His earlier calm had passed, and his hands were shaking uncontrollably again. After lunch he had left the garage early, claiming, truthfully, that he was feeling sick. Big Jack had gone to the club and Robbie had let Mick go, barely acknowledging him. Mick had got changed and left, feeling like a dead man walking.

He was out in his back garden. He had just finished telling Sharpie all about the visit from the two detectives.

'I don't fuckin' like it, I don't like it.' Sharpie paced up and down the garden, a cigarette jammed into his mouth. 'Fuck, how do they know we robbed that fuckin' gaff?'

He swore and kept pacing. Private detectives? Was it a trick? Did these detectives know they had robbed that guy's house? Did they know about Bo? What the fuck had led them to the fucking garage, of all places? 'How the fuck did he know Jack sent you? I don't buy it. You must have told him something.'

'I didn't. I never opened my mouth, but he knows.'

'This fuckin' week, I swear, if it's not one thing it's another.' Sharpie stamped up and down, his mind spinning.

'Big Jack's going to find out about the house,' Mick said, 'he's gonna know I lied, then he's going to fucking kill me. He will, I know it. He'll kill me.'

Sharpie slapped him upside the head. 'He ain't gonna do shit. He ain't gonna touch a hair on your head. He do, he die.'

'Sharpie, this is fucking serious. He's not what you think, he's not some fucking pushover. You think, 'cause of the stupid way he dresses and everything, that he's—'

'He's nothing, he's a fat fuck. I could ice him' – Sharpie clicked his fingers – 'like that, you know it. I could!'

'And when he works out the car was my fault, he's gonna really do a number on me. I'm fucking finished. I'll be found in a fucking bag somewhere. That's if they find me.' Mick sat down and rubbed his head where his brother had slapped him.

'Will you stall it!' Sharpie yelled. His cornrows wobbled and his voice trembled a little. He had never seen Mick acting so weird, so resigned. It was bugging the shit out of him. 'They don't know nothing.'

'I'll be lucky if he does it quick.'

'Jesus! Shut up, will you? You're wrecking me head!' Sharpie paced and smoked furiously. What was going on? He didn't believe in coincidences, and two people turning up asking about this Reid guy was too much coincidence for him.

On the other hand, maybe this was an opportunity. He thought of Big Jack: the way he had slapped him, the way he had tossed him aside like he was nothing… He jerked to a stop and turned to his twin.

'You know what we gotta do? We gotta make a… what the fuck you call it… a pre-empty? Yeah, that's it: a pre-empty strike. Like when they took out Biggy Smalls.'

Mick closed his eyes. An image of the grey pieces of brain showing through the blood and crushed skull made his stomach heave.

'Yeah, that's the way. Like what we did when Bo threatened us. Big Jack's threatening us, right? Fuck that shit. You can come work with me, we can be a fuckin' crew. We'd be unbeatable, for real.' Sharpie flicked his fag-end away and watched as it dropped, hissing, into a puddle of filthy water. 'Yeah, yeah. We gotta start steppin' up. We gotta stop takin' shit, waitin' for the other guy to strike first. We gotta be real.'

Mick groaned. It was bad enough that Big Jack was going to fucking kill them; now Sharpie had obviously taken a tumble straight off the deep end. 'Do you know who Big Jack's brother is? Do you?'

'No.'

'It's Tom Lawson. He's connected.'

'Man, no one's gonna know it's us. I am being proactive.' Sharpie paced away and came back again. 'Look, I got the Gat. We gotta protect ourselves. We under threat, Mick. Don't you see it?'

'No.'

Sharpie ran his hand over his cornrows, a malignant light in his blue eyes. 'We got to step up, Mick, make sure we don't get fucked with. We gotta earn respect. That fucker dissed me, and I'm gonna take him out.'

Mick groaned. This was a nightmare. He felt his stomach flip. 'What are you talking about?' he asked, even though in his heart he already knew the answer.

Sharpie smiled, but his glassy eyes stared into nothing; he was away. 'We take care of Jack. If he's dead, no one can connect us to the house. No one can connect us with Bo 'cept his old man – and, hey, we take out the old man too.'

Mick shook his head.

'What? What you shaking your head at? We can do it, make it look like a robbery or some shit. Hell, he's old, give him a shove down the stairs and the jakes will think he tripped or some shit.'

'You're fucking crazy.' Mick got up unsteadily and walked away. 'Crazy.'

'Shit, we can ice the fuckin' detectives if we have to. Can't no one point the finger if they dead. People like that, they musta got loads of people hatin'. No one would even think of us.' Sharpie made his right hand into a gun and said, 'Pow. Yeah, Mick, we got options, bro, we got game. Hey, where you goin'?'

'I don't want to do this no more,' Mick said softly. He went inside and closed the door on his brother.

# 26

Clive swung his golf club like he was chopping down a tree. He missed, and a divot of mud and grass flew into the air.

'Ohhh!' Max cat-called in mock horror. He was thrashing them and in tremendous spirits. 'He shoots, he scores! Shame that the actual aim is to hit that spherical white ball.'

Clive swore under his breath. This was the first game they had played together since the funeral. Both Max and Clive had come straight from work, and of course Larry could play whenever it suited him. It was a beautiful evening and the course was immaculate; it should have been a pleasurable game. But from the first hole it had been a disaster. It felt wrong, just the three of them. David's absence was like a great unmentioned albatross hovering over their heads.

Clive flattened down the ground and teed up again. This time he connected with the ball but sliced it into the rough.

'Not having your best game today, are you?' Larry took his glasses off and wiped them on his hanky. 'Wedding jitters?'

'No.' Clive pulled his tee out of the damp ground and stuffed it into his pocket. 'I don't know. It's everything.'

Larry cocked his head to the side. 'Such as?'

'Those detectives, for one, coming to the office asking questions like that – it's very off-putting. And then that stupid row with Sylvia…'

'She'll get over it,' Larry said kindly. 'Don't worry. This time next week you'll be married, and she won't even remember you ever exchanged a single cross word.'

'Mew-fucking-mew!' Max scoffed. 'What the fuck is this, a sewing circle? Come on, let's play some golf. Fucking women, they're more trouble than they're worth. Can't live with them, can't bury them at the bottom of the garden.'

Clive watched as Max swung his bag onto his back and strode off across the green. 'Remind me why it is we're friends with him again.'

'I don't know,' Larry said. 'Honest to God, I really don't.'

'How does he do it? How does he act like nothing's happened?' Clive said bitterly.

'Clive, come on.'

'I can't eat. I can't sleep.' Clive shook his head miserably. 'Sylvia keeps asking what's wrong with me.'

'Does she?' Larry glanced at him. 'And?'

'And what can I say? It's not like I can talk to her about it. Hasn't Dee said anything to you?'

'I don't think she's noticed.'

'Then you're clearly doing a better job of keeping shit together than I am. I can't seem to get that night out of my head. I see her, you know? I see her when I'm asleep. It's like… it's like she's waiting for me.'

'Jesus, Clive, don't talk like that. We agreed we wouldn't talk about that.'

'You know something?' Clive closed his eyes. 'I miss David.'

'Me too.' Larry placed his slender hand on his friend's arm. 'Everything will be okay, Clive. Just think: soon you'll be married and heading off on your honeymoon. Maybe a week or two in the sun will help you, I don't know, relax a little. You've been really burning up the hours lately.'

'I keep thinking about him. You know, he was so chuffed to be asked to be my best man. What the fuck happened to him, Larry?'

'I don't know. He was drunk, he fell.'

'Do you believe that? I keep thinking about it. And now his car is missing and shit. What if he had a fight with—'

'It was an accident, Clive.'

'But he was so angry. And you know David – he was so unpredictable sometimes, and Lawson—'

'Clive, stop. You're driving yourself crazy.'

Clive smiled at him then, and it was a smile of heartbreaking sadness. 'I really miss him.'

'Hey, ladies! Stop kissing and let's go,' Max roared from across the fairway. 'It's going to get too dark for me to whip you both.'

Larry and Clive grabbed their bags and began to walk.

'Sometimes I want to kick Max straight in the nuts, do you know that?' Clive said. 'At least when David was here, Max kept his fat mouth shut some of the time.'

'Only because David was too sharp for him. He didn't like being made to look a fool.' Larry pushed his glasses up his nose. 'Clive, if it weren't for the fact that he outweighs me by a hundred pounds, I'd kick the living daylights out of Max seven days a week, maybe twice on Sundays.'

Clive laughed. He looked fondly at his friend. 'Thanks for listening.'

'No problem.'

Larry smiled at him and patted him on the shoulder. 'We stick together, Clive, and everything will be all right. You'll see, we'll get through this.'

\*

Max, of course, whipped their arses. Later that evening, as he leaned against the bar of Davy Byrne's, gloating, Clive again swallowed his amazement that they even tolerated his company. And, worse still, now they were bound to him. He was even wearing Larry down at this stage.

Clive noticed that Larry seemed to be doing his level best to drink himself into a stupor.

By closing time, Clive discovered he had succeeded where Larry had failed. He was too drunk to drive his own car home, and he seemed to be experiencing some difficulty with gravity.

'You sure you don't want to come with me?' Larry said anxiously, holding him upright. 'I'm getting a lift with Murray. You can sleep it off at my house.' Murray was one of the bartenders.

'Nah, got work in the morning. I'll grab a taxi on the Green.' Clive leaned against him. 'Gotta make tracks, gotta make sure the little woman doesn't get any more pissed with me.'

'Fuck 'em,' Max said, stumbling over his own golf bag and almost landing on his snot. A passing gang of teenagers laughed at him, but moved on quickly when Max fixed them with a belligerent eye. 'That's what Atlee says.'

'What are you? His biggest fan?' Clive said, blinking furiously. One Max was bad enough; seeing two was making him sick. 'Atlee, Atlee, Atlee. You should marry him.'

Max glared, but he was too drunk to think of a snappy rejoinder. 'Screw this, I'm going home.'

'Bye, Max,' Larry said, relieved. Over the last hour, Max had been gradually becoming drunker and louder. It was a wonder they hadn't been asked to leave the pub.

Max waved over his shoulder with two fingers and staggered off into the night, his golf bag banging against his buttocks.

'You sure you're going to be okay?' Larry said, gripping Clive's shoulders to steady him.

Clive grinned. 'Yeah.'

'All right, then.' Larry let go. 'You can leave the clubs with me if you want.'

'Sure thing.' Clive looked at the bag by his feet and nodded. 'Do you think I'll be happy?'

Larry patted him on the cheek. 'Sure I do.'

'You're happy, right?'

'Sure.'

'David was happy.'

'Clive—'

'You're a good pal, Larry.'

'Yeah, yeah. Go on and get some sleep. Mind how you go.'

Larry watched as Clive wandered off down Duke Street, his hands buried deep in his pockets, singing softly under his breath. Larry waited for him to make it around the corner onto Grafton Street before he glanced at his watch. It was almost eleven. Dee would have gone to bed by now.

He picked up Clive's clubs and carried them back into the bar. Might as well have another. What the hell had he to go home to?

Happy... yeah, he was ecstatic.

*

Clive made it home in one piece and found the house in darkness. His initial drunken hope wore off when he realised Sylvia wasn't there. She was most likely over at her mother and the judge's house, sleeping in the shrine-like pink bedroom that they refused to alter. It was her escape route, held in suspended animation in case she should ever want it.

Clive poured himself a brandy and slumped down on the leather couch in the living room, the light from the hall the only illumination.

Man, he was tired. He rubbed his face and took a sip of his drink. Sylvia must still be seriously pissed off. Maybe he shouldn't have gone out with the lads, but fuck it, he needed some kind of release. He was under so much pressure lately. Didn't he deserve an evening to himself? Was this what marriage was going to be like? Having to explain every goddamned need?

Feeling angry and put-upon, he took another sip and set the glass on the floor. He threw his feet up on the couch and lay down, planning to rest his eyes just for a minute or two. Seconds later, Clive was asleep.

\*

Clive was standing in the middle of the car park at Johnny Fox's pub. He could see the lights of Dublin city twinkling in the valley below and smell the pine trees that surrounded him. His feet were bare and the gravel was cold.

Max and Larry were there, and David was too. Max and David were sitting on upturned beer barrels, playing chess on a trestle table. Larry was cleaning his glasses and doing his best not to laugh. Max was complaining.

'I don't like this fucking game. I told you that.'

'That's because it requires you to think.'

'Hey!'

David laughed, his handsome face lit up by the soft lights coming from the bar. He wore his favourite Hugo Boss suit and a shirt open at the throat. Clive wanted to run and throw his arms around him, but he couldn't lift his feet.

'David?'

'Hey, Clive. How goes it?'

'Good. I thought you were dead.'

'I am.'

'He is, you idiot. Look at his hands,' Max said, grumpily glaring at the board, his eyebrows knotted in confusion.

Clive looked at David's hands. They were grey and bloated, and the skin over his knuckles was shiny and had split in places.

'Jesus, David, does that hurt?'

'No, not any more.' David waited for Max to make a move, cheerfully whistling 'Anything You Can Do, I Can Do Better'.

'Stop that!' Max snapped.

Larry sighed. 'I'm going in to get another drink. Anyone want one?'

'Get me a Jameson,' Max said. 'No ice.'

'You know you shouldn't drink whiskey. Makes you a bigger jackass than you already are.'

'Hey, man, I want your advice, I can always beat it out of you.'

Larry sighed. 'Clive?'

Clive shook his head. Larry patted David on the shoulder. 'Sorry, old boy.' He walked off into the darkness. Clive noticed he was limping.

David rapped the trestle table. 'Are you ever going to move, lover boy? 'Cause I'd like to finish whupping your ass sometime this century.'

'Shut up.' Max grabbed his knight and moved it.

'Beautiful,' David said, and snatched it away with a tap from his queen. A fingernail fell off his hand and skittered across the board; he flicked it away absentmindedly.

'How are the wedding plans going?' he asked.

'Not so good, really. Me and Syl had a fight.'

'Oh?'

'Yeah, well, you know. It hasn't been easy. Not since…not since that night.'

'No, I can't imagine it has been.'

'David?'

'Yes?'

But Clive couldn't think of anything to say. He wanted to ask David if he missed them, if it had hurt when he drowned, but they seemed like stupid questions. David and Max continued to play, and in the distance Clive could hear a strange high-pitched sound that made the skin on his arms and neck prickle. He cocked his head. Was it getting louder?

'What is that? Can you hear it?'

Max carried on staring at the board as though he hadn't spoken, but David raised his head and smiled sadly. 'It's her.'

'Her?'

'You know.'

'What?'

'She's coming. It's too late now.'

'She? I don't know what you're talking about. I don't know anything. I was asleep, I swear,' Clive said, panicking. But he knew; he knew. 'David, please, I've got to hide, you've got to help me.'

'I can't, I'm stuck here. Don't you see?'

Clive looked fearfully over his shoulder. The sound was coming closer. The air was filled with sound, crackling, shrieking cries filled with horror and pain.

'David!'

'I'm sorry, I can't help you.'

Clive screamed. His bladder gave and he wanted to run, but his feet were rooted to the spot. David was disintegrating before his eyes. His skin was sloughing off in weeping, blistering chunks, and his gums had drawn back from his teeth. His shirt was covered in moss-stains and leaves, the skin on his hands had split open and fluid began to trickle from the wounds.

'David, what does she want?'

'Hey,' Max said, 'you're dripping shit all over the board.'

'Sorry,' David said. It was true: a puddle of fetid water was beginning to form where it dripped steadily from his sleeves. He shook his arms out, but more water appeared. Some of it slashed onto Max's cheek, and he wiped it off disgustedly. It left a huge smear.

The air around them grew thicker, the sound louder, and a smell began to rise from the ground – or was it coming from above? Clive gagged. He tried to back away, but to where? He bent forward and retched, but nothing came out.

When he straightened up, the car park was gone. He stood in a clearing in a dark and terrifying forest. The sound came from all around him. The air was rent with howls of such bone-chilling agony that he almost collapsed to his knees.

'David!'

But they were gone. Clive began to cry.

'David!'

Behind him; whatever it was, it was behind him. He couldn't move. The smell intensified, the air becoming so thick and viscous that he could no longer breathe.

'Please…'

The thing laughed. It was a thick, guttural sound, filled with rotting leaves and thick clay, a sound of hatred, utterly devoid of mercy. The air around Clive vibrated with intensity.

David was correct, of course. He knew; he knew who it was.

'Oh, Jesus, I'm sorry. It wasn't my fault. Please, you must believe me.'

'Turn around.'

Clive closed his eyes tight, squeezing them shut as he had when he was a child and terrified of the bogeyman. He shook so hard his teeth chattered in his head. He wept and clasped his hands together.

'Please. What could I do?'

A hand gripped him by the shoulder, lifting him up and turning his body with enormous strength. Clive smelled earth and something else, something putrid. He sobbed, his fear so great that he was beginning to hyperventilate.

Don't look at her, don't look.

But his eyes opened unbidden. Her eyes were black pools, no pupils, no colour. Her once-beautiful hair now hung limp and flat against her skull. He moaned when he saw the injuries, the rip over her eye where she had hit the radiator, the terrible bruising around her throat. The bloody tear on her upper lip where a drunken Max had bitten her as she struggled to get away.

She opened her mouth, and her swollen tongue lay black and rotted against her smashed teeth.

'Don't you want to kiss me?'

She jerked him towards her, and the tongue wiggled like a bloated eel. Clive screamed and struck out—

\*

'Jesus Christ!' Sylvia leapt back so fast she fell over onto her backside. 'Clive, wake up!'

'What? What?' Clive struggled to sit up, confused, disorientated, gasping for air.

'It's me, Clive. You were screaming. I came home and you were screaming in your sleep,' Sylvia said, her voice high and scared. She still wore her red coat and suede boots. Her handbag lay by her side and her face was white as a sheet.

Clive sat up and rubbed his face. 'Oh, Jesus.'

'Clive, what is it?' Sylvia regained some of her composure. She grabbed his knees and squeezed them. 'My God, darling, what is it? I could hear you outside. I thought you were being murdered—'

'I saw...I saw...'

'What? What? You can talk to me. What is it?'

But what could he say, what could he tell her? That they had murdered a girl, that Jack Lawson had buried her broken body in a ditch in the middle of the Wicklow Mountains? That the man with whom Sylvia was about to walk down the aisle had watched as his so-called friend forced the battered slip of a thing into a golf bag? That his feeble protestations had been just that – that he had, in fact, been slightly turned on by her cries, her powerlessness? That he had stood by and done nothing?

'I saw David. He was dead.'

'Oh, baby. You poor thing.'

Clive lifted his head and noticed for the first time the big terracotta plant pot. Sylvia had obviously carried it in from the garden as a weapon with which to save him. He started to laugh, but somehow the laughter gave way to tears. Despite a gallant effort to stem the tide, Clive began to weep openly.

Sylvia cradled him in her arms and held him until his anguish slowly subsided.

'I'm sorry,' he said, 'so sorry.'

Sylvia thought he was talking about the fight and the tears, and she squeezed him even tighter. 'All right, sweetheart,' she murmured, 'it's all right. Everything's going to be all right.'

# 27

That Friday, while a quiet and sombre Sarah worked her way through David Reid's financial records and learned what she could about Jack Lawson, John Quigley read, with growing disbelief, the extent of Brendan Whelan's injuries.

Ellen Savage – assistant coroner, close friend of Steve Magher and seriously good pool player – folded her arms across her chest and leaned against the wall of the corridor outside the morgue, looking a little pensive. She shouldn't really have been sharing personal information with John, as he was no relation to the deceased, but Steve had vouched for him and that made him okay in her book, even if what she was doing wasn't kosher. Besides, she admitted to herself, she fancied the arse off John, had ever the first time she had met him, the year before – not that he ever noticed her subtle come-ons, she thought with a sigh.

John winced as he scanned the sheet. 'Jesus Christ. Contusions, broken teeth, shattered cheekbone, cranial fractures...' He looked up. 'It's almost like he had his head kicked in.'

'I told you. Bullets look clean, but they do a phenomenal amount of internal damage while they whiz about looking for an exit. And it's on the increase. We're seeing more and more bloody messes like this.

'You reckon he was shot at close range.'

'No doubt about it. At a guess, I'd say fifteen feet max. The bullet nicked his index finger and struck him at a slight upward angle.'

'Upward? You think he was shot by someone smaller than himself?'

Ellen shrugged. 'I can't say. It could have been the angle at which the gun was held, or the shooter may have fallen.'

'Fallen?'

'I don't think the vic put up much of a struggle, but there are one or two marks that might indicate he had a physical encounter before he was shot. If we're lucky, we'll be able to get skin samples from under his nails, but this isn't like *CSI* on television, John, you know. It takes time to collect evidence and piece things together.'

'But he was definitely moved after death?'

'No doubt about that part.'

John finished reading and handed the report back to Ellen. He had tried to memorise it. He knew he'd be grilled about it when he got back to the office. Sarah was taking this hard: she blamed herself for putting the squeeze on the father.

'Poor fucking guy. Who would shoot an unarmed man in the face?'

'If only they could see the results,' Ellen said with a shake of her head. 'You should see this place on a Monday morning. People are animals, fucking animals.'

John offered his thanks and left, his head buzzing. Whoever had killed Bo had to have transport. Mick Quinn had access to cars; he worked in a garage, after all. And moving a body was a risky business. Whoever had killed Bo had done it somewhere where he was certain he wouldn't be watched or disturbed.

He thought about David Reid again. Was there any connection between the two deaths? John rubbed his head. He was starting to think of David Reid as a ghost, standing over their shoulders, shaking his head at how inept they were.

*

As John said goodbye to Ellen, Sarah waited irritably for Arthur Ward, assistant manager at AIB, to return to his office.

The office was overly hot, and Sarah yawned. She hadn't really slept much the night before. She had lain in her old bed, watching the lights from the cars on the road move over the ceiling, thinking about the case, her mother and her life.

Sarah yawned again. Where the hell was this guy? If he didn't come back soon, she was going to stretch out on the floor and take a nap.

'Miss Kenny?'

Sarah turned as the door opened and Ward and another man entered the office. 'This is our branch manager, Fergal Shaw.'

'Hello.'

'Good morning.' Fergal Shaw was a small, compact man with a high forehead and anxious eyes. 'Arthur informs me you are investigating a client of ours?'

'That's right,' Sarah said. 'I explained all of this on the phone earlier.'

'This is very irregular.' Shaw spoke with the self-importance of all little men in positions of power, big fish in small ponds. 'It is not our policy to discuss—'

'You spoke with my client and his solicitor?'

Shaw frowned, clearly unused to being interrupted. 'Well, yes.'

'And you know my client is named executor of your client's estate?'

'Yes, but—'

'But nothing. I work for James Reid, and he would like a complete history of his brother's banking for the last three months. You were authorised to give it to me, weren't you?'

Fergal Shaw's lips pulled into a thin, bloodless line. 'Yes.'

'Well, then, what else is there to talk about?' Sarah said, suddenly tired of the little man and his attitude.

'It could take a while to organise.'

'I'll wait.'

He smiled tightly and bustled back out of the office, Ward trotting in his wake.

Sarah settled back in her chair. A few minutes later, just as she was starting to yawn again, her mobile rang.

'Hey.'

'Hey, John. What have you got?'

'Bo was probably killed on Tuesday evening.'

Sarah closed her eyes and took a deep breath. 'That's the same day we put pressure on his father. Same day Brendan heard him talking to Sharpie Quinn. How did it happen?'

John hesitated, and Sarah sat up straighter. 'John, how was he killed?'

'He was shot in the face.'

'Oh, my God.'

'Hey, Sarah, it's got nothing to do with us. This guy was a fence and a thief, he met with a sticky end, it has bugger all to do with you. Okay? We don't even know who did it.'

'I know,' Sarah said. But she was thinking about Brendan Whelan's face. She was thinking of how defeated he had looked when Bo had attacked her, how powerless he had been. 'I think we shoud talk to Detective Stafford about this.'

'For what? What has Bo's death got to do with our case?'

'What if it has? The Quinns were planning on selling the stolen gear on to him. Maybe Jack—'

'We don't know the Quinns had anything to do with Bo's death. And I don't see why we should give anything to Stafford just yet. All we have is guesswork and speculation. We don't have anything to tie the Quinns to David Reid's death, any more than we can tie them to Bo's death. It's a big fucking jump from passing on stolen gear to shooting someone, Sarah.'

'Sharpie Quinn has plenty of history of violence.'

'Mick Quinn hasn't.'

Sarah didn't say anything.

'Look, let me talk to him again. He's only a kid. Maybe if he thinks he's going inside, he'll open up, tell me what's going on.'

Sarah closed her eyes. 'All right, but I don't like it. That guy Stafford made it his business to come to the office and remind us we were operating on his case. He won't like being kept out of the loop.'

'Soon as we have anything concrete, we can fill him in.'

Ten minutes later, Ward came back in with a handful of paper.

'Where's your boss?' Sarah asked.

'He didn't think you needed him for this. I can explain everything to you.'

'See, that wasn't so hard, now was it?' Sarah smiled, but it was a cold, hard parody of a smile that made Ward slightly nervous.

# 28

Big Jack shook hands with the two gardaí who stood in the middle of his garage. He nodded at what they said and gave them his card with all his telephone numbers, his face a perfect mask of concern and bewilderment. But as soon as the two detectives left, that expression was replaced by one of pure rage.

His nephew Billy – who had arrived only minutes before the gardaí, and who had been shitting it in case the two detectives took a closer look at the Ford he was driving – watched in amazement as Big Jack kicked a toolbox with such ferocity that the sixty-pound metal box flew halfway across the yard.

'Billy! Come with me.'

Big Jack ran up the stairs as fast as his bulk would let him. Startled, Billy glanced at Robbie, but Robbie only shrugged. He had no idea what was going on.

'Mick didn't show up today, and now I bet I know why! Those fucking eejits.' Big Jack ground his teeth together and fetched the bottle of Jameson's from his desk drawer. He poured himself a large one and offered a glass to Billy, who shook his head.

'What's going on? What did the police want?'

'They want to talk to Mick. They want to talk to him about some cunt who got himself shot.'

'Shot?'

'Aye, shot. A fucking fence. Found dumped in the Dublin Mountains. Reckon he was shot Tuesday.'

'A fence? Sure, God knows what type of wee dirtbird he was, or who he mixed with.' Billy sat down. 'But Mick, he's a soft wee cunt. I can't imagine him shooting no one.'

Big Jack's brain was whirring. The bruises on Mick's face, the Fiat burned out in Templeogue, Sharpie's newfound cocky attitude... He had to force himself to breathe normally. Shit: the Fiat. He had known Mick was lying to him, but never in his wildest imagination would he have guessed that it was about something like this.

Big Jack sighed. 'I gave Mick a job here because I knew his old lad, back in the day. I tried to give him a trade, keep him off the streets. I can't believe he'd be involved in anything like that. Mick's a grand young lad. But that fucker Sharpie, I wouldn't put nothing past him.' Jack jabbed his finger towards Billy. 'He's the one we need to be looking at. Cocky wee fucker, thinks he's a hard man, thinks he's one of them fellas in them gangs in America.'

Billy swallowed. The more Jack spoke, the more he looked like he wanted to pick up the desk and break it into a thousand pieces with his bare hands.

'Jack, calm down—'

'I knew there was something fucking funny about them two detectives coming here, looking for David Reid's car. How do I know they were looking for a car? A fence... Fuck.'

Billy frowned. He wasn't sure what Big Jack was talking about. 'Detectives?'

But Jack waved him silent. He eased his body slowly back in the chair and rested his head in his hands. He tried to think.

Big Jack didn't believe in coincidences. Private detectives asking about David Reid, a dead fence, and now the cops at his door looking for a nowhere-to-be-seen Mick. That little quisling Mick and his brother had taken the Fiat, Jack was sure of it. They had taken his fucking car. He couldn't believe the audacity of it.

Billy looked at his watch. He had been on the road half the day already. He was tired and he needed a shower. 'Jack, I—'

'Shut up.' Jack snapped forward in his chair. He should have known those detectives the other day weren't kosher. Maybe even David Reid's fucking friends were up to something. He grabbed the phone, pulled a phonebook out of his desk drawer and flicked through it rapidly, muttering under his breath.

Billy sighed and lit a cigarette.

'Aha!' Big Jack slapped the book down, put his finger under a number and began to dial.

'Ah, hello there, I'm looking for Larry Cole. He about? … No? Can you give me his number? It's a private matter… All right, then. Have you a pen handy?' Big Jack rattled off his number. 'Aye, that's right. Tell him to call Big Jack – and tell him it's urgent, and tell him to make sure he rings… Oh aye, urgent as hell. Good lass.'

He hung up and settled back in his chair, his massive face now devoid of any emotion at all. He would find out what was going on, he would find out if those detectives were after him, and then he would find out what Mick was up to, even if he had to beat the living shit out of him.

Two minutes later, a stuttering Larry Cole called back. Big Jack fired one question after another at him, his face becoming more terrible as each answer added to his fury.

'You listen to me, you wee cunt, you,' he roared finally, 'and you listen good. I don't give a fuck who asks who what. You don't, I said you don't fucking worry about that! You worry about getting me my fucking money. I had nothing to do with David's dying like that, and if any of you so much as breathes my name to any cunt or even thinks of it, I'm telling you on my mother's grave, God rest her soul, I will kill every last fucking one of you. We clear?'

He slammed the phone down with such ferocity that Billy jumped.

'Billy?'

'Yes?'

Big Jack didn't want to do it, not like this. He liked Mick.

But what choice did he have? Mick had lied to him and, in doing so, he had left Big Jack vulnerable. He sighed.

'I've got a job for you.'

*

Rose Quinn was not happy. She wrapped her bright-pink towelling gown tighter over her massive breasts and clamped down harder on her fag. She looked at the two plainclothes gardaí standing on her doorstep as if she might rip their heads off and use them for bowling. They were the second lot of gardaí that had called to her door that day, and her patience was wearing thin. At least the first crowd had left rapidly, leaving cards and firm demands that the boys get in touch ASAP. These two weren't budging, and she had a feeling they weren't going to go without what they had come for.

'Get out of it! What are you sayin'?'

'We just need to talk to them.'

'Is there no one else in this fuckin' estate you lot can call to?'

'Look, Mrs Quinn,' said the big, dark-haired detective. 'It would be better if the boys came in voluntarily—'

'I'm tellin' you the same thing I told the other cops earlier: they're not here. They're gone out. Are you stone-deaf or what?'

The detective's smile was becoming very strained. 'No, they're not gone out. Come on, now.'

'I don't know where they are.'

'Look, it's a very serious offence, lying to the gardaí,' the fat, sandy-haired one said angrily. 'You know you can be done for it.'

'You watch that tone. I know my rights.' Rose flexed her massive arm against the door, and the dark-haired detective took a hasty step backwards.

'You listen to me. You don't let us talk to them now, we'll be back with a warrant to search these premises—'

'You what?'

'A warrant, and if I have to—'

'A warrant? For what?'

'—I'll tear this place apart. You following me now?'

'Oh, that's right: threaten a poor woman, a single mother, a hard-workin', decent woman. Threaten her with tearin' up her Corporation house, that's right.'

'Look, Mrs Quinn, we—'

'Morning and night, I work. Look at me hands, scrubbed raw, they are. Is this what I work for, to be harassed in my own home?'

'We're not trying to harass you,' the dark-haired one said in exasperation. 'We only want to talk to them!'

Rose was a fast thinker, and at that moment she was thinking about the red silk bedcover Sharpie had given her. It lay draped across her bed upstairs, the first thing two detectives with a warrant might notice. They might also notice the DVD recorder he had given her the previous month, and various other gifts she had received from her generous son over the years.

A car pulled up outside next door's gate, and Rose spied her neighbour gawking at her through the windshield. Shit, she thought. Old Mrs Lynch, the biggest mouthpiece on the street, was in the passenger seat, her new perm and rinse making her look like a blue sheep.

That decided it. Rose opened the door wider and jerked her head at the two gardaí.

'You'd better come in. I'll go see if maybe they came home without my noticing.'

The two men, looking slightly bewildered, followed her into the small, cluttered living room. Rose didn't offer them seats, so they stood in the middle of the small room like two sycamores, their arms pressed by their sides in case they knocked something over. The air reeked of stale smoke. An ashtray filled to overflowing rested on the arm of the sofa. Judging from the deep indentation in the cushion, Rose Quinn spent a great deal of time there.

'You wait here, I'll see if they're in.' Rose turned on her heel and disappeared out the door.

'Jesus fucking Christ,' the fat one said.

The dark-haired one rolled his eyes and ducked back out into the hall. He caught a glimpse of Rose Quinn's huge arse disappearing up the stairs. He came back inside. 'Right, we get them and get out of here.'

'Suits me.'

'Don't answer any questions, just get them into the car.'

*

Sharpie was up and dressed and looking out the window. Mick was awake too, but he was sitting on the side of his bed, still in his boxer shorts. Rose did a double take when she saw him; she had never noticed how thin he was before. Normally he never let her see him without his clothes. You could have played the xylophone on his ribs, and the bones in his shoulders protruded clearly.

'Who is it?' he asked.

'Cops.'

'Again? Shit, for real?' Sharpie whispered. 'Where? I didn't see them go.'

'They're downstairs.'

'What?' He reeled away from the window and stared at his mother in amazement. Mick groaned and dropped his head in his hands.

'Get rid of them,' Sharpie said.

'I will not. They said they'll come back with a warrant. I'm not havin' my home tore up. What the hell have yous been up to, you little shites? And no bullshit. Why are the cops at my door talkin' about warrants?'

Sharpie took a drag from his cigarette and blew a smoke ring. 'It's nothing. It's a mistake, is all.'

'What is? What are they here for?'

'Nothing. How the fuck should I know what the bleedin' cops are on about? Will you get off my case? I can't fuckin' believe you let 'em in here.' He was so rattled that he completely forgot his hood vernacular.

Rose narrowed her eyes. 'Mick?'

Mick didn't look at her, just shrugged his thin shoulders. 'Dunno.'

'Well, you better get your arses downstairs. I'm not havin' that lot tearin' the house apart lookin' for yous two, so whatever the fuck yous got yourselves into, yous had better get yourselves out of it.'

Rose stuck her cigarette back into her mouth, went out and closed the door with a bang.

Mick slid down off the bed and sat as still as a statue. His squeezed his eyes shut and rested his head against his knees. He was having trouble breathing. It felt like the walls were closing in on him. 'Sharpie, what—'

'Shhh.'

Sharpie crossed the floor and glanced out onto the landing. His mother was still there, no doubt waiting for them to start talking.

'What?' he demanded.

'You get it sorted, whatever you've done.' She tossed her head back and made her way down the stairs, a plume of smoke trailing over her shoulder. 'They're coming,' he heard her say. 'You wait in there, now.'

Sharpie shut the door and turned to his brother. 'We've got to get the fuck out of here.'

'And go where?' Mick said miserably.

'I dunno, somewhere, least until this shit blows over.'

Mick lifted his head and stared at his twin in disbelief. 'It's not gonna blow fucking over.'

'Keep your voice down.'

'You fucking killed a man – we fucking killed him. You heard the news last night, same as me: they found him, they found Bo. Now the cops are here. What you think they're here for?'

'They don't know shit. They can't prove shit.'

'They must know something, or else why would they be here at the fucking house?'

'You heard Ma: they want to talk about some car. Shit, that could be anything.' Sharpie's eyes skittered furiously. He was getting a headache and he was starting to feel cornered. 'Look, if it was that serious they'd have arrested us, come with a warrant, right? They don't know we did shit; they can't.'

But he was thinking of the detectives who had called to the garage the day before. This could be a trick, the cops could know something. Maybe burning the car hadn't got rid of everything...

He pulled his bed aside, pried up a loose floorboard and retrieved the Glock.

'Come on, Mick. We're goin' out the back window.'

'What?'

'Get dressed, quick. We can go out through Ma's window, drop onto the grass. It's not that big of a drop.'

'Big enough to break your ankles.'

'Nah, come on.'

Mick looked at his brother's sparkling, demented eyes, the twitchy jaw, and suddenly he felt tired. He knew, with certainty, that he would always be in the shit with Sharpie. He would always be in some situation or other, he would always be trying to get them out of scrapes, always trying to keep Sharpie from fucking up big-time. It was relentless, it was exhausting, he was seventeen years old and he felt like a hundred.

'Sharpie, I don't want to go nowhere.'

Sharpie tucked the gun into the waistband of his enormous jeans. He looked at Mick as though he had suddenly started talking in German. 'Mick, come on.'

'I don't want to go nowhere. Do you not see? We're just gonna get in more shite. I'm so fucking tired. I haven't slept in days. What's the point of going out the window, anyway? Where are we gonna go? We don't have any money, we don't have a car, we don't have nothing.'

'Mick, we gotta split. Stop talkin' fuckin' stupid.'

'I'm not going.'

'Mick—'

'No.'

Sharpie darted across the room and grabbed him by the arms, trying to haul him to his feet. 'You've gotta come. I can't go on me own.'

Mick shook his head and wrenched his arms free. 'I'm not going. You go if you want. I won't tell them nothing, but I'm not going.'

Sharpie started to get angry. He jumped up and walked in a circle. 'Ah, fuck, Mick, this is no time to go fuckin' gaga on me. We gotta get out of here.'

'I'm not going.'

Sharpie kicked him. 'Get up.'

'No.'

Sharpie kicked him again, harder this time. 'Get up.'

Mick winced but refused to budge. 'What's the point?'

Sharpie, becoming more and more agitated, booted him again. 'Get up!'

'You can keep kicking me all you bleedin' want, I'm not going.'

Sharpie went to kick him once more, but he pulled it at the last second when Mick closed his eyes, waiting for the blow. Sharpie knew then: it was futile. His shoulders slumped.

'Mick, please. Don't do this, don't do this to me.'

Mick lifted his head. 'I'm sorry, Sharpie. I'm not gonna go nowhere. But I swear I won't tell 'em nothin'. I can promise you that.'

'Yo, fuck you, homie – fuck you for real,' Sharpie said, almost tearfully. He clamped his black beanie hat over his cornrows and grabbed his denim jacket from the end of the bed. 'I'm gettin' the fuck out of here. I ain't takin' no chances.'

And then he left. Ten minutes later he was crisscrossing the gardens in a neighbouring street, his head bursting with noise as he struggled to understand his brother's betrayal.

\*

Mick got dressed slowly and made his way downstairs. He pushed open the sitting room door. 'I'm—'

He froze when he found himself staring up into the flat eyes of Billy, Big Jack's lunatic nephew. He tried to back away, but Billy raced into the hall, grabbed him and yanked him forward so hard he fell.

'Boy,' Billy hissed softly, 'keep it fucking shut or I'll kill that fat old cunt, you hear me?'

Mick nodded.

'Where's the other one?'

'He's not here.'

The other 'detective' pushed past them and raced up the stairs. He came back a minute later, pink and furious. 'Gone.'

'I said you should have stayed in the hall,' Billy snapped. 'Of course he's fucking gone.'

The fat one flushed. 'It's not my fault.'

'Where'd he go?' Billy said, giving Mick a dig between the shoulder blades.

'Hey, get your fuckin' hands off my boy,' Rose said, stepping into the hall. Her anger towards cops was greater than her apathy towards Mick.

Mick shook his head, feeling very small between them all. 'I dunno where he is.'

'Fuck,' Billy said, and Rose frowned.

'Look, we got this one. Let's go. We can pick the other one up later.'

Billy grabbed Mick and sighed. 'Come on.'

'Wait a minute,' Rose said. 'What station are you goin' to?'

'Store Street.'

'And what was—'

'We don't have time for Twenty Questions,' Billy said, half dragging Mick towards the door.

Rose grabbed him by the arm. 'Hold on there. He's only seventeen, you can't just take him in without—'

Billy pinched the back of Mick's arm, so hard the boy whimpered.

'Ma, it's all right – it's all right. Don't worry.'

'Mick, you be all right, son?' Rose said, feeling strangely uneasy.

Surprised, Mick smiled at her. 'Yeah, Ma. Relax. I'll be back later. I didn't do nothing, this is all a big mistake. Don't worry.'

She followed them to the door and watched as they put her son into the back seat of a black Nissan Almera. The sandy-haired one climbed in next to him and they drove off.

# 29

'What have we got?' John asked, shaking brown sauce onto his fry up. They were in Bernie's Café, up the road from QuicK.

Sarah shrugged. 'Dead man, missing car, jumpy friends, a break-in organised by a crooked car dealer, forty grand missing, no concrete evidence of any wrongdoing – just a whole lot of things that don't really add up.'

'Gambling?'

'James says he didn't even do the Lotto.'

'So where did it go, then?'

'That's the forty-grand question right there. It hasn't turned up anywhere, he hasn't bought anything with it that I can see, there haven't been any major purchases except the car, and that was a trade-up – so where's the forty grand gone?' Sarah tied her hair back into a ponytail and stared at the bank printout. 'He ordered it over a week ago; you have to put in an order if you want that much cash. So why cash?'

'He's got to be giving it to someone. Paying someone off.'

'Who?'

'Jack Lawson.'

'Why?'

'I don't know.'

'Blackmail?'

'If it is, it has to be something to do with Juicy Lucy's. I hardly think it has to do with the cars.' John pulled the rind off his rasher and popped it into his mouth.

Sarah shrugged. 'David's mates are all married, or as good as. What if Lawson has them on tape carrying on with his workers or something?'

'I doubt David Reid was carrying on with female strippers.'

'True.' Sarah sighed in annoyance. 'Look, we know Lawson had those kids break in – but what if it wasn't that laptop they were after? What if they were sent to look for the money?'

'Anything is possible – and we're all about the possibilities,' John said with a wink.

Sarah put down the paper and went back to picking at her salad. 'I'm going to go see Brendan Whelan in a while.'

'What?' John frowned. 'Why?'

She shrugged. 'I feel I should go, pay my respects.'

'Sarah, he's not going to want to see you.'

'I'm going anyway.'

John went back to eating his fry, but after a few minutes he put down his knife and fork and looked across the table. 'What are you going to say to him?'

'That I'm sorry for his loss.'

'He'll tell you to get stuffed.'

'Maybe so.'

'You want me to come with you?'

'No, I'll be fine on my own. Maybe you can go see Mick Quinn.'

'I don't mind coming.'

'I don't need you to come.'

And there it was – the brush-off. John nodded and went back to his food. Whenever you thought you were on the same page as Sarah, she shut the book.

\*

Mick was trying to stay calm. 'Look, Billy, what the fuck? I mean, you coming to me gaff? What's going on?'

'Jimmy,' Billy said, 'think I should circle the block?'

'He's long gone.'

'I'll just swing round once.'

They drove slowly back around the estate. As Mick passed his mother's house again, he was surprised to find a lump in his throat.

There was no sign of Sharpie.

'Where'd that other little shit go?' Billy said, glancing at him in the rear-view mirror.

'I dunno. I—'

Jimmy punched him in the ear then, so hard he had almost blacked out. He slipped down sideways and moaned. Jimmy grabbed him by the back of his T-shirt and hauled him upright.

Mick raised his hand to his ear in disbelief.

'I'm going to ask you again,' Billy said. 'This time I'd come up with a better answer.'

'I don't know where he is. He thought you were cops and he legged it. He didn't say where.'

'He got a mobile?'

'Who?'

'Your brother.'

'I – I don't—'

Jimmy hit him again, in the ribs this time. Mick felt a crack, and then an excruciating pain flooded through him, as though he'd been struck by a train. He gagged and would have thrown up, but Jimmy grabbed him by the back of the neck and said, 'You puke, kid, I'll make you fucking eat it.'

Mick concentrated on holding his bile down where it belonged. He had no doubt the guy was serious. He had never been so afraid in all his life.

'Now, does he have a fucking mobile?'

Mick nodded.

'Good. Now you're learning.'

While he struggled for air, Jimmy leaned forward. 'Hey, this fucks up the whole deal. What are we gonna do now?'

Billy pulled out a mobile of his own and dialled a number.

'Howya... Yeah ... Nah, other one done a runner ... Yeah, hold on.' He looked in the rear-view mirror. 'You're sure you don't know where he's heading?'

Mick nodded.

Billy returned to his call. 'Yeah, well, that's the way it happened.' He held the phone away from his ear for a second as whoever was on the other end of the line blew a fit. 'What do you want to do? ... Uh-huh, uh-huh, right ... Yeah, sure. Okay.'

He hung up and threw the phone onto the dashboard.

'Well?' Jimmy asked.

'I tell you, kid, you're one lucky wee cunt.'

Mick held his broken ribs and lifted his eyes to the rear-view mirror. His ear was ringing and he still wasn't convinced he could keep from spewing. He wasn't feeling particularly lucky.

'That was a stay of your execution. Least until we can collar that fucking brother of yours.'

Mick closed his eyes and said a silent prayer. Please, God, keep Sharpie running, don't let him get us killed. Just this once, please, God, let him use his brains.

Jimmy tapped him on the side of the head again. 'Don't look so relieved, kid. Trust me: sometimes getting killed ain't the worst thing that can happen to a fella.'

'Yeah,' Billy said. 'We got a few questions for you, and you are gonna answer straight, boy. You don't, you are gonna wish you were dead.'

*

Sarah drove to Clanbrassil Street. Unsurprisingly, the pawnshop was closed, the metal shutter pulled down over the windows, the shade down behind the door.

Sarah rang the bell and waited, unsure of what to do. Finally, she rang again, keeping her finger on the buzzer long enough to annoy even the most patient of souls. A few moments later she heard a rattling. A woman about her own age, with short brown hair, unlocked the door and looked at her over the chain, a look of irritation firmly in place.

'I'm sorry, we're closed today.'

'Actually, I'm here to see Mr Whelan.'

'I don't think he's really up for visitors. Perhaps if you leave your name I can—'

'I really need to speak with him. Please – it's about his son, Brendan.'

'I see. I'm Mr Whelan's niece, Claire. Can I help you?'

'No.'

Claire's scowl deepened. 'I'm afraid I'm going to have to ask you to leave. My uncle has suffered a very tragic bereavement. His son—'

'Was killed. I know. That's what I'm here to talk to him about.'

'Oh?'

'I'm Sarah Kenny. I'm a detective.'

That threw Claire. She opened the door a little wider, and Sarah took her chance and slipped inside.

'I'm terribly sorry. You should have said. I didn't realise you were with the gardaí.'

'That's okay,' Sarah said, neither confirming nor denying that she was any such thing. 'How is Mr Whelan holding up?'

'He's upstairs, just sitting in Brendan Junior's room – it's terrible, really. To tell you the truth, he's taking it very hard.' Claire leaned forward and grasped Sarah by the arm, her eyes shining with questions. 'Is it true he was shot in the face?'

'Yes, he was,' Sarah said stiffly.

'Tell me, do you know who did it yet? Was it to do with drugs?'

'I don't believe so.'

'Oh, we thought it might be.' Claire looked over her shoulder and lowered her voice. 'Do you have any idea if it was to do with gambling? He was a ferocious gambler. Did you know that?'

'I knew.'

'Any idea who, you know, wanted him out of the picture?'

'Not yet, but I'm following a very definite line of inquiry.'

'Really? That's fantastic.' Claire's eyes gleamed, and her forehead almost touched Sarah's. 'Is it true he was, well, really badly beaten?'

Sarah took a step back. 'Not that I know of, but I'm afraid I can't give any details.'

'Oh, of course.'

'I'm very sorry for your loss. I won't intrude too much. If I could just have a quick chat with Mr Whelan…'

Claire hesitated, unwilling to let her captive go when she still had questions. 'He's probably not going to be able to tell you much. Dad called Dr Burke earlier, and I think he gave him a sedative. He's been very quiet – won't come down, not even for a sandwich.'

'I won't take up a lot of his time, but I do need to speak to him. It is imperative to the case,' Sarah added, somewhat pompously.

But pomp clearly worked: Claire nodded and managed to pull off a genuine look of contrition. 'Of course, Detective. Please follow me.'

Sarah followed Claire behind the counter and through an old-fashioned parlour behind the shop. Elderly people sat in small groups, chatting and holding drinks. They all studied Sarah with open curiosity as she passed.

'Detective,' Claire mouthed.

Sarah nodded to them and hurried along. Jesus, no wonder the poor man didn't want to come downstairs. Sarah had never understood why people felt the need to congregate at the home of the bereaved. It had been the same when her father died: endless rounds of sandwiches, tea, biscuits, beer, whiskey, Jackie and Helen whispering furiously whenever they got a chance, her mother weeping incoherently in the kitchen… That had not been a good time for anyone, least of all Sarah. She had arrived home the day before the funeral, stepping off the ferry exhausted, ill, almost two stone lighter than she was now.

She shuddered, physically shaking off the memory.

They climbed a set of rickety stairs covered with threadbare carpet and arrived on a small landing chock-a-block with dusty furniture and ancient, faded oil paintings. Claire tapped gently on a closed door.

'Uncle Brendan?'

There was no reply from within.

'Uncle B?' She tapped again. 'There's someone here to see you.'

Sarah fidgeted. The air was full of dust and mould. She wanted to crank open a window and take a deep breath.

'Uncle Brendan?'

This time there was a muffled response. Claire smiled over her shoulder at Sarah and reached for the doorknob.

Sarah stayed her hand. 'If you don't mind, I'd like to talk to him alone.'

The smile faded. 'Oh? But he might want family present.'

Sarah held her ground. 'If he does, I'll call you, of course.'

'Suit yourself. I'll be downstairs if you need me.'

Claire straightened her shoulders and tugged at the hem of her suit jacket, offended. She strode off, weaving her way through the furniture and stacks of papers like an angry Clydesdale. Sarah waited for her to turn the corner before she opened the door.

She stepped into a gloomy, rather old-fashioned bedroom. It was full of the same dark furniture that cluttered the hall and was painted a cold robin's-egg blue. There were posters on the walls, two of The Clash and one of Pamela Anderson lying half naked in the surf. The carpet was blue-and-green paisley. It reminded Sarah of the terrible stuff that used to carpet their office.

It took her a second for her eyes to become accustomed to the dark and locate Mr Whelan. He sat in an old armchair by the window. He wore a dark suit and highly polished shoes that looked very dainty on his feet. He was holding a football in his hands, turning it over and over.

'Mr Whelan?'

He lifted his head and stared at her, confused. Gradually that confusion was replaced by recognition, and then by rage. He dropped the ball, heaved himself out of the chair and took a couple of shambling steps towards her, his hand outstretched and trembling.

'You get away from here.'

'I'm very sorry for your loss.'

'Sorry! I don't want your sorry,' he hissed. 'Get away from here.'

'I only want to talk with you.'

'I don't want to talk to you.'

'Please. I'm really sorry – I'm sorry we pushed you, I'm sorry we threatened you. I didn't know any of this would happen.'

'What good is that to me now? My son is dead!' He lunged for her, his hand raised and balled into a fist. 'Will your sorry bring him back?'

Sarah closed her eyes, steeling herself for whatever was coming next. But nothing happened.

'He's dead,' Brendan Whelan said softly, as though the words were still a surprise. He turned away, walked unsteadily back to his chair and sank into it. 'Can you not leave me be? I'll call the gardaí on you. You've no right to be doing this. You've no right to be coming here today, no right!'

Sarah let him rant. Presently he stopped and began to weep, great, wracking, silent sobs. Sarah sank to her knees and put her hand on his arm. He smelled oddly comforting, of Brut and Brylcreem.

'I'm truly very sorry.'

Whelan pulled a hanky from his pocket and dashed at his eyes. 'Do you know what they did to him?'

'I heard.'

'I didn't even recognise him. His face was all shot and swollen. I had to identify him, and at first I couldn't even tell if it was him or not; it didn't look like him.' He took a shuddering breath. Sarah said nothing, knowing there was more to come.

'He was lying there, in that filthy ditch, thrown in there like a piece of rubbish. Just lying there in the grass like a piece of rubbish.' He wiped at the tears with his huge hanky. 'They shot my boy and then they left him there, like…like rubbish.'

Sarah swallowed her own tears and patted his arm. She knew it didn't matter what she said or did. There was no way to comfort this man. Parents were not supposed to bury their children: it was against the natural order of things. All the grief and pain that normally went with the death of a loved one was magnified. She sighed softly. He would probably never get over it.

After a while, she felt Brendan Whelan gain control and pull away from her. Sarah stood up and cleared her throat.

'Well, I'd better be going. I know you didn't want to see me, but, like I say, I…I wanted to come and… say I was sorry.'

The old man lifted his face and stared at her. His red-rimmed eyes were no longer furious, just exhausted. 'Was it them?'

Sarah knew exactly who he was talking about. 'I don't know.'

'But what do you think?'

'I think it could have been.'

'I've already told the gardaí.' He nodded slowly. 'Told them about the stolen items, too, and about you calling here. Will that interfere with your other case?'

'Maybe. I don't know.' She smiled. 'Doesn't matter, anyway.'

Whelan closed his eyes, took a deep breath and let it out slowly. 'Go over there to that chest at the foot of the bed.'

'What?'

'The chest – do you see it?'

Sarah looked around. The chest was a huge, old-fashioned piece of luggage with mouldy leather straps.

'I see it.'

'Open it up.'

Sarah lifted the lid slowly and looked inside. There was a jumble of old runners, magazines, earphones, a handful of cassette tapes that looked like they hadn't seen daylight in a number of years. But what stood out was the thing that rested on top of all this junk: a sleek grey Apple iBook.

Sarah looked over the lid at Brendan Whelan, but he had not opened his eyes.

'Is this what I think it is?'

'I don't know. I never saw it before today.'

Sarah lifted it out and placed it on the bed. She opened it up and hit the power button. After a few seconds, the log-in box appeared on screen.

Sarah switched it off and closed it. 'I think this is David Reid's laptop.'

Brendan Whelan nodded slowly. 'I thought it might be. Didn't think my Brendan would be interested in electrical goods, but there you go… it just goes to show.'

The sentence ended in a choked sob, but he pulled himself together again. 'Take that yoke out of here. I don't want to see it or you again.' And with that he closed his eyes again.

Sarah lifted the iBook and made her way quietly out of the room.

'Well? What did he have to say for himself?' Claire practically pounced on Sarah as she was shutting the door.

'Jesus!'

Claire looked down. 'What's that? Is that a laptop? Does that have something to do with the investigation?'

Sarah tried to sidestep her. 'I can't divulge any information at this point,' she said, using her best TV3 cop talk.

'It was drugs, wasn't it?' Claire followed her, talking in a stage whisper. 'It's okay, you can tell me. I won't tell a soul. It was drugs, wasn't it?'

'Oh, for fuck's sake,' Sarah snapped. She whirled around. 'That man in there has just lost his son. What is it you want? Something to talk about in the office tomorrow?'

'Well, excuse me for asking.' Claire reared back. 'He was my cousin too, you know.'

'Then show some decency. Have a little less glee about the details.'

Leaving a furious, spluttering Claire behind, Sarah made her own way out, happy to get away from the gloom and the dust and the overwhelming feeling that, despite what John said, she had played a significant part in the death of Bo and in the heartbreak of Brendan Whelan.

# 30

The lock-up was hot and dusty. Mick sat as still as possible and tried to make his mind go someplace else. There were parts of engines and other car parts scattered around the place. He tried to concentrate on them, guessing what type of car each piece came from, as though they were all part of a giant jigsaw.

'Call him.' Billy held the mobile against Mick's swollen lips.

Mick tried to take the phone, but his vision was so blurred that his hand grasped six inches to the left of it.

'He's fucked,' Jimmy said. 'Head's gone.'

'Ah, for… Here, you little prick. It's right in front of you.' Billy pushed it into his hand, hoping the kid stayed conscious long enough to talk. They had really worked him over. Billy was surprised that such a slight young lad had had the balls to keep his trap shut for so long. Of course, they had known he'd talk in the end – they always talked – but still, the kid had impressed them. He had only screamed for a while; after that he had merely whimpered.

Mick tried to keep as still as possible. He had lost two of his teeth, and Billy had kicked him so hard in the back that he was afraid his spine would snap if he moved. One of his eyes was so badly swollen that the skin had split and blood oozed down his face. He pressed Send on his mobile.

He listened as the call clicked and travelled. It went straight to voicemail again, for the third time in an hour – as he had known it would, because Mick was not dialling Sharpie's current mobile. He was dialling the old one that he knew was in a drawer back at his mother's home.

'Nah.' Mick held the phone up to Billy and slid over onto his side.

'Bollocks.' Billy took the mobile and wiped it clean on his trousers. 'No sign yet.'

Jimmy lit a cigarette and settled back down to shuffle the deck of cards. 'Then we got no choice but to wait. We got to get the other one.'

Billy's mobile rang. He glanced at the screen and cursed. It was Big Jack, for the third time.

'How you doin', Jack?'

'Did he tell you where the other one is?' Jack was slurring his words slightly, Billy noticed.

'Nah, but we'll get him. Jack, it's worse than you thought. He told us about the fence. He's some pawn guy, they shot him in your fucking yard. That's why they needed the car. It broke down, so they burned it out.'

'Jesus. Why'd they shoot him?

'They took shit out of some house you had 'em go to, and then sold it on to your man. But somehow he got wind that the gear was hot—'

'What gear?'

'Laptop, jewellery, that sort of thing.'

'He told you all this?'

'He took a bit of persuading, all right. Plucky little fuck, isn't he? He stayed quiet like a pro. We had to turn up the heat a bit.'

Big Jack didn't say anything.

'You want me to keep pushing him?'

'You think he's got anything else?'

'I doubt it.'

'Then leave him be. I'll call you back in a while. Keep trying to get the other fella.' Big Jack hung up.

Billy sighed. He had a hot date that evening with a barmaid from Fermanagh. At this rate, he'd be lucky if he even made it home before dark. 'What's he fucking like?'

'What's up with him?' Jimmy asked.

'Feeling guilty over this wee prick.' Billy toed Mick. 'Drunk, too.'

'Tom will go spare if he finds out all this shit is going on. Dead fence, detectives… It's a fucking mess, so it is.'

'Aye, well, that's for me da to sort out. He's queer that way, has a soft spot for Uncle Jack. Where could the other little fuck be?'

'Dunno, but you better hope he turns up before this one kicks it. He don't look so hot.'

Billy looked down at the kid by his feet. 'He doesn't, does he?'

'Tough little fuck, wasn't he?'

'Sure was.'

'Probably wouldn't have told no one nothing about Big Jack's business.'

'Can't take a risk. It needs to be cleaned up, you know yourself. Too much at stake to have the cops looking into the business. Something Big Jack should have thought of first.'

'Aye, we shouldn't have to be cleaning up Jack's stinking mess.' Jimmy dealt the cards and indicated the bleeding, dusty Mick with his head. 'That kid, he wasn't a bad little fuck. Why'd Jack use kids to do a job for him, anyway? What did he expect?'

'Who the fuck knows?' Billy slipped Mick's mobile back into his pocket. He grabbed the chair and sat down to look at his cards. Not a bad hand.

They went back to playing cards, while Mick Quinn slowly slipped into blessed unconsciousness on the floor by their feet.

\*

Sarah entered the office and plonked the computer down on John's desk. 'Look at what I have.'

John ran a hand over the laptop. 'Is that David Reid's computer?'

'It could well be.'

'Where did you get it?'

'Brendan Whelan found it in his son's room.'

'So at least we know Bo defintiely did deal with the Quinns,' John said. 'And he gave it to you?'

'Yup.'

John frowned. 'Sarah, if Jack Lawson sent those boys to get this, then why doesn't he have it? Why did they give it to Bo Whelan?'

'I…' Sarah sat down. 'Dammit.'

They sat looking at each other for a moment. Then Sarah shrugged. 'Then maybe it was money he was after. Shit.'

'Never mind. At least we have this. Let's open it up.'

'Brendan Whelan told the gardaí about the boys, anyway. We'll probably get a visit.'

'Yeah? I'd say bang goes any chance I have of wringing information out of Mick, so.' John rubbed the stubble on his chin. 'How is Whelan?'

'Devastated, as you would expect. Come on, let's have a look at this thing.'

John turned the laptop on and waited as it booted up. The log-in screen came up, prompting them for a password. John stared at it. 'How exactly are we going to get into this?'

'Guess the password, I suppose.'

'How the hell do we do that?'

'I don't know. Let me call James first, see if he has any idea.'

John glared at the blue screen. 'It could be anything.'

Sarah sat down behind her desk and picked up the phone. She smiled suddenly, a hopeful, radiant smile that knocked John's socks off. 'I know. But you know what, John?'

'What?'

'This could be it. We got it. Maybe now we can find the connection between Jack Lawson and David Reid. Maybe now we'll finally get some idea of who David Reid really was.'

*

Sharpie was tired. He was eating a burger and chips in Mario's Chipper and wondering why he hadn't heard from Mick. The fucking jakes must really be doing a number on him. Was it possible Mick had cracked, told them about Bo? Nah, he wouldn't do that. He had been acting weird and shit, but they were brothers, and brothers didn't stool each other out.

He looked at his mobile again, itching to call him, but he didn't want to take the risk in case the cops were listening. He had called his mother five times in the last two hours, and she knew even less than he did.

Sharpie licked tomato sauce off his fingers and took a swig of his Coke. He should have made Mick go with him, just made him. They were never out of contact for this long. It made him feel uneasy.

He finished his food, tossed the wrapper in the bin and made his way outside for a smoke. He sat on a wall and stared at the screen of his mobile. It was coming up to half five. Sharpie made a decision: if he hadn't heard from Mick by six, he'd call, cops or no cops.

*

Sarah ran her hands through her hair in frustration. They had tried about twenty different passwords and got nothing.

'Try "golfchair",' John said.

'Golfchair?'

'You know, work and pleasure.'

Even though she thought it was stupid, Sarah gave it a whirl. Nothing. 'That's not it either.'

'This is a waste of time.' John took his feet off his desk and stretched. 'We'll be here all night, and even then we probably won't get it. Look, let's face it: we need someone who knows how to bypass the log-in, someone who knows something about computers.'

'Like who?'

John thought for a minute. 'We could try Jackie's fiancé – what's his name?'

'No.'

'But he works with computers, doesn't he?'

'He works in IT, not the same thing. And I'm not asking him.'

'But why not? He might—'

'I said I'm not asking him.'

John closed his mouth with a snap.

'Okay?' Sarah demanded.

'Okay. No need to bite my head off.'

'I'm sorry.'

John said nothing for a moment. He patted his pockets, looking for his keys. 'Look, it's been a long day. Why don't we knock it on the head for tonight? I've got to get home and take Sumo out for a walk. And it's not like we're going to crack the code by sitting here sniping at each other.'

Sarah let the dig go, sat back in her chair and sighed. She was exhausted, and she wanted to get home to see if her mother was all right. 'What about Sharpie Quinn? Are you going to talk to him?'

'I'll track him down tomorrow. Meantime I'll take this with me, keep trying word combinations.'

Sarah shrugged. She was too tired to pretend to be anything other than pissed off.

They locked up the office and made their way downstairs, past the still-locked door of Rodney Mitchell's office. The bass was thumping from the Freak FM office, and they could hear voices and laughter inside.

John stopped so suddenly that Sarah collided with him.

'Ow.'

'Sorry,' John said. 'Wait here a second.'

'What are you doing?'

'Got an idea.' John approached the door of Freak and knocked.

Immediately the voices and music were silenced. John waited and knocked again, louder this time.

'Who is it?' a muffled voice finally asked.

'It's John from upstairs.'

They heard murmuring, and then the door opened a few inches and a guy of about twenty peered out. He was small and as skinny as an alley cat, with a bleached-blond mullet and three rings in his left eyebrow. His grey eyes did a quick scan of the landing before he opened the door and stepped out. A plume of smoke wafted out with him before he could close the door again. John sniffed; it sure as hell wasn't regular tobacco.

'Hey, man, how you doin'?'

'It's Click, isn't it?'

'Clique,' the young man said with a pained expression. 'DJ Clique.'

'Right, right. Listen, I got a favour to ask.'

'Sure, shoot.'

'You or any of your guys know anything about computers?'

Clique snorted, managing to look offended and smug at the same time. 'Whadda you want to know?'

'How to bypass a password.'

Clique didn't even bother to ask why. 'Sure, man, I know how. What type of computer you got?'

'A laptop.'

'Yeah, man, but what type?'

'Oh… Apple iBook.'

'Pfft…' Clique waved an arm laden down with plastic bracelets. 'Yeah, man, that I can do.'

John beamed at him. 'And when might you be able to do it?'

Clique shrugged. 'Gotta finish my show, but I'll be free after nine.'

'Beautiful. I'll come back, pick you up. We can do it at my place.'

'Sure, man, whatever. We gotta swing by my place first, to pick up a CD.'

'Where do you live?'

'Rathmines.'

'Perfect, it's on the way to mine.'

'Cool.'

Clique nodded to Sarah and went back inside. Another puff of sweet smoke filled the landing, and then the voices started up again and the bass kicked back in.

'How the hell did you know?' Sarah asked incredulously as John took the laptop from her and they made their way out. 'How did you know he'd know?'

'We were talking about it the other day, me and Mike,' John said with a wry smile. 'From twelve to twenty, that's all they do – GameBoys, computers, PlayStations, digital this, MP3 that. They're the next generation.'

'Jesus, that makes me feel really old.'

'We're not old, but, well, let's face it, we're no spring chickens any more.'

They walked to their cars in silence, contemplating how two people in their thirties could already be deemed a little over the hill.

'Will you call me if you find anything?' Sarah said as she reached the Fiesta.

'Why don't you come over and watch the next generation at work? I can ring for a Chinese, we can have a few beers, sit there feeling inadequate while Clickety-click talks down to us.'

'I can't.'

'Oh?'

'Sorry, I promised Mum I'd cook this evening.'

John frowned. It wasn't like Sarah to put a cooking commitment before a break in a case. 'Okay. I'll give you a call the second I learn something.'

'Thanks.'

Sarah climbed into her car, put on her seatbelt, checked the mirrors and drove off with a little wave.

John watched her go. She wasn't telling him something, and he was worried. He wondered just what the hell was going on with her dingbat family now.

# 31

Sharpie sat down near the bus driver, amongst the shoppers and tired workers, and wondered if he was losing his mind.

He tried to calm down, but he was incapable of stopping his knees from bouncing, or his hands from picking furiously at the peeling sunburn on his forehead. He had called Mick's number ten minutes before. When the man had said, 'We've got your brother,' it had taken Sharpie less than five seconds to realise he wasn't talking to a cop. He had hung up then and called his mother, demanding a description of the men who had called to the house that morning. After she had given it to him, sounding scared and confused, he hung up on her too. Feeling a strange, unfamiliar sensation in his gut, he had called the man back and demanded to speak to his brother.

The man had laughed. Mick couldn't come to the phone, he had said, but Sharpie should make it his business to come to them, if he ever wanted to see his brother alive again. He had given Sharpie the address of a warehouse in Ringsend and hung up. Further calls had gone ignored.

So here he was, on a bus into town. He rubbed his temples and groaned again. He couldn't abandon Mick, but what the fuck was he going to do? Who had him? What did they want? And why couldn't

Mick come to the phone? Had they hurt him? The thought of his brother being hurt filled Sharpie with a rage so white-hot that it was all he could do to contain it. He wanted to lash out, to strike down every fucking motherfucker that even looked askance at him.

Mick might even be—

Sharpie moaned aloud, so loud that the woman next to him got up and moved seats.

Think, think – what would Fifty do? He'd watched *Get Rich or Die Trying* a million times. Fifty would find those guys and blow them away. But this was not the movies, and Sharpie was not Fifty Cent. His brother was in the hands of fuck knew who.

It had to be a trap, something to do with Big Jack. Ringsend? Didn't Jack have places over there? He couldn't remember; he couldn't think. The fucking detectives must have told Big Jack about the break-in, and Mick had been right all along: Big Jack was gunning for them.

Big Jack. Fat Elvis-looking motherfucker. Sharpie hated him with a passion, but Mick…Mick thought he was cool, always going on about Big Jack's Mercedes and his fancy house. Mick wanted to own a garage someday. Stupid fucking Mick and his stupid fucking ideas. Kid deserved to be smacked down.

Sharpie thought of his brother's easy smile, the way he went scarlet whenever Sharpie called him a fag. And for the first time in Sharpie Quinn's miserable life, he knew what it felt like to be helplessly, hopelessly, truly afraid. Even when he had had his throat cut and he was lying on the waste ground feeling the blood drain from his body, he had not experienced anything like this fear.

Mick. His Mick. Stupid, nervous Mick. Sharpie shook his head. He loved him; he loved him more than his own self.

He got off the bus and ran the whole way to the garage, hoping – no, praying – that it would still be open, that he would find Mick there, that whoever had him could be reasoned with. If they couldn't, well, then he would take them out, he would ice them; he would save his brother.

He turned the corner onto Bridgefoot Street and almost wept with relief: the yard was open, and the tail end of Big Jack's Mercedes was clearly visible. He put a spurt on and galloped through the gates. Here I come, motherfucker; I'm coming for you.

'Mick's not here, didn't turn up today. But, sure, you know that, don't you?' Robbie was walking across the yard, rolling a tyre in front of him. 'What you doing here, anyway?'

'Where's Big Jack?'

'Upstairs in the office. And you tell that Mick he can go an' shite if he ever wants another day off. Leaving me stuck like that, without even a call, and me with a load of work on. Aye, he left me right in the shit, and I won't forget.'

Sharpie wasn't listening. He took the steps two at a time and burst into Jack's office.

Jack was slumped in his chair, a glass of whiskey in hand.

Sharpie pulled the gun from his waistband and pointed it straight at Big Jack's head. 'Where is he? Where's my fuckin' brother, you piece-of-shit motherfucker?'

Big Jack could hardly believe what he was seeing. He stared at Sharpie with pink, misty and clearly very drunk eyes. 'Jesus fucking Christ! Are you off your fucking head? Put that away.'

Sharpie kicked the door closed behind him. 'Answer me or I swear, man, I'll blow your brains across the fucking wall.'

'What the fuck are you doing here?' Big Jack tossed his whiskey back, set the glass down on the desk and refilled it sloppily from a half-empty bottle of Jameson's.

'Where's—'

'You need fucking help. You need your head seeing to, coming in here like this.'

'Yo, man, this is for real! Where are they? Where's the men that took Mick?'

'Mick? Who took him?'

'Two men.'

'What men?'

'They said they was cops, but they wasn't.'

'Sit fucking down there, now, and start from the beginning. No point shouting at me like a lunatic. Sit.'

'I don't got time to sit.' Sharpie waggled the gun. 'I know it was you, I know—'

'You know shite. You don't tell me what's going on, I can't help you.' Big Jack shrugged and took a slug of his drink.

Sharpie advanced on him. 'You – I know you done this.'

'Did what? What are you shiteing on about? I've been here all day. Ask Robbie if you don't believe me. Why would I send two fellas to pick Mick up? I thought he was sick, anyway.'

Sharpie stood staring at him, his finger tense on the trigger. 'You're lying.'

'Why would I lie? What would I want to pick Mick up for? What the fuck is going on? You come in here shouting about Mick, threatening me with a fucking gun…'

Sharpie stared at Big Jack. Big Jack stared somewhat blearily back. Sharpie felt sweat trickle down his back. He couldn't tell if Big Jack was lying or not. But if he wasn't, who were the two men? Could it be just something to do with Bo? What if he had got it completely wrong? He had beaten up that hash dealer recently… What if none of this was anything to do with Big Jack?

Sharpie's gun hand wobbled. The noise in his head began to subside.

'You didn't have Mick picked up?'

'Course not. Why would I?' Big Jack ran his hands over his face tiredly. 'Son, you and me don't get on too well, I know that, but will you stop sticking that fucking gun in my face and tell me what the hell is going on? I hope you haven't got Mick into trouble. He's a good fucking lad.'

Sharpie lowered the gun and stared at Big Jack. Was he telling the truth? He didn't seem too worried. Sharpie tried to think. 'Mick… We, we were…'

'You were what? Sit down there and start from the beginning,' Big Jack said to the agitated Sharpie. 'Why don't you help yourself to a drink there? You look like you could do with one.'

'I don't have time for no fuckin' drink, man! They got Mick—'

'Go on, it'll steady your nerves.'

'I don't want no fucking drink!' Sharpie took off his beanie and wiped at the sweat on his brow. If he hadn't been so panicked, he might have wondered why Big Jack was being so kind to him.

Big Jack leaned back in his chair and folded his arms. 'All right, then. But sit the fuck down, you're making me nervous, standing over me like that.'

Sharpie sank into the swivel chair on the other side of the desk, still keeping the gun trained on Jack, but without the same intensity. 'Look, if you didn't do this, then you gotta help me. They're expectin' me to show any minute. I gotta go. If I don't, fuck knows what they'll do to Mick. You gotta help us. Look, man, I know you and me got beef, but you gotta help Mick.'

'Who's expecting you? You need to start from the beginning. What the fuck have you and Mick been up to now? And no bullshit. I can't help you if you're not straight with me.'

'Man, I ain't go no time—'

'You better make time. I'm not going into anything half-cocked.'

Sharpie sighed heavily. 'All right, but then you gonna help me?'

'I'll see.'

Sharpie gave Big Jack a brief and heavily edited versions of events. He skipped anything that might anger him, such as the fact that they had shot Bo in his yard, but he confessed that they had 'borrowed' the Fiat, since he figured Big Jack wasn't that stupid. He talked and Big Jack listened, seemingly in stunned, angry silence, shaking his head now and then. He was plotting his next move.

He hadn't expected the lad to turn up here. He had been very specific to Billy about not mentioning any names. But here he was – and with a gun, no less. Sharpie Quinn was a stupid, dangerous thorn in his side, and he was not going to waste the opportunity to prune him. The question was, how? The gun was no longer pointed directly at him, but he was old and fat and it wouldn't take much for Sharpie to get the drop on him. He needed to use his brain. On that front, he was certain he had the advantage.

'Well,' he said when Sharpie finished talking. 'Looks to me like you've landed your brother in a heap of trouble. You even managed to drag me into your mess, taking the car.'

'I know, man, but look – we can go talk to these people. You know people, I know you do. You can help.'

'Why should I?'

'Look, if it was me – sure, man, I get it, ain't no love between us. But Mick, he don't deserve nothin' bad. He's on the level, you know it. He's straight up.'

Sharpie was pleading. Big Jack noticed he was no longer even tipping the gun in his direction. He had him now.

'If I do help you, you've got to make it up to me for the car. I don't give a goddamn about you or your troubles, but Mick… well, Mick's like a son to me.'

'I know, man, I—'

'And then I don't want to see you around here ever again, we clear on that? I see you, I'm going to go to the fucking cops and tell them everything you just told me. We clear?'

Sharpie was nodding even before he had finished the question. Big Jack unhooked a length of waven pipe he kept hidden under his desk in case of break-ins, slipped it up the sleeve of his jacket and hauled himself out of his chair.

'All right, then. I'm going to go tell Robbie to knock it on the head for the day, then me and you are going to call those bastards that have poor wee Mick, and we're going to see what they fucking want. Right?'

Big Jack made his way wearily around the desk, heading towards the door.

'Yeah, man.' Sharpie checked his watch, which was on his gun hand. 'But we don't have much time, they—'

Big Jack struck fast. He slipped the pipe down his sleeve and hit Sharpie on the side of the head with it. Sharpie jerked, and Big Jack whacked the gun out of his hands. It skittered across the floor and came to rest under his desk. Before the boy could register what was happening, Big Jack swung the pipe under Sharpie's chin. He grabbed the other end and pulled it tight, yanking the boy back towards him, almost lifting him to his feet. Sharpie's hands flew up and he grappled furiously, trying to wrench himself forward, making strange gurgling sounds. But Big Jack was too powerful. Sharpie tried to gouge at his eyes, raking Big Jack's face with his nails. Big Jack turned his head and kept the pressure on. In desperation, Sharpie lifted his feet and kicked out against the desk, sending them both crashing backwards into the wall. Big Jack gritted his teeth and tightened his grip.

It took minutes, but eventually Sharpie stopped struggling. His arms dropped away and his body sagged.

Big Jack, his muscles aching, his suit jacket torn and ripped under the arms, staggered forwards. He dropped Sharpie to the ground, slumped forward onto the desk and lay there gasping for air, saturated in sweat.

He reached for the bottle of Jameson's, but it fell from his shaking fingers, rolled off the desk and smashed against the floor.

'Bollocks.'

Really, he thought glumly, he was too old for this kind of shit.

Big Jack stood up and made his way unsteadily to the door. He went outside and leaned over the railing.

'Robbie!'

'What?' The little man appeared underneath him, wiping his filthy hands on his overalls.

'Take off there; good lad. Just shut over the gates. I'll lock up when I'm going.'

'What? But you wanted me to finish stripping the Opel, and then I've got to—'

'It'll wait until tomorrow. Go on now – here.' Big Jack dug into his pocket and tossed down a twenty-euro note. 'Why don't you head off and have a pint?'

Robbie glanced at his boss suspiciously. If there were two things Big Jack did not do, one was tell you to knock off early and the other was give you money for nothing. Something was up.

'You sure?'

'I'm sure. Got a bit of sorting out to do here. You head on now.'

Robbie stuffed the note into his pocket. There was something going on, all right, but it was none of his concern. Just as Mick talking to that detective was none of his concern, just as Billy racing out of the yard earlier that day with murderous intent in his eyes was none of his concern. Robbie had long ago learned to keep his beak out of thinks that didn't concern him.

'All right, I'll call it a night, so.'

'Good man. See you tomorrow.'

While Robbie put away his tools and changed out of his overalls, Big Jack went down the stairs – carefully – and opened the boot of his car.

*

Thirty minutes later, Big Jack pulled into a small yard in Ringsend – a yard he had used on so many occasions to strip down boosted cars – and tooted the car horn.

To the rear of the yard was a small lock-up with a red corrugate door. The door was rolled up, and Billy stepped out and squinted in surprise at Big Jack.

'What about ya? What are you doing here?'

'Got a surprise visit.' Big Jack squeezed himself out from behind the wheel.

'What's going on?'

'Never mind that. Where's Jimmy?'

'Inside.' Billy stared at the red marks on Big Jack's face where Sharpie's nails had raked him. 'What's wrong – what happened?'

'I asked you to take care of them boys. I asked you to make it quick and simple.'

Billy shrugged. 'Yeah, but one of them did a runner—'

'It was a simple fucking request. Pick 'em up, find out what's going on.'

'Look, I already told you, we got one of the wee fuckers – he's in there. We're just waiting on the other one. He called earlier and—'

'Come here.' Big Jack had made his way around to the back of the Mercedes. He opened the boot. Billy followed him warily, making sure he could see Big Jack's hands at all times. He peered over the lip of the boot and saw a body, partially wrapped in plastic.

Big Jack moved the plastic aside.

'That's the spit of the one we have inside,' Billy said. 'What are you doing with him? He's supposed to be on his way here.'

'He came to me first. He knew I was behind this,' Big Jack said quietly.

'You kill him?'

'Well, he's not going to leap up any second.'

Billy looked hard at his uncle. He didn't like Big Jack and frequently impersonated him when drunk, but right now his uncle didn't look so funny. Billy was impressed that the old boy still had it in him to do what had to be done. At this rate, he might make it back up North and get a crack at the busty barmaid after all. That cheered him up considerably.

'The one inside's pretty busted up. What do you want to do with him? Not much point letting him go. He'll want to know what happened to his brother, could kick up a fuss.'

Jack closed his eyes. He liked Mick, liked him a lot – but with Sharpie dead and the cops sniffing around, what choice did he have? He had to get rid of any risk. There was too much at stake. He had businesses to run. He had to be seen to be decisive.

'How bad is he?'

'You want to see him?'

'I…' Big Jack swallowed. 'No, just tell me.'

Billy shrugged. 'Wouldn't put much of a bet on him making it through the night, one way or the other.'

'I didn't want you to hurt him that bad,' Big Jack said angrily.

'What was I supposed to do? You wanted answers, and the wee shite wouldn't talk at first. No point crying over it now, Jack. You wanted it done different, you should have handled it yourself. Look, I'll put him out of his misery, make it quick.'

Big Jack ran his hand across his face. His heart was hammering in his chest. He thought of Mick's shy smile. But the little shit had brought all this on himself. Maybe it hadn't been his fault, but at the end of the day, Big Jack had to look out for Big Jack. There was no room for sympathy.

'We'll put the two of them in the back of your car, take them away out of here and get rid of them. You'll have to burn out that Nissan, too.'

'No problem. We roped it this morning, not even our plates.'

'Okay, then. Let's get going.' Big Jack turned away from the boot and staggered slightly.

Billy gripped him by the elbow. 'You all right there, big man?'

'No,' Big Jack said truthfully. 'Far from it.'

# 32

'Are you sure he won't bite? I don't like the way he keeps looking at me.'

DJ Clique was eyeing Sumo warily. The big dog was lying on a rug by the empty fireplace, chewing what looked like the shoulder-bone of a cow.

John glanced at his dog. Sumo – part Irish wolfhound, part German shepherd – was gnawing away on the bloody bone with fierce concentration and enjoying it immensely. Every so often a deep, rumbling growl escaped from his massive chest.

'No, he's fine.'

'He's growling.'

'Yeah, but that's a happy growl. Trust me, you'd know if it was an angry growl.'

DJ Clique was beginning to regret ever agreeing to come to John's house. But he had made a quick call to Mike Brannigan, and Mike had assured him John was a good guy and told him to help him out, so here he was. Mike hadn't mentioned anything about there being some kind of wolf in John's home.

'Okay, then.' Clique opened his bag, took out a leather pouch that held a stack of CDs, selected one and placed it beside the laptop.

'It's actually easy enough to gain access to these things, you know.

All you have to do is start up from the system CD and go through the process as if you were going to reinstall the system software.'

John opened two bottles of beer, passed one to Clique and kept one for himself. 'I have no idea what you said there, but it sounded pretty impressive.'

Clique sighed. 'Never mind.' He put his CD into the side of the iBook. 'You got a coin?'

'Sure.' John dug in his pockets and handed him a euro. 'Why do you need that?'

'We've got to shut it down manually because we don't have the password.'

'With a coin?'

Clique flipped the iBook over. He used the coin to open the cover and remove the battery.

'Oh,' John said, feeling like a fool.

Clique popped the battery back in and handed the coin back to John. 'Okay, now we power on, and I just need to hold this key here…'

He placed his finger on a key and hummed under his breath. John noticed his plastic bracelets had words printed on them: 'Make poverty history.' He looked at Clique's mullet and eyebrow-piercings again and shook his head: little hippie.

An install page came up on screen, and Clique gave a satisfied nod. A quick tippity-tap later, he brought up the utilities page. 'Now all we gotta do is reset the password.'

'We do?'

'Sure. Give me a password.'

'Like what?'

'Like anything you'll remember.'

'Sumo.'

'Better add a number or two to that.'

John frowned. 'Why?'

'Just safer that way.'

'Okay, add 06 after Sumo.'

Clique snickered a little. John glanced at him.

'What?'

'Oh, nothing. Least you didn't pick your birthday.'

'My birthday?' John said, thinking of every bank card and video card he'd ever owned.

'Yeah, everyone puts in birthdays or house numbers. It's stupid. First thing I'd check for.'

While John vowed to change his PIN numbers, Clique typed in the new password, quit the programme and pressed Restart. The log-in page came up on screen. Clique ejected his CD and slid the iBook over to John.

'There you go, man, she's all yours.'

'That's it?'

'Sure. Type your password in, and off you go.'

John goggled at him. 'But it only took you a couple of minutes.'

'Uh-huh.'

'These things aren't exactly secure, are they?'

Clique shrugged. 'Not much is, nowadays.' He glanced at his watch. 'Look, man, I gotta shoot off home and get changed for a gig. You need anything else, give me a shout.'

'I will. You need a lift?'

'Nah, man, I'm cool. Hey, you ever need me again…'

He handed John his card. His name and numbers were printed on beautiful embossed paper that must have set him back a fortune. John was impressed.

He saw Clique out, thanking him profusely. Clique seemed a little embarrassed by the praise. He gave John a complicated handshake and went off with himself, his giant pants halfway down his ass and his golden mullet glowing dimly in the gathering darkness.

John galloped indoors and grabbed the phone. He called Sarah's mobile.

It rang for what seemed like an age. Finally she answered, sounding dull and groggy.

'Hello?'

'Hey, it's me.'

'John? What time is it?'

John checked his watch. 'Nine-forty.'

'Oh, crap. I must have fallen asleep.'

'You're never going to guess. We got the password.'

'Really?'

'Man, that kid – he was in like Flynn. I swear to God, I never saw anything like it in my life. We would have been sitting there for months trying out combinations, but this guy, he was—'

'John, hold on a second, would you?'

'Sure.'

He heard her moving about, calling for her mother. He leaned against the wall, waiting, not exactly patiently, for her to come back on the line.

'John?'

'Hey. Anyway, like I was—'

'John, I'm going to have to call you back.'

'I— What?'

But she had already hung up on him. John stared at the phone in disbelief. They were about to enjoy probably the best break in the case thus far, and she had hung up on him. Pissed, John slammed his receiver down and made his way back into the sitting room.

'Women,' he said to Sumo. 'Can't live with them, period.'

Sumo paused for a brief second, then resumed turning his bone into mush.

John sat down at his table, tapped in his new password and, without the fanfare and praise he would have liked, entered into the private life of David Reid.

\*

Sarah ran upstairs, calling her mother's name. The house was in complete darkness and she knew, even as she checked all the rooms, that she was alone. She went back downstairs and raced out to the shed. Nothing.

'Mum!'

The side gate was open.

'Oh, no…'

Sarah ran back inside, grabbed her house keys and ran out again. She hurried onto the street and stood there in the twilight, searching frantically, hoping to catch some sight of her mother. Which direction had she taken? Maybe she'd called in to the neighbours? Sarah didn't want to start knocking on doors at this hour of the night, but what else could she do?

'Hello there, Sarah.'

Sarah jumped and whirled around. In the gloom she could make out Mrs Mackey from across the road, hanging over her gate. She was a small, chubby lady in her late fifties, and for as long as Sarah had known her she had always worn black stretch pants and twin-sets.

'Hi, Mrs Mackey. Sorry, I didn't see you there.'

'Are you looking for your mum?'

'Yes,' Sarah said. 'Have you seen her?'

'She walked past me earlier, when I was bringing out the bins.'

Sarah approached her and smiled, trying very hard to keep her voice calm. 'What time was that?'

'Would have been about twenty minutes ago.'

'Right.' Sarah felt the smile freeze on her face. 'Did she say where she was going? Which way did she go?'

'She went down towards the main road. She said something about catching a bus.'

'A bus?'

Mrs Mackey's chubby face puckered in alarm. 'Is everything all right? Oh, if I had known you were inside, I would have got you, but there were no lights on and I thought—'

Sarah patted her arm. 'Don't be silly, but listen, I'd better head after her.'

'Oh, dear, I know she hasn't been herself lately. I didn't… Perhaps I should have stopped her, but she did seem very determined. And she's been so… well, like I said, not really herself lately. I was only saying to Eileen across the way there yesterday that we ought to drop in more.'

Sarah winced. Christ, were all the bloody neighbours talking about her mother's mental health?

'Look, don't worry. I'm sure she's just going for a walk.'

Mrs Mackey didn't look too convinced, but she bobbed her head anyway. 'Well, I hope you catch up to her.'

Sarah thanked her and took off, walking as fast as her damaged ankle would allow. As soon as she was out of Mrs Mackey's view, she began to run.

The main coast road was over a mile away. Her mother had a head start of twenty minutes. Shit.

Even though her ankle and knee were beginning to throb from the exertion, Sarah ran as hard as she could.

# 33

'Slow down, will you?'

Jimmy clung to the handle of the passenger door to keep from being flung all over the place. They were driving along a pitted track in the middle of nowhere. Trees surrounded them on both sides, and the grass growing in the middle of the road was almost knee-high.

Billy slowed down a fraction. It wasn't too late. He was determined to get rid of the twins ASAP and make it to the bar and his barmaid. 'Sorry, ground's as hard as nails and there's fucking rocks all over the place.'

Jimmy grunted and glanced out the passenger window. The trees were dense and seemed oddly watchful. It was pitch-black, not a light or a house for miles. He didn't like it. He was a town boy through and through; all these trees bothered him. The darkness of the place bothered him. It was creepy.

'Where we going, anyway?'

'There's an old quarry in about another two miles. We drop 'em down into the water there, bye-bye, no one's ever gonna find them.'

'Hope you're right about that. Last thing you want is some kids swimming around in it or shit, and one of these bobs up.'

'They won't bob if we weigh them down properly. And trust me, no kid swims in this place. Water's stagnant, for a start, and fuck knows how deep it is. Truth be told, it's a creepy kind of hole even in the daylight. Nobody comes near it.'

Jimmy glanced out the window again. He could well believe it. 'The big man looked shook, didn't he?'

'Goin' soft. I'll need to talk to my father about this. Can't be soft in this game, Jimmy, can't be leaving yourself open like that. It's like that fucking girl. What would have happened if the cops had got wind of that?'

'Still, he took care of that other kid, didn't he?'

'Aye, there is that. I didn't—'

The car tore around a bend and hit a particularly large stone. Billy swore as the tyres skidded hard left. He spun the wheel and hit the brakes. The car slewed sideways, coming to rest with the boot in the ditch. The engine stalled.

'Jesus!' Jimmy was tight against the seatbelt, his two hands pressed on the dash. 'I told you – slow down and stop thinking with your cock. You'll get us killed.'

'Sorry.' Billy grinned sheepishly. He started it up again, spun the wheel and straightened up.

'We crash, I swear, I'm going to wring your neck. No way I'm walking back through this shit just 'cause you want to throw the leg over some big-diddied bitch.'

'You can say that because you haven't a snowball's of getting your dirty paws on them. That girl has the best rack I've seen in years.'

'Yeah, but the face of a fucking bulldog licking piss off a nettle.'

'Aye, right enough, but, sure, you don't look at the mantelpiece when you're poking the fire.'

'Just keep your fucking eyes on the road and slow down.'

'Aye, boss,' Billy said sarcastically, but he eased his foot off the accelerator.

In the boot, Mick Quinn opened his eyes.

He was in agony. He had been thrown against the hood in the tail-spin, and the pain had jolted him back to consciousness. He was disorientated and confused. He smelled petrol and tasted blood in his mouth.

He knew he was on the move, and after a second or two he managed to work out that he was in the boot of a car. He fought the sensation of claustrophobia as the memory of the two men came back to him. This was not the time to panic. He was in agony, but he was alive.

If he was in a car, that meant he was probably still with Billy and Jimmy. He tried to turn and take a bigger breath, but there was no room. He was pressed up against something soft. He ran his hands over it and froze.

It was a body. There was somebody in here with him.

Mick withdrew his hand and tried to breathe, but he couldn't. Trembling uncontrollably, he put his hand out again and touched it. He groaned as he ran his fingers along a chest, up to a neck. Finally, quivering harder, he ran his hand over the face. The skin was soft and cool to the touch.

He withdrew his hand and fought the rising hysteria. But he had to be sure. Sobbing softly, Mick reached out again and moved his hand shakily along the body. His fingers felt numb and clumsy as they moved up over the face and finally came to rest on the soft, cornrowed hair that could only belong to one person. The only person in the world who had loved Mick Quinn, and whom Mick Quinn had loved back.

\*

Sarah had run almost the whole way to the coast road before she saw her mother sitting on a wall, about ten feet from a bus stop. Deirdre Kenny looked confused and angry. She wore slacks and a blouse, but she had slippers on her feet and her hair was in disarray. Sarah suddenly saw her mother as others might see her: a confused old lady sitting on a wall, just another loony in a city full of them, more to be pitied than laughed at.

Sarah felt like weeping.

She slowed to a walk and tried to catch her breath. She was sweating and her ankle felt like it was on fire. 'There you are!'

Deirdre squinted at her as though she had no idea who she was.

'Mum... Jesus, you almost gave me a heart attack. Why didn't you tell me you were going out?'

Deirdre tilted her head and smiled slightly. 'There you are, now. What are you doing here?'

Sarah sat down on the wall beside her and took her mother's hand in her own. Even though it was a mild night, her hand felt cold, the skin thin and papery. But at least she still had the bandage on her other wrist. 'Mum, you left the house without a word.'

'I know that!'

'Okay, okay.' Sarah looked around. 'Why did you come down here? You shouldn't be walking around at this hour of the night.'

'I wanted to catch a bus into town, but the driver wouldn't let me on. He was very rude. He told me to go on home, as if I were a child.' She sniffed. 'I forgot my purse.'

'Why did you want to go into town?'

'I...' Deirdre pushed her hair from her eyes, her brow furrowed in concentration. 'Well now, there's a thing. I don't really remember. Isn't that odd?'

'It's late. All the shops will be closed by now.'

'Will they? Well, yes – I mean, Friday's late opening, but I suppose it is later than I thought.'

Sarah nodded, but inside the fear mushroomed. The idea of her mother wandering around the city centre at night in her slippers terrified her. Thank God she hadn't taken her purse. Thank God the driver had had the good sense to tell her no.

'It's getting late. Do you want to go back home?'

'It's nice here.'

Deirdre withdrew her hand and rubbed her daughter's back. Sarah

301

sighed and leaned against her mother, exactly the way she had as a child. She smelled the Dove soap her mother used and the fabric conditioner she preferred, but underneath it all there was another smell lurking, a sickly, milky, almost sour smell. Where had this come from?

'I'm so glad you're home. Do you know that?'

Sarah nodded. She was afraid to speak. She wasn't sure she could hold herself together, and she was afraid that if she started to cry, she might not stop.

'When you were with that awful man, I used to cry at night.'

'I know you did.'

'I worried so much.'

'I know.'

'And I'm sorry you're so unhappy.'

Sarah's breath caught in her throat. She sat up and turned to stare at her mother.

'What? I'm not unhappy.'

'I know you're worried. Do you think I can't see it?'

'It's this case. That's all I—'

'Oh, Helen, stop.'

Sarah blinked. 'Mum, I'm Sarah.'

Her mother frowned.

Sarah stifled a sob that rose unbidden to her throat. 'I think we should go home.'

'I'm sorry, Sarah. Everything is just so... it's hard right now.' Her mother's eyes were dark, like her own, but lately they had had such a faraway look in them that Sarah couldn't remember the last time she had noticed just how beautiful they were, how intelligent and kind they could be. 'It's all so hard to work out, do you see? Every day, it's just so hard.'

'Mum, everything will be fine, I promise you. I'm here now. I won't let anything happen to you.'

'You're a good girl.' Her mother reached out and smoothed a lock of hair from her cheek. Then she smiled again, and the moment was gone. 'Oh now, look at that: I forgot to put on any shoes. Look at my slippers, they're filthy. God, what must people think of me?'

'Is your wrist hurting?'

'No, it's fine, not sore at all. Let's go home. We'll make hot chocolate. You love hot chocolate, don't you?'

'Sure.' Sarah hated hot chocolate. It was her mother's and Helen's favourite drink.

She helped her mother up, and together they made their way home, Deirdre babbling about bus timetables and Sarah trying not to wince every time she took a step.

*

Billy parked the car beneath a huge mound of gravel, a couple of feet away from a large man-made pool. In the headlights the water looked black and treacly. Jimmy noticed with distaste that there were vast patches of greenish, furry-looking scum floating on its surface.

'I don't like the look of this shithole.'

'Pity about you. Now, we need to find some pretty heavy rocks.'

'How we going to do this?'

'We'll fix the rocks in the chicken wire and roll them into it, separately. Then we can toss them in from that ledge up there – you see it?' Billy pointed. 'The water there is fairly deep. And the rocks will keep them weighted down at the bottom.'

'You sure?'

'Never let me down before.'

Jimmy followed his finger and made out a ledge, just at the edge of the illuminated area. It was at least fifty feet above the still water of the lake, on a steep, narrow path. He looked dubiously at Billy. Unlike his colleague, Jimmy was not exactly in peak physical condition.

'How we supposed to get them up there?'

'They can't be that fucking heavy. We'll carry them. You take one, I'll take the other.' Billy opened the glove compartment and took out a pair of needle-nosed pliers and a roll of garden wire.

'What do we do about the one that's not dead?'

'Do? Nothing.'

'I thought you were going to put him out of his misery.'

'Look, I could put a bullet in the back of his skull, but he's gone, isn't he? What's the point?'

Jimmy shrugged and scratched at his belly. 'Seems fucked up, drowning him like that.'

'What you want to do? Shoot him up before we drown him?' Billy said incredulously. 'You think he'd prefer it? Maybe I should try and bring him round first, let him know we're about to kill him?'

'No, it's not that…'

'Fuck that, big man. Will you not talk shite? Come on.'

They climbed out of the car and made their way around to the boot.

'Shit, it stinks here,' Jimmy said. 'Smells like something dead.'

'Told you, that water's stagnant.'

Close by, a fox yowled. Jimmy jerked around and fell against the car. 'What the fuck was that?'

'Fox. Shite, you city boys are all the same.'

Jimmy glanced around, breathing heavily. He couldn't tell which direction the sound had come from. The steep quarry walls bounced the sound around, creating an eerie echo. He swallowed and let out a slow breath. He'd be very happy to get the hell out of here.

Billy unlocked the boot, and together they peered at the prone bodies. Billy checked to see if Mick still had a pulse. He did, and it felt strong enough to Billy, but then he was no expert. He opened Mick's left eye and peered in. The pupil contracted, but the eye was full of blood. He withdrew his hand.

'Told you. Probably bleeding in the brain or some shit. Shouldn't take much to lift them. Which one you want?'

'We should carry them between us.'

'Away with ya! Takes too long. Come on, which one?'

'Doesn't matter. I'll take the one Big Jack brought.'

'Right.'

Together they hauled Mick out and dumped him on the gravel. Then they dropped Sharpie next to his brother. 'What the fuck is he wearing?' Jimmy asked, toeing Sharpie. 'He looks like… what do you call him?'

'Who?'

'Your man, the comedian. Ali G.'

'He looks like a fucking eejit,' Billy said, taking a torch from the boot.

'Mad, that, isn't it?'

'What?'

'Big Jack being able to handle him like that.'

'Back in the day, he was a mean son of a bitch. You should hear the old lad tell stories some time. Put years on you.' Billy rolled his eyes. 'Let's get on with it.'

He grabbed the roll of chicken wire from the back seat and slammed the boot closed, plunging them into near-darkness again. He flicked on the torch and the shadows around them increased, making Jimmy all the more nervous.

'Right, we'll carry them up first, then we'll get the rocks.'

'Right.' Jimmy didn't give a shit what way they did it, as long as they could get the hell out of that quarry.

They each hoisted a twin over their shoulders in a fireman's lift and began to trudge over the gravel and up the stony pathway, towards the ledge. The angle was steep and the rocky ground hard and slippery. Even though the twins weren't especially heavy, they were dead weights, and both men were soon sweating buckets. Jimmy was puffing and blowing like a broken-down horse. He slipped numerous times, and by the time they reached the ledge he was staggering about like a drunk. He was very glad when Billy stopped and let Sharpie slide off his shoulder, his body hitting the ground with a sickening thump.

'This'll do here.'

Jimmy dumped Mick and bent over double with his hands on his knees, wheezing. 'I… don't get… fucking paid enough for this shit.'

Billy took out his pliers and wire. There was enough in the roll to wind around the body of each boy. It was true what he had said to Jimmy: he had done this before, and when a body was weighted this way it did not resurface.

'Scout around for some decent-sized rocks there.'

'Scout around where?' Jimmy straightened up and mopped his brow. 'It's pitch-black up here. What if I fall?'

'You won't fall. Give your eyes a minute to adjust and then have a look around you. Nothing too small – we don't want them slipping through the mesh.'

Jimmy began to feel about him. 'There's not much up here.'

'Try lower down, then. There was loads of fucking stones around the car.'

'The car?'

Billy swore under his breath. 'Jesus, will you give my head peace! Just go and get some fucking stones before we're here all night!'

'Go all the way back down?'

'What do you want to fucking do? Here, take the torch and get on with it.'

Jimmy grunted, but he made his way back down the path to the car. He moved slowly, taking serious care. He was wearing slip-on loafers and there were no grips on the soles.

Billy waited for a moment and then began to search around for suitable stones. The first few he found were too small, but eventually he located one about the size of a football. He carried it over, dropped it beside the bodies and resumed his search.

Mick heard him moving about in the darkness, muttering to himself. He tried to keep as still as possible. Jimmy had gone, there was only this one to deal with. Mick made a decision. He had a slim chance

– his only chance, really. If he didn't act now, he'd never make it out of this quarry alive.

He moved slowly, sliding his right leg from beneath Sharpie's body and easing his feet into position under him. He felt weak and light-headed. There was so much shooting pain in every movement, but he kept going, holding his breath, desperate not to make even the slightest sound. Even in the dark, he could see Billy's bulk, scrabbling around, searching for more stones.

Mick finally made it into a crouch. He had a choice now: try and creep over, or rush him.

He was afraid; he was afraid to move. Afraid.

I'll take the one Big Jack brought... He looks like a fucking eejit...

Mick rested his shaking hand on Sharpie's back. He thought of his brother's cocky laugh, his infernal banter. He thought of Sharpie, his brother, his best friend. A strange calm enveloped him. He stopped shaking and began to focus.

He had one chance, and he was going to make it pay. Never mind the fear, never mind the pain. The pain was terrible, but it meant he was alive. It meant he had a chance.

Mick dug his heels into the ground, gritted his teeth and charged.

Billy heard him at the last second. He spun around, but he was off balance. Mick hit him right in the chest with his shoulder. It was like being hit by a speeding train.

With a terrified scream, Billy Lawson fell through the air and landed with a splash in the black, stinking water below.

# 34

Big Jack was not a well man. Not only was he ferociously hung over, but he was worried that his whole life was about to go down the toilet, along with what felt like most of his insides. He was so angry and distraught at being woken in the middle of the night, he hadn't even styled his hair. It lay on top of his head like a dead crow.

He clutched the chair in front of him and tried very hard to understand what he was hearing from the two filthy men seated in front of him. A taxi had left them at his house not fifteen minutes before, and this simple action had screwed his day.

Billy had called him at ten past two that morning. It had taken them that long to walk the eight miles back through the woods to the main road and find a phone box. Billy's mobile had been destroyed by the swim in the filthy lake, and Jimmy's had been in the goddamned car – which Mick Quinn had stolen when Jimmy had gone to help Billy.

'So let me just see if I'm understanding this correctly,' Big Jack said, a tremble in his voice. 'What you're telling me is that a slip of a lad, battered to shite – dying, according to you – somehow managed to overpower you pair of cunts. And not only that: this battered, dying slip of a lad also managed to take off in your fucking car. Is that what you're telling me?' He gripped the back of his kitchen chair so hard that the wood creaked and groaned in his massive hands.

Billy scowled and nodded miserably. Despite the fact that he had vomited copiously after Jimmy had half dragged him from the stinking water of the lake, he was convinced he was about to die of some bacterial infection from swallowing so much filthy water – either that or pneumonia. He shivered. He stank to high heaven, too. In the heat of the kitchen, the stench was almost unbearable.

'Look, Uncle Jack, it wasn't our fault. He fucking ambushed me.'

'He is a kid, a fucking kid, and you muppets let him get away.'

'I didn't let him do anything. He pushed me off a fucking cliff, Jack. I could've drowned!'

'And you!' Big Jack turned on Jimmy. 'What the fuck were you doing?'

Jimmy shrugged. 'It was dark. By the time I'd figured out what was going on and dragged Billy out of the water, he was already halfway down the lane.'

'You should have stopped him first.'

'I didn't know he'd pushed him. I thought Billy had fallen in. Anyway, Billy can't swim. If I'd gone for the kid, Billy'd be dead.'

'Jesus.' Big Jack closed his eyes. Mick, the tough little bastard.

'You know, we wouldn't be in this fucking situation if you hadn't used them kids to do a break-in to start with.'

Big Jack let go of the chair and backhanded Jimmy across the face so hard that he fell out of his seat. 'If you say that once more, I'm going to take you out the fucking back and drown you myself, finish the fucking job.'

Billy shivered and glanced at Jimmy, who was picking himself up, a murderous expression across his fat face. 'No point beating on us, Jack.'

'Tell me this, now. What the fuck did you do with Sharpie?'

'What could we do? We tossed him in the lake.'

'Oh, Jesus.' Big Jack rubbed his hands over his face. If Mick went to the cops, and if he remembered how to get back to the lake, it was all over. There was bound to be evidence on Sharpie's body. He had scratched Jack badly – would the pond destroy DNA evidence? How would he explain the scratches?

Jimmy looked at the floor and Billy shrugged sullenly. 'What the fuck were we supposed to do, bring him here? Look, we didn't really have much of a choice, did we? I'm sick of this. Fuck, man, I almost drowned. My father's gonna be livid when he gets wind of all this.'

Big Jack stared at them for so long his eyes watered. This was a nightmare, a walking fucking nightmare.

He had to think. Mick was the key, he had to find him. The car was a ringer and not connected to him in any way. The two eejits in front of him had no records and therefore no fingerprints on record. Anyway, all of this worry was based on the idea that Mick would even go to the cops. He might be scared shitless and run for it. Of course, if the private detectives got wind of that, it would sound suspect, especially as they had been asking David Reid's friends about the boys over the break-in – but then again, with the fence dead, it would only be natural if the Quinns ran; it would prove their involvement. And then the private dicks could go swing for it. There was nothing to connect Jack to David Reid.

Unless they got to Mick.

'Fuck.' Big Jack stalked over to the sink, got a glass of water and stared at his reflection in the kitchen window. He had to find Mick, and fast. He had to finish the job.

He let out a deep breath. First things first: he had to get rid of this pair of clowns, get them back across the border fast.

'Right, I'll get ye a car. You got to get back up home.'

'Do you have any spare clothes?'

'Clothes?'

'Yeah. I can't go anywhere like this, I stink.'

Big Jack bit down on his bottom lip till it turned white. His eyes narrowed, and for a moment it looked like he might fly across the room and simply tear Billy in half, nephew or no nephew.

Billy shut his trap. Big Jack called Robbie and asked him – praying he was sober enough to do it – to deliver a car to the house.

*

When Sarah stepped into the office that morning, she was surprised to find John slumped in his chair, with David Reid's laptop open on the desk in front of him. John looked up at her arrival. He yawned and rubbed his dense stubble. He wore his usual attire – faded jeans and a pale-blue T-shirt – but he looked crumpled, more crumpled than normal. She thought he looked exactly how she felt. She was late because she'd had to go next door and ask her neighbour, Eileen O'Connor, to pop in on her mother and keep an eye out for her. It had been all she could do not to cry at the look of compassion and understanding on Eileen's face when she had said of course, it would be no problem.

'John? What are you doing here so early?'

'What happened to you? Why didn't you call me back last night?'

Sarah hung up her jacket. 'I'm sorry. Something came up, and by the time I'd dealt with it, it was kind of late.'

'Sarah, what is going on with you?'

'What do you mean?'

'You've been acting really strange lately. You're distracted, you look like shit, and what's with the phone thing? Are you in some kind of trouble? You know you can trust me.'

Sarah looked at him and smiled. He looked so genuinely concerned that she felt an overwhelming urge to blurt everything out. 'I'm having a weird sort of week.'

'Want to talk about it?'

'John, everything's fine. I'm sorry I forgot to call you back. So tell me – you got into the computer ?'

'Right.' John shrugged, knowing she wasn't telling him the truth and frustrated by the brush-off. 'Clique opened it up in minutes. I've had a look through most of it – pretty boring shit, really, mostly work-related stuff and whatnot. No mention of any gambling or debts. I haven't found anything that might make it worth stealing.'

'There has to be something.'

'There isn't, but feel free to prove me wrong.'

Sarah sighed. 'Really? I was sure there would be something.'

'Yeah, well, me too,' John said. 'But I've been reading through his e-mails half the night, and I've come up blank. You sure this is what those lads were looking for?'

'There has to be something on there. I heard them talking, they were definitely looking for something specific. And apart from the jewellery and stuff, that was the only thing missing from the house.'

'That you know of.'

'Right.'

'Here, take it; be my guest. I'm sick of looking at it.' He stood up and stretched. 'I'm making more coffee. Want one?'

'Please.' Sarah picked up the laptop and carried it to her desk. After half an hour of scrolling through the e-mails, she sighed.

'See? Boring, isn't it?'

'We need to narrow the search.'

'To what?'

'To just before David made the order for his savings.'

Sarah pulled out the bank statement she had collected the day before, ran a search for files from the previous month, and scrolled though them from start to finish. 'Damn it.'

'Nothing?'

'Nothing – nothing on the desktop, nothing in the files. Just work-related stuff... and a couple of porn sites.'

'Yeah, got a few eyefuls of that myself last night.'

Sarah clicked down further. 'The man liked his porn.'

'What man doesn't?'

'Guess he never thought anyone would be digging through his personal stuff. It seems kind of wrong.'

'Digging through personal lives is what we do, Sarah. Look, this is getting us nowhere.' John stood up. 'I'm going out.'

'Where?'

'To talk to Mick again.' John grabbed his keys and made for the door. 'I'm tired of stumbling around. I'm going to do what we should have done in the first place. I'm going to ask Mick Quinn exactly who sent him to break into David Reid's house, and why.'

'Are you going to the garage? What about Jack Lawson?'

'What about him?' John said. He ran his hands through his hair. 'Look, like you said, at some point we're going to have to tell Detective Stafford that we know who broke into David Reid's house, and that Mick works for Jack. The cops will want to talk to the boys about Bo. We have David's computer and we can connect them. So, one way or another, this will be out of our hands, and before that happens, I want someone to give me straight bloody answers.'

'Wait!' Sarah cried as he stepped out into the hall. 'Don't forget you've got that other job on today – Mrs Conway's husband.'

'I won't, I won't,' John said, even though he had completely forgotten about it. 'Call me when he's on the move.'

'Make sure you don't lose them this time,' Sarah said tiredly. 'We could do with the money.'

John looked at her. She looked pale and almost as dispirited as he felt. 'Are you sure you're okay?'

'I'm fine.'

'You know if you need to talk to me, I'm here, right?'

'I know that, John.' Sarah smiled softly at him. 'Thank you.'

'Okay, then.' John hesitated, but there was nothing more to say, so he left.

*

'You again.' Rose Quinn moved the cigarette to the other side of her mouth. 'They're not here.'

'Well, I called by the garage, there's no one there. Look, Mrs Quinn, I don't have time to—'

'Too bad. They were roped in by the cops yesterday.'

'Were they?' John said, thinking, Bang goes my chance to ask any questions.

'They took Mick in, anyway.'

'But not Shane?'

'No – and before you ask, I haven't seen hide nor hair of him since yesterday, either.' She folded her massive arms across her chest. 'Look, I don't know what the hell's goin' on, but it's not right. They were very rough with Mick, too, grabbin' him like that.'

'Which station was it?'

'Store Street, he said,' Rose huffed.

'Did you happen to get their names?' John took out his notebook.

'Detective Furlong, and the fat one was called – hang on… Sergeant Paddock.'

John looked up. 'Furlong and Paddock?'

'That's what they said.'

'They show you any identification, or a warrant or anything?'

Rose looked at John as if he was crazy. 'I didn't ask. I mean, they was cops, I just— Here, do you think they weren't?'

'What was the charge?'

'I don't know, do I? Nobody ever tells me nothing. They were pushy, but, like, cops.'

'Did they caution Mick, or ask you to go along with them?'

'No. Actually, they wouldn't hardly let him open his mouth.'

John glanced at his watch. If Mick had been brought in yesterday and not yet released, that meant they had to be charging him with something. Still, Furlong and Paddock?

'Look, I'll go and see if I can find out what the charges are. Thanks for your time.' He turned to go.

'Hey.'

He turned back. The cigarette was still there, but the attitude was not. Rose looked, if anything, a little nervous. Her small, washed-out eyes were fixed intently on his.

'Do you think there's something funny about them calling here? I mean, now that you say it out loud like that – Paddock and Furlong... And the blond fella, now that I think about it, he was awful fat to be a cop.'

'I'm sure it's nothing.'

'If you do get a hold of either of the boys, will you tell them to give me a call? I can't get them on their mobiles, and I'm, you know... Just... if you could just say it to them.'

'Sure, no problem.'

'Thanks.'

John went back down the path and got into his car. He rang Directory Enquiries and got the number for Store Street Garda Station. He spoke to a very pleasant and helpful garda who John just knew, from the sound of her voice, had to be a cutie. But, cutie or not, she informed him that there was no Michael Quinn being held there – and, more worryingly, there was no Detective Furlong or Sergeant Paddock working there, either.

# 35

Clive pulled back his curtains and glanced up at the sky. He yawned and stretched. It was still a bit grey, but starting to clear. The light rain from last night had stopped, and there was hope that by four o'clock the sky would be blue, blue and sunny.

A perfect day for a wedding.

A perfect day to put all his troubles behind him and start afresh. He checked his watch: eleven o'clock. Excellent – plenty of time to grab a shower and have a bite to eat. Sylvia had stayed over at her parents' house last night, so he was alone on this, his last morning as a single man. He glanced at his reflection in the bedroom mirror and smiled. This was going to be the happiest day of his life. He wasn't going to let anything take away from it.

He headed for the shower, whistling softly under his breath.

*

Big Jack was beginning to get a grip on his panic.

He drove into town and called into the showroom. He chatted briefly with the two girls at the front desk and spoke with the main salesman. But the whole time he was talking business, he was running an entirely different commentary in his head.

Okay, things weren't great, but it wasn't the end of the world. Mistakes had been made, but mistakes could be rectified. Billy and Jimmy had gone back up North, safely out of the way. Sharpie was dead, his body at the bottom of that lake. Robbie had seen Big Jack with him, but Robbie was no fan of Sharpie Quinn, and if he knew what was good for him, he'd keep his trap shut. There would be no way to connect Big Jack to Sharpie's disappearance – once he found Mick.

He swung by the garage and told the grouchy Robbie – who had arrived, sleepily, minutes before – that he would be back later on, and to give him a shout if Mick turned up. As he went over to the laundrette on the NCR, to pick up the money for that week, he started to make calls, making sure every person he knew was keeping an eye out for Mick, especially at hospitals.

Of course, even with Mick out of the picture, there would be questions and repercussions. Jack's brother Tom would be upset. The gardaí might visit, ask questions about Mick being missing, but he could deal with that. He'd say he figured that Mick must have been involved in the death of the fence and had fled rather than face the consequences. Big Jack would be shocked and appalled, of course, but resigned. He had tried to give the lad a chance in life, but sometimes even good lads could get pulled down by family…

He ran through it again. Two men had picked Mick up from the house? No, nothing to do with him. Well, like everyone always said, who knew what the hell Sharpie Quinn was up to? Sure, it was rumoured that he was involved in drugs. Then again, maybe it was connected with the death of the fence. People like that knew other people like that. It was unfortunate, but that's life these days: no values.

What if Mick was in a garda station right now?

Big Jack wiped his brow. He was sweating from a combination of heat, hangover and fear. He hadn't slept well, even with the drink. He kept hearing the strangling sounds Sharpie had made. It had been many a year since he'd taken a life, and back then it hadn't been anyone he'd known. No, no doubt about it: he was too old for this shit.

John drove back into town, his mind in turmoil. He had a bad feeling in the pit of his stomach, a bad, bad feeling. Something was not right. Why had someone come along and taken Mick like that?

He was turning onto Wexford Street when his mobile rang.

'Hello?'

It was Sarah. 'John, where are you?'

'Hey. I'm about to park the car.'

'Don't bother. Mrs Conway called: he left ten minutes ago. You need to get to the girlfriend's house and follow them.'

'Ah, fuck.' John looked at his watch and groaned.

'What's wrong?'

'The Quinn boys – they're missing.'

'Both of them?'

'Their mother said Mick was picked up yesterday by two guys claiming they were cops, and he hasn't been heard from since. Sharpie's dropped off the face of the planet, too.'

'What do you mean, claiming to be cops?'

'They didn't show her any ID, and they said they were called Furlong and Paddock—'

'That's got to be a joke, for a start. Racing names.'

'Exactly. And they said they were from Store Street, but Store Street has no one of those names working there, and they've never heard of Mick.'

'Jesus.' Sarah said nothing for a moment. 'Well, look, you get after Conway and I'll ring around a few of the other stations. Maybe it wasn't Store Street.'

'Will you?'

'Sure.'

'Thanks, Sarah.'

'No problem.'

Big Jack did the rest of his rounds with a headache building behind his eyes. By the time he made his way back to the garage, he was sweating profusely. The day seemed heavy and oppressive as the heat rose.

He frowned when he saw the gates to the yard were closed. He glanced at his watch and swore. Where the fuck had Robbie gone? He parked up on the kerb, heaved his massive bulk out of the car and went to the gates. They were unlocked.

Still puzzled, Big Jack stepped into the yard. He could hear the radio blaring from the big shed in the corner. The heat was unbearable. He mopped at his brow again. The sweat was pumping off him.

'Robbie? Why're them gates shut over?'

No answer. Big Jack smoothed his hair and hitched his pants up higher as he made his way across the yard. He grabbed the shed's massive sliding door, wrenched it back on its tracks and stepped into the gloomy interior.

'Robbie?'

The Corsa that Robbie had been working on was there, the bonnet up, waiting. Something rattled at the back of the garage, where the floor pit was.

'Robbie?' He probably couldn't hear, over that racket. 'Are you deaf or what? Why are them gates shut over? I told you before, I don't like them shut. People will think we're closed.'

Big Jack walked around the Corsa and saw Robbie sitting on the floor by the tyre-stand, his hands and feet bound by gaffer tape, another thick strip over his mouth. His bloodshot eyes were huge and dancing wildly in his head. He had an ugly welt on the left side of his head.

'Robbie! What the hell—'

'You fucking bastard!'

Big Jack swung round as Mick Quinn stepped out of the shadows behind him and swung the tyre iron with a magnificent upward stoke. The blow connected with the underside of Jack's lantern jaw and knocked him clean off his feet.

Mick stepped over his prone body. 'The bigger they are,' he said, and spat on his employer's face.

# 36

John drove slowly, keeping his distance in case he disturbed the two lovebirds in the car ahead. He had followed them from the blonde's house, and now they were cruising through the car park of Jervis Street shopping centre.

John's stomach rumbled. He'd eaten nothing that day and he was absolutely famished. He was seriously considering eating a half-melted Mars bar he had found in the glove compartment when Martin Conway nipped into a tight parking space.

'Shit.'

John drove past and luckily found a parking space on the next level. He parked the Manta, grabbed his digital camera and ran back downstairs just in time to see Conway and the blonde disappearing into the stairwell. John grinned. The chase was on, and this time he would make damn sure he had something to show for all this time.

He raced down the stairs and out onto the upper floor of the shopping centre. He spotted his quarry immediately, strolling amongst the other shoppers, chatting and smiling, looking innocent and sweet and not at all like two people about to engage in an illicit act.

John took a few pictures of them and strolled along, pretending to look into the shop windows. To his gut-rumbling delight, they entered a café and took a seat at the back. John bought a newspaper and followed. He took a seat near the kitchen, where he could observe them without being too obvious about it.

'Whatcanigetcha?' A bored-looking waiter with raging acne wiped the table, spraying crumbs everywhere, including over John.

'Coffee, and a cheese-and-ham toasted sandwich.' John craned his neck around the waiter. Shit, were they actually canoodling in full view of everyone? He lowered his camera, as if trying to work out the buttons, and tried to snap them.

'Ciabatta or regular?'

'Regular.'

'White or black coffee?'

'White.'

'Cheddar or Edam?'

'Jesus, I don't care. Cheddar will do.'

The waiter gave John a snotty look and wandered off. John angled his camera and took another few shots. They were canoodling – in broad daylight, too. Conway was grinning broadly, and as John snapped away he leaned across the table and whispered something into the blonde's ear. Whatever he said, the blonde giggled and gave his hand a playful slap. They ordered a pot of tea and ignored it when it came.

Moments later, Conway leaned across, whispered something else and then abruptly stood up and left the coffee shop. The blonde checked her watch and drummed her fingers on the table top. She opened her handbag and retouched her lipstick and checked her watch again. She fidgeted.

John had never been this close to her before. She looked older, brassier than she did from a distance. John felt the sweat run down his back. Now what?

Suddenly she got up, grabbed her handbag and left. Her incredibly high heels clicked loudly on the tiled floor as she swished past John in a cloud of cheap perfume.

'Shit,' John said. He got up to follow.

'Hey! Where do you think you're going? Your food is ordered.' The pimply faced waiter blocked John's exit.

'I have to—'

'You have to pay for it. It's ready. You ordered it.'

'Fine – keep the coffee, give me the sandwich to go.'

John dug around in his pocket for money and then waited another agonising few seconds for his change. He raced out of the café, but to no avail: Martin Conway and the blonde had vanished.

Cursing furiously, John ran to the upper level of the shopping centre and leaned as far out over the rail as gravity would allow. He peered up and down, but there was no sign of them among the shoppers.

'Damn it!'

He ran all around the upper level, looking in through the shop windows, and then took the escalator down to the ground floor. He checked the whole floor, from each entrance: no sign of them anywhere.

Disheartened, John sat down wearily on a bench and began to eat his sandwich. He couldn't believe it. He had lost them again.

He took out his camera and had a check through the pictures. Some of them were a little blurry, but the ones he had taken in the café were perfect. At least he had photos of them being a little bit fresh with each other – not kissing, but looking very lovey-dovey. John sighed. They were hardly concrete evidence of hanky-panky, and Mrs Conway wanted concrete.

He finished his sandwich, balled the paper up and flung it in the bin. He was beginning to wonder if Conway and the blonde were actually having anything more sordid than a mild flirtation. If she were his mistress, wouldn't he be trying to get his leg over at some stage? But he hardly spent any time in her house when he picked her up, and he always went straight home after he dropped her off. And every time John had followed them, they went somewhere very public – almost as if they wanted people to see them...

John stopped walking.

What if the trips were the foreplay, the lead-up? What if Martin Conway didn't need a bed to get his jollies?

John looked around him. Where would a couple go? Not the public toilets – too many people. Then where?

John walked around quickly, keeping a sharp eye out. He was beginning to grow frustrated when he spotted a familiar blonde head disappearing behind a railing in Debenham's.

'Gotcha!'

He made his way into the store and followed her at what he hoped was a discreet distance. Whatever she was doing, she wasn't shopping. Every so often she glanced around, acting suspiciously like a shoplifter. John managed to snap a few pictures of her looking his way. Then she was off again, heading at a decent clip to the back of the store, towards the Debenham's bathrooms.

John crossed his fingers and followed.

The blonde did another quick eye-sweep of the store before ducking into the ladies. 'Okay, okay,' John muttered to himself. It could be nothing, or it could be something. Either she was going to the bathroom, or she wasn't.

And there was only one way to find out.

John counted to twenty and ducked into the toilets behind her.

'Excuse me!' A middle-aged woman primping in front of the mirrors snatched up her handbag. 'You can't come in here. This is the ladies.'

'Sorry,' John said, holding his hands up. 'I'm looking for my wife. Honey?'

'You can't come in here.'

'Honey, I'll wait for you in the car! Sorry, sorry.'

John retreated. He spent a few minutes lurking about in the shirt department before the middle-aged woman came out. As soon as she was gone, he went back inside.

He ducked down, peeping under each stall door. The blonde had been wearing beige high-heeled shoes with an open toe. When he got to the very last stall on the left row, he found the shoes – but they were empty. However, John noted gleefully, there was another pair of shoes beside them – or, rather, between them – and unless the blonde had suddenly taken up wearing brown brogues in a size nine, John had found his evidence.

He nipped silently into the stall next door and climbed up on the toilet seat. He checked that his camera was operating perfectly, then he peered over the partition and said, 'Smile, folks! You're on Candid Camera!'

It was a cheesy line and he knew it, but somehow it seemed fitting.

The camera snapped. The blonde stared up at him in amazement and began to scream, as did Martin Conway. She had her legs around his waist and he seemed to be frozen, his grubby little hands wrapped around her bosom. It was a great photo opportunity.

Martin Conway recovered first.

'You dirty fucking pervert!'

John laughed, jumped down and made a run for it.

He was still laughing as he made his way back to the car. Sometimes he hated his job, other times he loved it passionately. This was a good day.

He was running through the car park when he stopped dead in his tracks. This was better than a good day. This day was tops.

'Oh, Lord, thank you. Feast or famine.'

Parked neatly in front of him, in Block D, row 8, was an Audi Quattro, silver, its registration number an exact match to David Reid's car.

John approached the car and looked in through the window. It was full of junk and McDonald's wrappers. He walked around to the front and put his hand on the bonnet.

It was warm.

Someone had, not too long ago, parked this car here.

John shook his head in wonder. He took out his phone, called Sarah, then settled in to wait.

# 37

Clive looked at his reflection in the mirror and re-adjusted his tie. He was still at it when his father came up behind him, his face split by a massive smile, his eyes misty.

'Aw, Dad,' Clive said, smiling fondly at him. 'Not you too.' His mother hadn't stopped sniffling since she had arrived half an hour before.

'I'm proud of you, lad. I wanted to tell you that. You and Sylvia are a great couple. Your mother and I…we wanted to tell you that.'

It was so heartfelt that Clive choked up. He wanted to say something in return, but he couldn't find the words. Instead he turned and hugged his father, as hard as he could.

*

Larry stared at Dee as though he had never seen her before.

'What?' she said, smiling.

'You're beautiful.'

'Oh, stop,' Dee said, but she was pleased. She knew she looked well. Her hair had been cut and styled the day before and rested softly on her shoulders, and the green Jil Sander she had bought especially for the wedding made her feel like a movie star.

Larry went to her and kissed her gently on the forehead. 'I love you.'

She smiled again and, to his surprise, lifted her head and smooched him like a schoolgirl on her first date.

\*

Max cursed as he struggled with his cufflinks. 'I hate these fucking things.'

In the en-suite bathroom, Laura Ashcroft opened the press under her sink and unzipped her make-up bag. She found the Xanax and dry-swallowed two of them. She was about to pop the packet back into the press when she noticed there were only three left. Damn. She'd only had that prescription two weeks.

She paused. A whole day with Max and his unbearable friends and their snotty, bitchy wives… She slipped the packet into her clutch bag. They, and as much vodka as she could sink without being described as a lush, should help her get through it.

'Hey!' Max shouted. 'Come help me with these, will you?'

Laura straightened up and rearranged her features as if by magic. 'Coming,' she said, in a cheerful voice that was as natural as her blonde hair.

\*

Big Jack opened his eyes and stared up groggily at the slip of a lad who had floored him. He moaned when he saw the state Mick was in.

Mick staggered a little. He was clearly horribly concussed, and he seemed to be having trouble standing. Jack could hardly believe that what he was looking at was Mick. One of the kid's eyes was completely shut, and his face was a mass of purple and black bruising.

'Why?' Mick raised the tyre iron again, and Big Jack raised his hands to ward off the blow. But Mick didn't seem to have the energy to hold it up. 'Why did you do this to me?'

'Mick…' The first blow had broken Jack's jaw. Blood ran into his mouth and down his throat; he choked and spat. The pain was almost unbearable. 'Mick, let me explain.'

'Why did you do it, Jack?' Mick wiped at his one open eye. 'I did everything you asked me to do. Why did you kill him? Why'd you kill Sharpie? Why did you kill my brother?'

'Mick, I don't know… what you're…' But it was almost incomprehensible even to his own ears.

'I heard them talking! I heard them. You did it, you, you, you.' Mick started to cry. 'I didn't… I wouldn't have said anything. I just wanted… just wanted to work.' Snot dribbled from his broken nose and mixed freely with the blood and dirt. He lifted the tyre iron and swung it as hard as he could. This time the blow broke Big Jack's radius. 'Why? Why'd you have to kill him? Why?'

Jack screamed and tried to roll out of the way and protect himself at the same time. Mick kicked his good arm away, and, screaming, he raised the iron in both hands and smashed it down, again and again and again, until there was nothing left of Big Jack Lawson's head but a pulpy, bloody mess.

Exhausted, Mick tossed the tyre iron aside and staggered away from Jack. He crashed into a metal shelving unit and dropped to his knees. He lifted his head and looked at Robbie through his destroyed eyes.

Robbie had been screaming behind his gag during the attack, but now he sat silent, his eyes huge and pleading. The sweat stood out on his forehead. He was splattered with blood.

'He killed Sharpie.'

Robbie nodded slowly, too terrified even to blink.

'He did it. He set us up, Robbie. Two men.' Mick toppled over onto his side. 'Sharpie…'

Then he passed out.

# 38

'Wonder who those guys were who took Mick Quinn away.'

Sarah glanced at John. 'Are you really worried?'

'I don't know. It's weird, though: a few days after Bo's old lad tells the cops about his suspicions, someone gets to Mick. And the other one's gone, too.'

'Maybe the mother was lying. Maybe they've just done a runner.'

'She was on the up-and-up. We thought Bo had done a runner, and look how he ended up.'

Sarah blanched. 'You don't think…'

John grunted and lit another cigarette. 'I don't know. I don't like it. I've got a bad feeling about it.'

Sarah shifted in her seat and looked across at the silver Audi. 'Are you sure the engine was warm?'

'Positive.'

'Well, it won't be now.'

'I'm telling you, someone parked it there not long before I called you.'

Sarah rolled her neck until it cracked. She broke her Mars bar and handed half to John. They were sitting in John's Manta, which was now facing the Audi. John had moved it when Sarah had arrived, in case they needed to follow someone. But so far there was no sign of anyone coming back to the Audi.

'I can't believe the neck of those two fellas,' John said through a mouthful of Mars bar. 'Just going up to the house like that.'

'It's a good ploy, if you ask me, long as you can pull it off. Who's going to mess with the gardaí?'

'Mm. I'm going to go by the garage again this afternoon, make sure Jack Lawson knows I'm looking into Mick's business. I'm gonna make sure that fat lump knows I'm watching him.'

'You don't think he has anything to do with it, do you?'

John shrugged. But he did. He had spoken to Mike Brannigan again, and Mike had assured him that Jack Lawson was not the sort of man who liked attention. If Mick and Sharpie were in trouble with the law, Jack would take a very dim view of it. But still, that didn't mean he would harm the boys. Maybe he would hide them. But then why send two men to the house? Why the garda act?

Sarah fidgeted, bored and fighting an attack of drowsiness. 'Show me your camera again.'

John passed her the digital camera. Sarah turned it on and laughed softly. She had seen the photos twice already, and yet they still made her giggle.

John raised an eyebrow. 'They're good, aren't they?'

'She wanted proof and, baby, is she getting proof.' Sarah particularly liked the shot where both parties were looking straight up into John's camera, a startled look on the blonde's face, a mixture of lust and terror on Martin Conway's shiny chops. 'Oh, she's going to have his balls for this.'

'Not exactly the sort of man I'd have pinned for the outdoor-loving type. A real little risk-taker. Just goes to show you can never judge a book by its cover.'

'Damn straight.' Sarah's mobile rang. She got it out, looked at the screen and hit Busy. Seconds later, it burst into life again. Sarah's lips whitened. She turned the phone off completely and set it on her lap.

John watched the little performance. 'Can I ask you a question?'

'Sure.'

'What's going on with the calls?'

Sarah looked at him. Her hair had been freshly washed that morning and it hung down loose, framing her face like velvet. 'What do you mean?'

'Look, I know you don't like it when people pry, but—'

Sarah frowned and looked out the window. 'It's nothing. Family business.'

'Anything I can do to help?'

'No.'

'Okay.'

They sat in silence for another moment or two. Then Sarah sighed. 'It's Helen, and I don't want to talk to her.'

That John could understand, but he knew there was more to this. 'Why not? I mean, apart from the obvious.'

'When Mum had that accident the other week, sprained her wrist...' Sarah tried to keep the misery out of her voice and failed. 'My sisters think it... they want to put Mum into a retirement community.'

'Because of a sprained wrist?'

'She's not sure how she fell. She can't remember. She's...she's showing all the signs of early-onset Alzheimer's.' And as Sarah said the words, she knew they were true.

'Oh, shit, Sarah, I'm sorry. Why didn't you say anything?'

'I don't know. I think. I thought if I didn't say it, then it wouldn't be true.'

'I'm so sorry.'

'I...'

John reached out to take Sarah's hand and was amazed when she collapsed across the handbrake onto his chest, sobbing bitterly. The tears she had been holding in check for the last few days finally spilled over.

Whatever John had been expecting, this wasn't it. He didn't know what to say. He scrambled desperately for the right words of comfort. He couldn't believe she had opened up to him – it was so unlike her. And now... what could he say? Maybe the best thing would be to say nothing, just hold her, let her let it out.

So he did. He held Sarah close and let her cry. But it wasn't long before he felt her stiffen and pull herself together. He only had one chance before she slipped away. He lifted her head and cupped her face with his hands.

'Listen to me.'

Sarah looked at him, tears streaming down her face.

'I am here for you, you understand me? You need me for anything, anything at all, and I'll be right there. If you need time off work, take it – take whatever you need. Just don't shut me out.'

She nodded. 'Okay.'

John brushed a tear away with his thumb. 'I mean it, Sarah.'

'I'm all right. I'm all right.' She straightened up and slid back into her own seat. She wiped her face with her sleeve and cleared her throat. 'Stupid, really.'

'It's not. It's not stupid at all. How long have you known?'

'Honestly? A while.' She sort of laughed. 'I knew something was wrong, but she's always been a bit... well, you know what she's like.'

'She can be a little eccentric,' John said, smiling to soften the words. As long as he'd known Sarah, her mother had always been a little nutty. John's mother used to say that Deirdre Kenny had one foot in this world and one in the next.

'Exactly, so I didn't really think anything of it at first. But the last few months... I thought I could help her. I didn't want to believe it. You know me – denial, denial, denial, until it hits me right between the eyes.'

'Is it really that bad?'

'I don't know how bad it really is. My sisters want her to do tests, and I'm afraid...' She dashed at her tears violently. 'I'm not ready to give up and just stick her in a fucking home, no matter what they call it.'

'I'm sorry.'

'Thank you.'

John smiled. He tried to think of some words of comfort, but he couldn't. Sarah was losing her only remaining parent, and nothing he could say would change that. Alzheimer's wasn't something he could even imagine. True, both his parents were dead, but they had been elderly and both had gone fast. Alzheimer's robbed you of a loved one long before he or she left this earth.

He was still trying to think of something to say when JJ Hutton came bobbing along, a set of keys swinging from his hand, a big fat joint tucked behind his ear. He was listening to his new iPod and singing along, badly, to Ce Ce Peniston. Two Champion Sports bags dangled from his wrist. He wore navy jeans with green stitching, a huge hoodie with front pockets and brand new Timberlands. He clicked his fingers in time to the music.

'Look at the state of that,' John said, trying to lighten the mood.

Sarah sniffed, but then she frowned. 'He's going towards the Audi.'

'You don't think he's our guy, do you?'

Sarah and John sat up straight. They watched as JJ lifted his arm and pressed the remote control on his key ring. The Audi flashed its lights twice in response.

'It is him! Quick, he'll get away.'

John leapt out of the car and walked quickly towards JJ, who was putting his purchases into the boot.

'Hey! Hey, you!'

Because of Ce Ce, JJ only noticed John coming at the last moment, and by then it was too late to do a runner. He slammed the boot closed and lunged for the driver's door. He had managed to get it open and dive in when John opened the passenger door, reached across the handbrake and slapped him upside the head so hard that he dropped the keys and his left earphone popped out.

'Ow – shit! Whoa, man – I don't have any money. Take the fucking bags, man, just don't hurt me.'

'I'm not trying to rob you, you bloody idiot. Give me the keys.'

JJ fumbled for the car keys. 'What's this about?'

'It's about you driving a dead man's car around, you dumb shit. With his keys. Want to explain that?'

'Who, me?' JJ squeaked, somewhat unconvincingly. 'I don't know what you're talking about. I don't know anything about no dead man.'

John rolled his eyes. At least he hadn't said, 'What car?' 'Give me the keys before I whop you another one.'

JJ's shoulders slumped. He picked the keys up and reluctantly handed them to John. 'Hey, be cool, man, be cool.'

'You be cool, and shut up.'

'Are you a cop?'

'What do you think? If you try a runner, I swear to God I'll rip every mat out of that head of yours. Now, what are you doing driving around in David Reid's car?'

'I bought it, man. Off a guy in a bar.'

'Yeah? For how much?'

'I don't know, couple of thou. He said he was going abroad, needed a quick sale.'

'Yeah? Which pub?'

'I...'

'Think quick, now.'

'I can't, man, not with you breathing down on me—'

'Did he have wings?'

'What?'

'This guy who sold you the car. Did he have wings?'

'Wings?'

'Yeah, wings – maybe some kind of wand?'

JJ blinked slowly. 'I don't know what you mean.'

'You know, was he dressed as a fairy? Is there a car fairy I don't know about?'

'Look, man, I didn't do anything wrong, you know? I mean—'

Sarah tapped on the driver's window. JJ jumped and whirled around, dreadlocks flying.

'Roll your window down,' John said, slapping JJ on the back of the head again. JJ did as he was told.

Sarah peered in at JJ, taking in the joint behind his ear, the bloodshot eyes.

'What we doing, John?'

'He had the keys.'

'Interesting.'

'I think so. I'm going to take the car fairy here back to the office in my car. You follow behind in this.'

'Great. What's your name?'

'No way, man. I want a solicitor.' JJ shook his head. 'I'm not talking to no one.'

'I'm Sarah Kenny from QuicK Investigations. The man about to slap you upside the head again is my partner, John Quigley. So let's try again. Name?'

'Private detectives?' JJ looked relieved at first. He sniggered into his hand, then straightened up and looked pissed off. 'Hey! Who do you people think you are? I don't have to tell you nothing.'

'Okay. John, forget about the office. Just bring him straight to the cop shop. Let them charge him and be done with it.'

'Whoa! Charge? What charge we talking about here?'

'I don't know – robbery, carjacking, manslaughter... although they might bump it up to murder.'

'Probably be able to add possession of narcotics,' John said, yanking the joint out from behind JJ's ear and snagging more than a few hairs in the process.

'Right, then—'

'I didn't do no fucking murder! Hold on, now.' The colour had drained from JJ Hutton's face. He grabbed John's arm, and John noticed he had lost his devil-may-care look; even his dreadlocks seemed deflated. 'Look, man, I swear it. Bring me to your office. I'll tell you everything I know. But you've gotta believe me, man, I didn't do no murder. We don't have to involve no police. I'll tell you what I know.'

'Beautiful.' John slapped him on the back of the head again, just for the hell of it. 'Out.'

# 39

'Can I light this?'

'No,' Sarah said. 'Sit there and be quiet.'

JJ put the cigarette back in its box. He put his hands on the desk, then took them off and rubbed his legs, then put his hands back on the desk, his leg jiggling up and down.

Sarah sighed. 'John, can I talk to you outside for a second?'

'Behave.' John wagged his finger at JJ.

'Yeah, man, whatever.'

John and Sarah stepped onto the landing, and Sarah closed the door.

'Look, before we talk to this idiot, I want to know what we're going to do with him.'

'What do you mean?'

'He's going to say anything to wiggle out of being taken to the police.'

'Right.'

'John, I don't fancy any more run-ins with the gardaí. We need to give him to Stafford.'

'But we talk to him first, right?'

'I don't know. We should be ringing Stafford right now to say we

337

have the car. I think they might actually lock us up if we withhold information from them again.'

'We don't have any real information at the moment.'

Sarah narrowed her eyes. 'We have the car. And not just that – he had the keys. For all we know, he murdered David Reid.'

'Come on.'

'He could have.'

John sighed and folded his arms. He leaned against the wall. 'Okay, this is what we'll do. First we talk to this eejit in there and see if he has anything to offer, then we see how we play it.'

'Now you're splitting hairs.'

'I'm not.'

'John, don't be stupid.'

'Come on, ten minutes – we talk to him for ten minutes. What harm can it do?'

Sarah frowned and chewed her lip. 'All right. Ten minutes, tops. But then we're calling Stafford, I don't care what you say.'

John grinned at her. 'That's why I love working with you.'

'Yeah, yeah.'

*

Clive beamed at Sylvia and took her hand in his. They were sitting in the back of the Rolls, on their way to the reception.

'How are you doing, Mrs Hollingsworth?'

'Pretty good, Mr Hollingsworth.'

Clive lifted her hand and kissed the back of it. 'You look beautiful.'

'Thank you.' Sylvia kissed him on the mouth.

And it was true, Clive thought. He had never seen her look so lovely, so radiant. In her Vera Wang gown, with her hair so sleek and elegant, she looked like a delicate, rare orchid.

Clive let his head fall back on the rest and took a deep breath.

Maybe he could finally relax. Maybe Larry had been right. Maybe he could finally put the nightmare of the last few weeks behind him and start to live again.

'The ceremony was wonderful,' he said.

'Didn't the choir sound amazing? The soprano – oh my God, I literally got goosebumps all over when she sang "Vide Cor Meum".'

'Larry told me she sang at another wedding he went to. He said there wasn't a dry eye in the church when she finished.'

Sylvia smiled. But she didn't want to talk about Clive's dreary friends or about other weddings, not on this, the most important day of her life. 'Did you hear Mum? I thought we were going to have to stop for a few minutes.'

'She was really crying, wasn't she?'

'So was yours.'

'Not quite so… vocally.'

They grinned at each other. Mrs Cockburn's dramatic weeping had been ridiculous. Father Roche had had to raise his voice to cover it.

'I love you, Mrs Hollingsworth.'

'I love you too.'

They kissed so long and so passionately that the driver had to force himself to keep his eyes on the road.

\*

'Okay, JJ, let's hear it. Tell us how you ended up driving around in David Reid's car.'

'Look, the thing is…' JJ Hutton looked nervously between John and Sarah. 'I didn't really do nothing wrong, not really.'

Sarah sighed and sat down. She was getting pretty sick of hearing him say that. 'For all we know, you killed David Reid.'

'Man, I told you, I didn't kill no one. I swear. I wouldn't hurt no one. You can ask whoever, man: I'm non-violent. I swear.'

'Yeah, yeah, you swear. We get it.' John leaned against the window ledge and crossed his arms. 'Don't give me any more crap about buying the car in a pub. I don't believe it.'

JJ ran his hands over his dreads. 'Look, if I tell you what happened, will you keep me out of it? I don't want no trouble. I don't want the cops talking to me.'

'We can't do that,' Sarah said.

'But I didn't do nothing.'

'Stop saying that,' John said. 'You did something, otherwise you wouldn't be sitting there sweating up a storm.'

'I told you this was a waste of time.' Sarah reached for her phone. 'I'm ringing Inspector Stafford. You can feed him this line of bullshit until you're blue in the face.'

'All right, all right. Stall it.' JJ held out his hands in front of his face. Sarah paused with her fingers on the receiver. 'And no lies, either.'

'Yeah, all right.' JJ nodded and licked his lips. His mouth was bone-dry. He wished he hadn't gone into town in the car – that had been stupid. He also wished he weren't carrying almost a pound of grass in the inside pocket of his hoodie, grass he had bought that very morning from Joe, Triona's cousin, a hard-nosed little dealer JJ was half afraid of. If these two brought him to the cops and they searched him, he was fucked. He'd be caught for intent to supply as well as possession.

'Why didn't you even change the plates?'

JJ shrugged. 'Cops stop you and you got false plates, they're gonna find out straight off. I figured no one would have reported it stolen.'

'So you knew the owner was dead, then,' John said with a sly smile.

JJ swallowed and vowed to get his fucking wits about him.

Sarah opened a red spiral-bound notebook and plucked a well-chewed Biro out of the jam jar on her desk. 'Okay, let's go. Name?'

'JJ.'

'JJ what?'

'Hutton.'

'How old are you, JJ?'

'Twenty-two.'

'Where do you live?'

'Got a place over in Kilmainham.'

'Where?'

'Kilmainham Heights.'

Sarah and John exchanged glances. Kilmainham Heights was within view of the spot where David Reid had been found.

John went to Sarah's desk and sat on the corner of it, towering over JJ. JJ swallowed and licked his lips again. 'Look, I swear on me ma's life, I didn't go near your man.'

'Kilmainham Heights?'

'What?'

'Kilmainham Heights? That's where you live?'

'Yeah, the apartments there on the—'

'I know where they are. David Reid died right outside them. You sure you didn't run into him that night? Flag him down, rough him up a bit?' John grabbed JJ by the front of his jacket and jerked him closer. JJ squeaked in fright. 'Maybe you only meant to rob him, but he was so fucking wasted he fell in.'

'I didn't.' He looked pleadingly at Sarah. 'Don't let him hurt me.'

'Tell us why you're driving around in David Reid's Audi, with his keys. And no more bull. If you don't talk, I'm bringing you straight to the cops.'

JJ blinked rapidly, trying to think and failing miserably. 'Look, there was two of them. I didn't do nothing. I was having a spl— a fag under the bridge, and I saw the whole thing.'

John let go of him and shoved him back into the chair. 'What were you doing under the bridge?'

'All right, I was having a spliff. Triona—'

'Who's Triona?' Sarah asked.

'My girlfriend. Look, I swear to God, I didn't do nothing. There was—'

'What time was this at?' Sarah said, writing in the notebook.

'I dunno, exactly. I can't think.'

'You'd better,' John said menacingly.

'Yeah, yeah… around eleven or thereabouts.'

Sarah nodded. 'Right, go on. Go from the beginning, and don't leave anything out.'

'And if you lie about anything,' John said, leaning in, 'I'll know, and I swear to God, I'll kick you down those stairs outside so fast your feet won't even touch them.'

JJ flicked a quick look up at John's face and sighed. He was caught between a rock and a hard place, and he knew it. It was either spill to these arseholes or face the cops. No contest.

'All right. Look, me and Triona had a row, and I said I was going out to get some beers…'

It took him the best part of ten minutes to tell his story. When he was finished, you could have heard a pin drop in the stuffy office. Then John lurched forward and yanked JJ straight out of the chair by his dreadlocks.

'Right, we're going down to the station. You're a Grade A fucking bullshitter.'

'I'm telling you, that's what happened!' JJ said, struggling to free himself. He jerked away from John, losing quite a few hairs in the process. He wiped at his brow. He was sweating like a mad thing. He wished he could take off his jacket, but he didn't want to risk them seeing the grass.

'I don't believe you,' John said, advancing on him again. 'I think it's a bullshit story you concocted to make yourself look innocent. You expect us to believe you were sitting under a bridge like a fucking troll? You expect us to buy that?'

'I swear, that's what happened. The guy was wasted, all wobbly and shit, couldn't keep his feet under him – he looked totally out of it. I swear. They were fighting and he fell, and next thing I know, he's in the water and the other guy's holding him down. Then he high-tailed it.'

'And who was this guy with him? What did he look like?'

'I dunno.'

'Tall, short, fat, thin, long or short hair?'

'I don't know. Normal-looking.'

'Normal? That's the best you can give us?'

'I keep telling you, it was dark.'

Sarah stared at JJ with something approaching real revulsion. 'You're telling us you stood there and watched a man being drowned? Is that what you're telling us?'

'Wasn't that simple, you know?'

'You watched a man drown, and then you picked his body clean, like a… like a bloody vulture.'

'Hey, what was I supposed to do?' JJ looked offended. 'It was fight or flight, man. Survival.'

'Except you did neither. You waited.'

'Yeah, well…'

'You could have called an ambulance, you could have… you could have shouted for help. Jesus, you could at least have shouted "Stop!"'

JJ looked as Sarah as though she had suddenly dropped on all fours and begun barking. 'Are you fucking soft? What if he'd come after me?'

Sarah shook her head. 'He probably would have run for it.'

'Yeah, lady, right.' JJ huffed. 'Look, you asked me what happened, and I told you.'

'What did the man look like?' she asked.

'I told you, it was dark. He could have been tallish.'

'You see what kind of car this "tallish guy" was driving?' John snapped.

'Nah, didn't get a good look – it was up on the road. But I heard it. Sleek-sounding motor.'

'How did you find the Audi?' Sarah asked.

JJ looked uncomfortable. 'I used the car park ticket, man. It was in his wallet.'

'You still have it?'

'The ticket?'

'The wallet.'

'Nah.' He waved a hand dismissively. 'I got rid of that.'

'Where was the car?'

'Drury Street car park. Look, I've told you everything I know, I swear.'

Sarah wrote that down. They had checked that car park; no wonder they hadn't found the Audi. And it fitted in perfectly with where David Reid had been earlier that evening. He had left his car in Drury Street because he was drinking. JJ was probably telling the truth when he said that there was another car involved.

She picked up the Audi keys from her desk and studied them carefully. JJ's keyring was an ugly plastic affair, with a picture of a Rastafarian smoking a massive joint on the back.

'Is this your keyring?'

JJ looked at her sulkily. 'Yeah. So?'

'Was there anything on these keys when you got them? A silver globe, maybe?'

'Globe?'

'Yes, a globe – a silver ball. It had the words "Meridian Club" on it.'

'Oh, that.'

'Yes, that. I thought it might have come off in a struggle, but now you're saying the keys were in his pocket all along. So did you take it off?'

JJ blinked at her. 'What? How'd you know?'

Sarah looked at John in exasperation. 'Am I still talking in English?'

'Yep.' John slapped JJ on the back of the head. 'Pay attention.'

'Ow! Stop fucking hitting me!'

'Then answer the question.'

'I don't know, it was heavy and kind of stupid-looking. I just took it off. What's the big fucking deal? You can have it back. Shit, it's just sitting at home, anyways. You can have it back.'

'What did you say?' It was Sarah's turn to look confused. She opened her desk drawer and rummaged inside. She found the globe, took it out and tossed it to JJ.

He caught it neatly and looked down. 'Yeah, this is exactly the same. So?'

Sarah sat forward, her eyes alert and sharp. 'JJ, listen to me carefully. Are you saying that you took a globe exactly like that one off David Reid's keyring, and that you have it at home?'

JJ scowled and rubbed at the back of his head. 'I said that, didn't I? That's why I didn't know how you knew about it. No need to be slapping me and shit. You asked me and I told you.'

'Lying sons of bitches.'

Sarah opened her drawer and pulled out David's file. She flicked through the pages quickly and pulled out the photo she had found on the day of the break-in – the photo of four friends, taken on a beautiful sunny day at La Manga Golf Club.

She slapped the picture down on the desk in front of JJ. 'Look at that photo.'

JJ glanced at John suspiciously. 'You gonna hit me again?'

'Not unless you want me to.'

JJ huffed and bent over the photo.

'You see anyone here you recognise?'

'Shit, they wear some goofy-looking clothes, don't they?'

'Do you recognise—'

'Yeah, yeah, keep your shirt on. I seen one of these guys before.'

John and Sarah waited with bated breath. But JJ said nothing.

'Come on!' Sarah snapped eventually. 'Which one is it?'

But JJ's street brain had kicked into gear at last. He crossed his legs and looked at the two detectives, smiling slyly. 'Look, I don't know about this, you know? I could get in a lot of trouble here. If I tell you everything I know, how do I know you're not gonna drag me in and hand me over to the fucking cops?'

'Why would we do that?' John asked sarcastically. 'You being so helpful and all.'

'Look, I didn't do nothing wrong.'

'Ah, not this again. You robbed a man, you little fucking shit,' John said, cracking his knuckles.

'He was dead. Wasn't like he needed it where he was going.' JJ took out his cigarettes and lit one, without asking. The worm had turned.

John was staring at him, considering whether another wallop to the head might alter his thinking, when Sarah said, 'Okay. Deal.'

John looked at her in surprise.

Sarah leaned across the desk, her face deadpan. She didn't want JJ to doubt her. 'But you listen here: if you're bullshitting us, we will make it our business to hunt you down, no matter where you are. And you owe us. Is that clear? You owe us a huge favour.' It was Sarah's turn to smile slyly. 'And, JJ, I always call in my favours.'

JJ stopped smirking. He knew this dark-haired piece wasn't pulling his chain. Damn, why had he taken the car into town that morning? Life was not fair.

'You serious? No cops?'

'Look, I don't want you, I want the man who drowned David Reid.'

'All right, we got a deal.'

He held out his hand to shake on it, but Sarah ignored it. 'All right, then, Mr Hutton. Point him out.'

JJ withdrew his hand and jabbed the picture with his index finger. 'Him. That's the guy. He's the one I saw drowning the other guy.'

'You sure?'

'I'm sure.'

Sarah stood up. 'Come on, John. We're going to give our new friend here a ride home. Then we're going to go talk to a man about a globe.'

# 40

The reception was in full swing. The Glen Acre Hotel in Howth had laid out champagne for the guests on arrival, and a six-piece classical band had played softly and discreetly during the meal. A second band was scheduled to take over when, hopefully, the guests would be relaxed and drunk enough to dance to songs like 'Come On, Eileen' with barely restrained passion.

The speeches had been short and relatively ribaldry-free, and now, as the staff cleared the plates and the men made a dash to the free bar, Clive felt a burst of pride and happiness and, yes, relief – relief that the day had been more than he could have imagined.

He looked around the room and basked in the moment. Everyone was talking and eating and having a blast. The judge was propping up the bar, telling stories to a crowd of men, including Clive's father. Sylvia's mother had finally quit sniffling and was deep in the middle of a bitchy conversation about outfits with her two sisters and her three nieces. Clive's mother had moved down from the head table and was chatting with some society friend of Sylvia's. From her expression of rapt attention, he knew she was getting the goods on a few notorious party revellers.

'Larry, have you seen Max anywhere?' Laura Ashcroft stumbled slightly as she walked over to where Larry sat watching Dee chat to some cousin of Sylvia's.

'Hmm?'

'Max! He's got the camera.'

Larry looked around, trying hard not to show that he noticed Laura's huge pupils. 'I don't see him anywhere. Why don't you sit here and I'll have a look for him?'

Laura didn't need to be asked twice. She collapsed into the chair beside him and leaned her head on her hands. 'God, I'm…I'm tired.'

'I'll go see if I can find him.'

'Thanks, Lar.'

Larry wandered around the hall, then went across the foyer to the main hotel bar. He found Max propping it up, a huge brandy glass half empty by his elbow. He was watching the rugby on the bar TV.

'Max, your wife is wondering where you went to. She wants to get some photos, and she says you have the camera.'

Max turned from the bar. 'What?'

'Are you all right?'

'Sure. Come have a look. We're getting hammered.'

'Max, don't you think we should go back to the party?' Larry felt his skin begin to tighten around his body; even his scalp prickled. 'It's bad form to leave it like this.'

Max put his hand into his pocket, fished out an incredibly slim camera and passed it to Larry. 'Here. I'm going to watch this half.'

'Max, it's Clive's wedding.'

'So?'

Larry Cole was not a violent man by nature. But at that moment, if he'd had a gun in his hand, he would have put a bullet between Max Ashcroft's jiggling eyebrows.

'Max—'

'Lar, fuck— Hey, what's this about? What are they doing here?' Max looked over Larry's shoulder, his expression suddenly very, very troubled.

Two people were walking across the foyer towards the bar, not fast, but with definite purpose. Larry wondered for a moment if they were friends of Sylvia or guests from the wedding, although they didn't look like they were dressed for the occasion. But he knew them from somewhere.

They pushed open the glass door of the bar, their expression grim and serious. As they did so, Max said, very distinctly, 'Fuck.'

'Nice place,' Sarah said to Larry. 'Lillian Daly was very put out that she wasn't invited.'

'Was she?' Larry said, a little confused. 'And she sent you?'

'Nope, we're here for your good buddy Mr Ashcroft,' John said. 'Hey there, Maxie boy. We'd like to talk to you about the death of David Reid.'

Larry turned his head. 'Max?'

Sarah reached into her bag and withdrew both globes. She set them down on the bar with a clatter. 'You know where your one of these is, don't you, Larry?'

Larry squinted. 'Yes, at home somewhere.'

'And Clive's is on his keyring; I've seen it.' Sarah smiled. 'Max, sweetheart, how about you?'

And then Max made a run for it.

He got as far as the French doors leading out into the beer garden before John tackled him from behind, knocking him out through the doors and into an ornate wheelbarrow filled with flowers. The wheelbarrow's legs buckled under their combined weight and the two men toppled over, scattering soil and flowers everywhere.

Larry watched open-mouthed. He turned to Sarah, who watched as John gave Max a dig to the face and dragged him to his feet.

'What on Earth?' Larry passed his hand over his head. Really, he was feeling rather odd. 'We're having a wedding here.'

John's jaw tightened as he yanked a filthy and stunned Max back indoors towards the bar. 'He killed David Reid.'

The air seemed to freeze around Larry, a snapshot moment. He could hear his own heart hammering in his ears. 'What are you talking about?'

'Larry, it's crap – I don't know what they're talking about.' Max's lower lip was bleeding where John had struck him. There was a huge rip down the leg of his pants. 'You fucking arsehole' – he wrenched his arm free from John's grasp – 'I'm going to sue you!'

'Shut the fuck up,' John snapped, 'or I'll hit you again.'

'Max?' Larry said. 'What are they talking about?'

A small, dark-haired man with enormous eyebrows opened the bar door and came in, followed by two uniformed gardaí.

Max saw them and seemed to wilt.

'I should have known you two would be here already.' Detective Inspector Stafford eyed the group up and down. 'I thought I told you to stay out of it and leave the police work to me.'

'Hey,' John snapped, 'we called you, remember? Without us, you wouldn't have any work.'

Stafford glared at John. But it was true: after they had collected the other globe at JJ's filthy dump, Sarah had called Stafford and given him everything she had, including JJ.

Stafford jabbed a stubby thumb at Max. 'Why is his lip bleeding?'

'He tried to make a run for it. John caught him,' Sarah said. She handed him the two globes. 'Here. You're going to need these.'

Stafford handed them to a uniformed garda. 'Here, put these in an evidence bag.'

'There has to be some mistake,' Larry said. 'Max, tell them you didn't do this. Tell them! David was your friend.'

'Larry, there's been some mistake here.'

'You were seen that night,' Sarah said. 'We have a witness.'

Larry reeled against the bar. He looked like he was going to vomit. 'Oh, Jesus.'

'Don't listen to them!' Max yelled. 'Don't—'

'Max Ashcroft, you are under arrest. You are not obliged to say anything unless you wish to do so, but anything you do say will be taken down in writing…' As Stafford read him his rights and the two gardaí jerked him towards the door, Max struggled for a second, until Stafford said, 'You want to walk out of here, or do we need to do this the hard way?'

'Hold on there, Stafford – I want a word with you,' John said, and followed the group out to the main car park.

Larry sagged against the counter. 'This has to be a mistake. Max couldn't have done this, he couldn't have. We're friends, all of us. We play golf together. We…'

Sarah nodded. 'We found David's car.'

'You did?'

'Yes.'

'Where was it?'

'Some kid was driving it around.'

Larry frowned. He wasn't sure what to make of this news. Was she saying that some kid had found David's car and stolen it? It made a kind of sense; certainly it explained why it had never shown up. 'What has that got to do with Max?'

'The keyring we found near where the body—'

'David's keyring. Yes, what about it?' Larry felt sick. He had the strange sensation that he was an actor and this was some kind of role he was playing. These detectives asking him questions, Max in handcuffs… it was surreal, a stage show. He wished Sarah Kenny would stop looking at him like he was some kind of specimen on a slide.

'It wasn't David's.'

'What's that?'

'It wasn't David's. The kid had that one.'

Larry could scarcely bring himself to breathe. Max had killed David? Hadn't he always known, somewhere? Hadn't he always suspected?

Sarah leaned her elbow on the bar, her dark eyes fixed firmly on her target. 'Why would Max kill his friend, do you think?'

'I really… I…' Larry took his glasses off and began cleaning them again. He thought of Jack Lawson calling him the day before, how angry and vicious he had been. He thought about the money. How would he and Clive pay it now, with Max gone too? How long would it be before Max hung them all to dry? His whole world was unravelling before his eyes.

There was nowhere left to turn.

'He identified him,' Sarah said softly. 'The kid with the car. He was under the bridge the whole time, he saw the whole thing. Max murdered your own friend. He murdered David Reid.'

'No.' Larry swallowed. It was funny: now that she had uttered those words, he felt strangely calm.

'The kid says Max dragged David down the bank and held him under like he was drowning a dog. What I want to know is, why? Why would he do something like that? And I think you know why. I think you know exactly why.'

'He… I…' Larry was trembling slightly. 'Oh, my God.' He stopped talking and licked his lips. There was not a drop of moisture left in his mouth, and he was getting a headache. David.

'What are you hiding? What are you afraid of?'

Larry tried to swallow again, but he couldn't. So this was how it happened, when the world collapsed around your ears. Maybe this was how everyone felt, tingly with adrenaline, heart beating and sweat pumping. It was really very unpleasant.

He closed his eyes and thought about Dee's lips on his earlier, how pretty she looked in her new dress. He thought of Clive, beaming and proud.

John came back. He was limping slightly and he looked pleased with himself.

'Everything all right?' Sarah asked.

'It is. I was just making sure Stafford knows it was QuicK Investigations who caught Max Ashcroft, not him.'

'Because?'

'Because I want James Reid to pay us, and I want it in the papers. That's a shitload of publicity for us.' John dusted his hands on his jeans and looked Larry directly in the eye. 'Max has gone off babbling a mile a minute. It won't take long for him to open up. You sure you don't want to fill us in on what the hell's going on?'

Larry sighed. He should have known this day was coming. His house of cards had toppled down.

'You asked me what I was afraid of.'

Sarah nodded.

Larry put his glasses back on. 'Can you wait for me for a moment?'

Sarah and John exchanged glances. 'Why?'

'I want to tell my wife I'm going. I'll tell her... I don't know, something. I don't want to upset her.' He straightened up. He was pale and sweating. 'Will you wait for me?'

'Sure.'

Larry nodded. 'Okay. Thank you.'

They trooped back out of the foyer and back to the banquet hall. John and Sarah stood by the main doors and watched as the waiters began clearing away the tables to make room for the dancing. 'Looks like it was a nice wedding,' Sarah said.

Larry Cole leaned in and kissed his wife, with more fervour and passion than Dee had ever imagined he could produce. When they broke apart, she was flushed and startled. She looked at her husband and listened, growing more and more confused, as he spoke quietly. He must have mentioned that John and Sarah were waiting, because she looked around angrily, seeking them out.

Clive Hollingsworth was watching Larry and Dee's exchange, too. His expression froze into one of sheer terror when he saw Sarah and John by the door.

'You think he knows something?' John said softly.

'I don't know.'

'He looks like he's about to shit himself.'

'Guilty conscience.'

'Yeah, but about what? What the hell have these men got involved in?'

Larry straightened up and turned away from his wife. He nodded to Clive and made his way back to Sarah and John. He did not say goodbye to anyone else. When he reached them, he was saturated with an air of weary resignation.

'Okay,' he said. 'You might as well bring me to the same station as Max.'

'Why would we want to do that?' Sarah asked.

'I'm his solicitor, for one. And… I'll explain in the car. Please.'

'You're his solicitor?' John laughed. 'Man, do you have your work cut out for you.'

# 41

John drove slowly for a change. Sarah sat quietly in the front of the car. She didn't want to rush Larry Cole or prompt him in any way. She wanted him to open up completely on his own, and she knew from past experience that silence was the best way to achieve this. She settled in to wait for as long as it took.

'So why did he do it?' John asked, reaching for his cigarettes on the dash. 'David was your pal, wasn't he? Why'd Max kill him?'

'What?' Larry Cole looked startled.

'You want one?' John offered him a cigarette over his shoulder.

'I don't…' Larry shook his head, but then a strange look came into his eyes. 'You know, I think I will. I used to smoke years ago, in college.'

He slid one out and accepted the lighter. 'I gave up after the kids were born – didn't want to be a bad example.' The irony of that statement struck him and he began to laugh bitterly. That, combined with the smoke, caused a furious bout of coughing that went on for almost a minute.

John glanced in the rear-view mirror. 'You all right there, bud?'

'Fine.' Larry nodded. When he finally stopped spluttering, he was pink in the face and his eyes were glassily wet. 'You think everything is under control, don't you? That everything is, oh I don't know, that it's going to work out.'

'That what is under control?' Sarah said, turning slightly in her seat.

He took another drag on his cigarette and exhaled. 'We want, don't we? We want things – houses, fancy cars, holidays, private schools. Everything has to be bigger and better.'

Sarah shrugged and raised her eyebrow. 'Some people call that progress.'

'It's a honeytrap. We're lured in, and once we're in, we're trapped. You know there are solicitors at my firm who refuse point-blank to drive a car over two years old? Most of them change cars every year.'

'So people like new cars.'

'And we're afraid all the time, aren't we? Afraid we're going to slip up, lose a contract, a client, have to cut back, have to move to a smaller house, downsize. We're afraid our peers will surpass us, have more than we have. We use credit like oxygen. We want, we need. It's relentless.'

'Not me,' John said. 'I'm happy with my lot.'

'Then you're a lucky man.'

'And what do you want?' Sarah asked.

'Nothing.' Larry shrugged and glanced out the window at the passing scenery. 'To provide for my family. For my wife to love me like I love her.'

'And does she?'

He took another drag on the cigarette. He didn't answer.

'Well, that's all good and well,' John said, 'but why did Max drown David Reid?'

'You're very blunt, aren't you?'

'Yep.'

'I don't expect you to understand. You don't know what we've been going through. I don't think you know what fear is.'

John kept his eyes on the road. He remembered the sound of a gunshot one wet, dark night, how his heart had thumped as he ran slipping and sliding through the muck, convinced he was too late, convinced Sarah had been blown away by Patrick York. Damning himself for having left her behind.

'I know fear,' he said. 'Trust me on that one.'

'You have to understand something. I'm not making excuses for Max.' Larry took off his glasses and polished them with his tie. 'I loved David, he was like a brother to me.'

'Right.'

'We've been struggling; it's been terrible. And Max – well, he must have thought he could, I don't know, protect all of us from…'

'From what?' Sarah asked angrily. She despised the whiny, self-pitying note that had crept into Larry Cole's voice. It made her want to slap him. 'Why the hell did Max Ashcroft kill David?'

Larry tossed the smouldering cigarette out of the driver's window. He sat back and began to laugh, so hysterically that John and Sarah exchanged worried glances.

'What's so funny?' John asked.

Larry wiped his eyes with the balls of his hands and got himself under control. 'You want to know why he did it?'

Sarah and John nodded.

'To protect us from scandal.'

'What are you talking about? What scandal?'

He sighed. 'We were on a weekend away, our last hurrah before Clive became a married man…'

*

'When does the entertainment get here?' Max said drunkenly from the red love-seat. Even though it was only eight o'clock, he had consumed the best part of a bottle of Absolut vodka and he was already beginning to get that mean-eyed look. Of course, he had been acting like a spoiled shit all day, ever since David had hammered him at golf.

Clive glanced over. 'What entertainment?'

He and David and Larry were in the middle of a poker game. Max had folded, claiming they were all cheating bastards and he didn't play with cheating bastards.

'You all right, Max?' Larry asked. 'Why don't you ease up on the drink for a while? You don't look so good.'

'Yeah,' David said, laughing. 'Sure you don't want anyone to hold your hair back while you puke?'

Max glowered at him. 'Shut up, you fucking queer.'

'What entertainment is he talking about?'

David and Larry threw their eyes up to heaven.

'It's nothing,' David said. 'A present from us to you.'

Clive frowned. He was fairly well on himself, at that stage, and was having trouble keeping his eyes focused. 'Huh?'

Max staggered over to the glass coffee table where two trays of sandwiches were laid out. He wasn't really hungry, but he figured he needed to eat something to sober himself up. While he was there, he mixed himself a good shot of whiskey with soda.

'Max, you stay away from that stuff,' Larry said. 'It's too early.'

'Hey! I brought it, didn't I?'

'You're going to knock yourself out.'

'Yeah, yeah.'

Max took a bite from a chicken-and-stuffing sandwich and a slug of his whiskey. Then he veered off towards the bathroom to run cold water over his wrists and splash his face.

They had arrived at the country hotel on the Friday evening and had an easy night – dinner, a few drinks, nothing too hectic. They had played golf all Saturday and had a few drinks at the bar. Now they were in the living room of the suite Max had picked out, playing cards and generally having a good time. David had organised the entertainment, through Big Jack Lawson, a car dealer who also owned a strip club down on Leeson Street. Larry had booked the hotel. They were going to give Clive the send-off of a lifetime.

'What entertainment is he talking about, Lar?'

'Nothing. Keep your cards up, I can see them.'

Clive raised his cards and squinted at them. He closed one eye. When that didn't work, he closed the other.

David watched him, the fond smirk of an older brother playing on his lips. 'You know, maybe we should all take it easy. I'm getting a bit sloshed here myself.'

He winked at Larry. Larry knew he was no such thing, but he nodded and put down his cards. They didn't normally drink so much – and, truthfully, Larry was always a little nervous about how ferocious Max became when he was twisted. It made Larry nervous and anxious to please. He realised that of late he had been beginning to dislike Max's company, and he wondered why on Earth he put up with him.

David, of course, held no such fear. It was almost as if David enjoyed winding up the big lug. Certainly his mild ribbing on the green today had been like a red rag to a bull. Everyone knew Max hated to lose. And he hated having his nose rubbed in it – no matter how jokingly – even more.

David nodded at Clive. 'You think he'll stay awake long enough to get some kicks?'

Larry ruffled Clive's shaggy hair. 'Come on, bachelor boy, let's grab something to eat.'

'Huh?' Clive looked at him and blinked slowly.

'Oh, man.' Larry laughed. 'Come on.'

They had some food and made Clive drink two cups of strong coffee. When Max returned from the bathroom, he didn't seem as volatile. He seemed almost eager to get into the spirit of things, and after a while Larry began to relax, David became more animated and Clive sobered up a little.

They played a few more games of poker, laughing about some of their other weekends away and the high jinks they had got up to over the years, ribbing Clive mercilessly about joining Judge Cockburn's family. David produced some cigars and they opened a bottle of Bombay Sapphire gin. By the time Big Jack Lawson called from downstairs at eleven o'clock to say the 'entertainment' had arrived, they had almost completely forgotten she was coming.

David snapped his phone shut and blearily rose from the table.

'That was my man Jack. Come on, you guys. Straighten up a bit. She's on her way up.'

'What?' Clive looked up. He was sweating up a storm. The two gins and bitter lemon he had consumed during the last card game had topped off what he'd consumed earlier in the evening. Despite David and Larry's best attempts, he was now hopelessly drunk. 'What's... er, what's going on?'

'What do you think?' Larry slapped him on the back harder than he meant to, making Clive spill his drink all over his shirt. 'You're getting married, old man, soon. We've decided to get you a bit of action. After all, it's your last few weeks of freedom. Last throw of the dice.'

'Huh?'

David started to laugh. 'Jesus, he's really wasted. Better clean him up a bit, or she's not going to go near him.'

Clive blinked. 'She?'

'Jesus.' Larry took the glass from him and hauled him to his feet. 'Are you sure this is such a good idea, Dave?'

'He'll be fine.'

'Come on, Clive, let's go get cleaned up a bit.' Larry managed to half lead, half drag Clive into the bathroom.

'What's she like?' Max asked, tossing back his whiskey and frantically trying to smooth his hair and button up his shirt. 'She nice?'

'Gorgeous. Brunette, green eyes, young, absolute beauty.'

'Surprised you'd know what to look out for.'

'A man can appreciate beauty and still like a bit of cock, Max.'

Max pulled a face. It annoyed him that, no matter what he said, David never seemed to get offended. When he was jazzed up like this, he found himself questioning whether he even liked David Reid.

'All right,' David said. 'I'm going to head downstairs and have a drink at the bar. You coming?'

'What? But what about the girl?'

'What about her?'

Max staggered to his feet, knocking his cards everywhere. 'I thought she was going to do a strip and stuff. That's what we paid for, isn't it?'

David frowned. 'For Clive.'

'Fuck that,' Max said angrily. 'I paid to see a show.'

'It wasn't for you, Max.' David turned to Larry, who was emerging from the bathroom, drying his hands on a paper towel. 'Larry, tell him.'

'Tell him what?'

'That this is not a fucking free-for-all. We hired the girl for Clive. She's paid to do a striptease and give Clive a bit of a send-off.'

'Right.'

'Well, tell this walking cock-jockey here.'

'What did you call me?' Max said, lurching towards him. 'No fucking wonder you're not interested. Not your type, eh, David? Too fucking female for you, you big bender. Hey, you should try it, you never know, maybe it'll cure you.'

'Oh, here we go—'

'Lads, come on,' Larry said, trying to calm the situation.

But David, whether from the drink or from listening to Max bitch all day, finally had his dander up. 'It's always the same with you, Max: you ruin every night out with your bullshit carry-on.'

'My what?' Max had balled his hands into fists. 'You fucking ponce, who are you to say that to me?'

'I'm sick of you, sick to the teeth of you. It's always the same. You're a fucking bully.'

'Lads, stop—'

Max took a step towards David, and David dropped one foot behind him as though getting ready for a lunge. All hell would surely have broken out if it hadn't been for the sound of soft yet urgent knocking on the door of the suite.

Larry splayed his hands. 'Look, that's the girl. David, you let her in and talk to her, I'll go get Clive.'

David smoothed his hair with his hands, took a deep breath and rearranged his expression. Max stepped back too, but he was still clearly furious.

'This isn't fucking over, you know,' he said in a tight voice.

David looked at him with contempt. 'Our friend is getting married in a few weeks. You think we could keep the testosterone level to a minimum for one night, Maxie?'

Max went back to the coffee table and grabbed his wallet. 'Yeah, I'll keep it down – but after this weekend, that's it. You and me are finished.'

'Lads, come on, there's no need for this.'

'Don't worry, Max,' David said, and smiled coldly. 'I couldn't have said it better myself.'

Larry hurried to the bathroom to get Clive, sensing that the night was blown, but not knowing what to do about it.

*

'All right,' Sarah said, 'so you had a golf-stroke-drunken weekend and your friends had a row. What has that got to do with anything? I've met Max Ashcroft; he's a dickhead. The real wonder is that someone as easy-going as David Reid tolerated him as long as he did.'

Larry snorted gently and waved his hand. He was on yet another of John's cigarettes. It seemed telling this story had turned him into a chain smoker.

'Oh, Max – he can be a boor, but he can also be quite fun, or he used to be. Truth be told, ever since he was promoted, a new Max has emerged: a not-so-nice one. Power can do that to a person, you know; it corrupts.'

'You're saying he's corrupt because of his job?' John asked as they sailed through a roundabout and hit the coast road.

'No, but…he doesn't have the same way of thinking as most people.'

'No shit, Sherlock.' Sarah stared disapprovingly at Larry. 'I think you probably have a lot in common.'

Larry looked away. 'Well, anyway, the girl came in…'

*

She said her name was Ivanka. She was very small, barely over five foot tall, with wide green eyes and waist-length brown hair shot through with natural copper highlights. Her features were very delicate, and when she smiled she had the slightest gap between her front teeth. She wore a long, pale-grey coat that almost reached the floor, and high-heeled boots. Even with her heavy make-up, she could only have been about nineteen at the most.

'Hello, I am here see bachelor boy.'

Max gawked at her openly, lustily and somewhat blearily. Her accent was pure Doctor Zhivago.

David smiled and shook her hand. 'Remember me?'

'Yes, we meet at club.'

'Right. It's my friend Clive who's getting married, Larry's gone to get him.' David leaned in a little closer. 'Between you and me, he's a little under the weather.' He made a drinking gesture with his hand, and the stripper laughed, a silvery, tinkly sound that made Max horny.

'What you wearing under that coat, sweetheart?' he said, leering at her. The stench of whiskey on his breath was so strong it was a wonder she didn't become drunk from breathing it in.

'Policewoman.' The stripper smiled, but her eyes were alert and wary.

'Yeah? Give us a gander, then.'

'Gander?' She frowned. 'I don't learn this word.'

'It's nothing.' David scowled and put his hand firmly on Max's arm. 'Max, we're going downstairs. Now.'

'Hey,' Max snarled, shaking him off. 'I'm only asking for a fucking peek at what I paid for.'

Ivanka was young, but she had experienced her fair share of drunks, and she knew a situation when she saw it developing. She could decipher people faster than a psychologist. She opened her coat quickly, flashing her tacky PVC uniform, complete with badge, handcuffs and rubber baton. In her shoulder bag, she also carried a hat and a little rubber whip, her stereo, scented oil and a collection of novelty condoms. She waggled her finger at Max. 'Look – policewoman. You be good or I arrest you, bad boy.'

Max almost slobbered. 'I bet you would.'

Behind them, Larry came into view, looking slightly sheepish. 'Oh, hello there. Er… David, can I have a word?'

'What's wrong?' David excused himself and went back into the bedroom with Larry. 'Where's Clive?'

'He's in the bathroom, cleaning the vomit off his shirt.'

'He was sick?'

'Everywhere. I got most of it up. Lucky it's all tiles.'

'Jesus. What about the girl? She's here now, we paid for the hour.'

'I know. And Clive knows she's here, he keeps giggling about it.' Larry thought for a second. 'He'll probably be okay. We'll put a clean T-shirt on him and sit him in a chair. She can do her strip or whatever, and we can meet up with him in the bar after.'

'I need to get Max downstairs.'

'Tell you what: I'll bring Max down – it might be easier if I deal with him – and you get Clive into the chair.'

David raised an eyebrow. 'You think I can't deal with Max?'

'Dave, Max is a bollocks with whiskey in him. You know that.'

David hesitated, but then gave in with a sigh. 'All right, you take him downstairs and I'll get Sick Boy into a decent state.'

Larry patted him on the back. 'Good man.'

'Yeah, yeah.'

\*

Ten minutes later, Larry had persuaded the lovestruck Max to go to the bar with him, and a glazed-eyed Clive had been shoved into a chair. The stripper eyed him disparagingly. David had cleaned most of the crap off his face with a wet towel and put a clean T-shirt on him, but he still looked wasted. His head lolled from side to side and his tongue was sticking out.

'He very drunk,' Ivanka said, shaking her head.

'I know, I know,' David said, rolling his eyes. He shook Clive gently and leaned in so close their noses were almost touching. 'Clive? Clive!'

'Dave. Buddy.' Clive grinned and patted David sloppily on the face.

'Clive, this is Ivanka.'

Clive rolled his head in the general direction of the stripper. 'Hiya, 'Vanka.'

'Hello. I do good show for you, yes, marry boy?' Ivanka said, stripping off her coat.

Clive grinned like a loon when he saw the uniform. 'Oh, boy.'

'Oh, boy,' David repeated. He had seen Clive like this before, and he knew that, no matter what Ivanka could do, this man was going to be sound asleep in less than twenty minutes – if he even lasted that long.

'Okay, Ivanka, do your thing. I think this is going to be the easiest money you've ever earned.'

The stripper shrugged her small shoulder. 'I do dance.'

David nodded and ruffled Clive's sweaty hair. 'Yep. Have fun.'

'Yep,' Clive said, and belched softly.

David laughed. 'Come downstairs when you're finished, Ivanka. Have a drink.'

'And him?'

'Oh, he'll be all right where he falls.'

Ivanka glanced at Clive again, a little unsure. She had gone on these excursions before for Big Jack, but never to anyone so obviously plastered. 'I start now?'

'Fire ahead.' David left the room to join the others downstairs.

'Okay,' Ivanka said, standing splay-legged in front of Clive. 'I put music.'

'Oh, boy.'

'You like Jennifer Lopez? You know, J-Lo?'

Clive didn't say another word, but his grin widened.

'Oh, boy,' Ivanka said, rolling her eyes, and off she went to look for a socket to plug in her stereo.

\*

Max, David and Larry sat downstairs at the bar. It was busy. There were two weddings in the hotel that weekend, and the bar was packed. David and Larry were drinking brandy, sipping it slowly, enjoying it, chatting about the improvements that the hotel had made to the golf course. Max was knocking back the whiskey, brooding, refusing to be drawn into the conversation. When he excused himself to use the bathroom, both of the others were slightly relieved.

'What the hell is his problem?' David said, putting his glass down.

'He's competitive. All those corporate types are. I see them at my firm sometimes. Alpha-male syndrome.'

'It's a syndrome?'

'Only if being a bollocks is a syndrome.'

'It there a cure?'

'Shooting helps, I'm told.'

David threw back his head and laughed. 'Oh, man, his face when I won the game today…'

'I know, especially when he started to drop shots,' Larry said, shaking his head. He was starting to feel a bit better, not quite so nervous.

'That's it, isn't it? He can't accept failure, even from himself.'

'None of us like to lose.' Larry shrugged. 'But Max is an extreme example.'

'He's a jumped-up little bollocks that wants a good hiding. Want another?'

'Sure.' Larry tried a smile and almost pulled it off.

David nodded and went to the bar. He knew the weekend away was not doing Larry any good. He knew Larry was having trouble of some kind at home, and if Larry wanted to talk about it, he'd listen, but if he didn't, what could David do? They were men, they didn't barge into emotional shit unless an invitation was offered.

They reminisced about previous trips and games until, suddenly, Larry looked at his watch. 'He's gone a while, isn't he?'

David frowned. 'I'll go see if he's all right. With any luck he's fallen down the toilet.'

'You never know. He was fairly well on.'

David tossed down some of his brandy and headed for the toilets. Larry picked up his own drink and took a sip. There was a live band playing in the annex off the bar, and he could see couples of all ages making their way to the small wooden dance floor. One couple in particular caught his eye. They were about the same age as him and Dee. She was chubby, and her short ash-blonde hair glowed under the lights. The man was short, wearing brown cord slacks and a white-and-brown checked shirt. They didn't look rich and they didn't look glamorous, but, Larry noted as the woman led the grinning man to the dance floor amid his mild protestations, they did look happy.

He thought of Dee, drifting around their big house – her thin shoulders, her tired, bored expression – and he felt a wave of anger wash over him. What was wrong with being happy? It wasn't hard. Life wasn't that hard. All you had to do was live it.

'Larry.'

He looked up. David stood there, his expression tight and angry.

'What is it?'

'He's not there. He's not outside getting some air, either; I checked. He's probably gone back upstairs.'

Larry sighed and pushed his glass away. 'I told you he doesn't like to take no for an answer.'

*

Larry closed his eyes and rested his forehead against the car window. His voice had begun to shake slightly, and he wanted to gain some modicum of control before he continued with his story.

Sarah and John exchanged glances. They had almost reached Clontarf and would soon be in the city, and they wanted to know the rest of the story before they handed this man to the gardaí. James Reid deserved answers.

'Mr Cole—' Sarah began.

'You can call me Larry.'

'Larry, we're going to be there soon. I'll be contacting James Reid as soon as I drop you off at the station, and I'd like to be able to give him some answers. He's got a right to know what happened to his brother.'

Larry opened his eyes again. 'I'm getting to it. This is very hard, you know.'

Sarah checked to see if she had a shred of sympathy going spare. She hadn't.

He took a deep breath and began again.

'We ran to the elevators. David was in front…'

*

'I should have known he'd pull a fucking stunt like this,' David fumed.

'David, slow down,' Larry said breathlessly, trying to keep up. They passed the reception desk and Larry muttered, 'Good night,' to the receptionist, who was watching them with interest. David marched on, his little legs like pistons.

'I should have known. If he lays a hand on that girl, I'll kill him. I gave Big Jack my word we wouldn't do anything fucking stupid.'

'David, Clive is there.'

'You didn't see Max earlier. You didn't see the way he looked at her.'

'Of course I did. It's the whiskey. You know what he's like with whiskey.'

They reached the lifts, and David jabbed every button he could find. 'You're always making excuses for him.'

'I know.'

'He acts like a fucking knob on every trip.'

'I know.'

'We should have known this was a bad idea. You can't do anything with him.'

'I know.' Larry sagged against the wall. 'Look, we'll get him and bring him back downstairs. It'll be okay.'

'I told him she was for Clive. I'm not a fucking pimp.'

Larry flinched and darted a glance towards the reception desk. 'Jesus, keep your voice down, will you?'

The lift pinged, and David was in before the doors had fully opened. In silence they rode to the top floor, Larry growing ever more uneasy, David's foot tapping in barely contained fury.

As soon as the doors opened, he was off, his card key out, Larry chasing after him. He swiped the door, and Larry heard music: 'Waiting for tonight, ohhh…'

David stepped inside the hall. Larry followed and closed the door behind him. The sound of music increased.

'What if he's not here?' Larry asked. 'What if she's, you know, with Clive?'

'Then we apologise and leave,' David said, and opened the door to the living room.

\*

'And then?' Sarah said, almost on the edge of her seat despite herself. 'And then what happened?'

'And then,' Larry said softly, 'the nightmare began.'

*

'What the fuck?'

Clive was sitting on the floor by the sofa, his head in his hands, sobbing. Max paced the room like a crazed animal, his shirt in disarray, blood dripping from four long, vicious-looking scratches on his cheek. In the background, Jennifer Lopez was still singing at full blast.

'I knew it! What's going on here?' David snapped. 'Max, if you've laid a hand on—'

Clive lifted his head and looked at David. His face was smeared with lipstick and covered in snot and tears. 'David… I was… they were fighting.' He started crying again.

Larry felt his pulse in his ears. He looked over at Max and he knew: he knew something very bad had happened.

'What have you done?'

Max paced back and forth, muttering under his breath, but he didn't answer.

David took another step into the room. That was when he saw her. She lay in a crumpled heap, behind the overturned, smashed glass table that had held their sandwiches earlier in the evening. She was pressed against a blood-splattered radiator. Even from where he stood, David could see that her head was at an unnatural angle.

'Oh, no.'

He ran over to her and pushed the table out of the way. She wore only red lacy knickers, red suspenders and her boots. She was lying half against the wall, her body angled towards the bathroom, her head facing the door. David brushed her beautiful dark hair away from her face and gasped at the damage.

'Oh, Jesus.'

Her eyes were partially open. She had two cuts on her right cheek and her lip was split. Over her left eye was a gash so deep and raw that David was convinced he could see part of her skull through the ragged tear in her once-beautiful skin.

'Oh, Jesus Christ.'

One of her arms was trapped beneath her body. The fingers of the hand he could see were bloody, and she had lost two of her gaudily painted fingernails. She looked like a doll, a doll that had been flung away by a screaming child in a tantrum. He pressed his fingers against the white skin of her neck and closed his eyes, praying.

It was no use. She was dead.

'...Ohhh, waiting for tonight...'

David stood up and looked around wildly. He grabbed the stereo cable and ripped it from the wall. The music died instantly.

'What happened here?' he said, in a voice unlike his own.

That was when Larry moved closer and saw the girl. He gasped.

'David, is she...'

'She's dead, Larry. She's fucking dead.'

Clive began rocking back and forth and wailing softly.

'Max, what have you done?' David demanded.

Max stopped pacing and faced them. 'Look, it was an accident! I didn't mean to hurt her! The bitch scratched me, on my fucking face.'

'Why? What did you do?'

'I defended myself, didn't I?'

'What did you do, Max?'

'Nothing! He was passed out, and she was getting ready to go, and I came in and, you know, we were kidding around, and I said, look... I mean, we'd paid for the whole works, and... we're...we were kidding, and then she started getting all uppity.'

'And?'

'And nothing. Next thing I know, she's all hissing and scratching and shit. I hit – sort of pushed her away. Then the bitch comes at me, says she's going to get her fucking boss, going to press fucking charges, so...so I... there was a bit of a struggle.'

'Oh, Jesus,' Larry said, and fell back against the wall as though all the strength had evaporated from his legs.

'A struggle?' David said incredulously. 'She weighed, what, about seven stone? How could there have been a fucking struggle?'

'She was going to ring the cops!' Max yelled suddenly. 'What was I supposed to do? I hit her, she went over the fucking table and she hit the fucking radiator. Next thing I know, she's not moving.' He started pacing again. 'It was an accident.'

David raised his hands and tugged at his hair without realising it. 'Oh, Jesus, you fucking killed her.'

'David, what are we going to do?' Larry said.

'Do? What the fuck can we do? We've got to phone for an ambulance.'

'No!' Clive screamed, and they all jumped. He staggered to his feet and gripped David's shoulders. 'You can't! Sylvia... I'm getting married in a few weeks, to a judge's daughter. You can't get an ambulance, they'll bring the police. We'll all be arrested.'

'What else can we do?'

'He's right,' Larry said in a strange, colourless voice. 'We can't get the cops involved.'

David shoved Clive aside. 'What are you talking about?'

'I can't. If Dee ever found out about this... I can't.'

'Me neither,' Max said. 'I could go to jail for this.'

'You deserve to go to jail, you fucking animal,' David said angrily. 'What are you suggesting we do, Larry? The girl is dead.'

Larry wiped his forehead with his hands and took a deep breath. 'Look, she was Eastern European or something, wasn't she?'

'She said she was Ukrainian,' Clive mumbled.

'Right. So she's probably, I don't know, here illegally or something.'

Max was listening keenly. 'Go on.'

'Well, I don't know much about this type of thing, but we can, I don't know, talk to her boss. Explain that there was an accident. You know him, right? He's not going to want the gardaí looking into him either, is he?'

David stared at his friend in appalled astonishment. But Clive and Max were hanging on his every word. Larry looked at all their faces and felt oddly calm and together. 'This is what we'll do. David, you ring that Lawson man, get him up here. We'll talk to him, see if we can't organise something. If she was an illegal, then chances are nobody really knows her and nobody knows she was here.'

'Why do we have to get the man involved?' Max asked.

'Because he does know she was here. And because he knows David. It would be no problem for him to check who else was here.'

'Shit.'

'Okay, we need to get her up off the floor and make sure we get all her clothes, and we need to find some way of getting her out of here without the doorman or somebody seeing. Max, see if there are any spare blankets in the wardrobes.'

Max did as he was told, as compliant as a child.

'We need to straighten up this room a bit. We can pay for the broken table, say one of us fell over it – Max, because he's got those cuts to his face—'

'Larry, you have to stop this,' David said. 'You can't be serious.'

'Do you want to go to jail, David?'

'Jail? I didn't do anything!'

'What about your business, your rich clients? How many of them do you think you'll have left if word of this gets out? Four drunken middle-class men and a dead hooker in a hotel room on a stag weekend?' Larry laughed, more than a little hysterically. 'Think about that splashed across the newspapers.'

David thought about it, and he went grey under his perma-tan.

'We'll be ruined, all of us,' Larry said. 'It won't matter who did what.'

'But she—'

'She's dead, David. There's nothing we can do for her now. Ring the man, what's his name – Jack, is it? You've got his number.'

'Larry, please, tell me you're not serious.'

But he was. Larry Cole had never been more serious about anything in his whole life.

# 42

'You realise what you're telling us?' Sarah said in amazement. 'You're admitting to an assault, a murder, a cover-up, conspiracy, God knows what else. Do you realise that everything you tell us, the gardaí will get us to put in a statement?'

'I know.'

Larry Cole looked exhausted, as though every word sucked another drop of energy from his already depleted body. Sarah would later swear she saw him age before her very eyes.

'I know,' he repeated. 'But you don't understand. I can't do this any longer. I've had Jack Lawson on the phone. He was asking about you and about this Sharpie and Mick, and I said you had asked about them, and then he threatened me – and what about Dee? If I don't, it will never end, don't you see?'

'And did he go along with this plan? Jack Lawson?' John said, his voice tinged with more than anger. He was thinking of connections. He was thinking of Mick and Sharpie and how no one had heard from them in twenty-four hours. He was thinking of the two men going to Rose Quinn's door and hustling Mick out. He was thinking of Mick Quinn's smile as he had climbed out of the car that day. The kid had known. He had known, right then, that his days were numbered.

He was thinking of how badly he wanted to slap Larry Cole in the kisser.

'Of course,' Larry was saying. 'I was right: he didn't want the gardaí anywhere near it, any more than we did.'

'It?'

'The situation.'

'How nice for you that it all worked out.'

Sarah looked over at John. His knuckles were white on the steering wheel and his jaw muscles were bunched tightly. He was furious, beyond furious. At this rate, Larry Cole would be lucky if he made it to the garda station in one piece.

'So what happened?' she asked. 'How did you get her out?'

Larry rubbed his eyes. 'She was very... tiny. We were able to fit her inside one of the golf bags, and then...then Lawson took her away.'

'Carried out like the trash, eh?' John said. 'Nothing more than fucking clearing up the rubbish.'

'John,' Sarah said, and put her hand on his arm. He stopped talking, but when he lit another cigarette, his hand shook so badly that it took a couple of seconds for the flame to catch.

'What did he do with her?' Sarah asked.

'Buried her somewhere, I believe.'

'Where?'

'I don't know. But I'm... well, we think she was found. There was a body found in—'

'Wicklow,' John said. 'A body found there a few weeks back.'

'That's right.'

'You pack of cunts.'

Larry lowered his head. 'Yes, I suppose we are.'

'But what has this got to do with David?' Sarah said. 'Why did Max murder David?'

'Do you think I could have another cigarette?'

'No,' John snapped. 'I've only a couple left.'

Larry flinched slightly. He swallowed and pushed his glasses up his nose with his thumb. 'Well, it was about a week later...'

*

'David Reid on line one for you,' the secretary said over the intercom.

'Okay, put him through.'

Larry, who was spending a rare day in the office sorting out a land registry dispute, lifted the receiver and punched a button. He was a little surprised to hear from David. Almost a week had passed since that fateful night, and so far David had refused all calls and attempts at contact.

'David?'

'Jesus Christ, thank God I found you. Can you talk?'

'Of course.'

'I mean, can anyone else hear you?'

'No, it's fine. What's going on?'

'It's Jack Lawson. He was here earlier, some crap about dropping off a logbook, but he's after fucking money.'

'What?' Larry felt a huge weight descend on him. 'Are you sure?'

'Of course I'm sure. Look, I don't want to talk over the phone. Call the others and tell them we need to meet tonight to discuss this. I'm not going to be blackmailed by that fucker, no way, no how.'

'Okay, okay. I'll call you back.'

Larry hung up the phone and sat back in his chair. A whole new circle of hell was waiting for him to slip up again. He picked up the phone and began to dial.

*

Later that evening, the four men met up in Dicey Reilly's pub. It was a stiff and charged gathering. Nobody wanted to be there, and nobody – least of all David – wanted to discuss what had happened.

'Are you sure?' Clive said, clasping and unclasping his hands between his legs.

'He says he's out of pocket since he lost her. Says he paid a lot of money to have her brought over, and people are asking questions about where she is. He reckons he can quell any suspicions, but he says he should be – let me see how he put it – recompensed for all of his trouble.'

'Jesus,' Larry said. 'The bastard's blackmailing us.'

'What did he do with her?' Clive said softly.

'What does it matter what he did with her? How much does he want?' Max said.

David took a long sip of his pint before he spoke. 'He wants two hundred thousand euros.'

'What?' Larry and Clive said in unison.

'That's un-fucking-believable,' Max said, shocked. 'He's putting the squeeze on us.'

'No, Max, what is unbelievable is that we should be in this situation in the first place,' David said, refusing to look at him.

'I can't…' Clive looked panic-stricken. 'I don't have that kind of money right now. I'm… I've just bought a house.'

'What happens if we don't pay it?' Larry asked David. 'What can he do to us, anyway? He's involved too. He took her body away, for Christ's sake.'

'Keep your voice down,' Max hissed.

'Shut up, Max,' David said. 'Look, Larry, I don't know what he can do, but he's the type that can cause trouble, that I'm sure of. And I'm not fucking willing to spend the rest of my life dealing with him. None of us can. And I don't see why I should pay a red cent. I didn't do anything.'

'Well, you're the one who brought her,' Max snarled. 'You're the one who put us in bed with a blackmailing scumbag.'

David didn't hesitate for a fraction of a second: he flung his drink straight over Max, and before anyone had had a chance to register what had happened, he struck him in the face as hard as he could, knocking Max backwards off the stool.

Five minutes later, they were all out on their ear.

'You son of a bitch,' Max said, holding a wad of tissue against his rapidly swelling nose. 'I think you broke it.'

'Good,' David snapped, holding his hand under his armpit. 'If you ever try to lay this situation at my feet again, I won't be responsible for my actions.'

Larry hauled David away. 'Look, what are we going to do?'

'I don't know, I really don't,' David said miserably. 'Even if we divide it between the four of us, I don't have anywhere near that kind of money to part with, do you?'

'No – well, I could probably get it, but not without a lot of questions being asked.'

'I don't see why we should be the ones to pay it, anyway. We didn't hurt her.'

Larry thought of the way they had bundled that slip of a girl into Clive's canvas bag and hauled her out of that room. How light she had been when they had lifted her up. 'No, but we're all involved,' he said sadly.

'But we didn't do it.'

'David, we're either all in this together or we're sunk.'

'What if two hundred grand isn't enough? What if he hits us up again? What then, Larry? Are we going to keep paying? For Max?'

Larry blanched; he hadn't thought of that. 'But you know this man, don't you? You've got to talk to him, reason with him – tell him that, if we pay him, that has to be it.'

'How?'

'I don't know. We need proof of the deal, I suppose. Evidence that he's blackmailing us, in case he tries again.'

'How?'

'I don't know. I need to think about it.'

'I don't have that kind of money, Larry.'

'I know. Max should pay the lion's share, but we—'

'We nothing.' David pushed him away and shook his head. 'We're fucked, don't you see? We're fucked.'

'We are not fucked,' Larry said in a surprisingly strong voice. 'We just need to think, formulate a plan.'

*

'And did you?' Sarah asked as they whizzed by Fairview Park. 'Did you come up with one?'

Larry smiled. 'Well, it was a sort of a plan. We decided to get evidence. We had David talk to Jack Lawson, get him to put it in writing.'

'Excuse me?'

'At first he wouldn't go for it. Finally David went to see him and said we agreed to his asking price, but to protect us, I drew up a, well, a sort of contract stating what happened that night, including Lawson's involvement. We all signed it, and he was to sign it when we handed the money over. It was the only way we could be sure he wouldn't try to hit us up again. If we went down, he would go down with us.'

'A contract?' Sarah asked.

'Yes. I drew it up.'

'A blackmail contract?'

'It was the only protection we had.'

Sarah was incredulous. 'I've never heard the like—' Then she slapped her forehead. 'Shit – the contract. It wasn't the blasted laptop or the money they were after at all. Damn it!'

'Jesus, how the other half live,' John said disgustedly.

Larry shrugged. 'But the day we were planning to give Lawson the money, David changed his mind. He met Max in town and they had words. Max called me in a panic: David was threatening to call the whole thing off and go to the gardaí.'

'At least somebody had a conscience,' John said.

'Well, either that or he wasn't ready to part with his money,' Sarah said. 'Then what happened?'

'Max told me what David had said, and I went to go reason with him.'

'You saw him that day too?'

'I found him in the George.'

'So you reasoned with him. And then Max reasoned with him by holding his head under the filthy water in the fucking canal. Yep, bunch of reasonable guys,' John said, braking for a red light before the Ossery Bridge. Every word out of this man's mouth was nothing more than a whiny, self-pitying drone. It was all John could do not to snack him one in the gob.

'I know how it all looks. But by the time I found David he was plastered, and I mean really, really drunk – I'd never seen him so bad. I tried to talk to him, reason with him, but he was…' Larry took a deep breath, clearly distressed. 'He wouldn't listen, he wouldn't even look at me. Then he started shouting and cursing at me, going on about how he'd worked all his life to get where he was and he wasn't going to be ruined because of Max. It was relentless. I knew he was serious.

'I went to the bathroom and called Max. I told him that there was no way – you know, no way David was going to go through with it. And Max… well, he was furious. Lawson had been hassling him too, and he wanted the whole thing taken care of. I came back out of the bathroom and David was gone. I went outside, and he was there, just weaving around with his phone in his hand. He said he was trying to ring the gardaí to come pick him up. I couldn't believe it.'

'You were the one who smashed his phone, weren't you?'

'Not on purpose. I knocked it out of his hand.' Larry looked away, but Sarah could see his eyes were brimming with tears. 'I picked it up and put most of it back in his pocket.'

'And then?'

'He was too drunk to drive home. I mean, Jesus, he was too drunk to stand. So I went to get my car, and by the time I got back he was gone. I didn't know if he'd got a cab or what. I drove to his house, but there was no one there. I waited for a little while and then… I went home.' He rubbed his face. 'Max – Max must have found him first.'

Larry lowered his face into his hands and began to cry softly.

The lights changed, and John drove over the bridge and down past the Five Lamps pub as fast as he could. He wanted to get this man out of his car, and then he wanted to go see Jack Lawson, and then he was going to go home and take a long hot shower. Then maybe, just maybe, he'd feel clean again.

# 43

At Kilmainham Garda Station, John pulled right across a line of unmarked cars and sat with the engine idling, gaining a shooing gesture from a detective sitting behind the wheel and smoking a cigarette. John ignored him. Sarah climbed out of the car and looked back in at him.

'You coming?'

'No.'

'Why?'

'I need to go see someone.'

'John, I—'

'Sarah, get him out of my car, will you?'

Sarah said nothing for a moment. Her dark eyes searched John's face, but he wouldn't meet her eye. She pulled the passenger seat forward. 'Come on.'

Snuffling, Larry climbed out of the back of the Manta. Sarah dropped the seat back into place. 'John, I'm going to be a while. You know they're going to want full statements.'

'Yeah.' John nodded. 'Call me when you're done, I'll pick you up.'

Sarah looked at him, worried. 'Where are you going?'

'Just ring me.'

'What is it? What's wrong? It's about Lawson, isn't it? John, listen—'

'Close the door.'

'John, wait – just wait for a second.'

'Close the door.'

Sarah closed the door and watched as he drove off without another word. Behind her, Larry sniffed loudly and dabbed at his eyes with his scarlet handkerchief. 'I can't believe this is happening to me.'

'Oh, shut up,' Sarah said, and jerked him towards the front steps. 'A toilet would be ashamed to find you floating in it.'

\*

As John reached the Ha'penny Bridge, there was an enormous crack of thunder and heavy rain began to fall, large drops splattering hard against the windshield. John turned on the wipers. He felt the sick knot of fear in his stomach expand, growing faster with every new thought.

If Jack Lawson had sent Mick Quinn to get that contract, then John had dropped Mick right in it by going to Big Jack. But how could he have known? He thought of Rose Quinn's puffy face and worried eyes. She hadn't been lying to him at all. Her sons were missing, and John had a sinking feeling he knew why.

He pulled up at the garage and parked behind Jack Lawson's green Mercedes. The gates were closed. John got out and approached the car, getting saturated in the process. It was empty. He put his hand on the bonnet: it was cold.

He rang the bell and waited. After a minute he rang it again, leaving his finger on it. He could hear it jangling in the yard. When no one came, John kicked the gates in frustration, and as he did so, the gate opened a fraction before closing again.

John's antennae went up. He eased open the gate and stepped inside. The yard was deserted, but the doors of the massive shed were open slightly. He crossed the cobbled yard, walking slowly and keeping his eyes and ears open. Something wasn't right, he could feel it. The rain beat down, drenching him.

He slipped inside the shed and waited for his eyes to become accustomed to the gloom. There was music coming from the back somewhere. John followed the sound past a car and around a stack of tyres. He could hear something, a muffled grunting. Something was definitely back here.

He rounded a stack of metal shelves and saw Robbie, bound and gagged and half out of his wits, staring at him over a strip of silver duct tape. Between them lay a smashed and bloody corpse.

John stared at it in shock. The head had been all but obliterated. There was virtually nothing left, just a mass of bone and matter and congealing blood. John recognised the matted black hair and the hideous suit. That mound of blood and bone had once been Big Jack Lawson.

'Mmmphh!' Robbie said.

John tore his eyes away and carefully made his way around Big Jack. He reached Robbie, squatted down and yanked off the duct tape, none too gently. Robbie stretched his jaw gratefully.

'What the hell happened here?'

'Thank fuck! The young lad, Mick, he went fucking crazy. I didn't even see him. He clocked me when I came in to work. Next thing you know, I'm tied up and he's just sitting there, waiting. When I tried to talk to him, he put tape over my mouth. He…he just sat there until Big Jack came, then he attacked him.'

'You saying Mick did that, on his own?'

'He was like a madman. Kept screaming something about his brother.'

'How long ago was this?'

'A few hours ago.'

'Where is he now?'

'I don't know. Look, are you going to untie me or what?'

'In a minute,' John said, frowning. 'Where did he go?'

Robbie sighed. His left eye was bloodshot from the blow to the head, and he had a ferocious headache. He had pissed himself when Mick was beating Jack, and now his pants were stiff as a board. 'I don't know. I wouldn't say he went far.'

'Why not?'

'He was… well, he looked fairly wrecked himself. He sort of collapsed after he… did that to Jack, but then after a while he got up. I couldn't tell you where he went after that.'

John stood up. Robbie scrabbled around, suddenly panicked. 'Hey, wait! You have to untie me – you can't leave me here.'

John glanced around. For all he knew, Robbie was in on the whole thing. There was no way he was untying him, not just yet. Mick could be anywhere. He needed to find him first. 'I'll come back in a second.'

'No, wait, you fuck! I've been here for hours. Come back, you dirty bollocks – come back!'

John ignored him and skirted Jack's corpse again.

'Don't leave me here with him!' Robbie shrieked. 'Please!'

John crept slowly along the wall of the shed. The rain hammered on the corrugate, and Robbie's cries mingled with it. Mick Quinn, thought John, was barely five foot seven and as thin as a whip. For him to have attacked Big Jack like that… it was unthinkable.

John moved slowly, searching methodically. At last he stepped outside into the yard. He did another quick scout: nothing. He looked at the steps leading up to the offices. If he was still here, he had to be up there.

John crossed the yard and began to climb the steps. He moved slowly, carefully, his ears pricked, the sweat running down his back despite the rain. He was sure that any second Mick would leap out, wielding something, and cave his skull in.

He needn't have worried. He found Mick Quinn outside Big Jack's door, collapsed in a puddle of blood-streaked vomit.

As John approached him, Mick opened one eye – the other was swollen shut. John wondered if the kid even recognised him. His face was so battered it was almost unrecognisable. Through his thick black hair John could see a nasty head wound oozing blood. He lay there like a dog, on his side, barely breathing. His flimsy T-shirt was soaked, and his ribs protruded through it. The bloodied tyre iron lay beside him. Whatever Herculean strength he had summoned to dispatch Jack Lawson, it had long gone.

'Mick? It's me – it's John Quigley, the private detective. Remember me?' John knelt down beside him. 'Jesus Christ, lad, who did this to you?'

'Sharpie…' he whispered.

'Your brother did this?'

Mick shook his head, just once, and licked his puffy lips. Flecks of blood smeared him. John could see some of his teeth had been smashed.

'Don't try to talk, son,' John said. He yanked his mobile out of his pocket and dialled 999. 'Just hold on.'

'Sharpie.'

'Shush – it's all right. Try to relax.' John stared at him. There was hardly an inch of his face and neck that wasn't black and blue. What the fuck had happened to this boy?

'Hello? I need an ambulance, please – and hurry.'

# 44

Sarah shook out her paper and folded it. 'Can you believe it? They're finally talking about building a metro to the airport.'

John looked over at her. 'I read that this morning.'

'Know how much that's gonna cost us?'

'Couple of billion.'

'Exactly.'

'It's a bargain.'

'Oh, sure. Wait for the next budget and tell me that.' Sarah looked at her watch. 'Are you not going today?'

'What time is it?'

'Ten to two.'

'Shit.' John jumped up and grabbed a paper bag off his desk. It contained the latest addition of *Auto Trader*, two blackcurrant muffins, a bottle of orange juice and *The Sun*. John grabbed his keys and his light jacket. The heatwave was well and truly over, and already he could feel the tentative fingers of autumn creeping in. 'You sure you don't need me for anything?'

'No, no.' Sarah shook her head. 'You go ahead. Give me a call later, I'm going to be over in Sutton.'

'Sutton?'

'The guy with the neck brace, remember?'

'Oh, you mean Mr Whiplash.'

'Yes, him. Mr Owens reckons he's helping his brother build an extension. And if he's able to lug a wheelbarrow around, he should be able to sit in a hackney cab for a couple of hours.' Sarah rolled her eyes. 'Imagine pulling the same stunt five times in two years. Some people never know when to quit while they're ahead.'

'That's the truth.' John was smiling, but Sarah noticed the smile didn't reach his eyes. It hadn't for the last few weeks.

'So we'll talk later?'

'Sure. See ya.' And he was gone.

Sarah listened to his footsteps retreat down the stairs. She put her paper down and went to the sash window James Reid had liberated from the gloss paint, that first day.

James Reid... He had been so happy with them, it was unreal. Sarah could still see him sitting there, beaming, while he explained that the gardaí had recovered the rest of David's money from JJ Hutton, who had found it in a briefcase in the boot of David's car.

JJ had been cute enough not to mention it the day Sarah and John had caught him, but not clever enough to work out that Sarah was going to give his name to the cops at the first opportunity – and not clever enough to keep the money somewhere other than under his bed. James Reid kept thanking them profusely for proving everyone wrong, thanking them for proving what he had known all along: that his brother had been murdered. He said that proved David had wanted no part in what was going on with 'the other shower', and that he had been a good man.

John had said nothing to that. Afterwards, he had said that he didn't know what the definition of a good man was, but whatever it was, David Reid had failed spectacularly to fit the bill when he had not reported that poor girl's death from the word go. Sarah had agreed.

She opened the window and craned her neck to look out. After a few moments, John came into view, walking up Wexford Street, hands in his pockets, bag tucked under his left arm. She watched him walk away.

She was worried about him. It had been almost a fortnight since he had found Mick Quinn lying on that balcony. Almost a fortnight since they had discovered the truth about the death of David Reid. Almost a fortnight – and still John was beating himself up. He never said anything, but she could see it: he was wracked with guilt. She wasn't sure why. It wasn't his fault that Big Jack Lawson had tried to do away with Mick. But John had taken a liking to the kid. He said he thought the kid might have had a real chance if only every single person around him – including his own brother – had not been as crooked as a country mile. He said he didn't know why, but somehow he felt sorry for Mick Quinn.

When the garda divers had pulled Sharpie Quinn's body from that filthy quarry, John had been there, waiting on the banks. The cops hadn't wanted him there, of course, but Stafford had pulled a few strings. John had insisted he should be the one to tell Mick that his brother's body had been found. Detective Sergeant O'Connor, the man in charge of the case against Mick, had initially been reluctant, but had agreed in the end. After all, what difference did it make now? And it wasn't like Sharpie's body was the only one that had come up in the drags.

When John had returned from the hospital that afternoon, Sarah had read his face and known that what he had witnessed weighed heavily on him.

He went every day to visit Mick Quinn, never missed it. Somehow the boy pulled through the initial few days. The surgeon who had removed his spleen said he had never seen anything like it. He had literally been beaten to a pulp. He had been in a coma for two days, during which time they had discovered that all the fingers on his left hand had been broken and he had five broken ribs, a broken collarbone, a broken nose and two broken toes, not to mention the injuries to his head and teeth.

John had been stunned. And yet, Mick had pulled through.

He still couldn't remember a great deal of what had happened to him, but he had been able to give an amazingly accurate account of where he and his brother had been taken. The gardaí had no option but to press charges against him for Jack Lawson's murder – it had been cold-blooded and premeditated – but for some reason this didn't upset Mick. Very little seemed to upset him. He admitted to John that he didn't see the point any more. He had tried to go straight, tried to be as good as he could be, and he had been beaten, lied to, rejected – his mother had refused to see him ever since she had learned of Sharpie's death – and now he was being punished again. Tom Lawson had men on the inside, Mick told John in a dead, flat voice. He was a corpse, he said, his body just didn't know it yet. Mick Quinn, a plucky kid with a good heart, had finally given up.

That was what burned John the most: he could see that this kid might have had a chance, the same as he had had chances when he was growing up. This kid was worth ten of Max Ashcroft or Larry Cole or Clive Hollingsworth. This kid had faced up to his responsibility; he had told the gardaí, in chilling detail, how he had planned to murder Jack Lawson. He said it didn't matter that they knew. He had done it, and that was that.

That was why John went to visit every day and tried to engage Mick in things he might like, trying to make him see he was not alone. But even John could see that he was fighting a losing battle.

Sarah sighed and closed the window with a soft thump. The outcome of their original case was far more satisfactory. Max Ashcroft had been charged with the manslaughter of one Petra Noviska and with the murder of David Reid. Larry Cole was being charged with conspiracy to prevent the course of justice. The contract he had drawn up, in a vain effort to protect his family from scandal, was the most damning evidence of all. Clive also faced the charge of conspiracy. Judge Cockburn was using every means at his disposal to get the charges dropped, but that wasn't looking likely. The press were loving every salacious moment of it.

Jack Lawson's home and business had been raided, and in a safe under his floorboards the gardaí had found guns, over three million euros in cash and, best of all, four passports. Three belonged to girls found working at Big Jack's strip club. Not one of them was over eighteen. The fourth passport had belonged to Petra Noviska, and because of it the gardaí had finally been able to put a name to the young girl found by an eager basset hound named Flash.

Mr and Mrs Noviska had had their daughter returned to them. It was not a happy outcome, but at least they could stop wondering where she was and begin their grieving process. Maybe they would learn to live again, in time. Petra's son no longer remembered what his mother had smelled like or the songs she had sung to him at night. The young move on, but they do not fare as well as you might think.

Life is fraught with dubious decisions, Sarah mused. She thought of her mother. After another ferocious fight with Helen, her two older sisters had relented and agreed that a nurse, paid by the three of them, would live at the family home. It was not what Helen or Jackie really wanted, but as long as their mother had days of clarity and Sarah was willing to live in the house, they felt they had no option but to agree.

When the nurse arrived, Deirdre had objected, claiming that she was perfectly able to look after herself, thank you very much. That evening, while the nurse helped do her hair, Deirdre had called her Doreen – her own sister, who had died at the age of seven. Sarah had smiled and gone upstairs when she heard that. She hadn't come down for an hour.

Sarah sat back down at her desk and massaged her leg. It was never easy being a grown-up, making decisions that you had to live and stand by. It didn't seem to matter what age you were. The decisions the four men had made about Petra Noviska had destroyed lives – theirs, hers…

so many. People were people, Sarah thought, but people could be monsters.

Bo Whelan was dead, Big Jack Lawson was dead, Sharpie Quinn was dead, Mick Quinn might as well be. Brendan Whelan was a ghost in his dusty old shop. Sarah had seen clips of the four men's families on the news when the story broke: they had all looked stunned, shattered, pale-faced, in denial, angry, suffering. And for what? A weekend of fun, some risqué action, money, social standing... Had it been worth it?

Sarah's phone rang. She picked it up, and as she listened, a wry smile broke out on her face.

'Really? He said that? ... Uh-huh, and is that what you want to do? ... Well, of course, twenty-five years is a long time. Sure, I'm delighted for you... Oh, yes, I do believe in second chances, Mrs Conway... Why not, indeed? Thanks for calling. Enjoy Antigua. Send me a postcard.'

Sarah hung up. She popped her stiff foot up onto her desk and laced her hands behind her head, unconsciously mirroring John's usual pose. Mr Conway, when faced with pictures of his bathroom excursions, had apparently realised the error of his ways. Now that was a man who had taken responsibility for his actions. He had thrown himself at his wife's mercy and proclaimed undying love for her. To prove his repentance, he had bought tickets to Antigua. He had even ditched the blonde.

Mrs Conway had asked whether she should give him a second chance, and Sarah knew she wasn't looking for a negative answer. Sarah wasn't sure she did believe in second chances, but Mrs Conway had sounded deliriously happy, and at the end of the day, Sarah had no right to rain on her parade. Their job had been to provide evidence of Conway's infidelity. What Mrs Conway did next was up to her.

And maybe there was something to be said for second chances. Sarah had taken one with John, and that had worked out. Oh, sure, it wasn't one that everyone understood, and of course there were still days when she questioned her own sanity...

But then she thought of that day in the car, when they had been waiting for JJ Hutton to come back. She thought of how John's hands had felt on her face, of how she had absolutely and utterly believed him when he said he would be there for her. She knew he meant it. John Quigley wasn't a boy any more; John Quigley was a man, and he was a man in whom a woman could put her faith.

Maybe it was time to give John a real second chance.

She closed her eyes. Being a private detective was not what she had ever expected. They had made mistakes, both of them, but they were still learning. And if they got the odd phone call from a happy housewife on her way to Antigua, Sarah knew that, no matter what life threw at them, the lessons were worthwhile.

# Epilogue

The ferry pressed on silently through the night, her sleek bow slicing effortlessly through the gentle waves of the Irish Sea. A man stood alone on deck, smoking an unfiltered Sweet Afton, oblivious to the chill in the air. He inhaled the rich smoke and held it deep in his lungs. They were strong cigarettes, known as black-lungers; he had developed a taste for them on the inside, and now everything else tasted like shit.

He hunched inside his coat and watched the light from the pale moon turn the water silver. How treacherous the sea was: all calm on the surface, while underneath currents waited, grasping, twirling, waiting to swallow you whole, drag you beneath, press the air from your lungs, her cold, deadly fingers encircling and capturing your heart. No wonder the sea was referred to as 'she', he mused. Everything lay beneath the surface.

He took a last drag and pitched the cigarette over the side. He leaned against the railing, his massive, scarred hands holding the top rail lightly. He didn't really need to hold on; his balance was excellent – as was his hearing, as was the sight in his one good eye. The remaining eye was the colour of week-old milk. He didn't miss it. He had adapted.

He raised his head and sniffed the night air. Perhaps he was mistaken, but he felt certain he detected a change, a hint of smoke and earth on the breeze. He could not see the outline of the distant shore, not yet, but he knew it wouldn't be long before the lights of Dublin beckoned to him.

He reached into his pocket and pulled out the fold of newspaper that had been sent to him not three months before. Good eye or not, he could not read the print in the dark – but then, he didn't need to: he had memorised every single word.

The sisters had lied, as he had expected they would. Not that it mattered. She had made a mistake. Grown too sure of herself. QuicK Investigations… He shook his head. What a stupid name. He ran his fingers over the paper and closed his eyes. She had always been a sucker for the corny… or had she? He had thought he knew her, he had thought she was an open book, and look where that had landed him. He wouldn't make the same mistake again. This time he would be prepared. This time he would be sure of his mark.

He would take everything she held dear from her, as she had from him.

He would make her suffer as he had suffered.

His lips twitched and he returned the paper to his pocket. He lit another cigarette and urged the ferry on, his heart beating in time with every gentle roll and swell.

# Acknowledgements

Thanks to my agent Faith O'Grady for her constant support.

Thanks also to Ciara Considine, Ciara Doorley, Tana Ellis French and Breda Purdue at Hodder Headline Ireland for their absolute sterling work in shaping the usual rambling manuscript into the book in your hands.

My friend Anna, I know you've had a tough year and I hope this year proves I was right when I told you things always get better.

My girls, Sarah and Tara, looking forward to another few weekends of chatter, kissy kissy.

Thanks to Bryan for answering panicked phone calls demanding information with such good grace.

Antonia, *para siempre*.

For relief on Fridays, for making me laugh so hard I almost fell of a stool and for a beautiful sunflower, I'd like to nod in the general direction of Matteo, Enrique, Luigi & Victoria. *Viva La Tienda*!

As always to Terry and family for all the love and support. I'm a lucky lucky girl to have you and I love you all to bits.

And finally thank you to Andrew for everything and Jordan for finally cleaning her room. I love you two most of all.

Arlene Hunt
April 2006